PASTOR FORD TOOK ANYA'S HANDS, BOWED HER HEAD AND BEGAN TO PRAY.

Anya closed her eyes and tried to stop the trembling that was beginning deep inside. Within seconds, the shaking reached her skin; every inch of her body quivered. But Pastor Ford continued to pray, not stopping even when sobs heaved from Anya's chest.

"Let her feel your power, Father." Pastor Ford raised her voice and gripped Anya's hands tighter. "Free her from the hold that still controls her. You said in your word that *if the Son therefore shall make you free, ye shall be free indeed.* So I pray, in Jesus' name, that Anya be freed here, Lord."

The pastor began to pray in the spirit and Anya's sobs became louder.

"Oh, God. How could this happen to me?" Anya cried.

PRAISE FOR VICTORIA CHRISTOPHER MURRAY

D0963054

ALSO BY VICTORIA CHRISTOPHER MURRAY

Temptation

JOY

Victoria Christopher Murray

Walk Worthy Press

West Bloomfield, Michigan

WARNER BOOKS

NEW YORK   BOSTON

Copyright © 2001 by Victoria Christopher Murray
Reading Group Guide copyright © 2002 by Warner Books with Walk Worthy Press. All rights reserved.
Excerpt from *Temptation* copyright © 2000 by Victoria Christopher Murray. All rights reserved. No part of this book may be reproduced in any form or by any electronic or mechanical means, including information storage and retrieval systems, without permission in writing from the publisher, except by a reviewer who may quote brief passages in a review.

The song "Your Love" © 1990 Dawnn Lewis, Donald Robinson, Randy Bowland
The song "Perpetual Praise" © 1996 Jacquelyn Gouche-Farris

Cover design by Diane Luger
Cover photo by Sean Drakes / DK Stock

The Walk Worthy Press name and logo are registered trademarks of Warner Books.

Warner Books

Time Warner Book Group
1271 Avenue of the Americas New York, NY 10020
Visit our Web site at www.twbookmark.com
Visit our Web site at www.walkworthypress.net

Printed in the United States of America

Originally published in hardcover by Warner Books with Walk Worthy Press
First Mass Market Paperback Printing: September 2005

10 9 8 7 6 5 4 3 2 1

To Ray and Monique—my joy

Acknowledgments

First, as always, I give glory and honor to my Lord and Savior, Jesus Christ. The gift of writing comes from Him, the stories come from Him, the discipline comes from Him . . . need I go on?

There are so many people who stand with me, encouraging me and making sure that I continue with God's plans for my life. Thank you to my parents, Edwin and Jacqueline Christopher, who always believe. I love you two so much. To my sisters, Michele, Cia, and Cecile, and my brother-in-law, William, who tell everyone they know about their sister. To my uncles Herbie and Danny, who beam with pride and make me feel so good.

To the best friends God could have ever placed in my life: Tracy and Walter (thank you for that incredible tea!), Veronica and Joseph (I hope you guys have to come back to L.A. next year), and Lolita Files (thank you for believing in me so much and always telling me so).

To Dawnn Lewis and Jacquelyn Gouche-Farris. Thank you not only for your friendship, but also for allowing me to use your words. You inspire me and so many others with your beautiful songs.

The Murray clan is always so excited for me. Thank you, Grandmother, Nana, Jim, Dad and Ercelle, Michael, Elvis and Ruth, Victoria, and my nieces and nephew—especially Ta'shara (you too Allen), and Victor and Janaya.

To everyone at Warner Books, especially Jamie Raab and Christine Saunders. And a major thank you to Frances Jalet-Miller, who worked on every word of this novel. I learned so much from you.

Thank you to all of the authors who walk this road with me and who always have a word of encouragement and love: Kimberla Roby, Stephanie Perry Moore, Eric Jerome Dickey, E. Lynn Harris, Timmothy McCann, Jacquelin Thomas, Parry Brown, Franklin White, La-Joyce Brookshire, Yolanda Joe, and the many others.

To the book clubs across the country, I cannot thank you enough for your support. But especially to Denise, Cheryl and Tabahani, Dorothy and Minds in Motion, Jan and The Reading Group of Sisters and Friends, Tori and A Room Full of Sistas, Vanessa, Tina and Journey's End, and Wilma Wilkerson, who is my Texas connection all by herself. I thank you all for your never-ending support.

To all my sorors in Delta Sigma Theta. Thank you for coming out in every city and giving me much sisterly love!

Finally, to my top four:

Denise Stinson, my publisher. From the beginning you've had total faith in me and constantly encourage me to keep moving down this road. Not one of these pages could have been written without you. Thank you for your vision, your prayers, and your friendship.

Pastor Beverly "Bam" Crawford, my shepherd. Every time I listen to you, I learn. I cannot thank you enough for your spiritual leadership and guidance. I am stronger in the Lord because of you, and I love you so much.

Ray Allen Murray, my husband. You always believe, don't you? Thank you for thinking that your wife is the best and for encouraging me to believe the same. And thank you for walking this walk alongside me, for dreaming these dreams with me and loving me throughout it all.

To the readers who continue to overwhelm me (in a positive way) with their thoughts and love. Nothing is possible without you. Thank you.

Joy

Prologue

The man entered the apartment, secured the upper and lower locks, then chained the door. Only then did he feel it was safe to turn on the lights. His eyes adjusted to the bare overhead light and he scanned the concrete-gray, paint-chipped walls, trying to soak up every picture. There were photos of her all over, probably at least one hundred, if he'd taken the time to count them. One day he would. He stood with his back to the door, admiring his sanctum.

The heels of his shoes clapped against the planks of the wooden floor as he walked to the center of the room. He took off his tailored suit jacket, loosened his red tie and threw both on the iron cot. He turned and took twelve steps to his kitchen.

A sudden swell of revulsion hit him as he opened the microwave. The stench from the half-eaten dinner he'd left there almost scurried to meet him. With his nose upturned, he used the tips of his fingers to dump the brown-green furry object into the sink. The two-shelf refrigerator tilted as he opened the door. It was empty. He'd forgotten to buy food. No matter. He was too tired to eat anyway.

He opened a drawer from the old dresser, and pulled out the photo album crammed with pictures. He flipped through the images of her at work, jogging on the beach, leaving church, going into her townhouse. But even though he had come here to look at the pictures, he didn't have the energy to do it tonight. He slammed the book shut and dropped it to the floor.

Walking back to the cot, he counted the steps in his mind. He always did this, though he didn't know why. Out of habit, he supposed. He knew how many steps it took to get to each part of this room. Five steps to the bathroom, eleven to the clothing rack; thirty-eight steps and he could walk around the entire apartment.

The cot creaked under his weight as he fell onto it. He thought about changing his clothes, but there were no more steps in him. He lay back, making a mental note to buy a pillow, but only if it didn't cost more than five dollars. No need to splurge on frivolous, unnecessary items. He wouldn't be keeping this place much longer anyway.

He picked up the towel from the floor, threw it over the clock and wondered if he'd be able to sleep with the light. He'd have to—he wasn't getting up now.

Finally, he closed his eyes. It had been a long day. He'd spent his free time watching her—sometimes up close, sometimes from far away. But that was the best part; she never knew it.

The man felt himself drifting off to sleep, comforted by the muted, steady tick-tick-tick of the alarm clock. A vision slowly filled his mind. She was dressed in a suit, the burgundy one—his favorite—the one that made her look like a real woman.

She was looking straight at him, unbuttoning her

blouse. Her face was soft with desire. All signs of her usual arrogance were gone. Now she was just a woman, doing what she was supposed to do: preparing herself for him. He smiled in his slumber. It would only be a matter of time. Then Anya Mitchell would be completely his.

Chapter 1

"ny day now!" Anya shouted, as the car in front of her remained motionless even though the other lanes were inching forward.

Anya leaned on her horn, the blaring sound startling drivers around her, causing them to turn and stare. The driver in front of her looked back through his rearview mirror, held up his hands, then rolled down his window.

"Where do you want me to go?" he yelled.

Anya almost smiled. He *really* didn't want her to answer. She honked again—just a little, to annoy him, but she felt bad the moment she did it. She couldn't help it though—it was one of those habits that lingered from her college days in New York. Twenty years later, she used her horn as if she were still in Manhattan.

She bounced back in the seat of her BMW and tapped her fingers on the steering wheel, praying for a break in the traffic. She only had ninety minutes to get back to the office and then to the restaurant.

"Ahhhh!" she yelled. She squeezed her fingers around the steering wheel and a pinpoint of sunlight burst through the windshield, hitting her ring at the perfect angle. Her emerald-cut engagement ring sparkled like lightning, and the rainbow hues danced across her slender mocha finger. Anya stared at the flawless diamond, hypnotized for a moment by its brilliance.

Her cell phone rang and she jumped. She clicked the speaker button.

"Hello," she said, forcing a smile into her voice.

"What are you wearing?"

His seductive tone put a smile on her face. "My burgundy suit."

"The one with the short skirt? Umm, my favorite. How's your day?"

"Don't ask. What about you?"

"I've been in front of the computer all day, but now I want to see you. Are you going to be on time tonight?"

She detected a sprinkle of sarcasm in Braxton's tone and her smile faded a bit. "I'll be on time, Braxton, I promise," she said, running one hand through the tight curls on her head.

"Good, 'cause I can't wait to see you. We haven't spent enough time together lately."

"That's not true."

"Seems that way. That's why we should live together now. Waiting for the wedding doesn't make sense."

Her smile disappeared. "Braxton." She exhaled his name in a whine.

"Never mind. I'll see you in an hour. I love you."

She clicked off the phone and tightened her grip on the steering wheel. She shook her head to clear it of thoughts of her fiancé. There were more pressing issues in front of her.

Cars were beginning to creep forward and as her speed increased, she looked across the freeway's lanes. No three-car wreck, no stalled big wheeler. Nothing to cause the hour-long backup. She put her foot down on the accelerator and zipped her sports car across the lanes and around snail-paced cars. Maybe she could salvage the rest of the day. But the twisting in the pit of her stomach made her seriously doubt it.

"Hi, Anya. I have a couple of—"

Anya raised her hand, stopping her assistant midsentence. She skimmed through the pink slips Dianna handed her and sighed deeply. "Just take messages for the rest of the afternoon."

Without saying another word, Dianna nodded knowingly. The entire office had been tense as the date approached for the final pitch to Linden Communications.

Anya threw her briefcase on her desk and flopped into her leather chair. She swiveled and turned to face the large floor-to-ceiling glass windows that extended over two walls of her corner office.

It was a sparkling clear southern California day. The day after one of those El Niño storms that washed all the smog and dirt from the air and removed much of the shoreline from the southern Pacific Coast as well.

Anya stood, pulled her silk suit jacket over her hips, and strolled to the windows. This was why she had chosen this space. When she'd needed to expand her office, she'd been determined to find one with a breathtaking view of the city. These windows removed her from the present and took her to a faraway place when she needed to escape.

What is wrong with me? Anya wondered, as she looked down at her ring. She wanted to feel it—all of the blessedness that had been there at the beginning. But all she felt was what she'd been feeling the last few weeks: She was falling headfirst into an abyss.

She did remember the happiness that consumed her the day Braxton proposed. They were in church, in the middle of the service, right after the offering, when Pastor Ford had called his name.

"Braxton Vance, can you come up to the altar?"

Anya had frowned and pulled Braxton's hand. "What's going on?" she whispered with narrowed eyes.

He stood, looked down at her and smiled but wordlessly slipped away. Her eyes focused on him, as he trotted down the green-carpeted aisle.

Braxton moved up the two steps to the altar and took Pastor Ford's outstretched hand. She led him to the podium.

Clearing his throat, he pushed his thin gold-rimmed glasses up the bridge of his nose, then ran his hand across his almost bald head before he spoke. "Good morning, family." He paused as the congregation responded. "As many of you know, I'm a writer and this isn't the easiest career. In the beginning it was a struggle, but I am blessed that it is no longer. And now that the trial has passed, people everywhere remember me when and want to befriend me now. But most important to me are the people who were with me when times were thin—people who never cared about what I did for a living, where I lived, or what I drove." He looked directly at Anya. "Anya Mitchell, would you please come up here?"

It took the nudging of the woman next to her to make Anya stand. She moved haltingly through the silent congregation until she was by Braxton's side. Her trembling hands were hidden behind her back. What is he doing? she thought, as possibilities ran through her mind.

Braxton took her left hand. "Anya, you've always been there for me and our friendship has turned to love. So now . . ." He slowly lowered himself until he was balanced on one knee. Then he removed a glinting object from his sports jacket.

Anya was frozen in place. Her glazed eyes fixed on the image in front of her. But she could hear the soft, growing rumble that moved through the six hundred or so parishioners sharing this moment with her.

"Anya Mitchell. In front of God, Pastor Ford, and our church family, would you make me the happiest man on earth and agree to become my wife?"

While the congregation cheered, Anya just stared. Pastor Ford's voice brought her back to consciousness.

"Anya, you haven't said anything," Pastor Ford said, as she joined the two at the altar.

Anya allowed herself to smile but didn't trust herself to speak. She nodded.

"Braxton, I think you can take that as a yes!" Pastor Ford laughed.

The congregation roared when Braxton slipped the ring onto her finger. As the cheering continued, Anya allowed herself to relish the moment in front of hundreds of onlookers.

Anya smiled now, as she remembered that moment a little more than six months ago. She'd loved Braxton so much then and she certainly loved him now—even more. So what was wrong? Obscure emotions had unnerved her for several weeks, making her believe something bad was going to happen. But there was nothing specific she could pinpoint causing all of this doubt.

Braxton Vance was everything she'd hoped for—he was a man of God, professionally successful, and financially stable. And there didn't seem to be any dirty secrets or angry women lurking in his background, waiting to pounce upon them. Topping it all, he was certainly easy on the eyes, as the women in her office told her whenever he came to visit. He was the perfect package.

Anya sighed deeply, and walked back to her desk. As she sat, her fingers did a syncopated dance atop her marble desk and she let her eyes wander around the office, finally settling on her brass desktop clock. Hastily, she pulled the Linden Communications folder from her briefcase and turned on her computer, determined to work efficiently during the next half hour. But within moments, she was leaning back in her chair, twisting the ring on her finger.

Two short knocks at the door interrupted her thoughts. Before she could utter a word, the door opened and David Montgomery strolled in. Anya hated when he did that, just walked in without her permission. But no matter how many times she brought it to his attention, he continued doing it.

"Alaister finished all the numbers for the presentation." David sank into one of the cream-colored leather chairs in front of her desk and crossed his legs. "I've looked it over, but you can glance at it before tomorrow's meeting."

Anya gazed at him, sitting so casually, decked out in one of his tailored suits that looked like it had been sewn directly onto his muscular frame.

"How does it look to you, David?" Anya asked in her most professional voice.

"It's fine, I'm just giving you this professional courtesy."

Anya cringed, took a deep breath, and willed herself not to blow like an over-inflated tire. David had been working with her for a bit more than a month, but this wasn't the first time he had spoken to her in a tone bordering on insubordination.

She had to remind herself why she had hired David in the first place—University of Virginia M.B.A., certified financial planner, ten years of financial-planning experience with American Express in the Dallas office, national top-producer awards. Anya knew that David could help Mitchell & Associates Financial Services achieve all of her objectives.

Still twisting her ring, she stared at him, hoping her eyes delivered her message. She took off the ring, placing it on the desk before she spoke.

"Is this the complete report?" Her voice was stiff.

"Yep, all numbers have been triple-checked. You know I never bring you anything unless it's perfect."

Anya pursed her lips, leaned across the wide desk and took the report from David's outstretched hand, tugging at it just enough for him to feel it, and just enough for her to regret it. She shouldn't be acting this way—it wasn't David's fault she was in a bad mood.

"I'm getting ready to leave, so I'll take this home." She tried to soften her voice.

David raised his thick eyebrows. "You're leaving? I thought you'd review this right now. The meeting is set for nine. So if you have any changes . . ."

Anya lifted her chin. "If I have any changes, *I'll* handle them in the meeting."

David held up his hands in surrender. "Whatever you

say, Boss." He walked to the door, then turned back suddenly. "You know we're going to get this account. All of the numbers show that we can save them almost $100,000 a year on their benefits. I know Linden will be ours." He grinned, his deep-set dimples becoming even more visible.

The moment she was alone, Anya stuffed the report into her briefcase. He probably thinks I'm suffering from PMS or something, she thought. But she didn't have time to think about that now. If she hurried, she would still be on time for Braxton. She picked up her briefcase and rushed out, without saying a word to her flustered assistant.

Anya leaned into the soft seat and the tension of the day began to ebb from her shoulders. The traffic flowed easily down Wilshire—a surprise because she'd expected the trek from Wilshire to Melrose to be, at best, sluggish and stressful.

She popped the CD of her church's choir into the player and started swaying as the melodious sounds filled her car. This is what I should have done before, she thought. Praising the Lord always took her back to where she was supposed to be.

She drummed her fingers against the steering wheel pretending she was Sheila E., when she was jolted by the shrill ring of her cell phone. She debated whether to answer. It was either Braxton checking on her or Dianna calling with an urgent message that she didn't want to know about. "I'm not going to answer!" she yelled at the portable phone. On cue, the ringing stopped.

With a wide smile, she continued tapping her fingers to the music, but groaned a few seconds later when the phone rang again. She picked it up on the second ring. "Yes!"

"Anya?"

Who else would be answering her cell phone? "Yes, Dianna. What is it?"

"God, I thought I would never get you. You ran out so fast and you didn't tell me where you were going. So I figured the only way to get you would be on your cell phone and I am glad—"

Anya rolled her eyes. She loved Dianna, who was more than competent. But sometimes . . . "What is it?" she interrupted.

"Oh, you left your ring."

Dianna spoke so casually, it took a moment for Anya to realize what she was saying. Confused, she looked down at her left hand as her right one clutched the steering wheel. The third finger was bare.

"Oh, no," she groaned, vaguely remembering when she'd taken it off.

"I went into your office to straighten your desk and your ring was just sitting there, sparkling. I still think it's one of the prettiest rings I've ever seen. I can't wait until—"

"Di-an-na!"

"Sorry."

Anya considered her options. "Look, I'm supposed to meet Braxton"—she glanced down at the clock and moaned—"in five minutes. And I'm five minutes from the restaurant."

"I'll bring it to you! Where are you and Braxton going to be?"

"No!" Anya shook her head at the thought of Dianna

popping into the restaurant saying "Surprise! Here's your ring." What would Braxton think?

"I'll turn around and drive back down Wilshire. Meet me at the corner of . . . Wilshire and LaCienega. I'll be waiting for you right in front of the Red Lobster."

"Okay." Dianna seemed to sing the word.

"And, Dianna"—Anya softened her voice—"thank you." Anya clicked off the phone and looked at her naked finger once again. How would she have explained it?

She made an illegal U-turn and headed back toward her office, shivering as goosebumps rose on her arms despite the closed car windows. Just the other day, she had found her ring on the edge of the kitchen sink.

Is this a sign? she asked herself. She shook her head and sighed deeply. The tension of the day was gone, but replacing it was a feeling of deep uneasiness.

By the time Anya pulled up in front of Crossroads, she was thirty minutes late. She jumped from the car and tossed her keys to the valet. "Thanks, Michael," she called to the young man who often parked her car when she and Braxton came to her favorite restaurant.

Her heels clicked against the brick walkway as she rushed through the entrance, then stopped short behind a couple talking to the waitress. She squinted into the dark room and, seconds later, saw Braxton waving at her. She tried to read his expression, but he was too far away for her to discern his mood. The hostess motioned for Anya to follow her.

Heads turned as Anya made her way to the table. She

strolled with the confidence of royalty, gliding by the restaurant's packed tables.

Anya kept her soft brown eyes fixed on Braxton and never noticed the admiring glances from men and women alike. When she was close enough to see Braxton's smile, she exhaled.

Braxton took her raincoat and handed it to the hostess. "I got a call from my editor just as I was leaving, so I just got here myself."

Anya was relieved when Braxton pulled her close, hugging her. He was a head taller than she was, and he had to lean over slightly to rub his smooth face along her cheek. She eased her hand up his back, feeling the toned hardness, and closed her eyes trying to enjoy the moment. Braxton had a way of contacting her emotional nerve-endings with one gentle touch. But she didn't feel it today, and pulled back.

He hesitated for an instant, then brushed his lips against her cheek.

Anya responded with a smile. "How are you?"

"Wonderful, now. You sound like you had a tough day." He pulled the chair out for her, then moved his chair closer to her. With gentle fingers, he massaged her shoulder.

She nodded and closed her eyes, enjoying the feeling of her muscles relaxing. "We're jamming in the final changes for the presentation tomorrow, and I got stuck on the 405 and then I got into a little thing with David." Anya's words rolled over each other. She opened her eyes, glanced at the ring, then said a quick, silent prayer of thanks.

"Another little thing with David? What was it this time?"

"Oh, nothing," Anya said, waving her hand and ring in

the air. "Just the usual . . ." She left the sentence unfinished and picked up the menu. The aroma of the Creole spices teased her, reminding her just how hungry she was.

"Well, I don't want you to think about work. I have something that will take your mind off it." He reached to the chair next to him.

A bunch of yellow roses suddenly appeared on the table. She dropped the menu and brought the bundle to her face. "Thank you!" She smiled. "But what's the occasion?"

Braxton kissed her fingers. "The same as every day. I love you."

His light brown eyes enveloped her. She did love this man.

"Oh, those are beautiful!" the waitress exclaimed as she came to their table. "Are you guys celebrating something special tonight?"

Anya looked directly at Braxton. "We're celebrating our love." She laid the flowers on the table.

"Hey, now, that's a good reason. Would you like something to drink?" the waitress asked Anya.

"An iced tea." The waitress nodded and left them alone. Anya picked up the menu again. "I think we should order."

"I already ordered, honey," Braxton said, taking her hand. "When I realized you were running late, I thought I'd better. That's okay, isn't it?"

It was a moment before Anya responded. "What are we having?"

"I ordered the Georgia salad for you. I didn't think you'd want anything heavier."

Her smile drooped, and she pulled her hand away. From a nearby table, the aroma of the crawfish stew drifted over to her. She inhaled, then picked up her glass of water and took a long sip.

Braxton took her hand into his once again. "Anya, there is something we need to talk about."

She chewed on a piece of ice. "What is it?"

He sighed and dropped his head, dropping her hand at the same time. "I've been thinking about this marriage counseling."

It was Anya's turn to sigh. "Braxton, not again."

"I don't want to fight," he said, holding up his hands. "But I think we should really think about this before we start. It will be harder to get out once we begin."

Anya shook her head, but remained silent.

"Counseling is going to be a waste of time," Braxton continued. "You haven't gone through this before, but I have."

Anya closed her eyes and held her head in her hands. Around her, glasses and silverware clanked and laughter rose. But all she could hear were the words of the many discussions they'd already had on this subject. Some time passed before she opened her eyes.

"Braxton, just because you think counseling didn't work for you before, it doesn't mean it won't work now. If that were true, then you shouldn't even be thinking about getting married again, because your first marriage didn't work out."

He shook his head. "I'm not saying that. I'm saying that counseling is for kids just starting out."

"This has nothing to do with age. This is about taking time with our pastor to discuss all of those issues that come up in marriage. It's about being prepared, Braxton."

"We don't need outside help with our relationship."

"Obviously you could have used some help before." She softened her tone when he winced. "Braxton, just look at this for what it is—a way for us to learn how to keep God in the center of our lives. Why are you so against this?"

"Honey, I'm not against anything. I'm just saying that we already have God in our lives. We're two born-again, spirit-filled, committed-to-God people. That's all we need. We don't *need* counseling." He paused. "But if you're going to force the issue . . ."

She sat straighter in her chair. Her voice went up an octave. "You do remember that Pastor Ford requires this counseling if we want her to marry us."

He nodded.

"So, maybe you're saying something else." She twisted her ring with her words. "Maybe you don't want to get married at all."

Braxton shook his head. "That's ridiculous. We don't agree, but you know that I want to marry you. All I'm saying is that we can tell Pastor Ford that we're too busy right now, get out of counseling, and she'll *still* marry us."

"I can't believe you are actually willing to lie to Pastor," she said through clenched teeth. "We keep talking about this—going over the same thing. How can taking one hour a week, talking about putting God in the center of our lives, be a bad thing?"

"Here we go," the waitress sang, silencing their argument. The plate in front of Anya was filled with lettuce, tomatoes, cucumbers, and carrots, while an overflowing dish of pasta topped with peppered jumbo shrimp sat in front of Braxton. Her eyes darted between her plate and Braxton's, and her stomach growled.

Braxton took Anya's hand, and they bowed their heads

while he blessed their food. When he lifted his head, his smile had reappeared.

"Okay," Braxton said, motioning with his fork, "if I have to live with counseling, then I want you to do something for me."

Anya stabbed at a plump cherry tomato.

"I want to set our wedding date," Braxton continued, not noticing Anya's silence. "Let's go in there tonight with an announcement. I think we've put off setting the date long enough, don't you?"

Anya swirled a piece of lettuce in the vinaigrette dressing. Ever since their engagement, Braxton had been pushing to set a date. But she had continually put him off, saying that there was no need to rush. She was just too busy with her business and he was too busy with his writing.

She looked up at him. Now, as Braxton looked into her eyes, Anya knew there were no more excuses. What was she waiting for anyway? "Do you have a date in mind?"

"Tomorrow," Braxton chuckled.

Anya flinched. "Can't do it that fast."

"Just kidding—and hoping. How much time do you think we'll need? It's not going to be a big affair."

"It will still take time to plan, Braxton," she said coolly.

"Let's do June. That gives us six months, and Junior will be out of school so he could spend some extra time with us." Braxton smiled widely as he mentioned his son.

Anya hesitated. "That's fine," she replied, with as much enthusiasm as she could muster.

Braxton leaned over and kissed her, leaving the savory taste of the peppered shrimp on her lips. "Great! We'll tell Pastor tonight and then we can tell Madear."

Anya couldn't help but smile when he mentioned her

grandmother, the woman who had raised her since she was thirteen. Madear was so happy that Anya had found herself "a good Christian man."

"You do know how much I love you?" Braxton ran his palm across her cheek.

"I know," Anya said honestly. She never doubted his love.

Braxton talked throughout dinner, while Anya smiled and nodded. She watched as Braxton swept the last shrimp through the sauce on his plate and popped it into his mouth.

He smiled at her. "Are you finished?"

She munched on one last piece of flavorless lettuce. "I've had just about enough."

"Great, let's get to church!"

Anya wasn't surprised at Braxton's newfound eagerness. After all, she had given in. Well, she thought, as she backed away from the table, isn't that what a relationship was about . . . compromise?

The wheels of the metal cart creaked along the carpet. The cleaning lady paused outside David's door.

"Good night, Mr. Montgomery." With her thick Spanish accent, she always spoke slowly, drawing out every word to make sure she was understood.

David raised his head and squinted through tired eyes. "Good night, Gina."

Since he'd joined this firm, it had been this way— even the late-night cleaning people came and left before he did.

"I will lock the doors." The older woman gave David a toothy grin, then ambled toward the front of the office.

David knew what would come next. He waited, counting the seconds and her steps, and then heard her voice.

"Don't work too late, Mr. Montgomery. It's not normal for a handsome young man like you to be working so late. You should be home right now, taking care of a wife and some children. You shouldn't be alone." Gina tisked and continued mumbling indecipherable words.

David massaged his temples, trying to relieve the headache that had taken up permanent residency there. He waited to hear the office doors close and lock, the signal that Gina had completed her nocturnal soliloquy. Finally, he leaned his tall, ex-tight-end football player frame back in his chair, as Gina's words played in his head.

She'd said he was young and handsome. Young—that was hard to believe because he felt well beyond his thirty-two years. He moved forward so that he could glance at his reflection in his oversized glass-and-chrome desk. Many people said that he was good-looking, at least in recent years. When he was younger, girls preferred the fair-skinned boys. With his dark skin, he was the last one anyone looked at. But times had certainly changed. He was one of the handsome Black men of the new millennium. Chocolate brothers were in demand, and his smooth dark complexion was disturbed only by the close-cut beard that he'd recently started wearing. He guessed he could be considered good-looking, if the way women now reacted was any indication.

But Gina was right about one thing: He was alone. And going home to his Huntington Beach condo served only to remind him of decisions he'd made. It was there that he seemed to remember all the things he tried so hard to forget.

Mitchell & Associates was another attempt for him to start anew. But though he had been in Los Angeles for more than a month, he felt like he was still in the middle of Manhattan.

He glanced at the Linden presentation laid out before him. Seven-day weeks filled with fourteen-hour days had delivered what he knew was a flawless proposal. The office's atmosphere had been electric today, charged with expectation as everyone felt this million-dollar account was about to become part of Mitchell & Associates.

He had brought Linden Communications to Anya the first week he was here. He remembered her face when he told her the numbers this account would bring. She'd shaken her head and called him Mr. Boy Wonder. David exhaled loudly. "Mr. Boy Wonder." If she only knew.

The miniature walnut grandfather clock chimed softly eleven times. He didn't have to raise his head to know that, finally, it was time to go home.

Slowly, he stuffed papers into his briefcase. He never looked at anything he took home. He was always too tired. But he took them just in case he awakened in the middle of the night.

He stood, closed his eyes, and released a long sigh. He couldn't wait to fall asleep; unconsciousness was his relief.

He turned off the lights and walked through the capacious office, stylishly decorated with glass desks and black lacquer furniture. Moving silently along the rich mauve carpet that Anya had installed when she'd rented this space, he paused in front of one of the positive affirmation posters she had hung throughout the office.

DON'T QUIT, he read silently. That was the only thing he hadn't done.

It would be midnight by the time he got home. He would sleep for a few hours, then be up at five for his normal hour run on the beach, before returning to the office by eight—always before anyone else. He knew he was pushing himself, but it was the only way for him to survive.

Chapter 2

It felt like it was one hundred degrees in the conference room. The sun wasn't even shining through the paneled windows, but Anya knew if she didn't get relief soon, her satin blouse would be permanently affixed to her skin. She sat stiffly at the head of the long cherrywood table with her hands folded, waiting for Jon Green, the president of Linden Communications, to complete his perusal of the proposal.

Anya took a deep breath, hoping that would provide some ease, but the longer Mr. Greene kept his head lowered, the higher the temperature in the room seemed to rise. With just the slightest nod of her chin, she motioned toward the wall panel and Alaister, her manager for Group Accounts, stood and adjusted the air controls.

Alaister's movement made Jon Greene lift his head. "Anya, this looks good, but I want a few minutes to review these numbers with Charles. Is there an empty room we can use?"

Although surprised by his request, Anya said, "Of course, we can leave you alone in here." She looked at David and Alaister, and they nodded.

"No, let us go to another office."

As Alaister led them from the conference room, Anya removed her suit jacket, hoping that the perspiration lines on her blouse weren't noticeable.

"Is it hot or is it just me?"

David smiled and folded his hands behind his head, looking as cool as if he were on a Jamaican beach. "What're you stressing about? We've already won."

Anya squinted at David's grin. "Cocky, aren't we?"

He shrugged and unfastened the single button on his jacket. "I just know this business and I know the signs."

A bit too eagerly, Anya leaned toward David. "Signs? What are they? How do you know? Are you sure?"

David chuckled. "The first sign is that they are very impressed with *you*."

Anya stood and paced the long length of the room. She stopped in front of the mahogany panels, which hid the large-screen television they often used for presentations. "Usually I can read body language," Anya started. "But Mr. Greene never even blinked his eyes."

"Because he was staring at you."

She ignored his comment. "And his sidekick—it's amazing to me that Charles is one of the partners. He's barely out of high school. I don't think he understood any of the numbers."

"It is a curious team, but Jon's the numbers-and-decision man. There's nothing to worry about. They'll come back, tell us they want a few hours to compare our proposal to the others, and they will get back to us tomorrow or the next day—"

Anya jumped as the door of the conference room opened and Alaister returned. His normally put-together façade had melted in the heat. His tie was loosened and his blond hair stuck to his neck.

"Did they say anything?" Anya asked.

Alaister hunched his shoulders. "They hardly said a word. Just thanked me for the room, then closed the door in my face. I put them in Matthew's office."

Anya sighed deeply. Suddenly she felt drained by the anxiety. She wanted this account. Her business had grown steadily every year since she'd opened, but Linden would bring in an annual premium of more than a million dollars. Winning this account would be the perfect celebration of her tenth year in business.

"We'd better start thinking about hiring at least two associates to execute this business," David said, breaking the silence.

Anya shook her head. "I wish you would stop—"

A quick knock on the door interrupted her, and the three stood as Mr. Greene reentered the room.

"I thought I might have some questions, but you did such a good job, it's all clear." Mr. Greene took Anya's hand. "It's about the numbers for me, so let me compare yours to the others and I'll get back to you tomorrow or the next day."

She felt like her hand was drowning inside his and she softly pulled away.

"That's quite a little ring you've got there," Jon Greene said suddenly.

Anya looked at her hand, then back at him. "Thank you. Well, Mr. Greene, we'll be looking forward to hearing from you." Anya stood firm under his steady gaze. She turned to David. "Do you have anything to add?"

David shook his head and stepped forward. "Mr. Greene, let me walk you out."

Jon Greene took a long final look at Anya, then shook his head slightly. As David led the way, Mr. Greene turned back and smiled at Anya once again.

"That guy really likes you," Alaister said when they were alone.

"What are you talking about?" Anya had hoped that no one else had noticed the lewd looks the president of Linden had been giving her. She moved around the conference table, pushing in the chairs.

"Whenever you talked, Mr. Greene acted like he was hearing the voice of God. We got this account for sure."

"Well, *if* we get it, I hope it's based on more than that. Alaister, you guys did a great job."

He nodded his thanks.

"Let's get back to work. We have other clients depending on us."

Alaister left Anya standing in the middle of the room, rubbing her arms to ward off a sudden chill.

Chapter 3

The sun fought valiantly, but the clouds moving along the coast proved to be more powerful. Anya blew on her hands, hoping that her breath would warm her. She'd forgotten her running gloves this morning, but she'd be fine once she started moving. One last stretch to the side, forward, hamstring stretch—and she was ready to go. Zipping her jacket to the neck, she began to move. She ran without headphones, not needing music. The pounding surf provided both rhythm and melody.

She began jogging slowly, barely keeping ahead of the early morning walkers. Her sneakers tapped the pavement as she passed the eclectic mix of boarded-up T-shirt shops, jewelry stores, and eateries lining the Venice beach. Nothing would be open for hours. The strip belonged to the diehard health enthusiasts.

"Hey, Anya." Two male joggers came alongside her. "We haven't seen you recently."

Anya merely waved, saving every morsel of energy.

"See ya on the way back," one runner said, as they moved ahead of her.

The air felt good pushing against her lungs. She'd only

been running since she met Braxton, and most of the time, they shared these morning runs. But Anya hadn't called him this morning; she wanted this time alone.

She'd barely slept twenty minutes last night, settling instead for watching reruns on Nick at Nite. As soon as the dark slipped into dawn's light, she was up, feeling strangely rejuvenated and filled with the desire to return to her morning routine.

Now, as she reached the Venice Boardwalk Tee-Shirt Factory, she jogged in place, taking a sip from the water bottle hanging on her belt. She couldn't keep herself from thinking about the Linden presentation. Mitchell & Associates was no doubt a top contender but, still, it was a long shot.

"I'm not going to think about it anymore," Anya said aloud. She had prayed over this for weeks; it was in God's hands now.

As she passed the steel-gray condos, she let her mind drift to Braxton. Yesterday, the presentation had given her a reprieve. But now, remembering how well the counseling session had gone, she smiled. Just as she predicted—things got better once they saw Pastor Ford. Counseling and prayer—that was all she and Braxton needed.

At the top of the Santa Monica pier, Anya paused, resting her hands on her knees. Suddenly she raised her head, and her eyes darted from the deserted pier to the boarded-up buildings. Usually there were other joggers around her but today, she was alone. She straightened her body and shook her head, trying to dislodge the feeling of uneasiness. She quickly turned around and began her trek back, running faster now. It was time for her to get home.

Chapter 4

*H*e couldn't believe it when he saw her. He followed, jogging slower than his normal pace, staying a safe distance behind, just like he'd been taught all those years ago.

"There's a science to this," his sixteen-year-old friend Sean had told him. At fourteen, he listened attentively. "You have to be close enough not to lose sight, but far enough away not to be recognized." Sean spoke with the authority of a teacher, one who had practiced his craft.

His friend's words had seemed simple, but as they followed the young girl that day, he'd learned that this wasn't like the other games they'd played.

But now he followed Anya with the expertise that the years had given him. He watched as she ran with an attitude, barely acknowledging a male runner who he knew she saw frequently. She kept her face forward, as if she was the only one on the planet with a purpose. Sometimes, he admired that—sometimes, it made him sick.

When she got to the parking lot, he lowered his face

from her view and pulled his sweatsuit hood over his head. He leaned against the brick building and waited. She stretched her legs against the bumper of the car, then drove from the lot. Slowly he walked to his car. There was no need to keep her in sight. He knew where she was going.

nya was into her rhythm. Coffee in her favorite Delta Sigma Theta mug, subdued music flowing from the small speakers behind her desk, and papers strewn across her desk. She'd been in the office for almost two hours, but hadn't seen David or Alaister. They were all trying to pretend that everything was normal, though the Linden decision weighed heavy in the air.

Rapid taps on her door broke Anya's concentration. Dianna appeared, with both hands clutching the door.

"It's them. On the phone!"

Anya leaned back, waiting for her heart to beat a hole through her chest. Behind Dianna, she could see that half the office had gathered around Dianna's desk.

Anya inhaled, swiveled her chair so that her back was to the door, picked up the phone, and smiled into the receiver. "Mr. Greene," she greeted him, with as much calm as she could manage.

He told her a joke about how he'd been on the phone all morning, feeling like the Grim Reaper. She had not yet exhaled, but she chuckled along. Behind her, she could feel her team edging their way into the office, and she wondered if all twenty-five associates were present.

"Yes, Mr. Green," they heard her finally say. "Yes." Her voice was flat.

"I can't take this," Dianna whispered.

No one in the room seemed to breathe as they waited to hear the verdict.

"Thank you very much, Mr. Greene," Anya said. "I understand." As she hung up the phone, she faced the anxious group, her face expressionless.

Everyone held still, waiting to hear her words.

"David, may I speak to you . . . alone?"

The group backed out in noiseless disappointment.

"Anya, I should stay," Alaister said.

"No, let me talk to David. Then I'll meet with you."

Before Alaister closed the door, he glanced back and shook his head.

David sank into a chair and held his head in his hands. "I am so sorry, Anya. I was sure—"

"Sorry?" Anya kept her voice steady. "Is that all you have to say?"

He nodded, keeping his head down.

"Which part are you sorry about?" She walked around her desk, perching on it in front of him. "Are you sorry that you won't have any time for leisurely lunches? Or because you'll probably ask me for a raise?"

His head jerked up and his eyes blinked rapidly. "Wait a minute . . ."

Anya smiled.

David jumped from his seat. "You mean we got it?" His voice was barely a whisper.

Anya bobbed her head like an excited child.

"Whoopee!" David yelped and grabbed Anya, hugging and lifting her off her desk.

The door immediately opened, and Dianna tiptoed in. "Did you just say, 'Whoopee'?"

Anya and David ignored her as they danced a jig. The associates cheered and tried to enter the office all at the same time to join in the jubilant dance. Alaister was the last to enter, and Anya rushed to him, hugging him. He drew back a bit and Anya frowned slightly, then smiled when he hugged her back.

"Congratulations," she said. "You did a great job, Alaister."

He seemed almost breathless. "I thought we had it, then I wasn't sure—"

Anya motioned with her hands to silence the group. "There's something I'd like to say." She paused. "We got the account!" She held up David's and Alaister's hands in victory and everyone applauded. "And though this business belongs to Alaister's group, I thank all of you because this was a team effort." She smiled into the sea of black, white, and brown faces that grinned back. "This is one of the best teams I've ever worked with."

"We love you too, Anya," Mark Simmons yelled, and more cheers followed.

Her smile widened. "We have to celebrate." The group muttered their agreement. "Well, what about tonight, since it's Friday?" Anya asked no one in particular.

In unison, the group howled and hooted their approval. "Dianna?"

"Don't worry about a thing." Dianna waved her hand in the air as she headed back to her desk. "I'll get right on it. I can have something set in an hour or two. This is so exciting."

"Okay, let's get back to work." David ignored the groans as he ushered the group from Anya's office. He was the last one to step out, and before he did, he turned back. "Congratulations . . . Boss," he said with a deep-dimpled smile.

Alone, Anya leaned against her closed door. Her body trembled as she absorbed this news. She wanted to sing. She wanted to dance. But most of all, she wanted to praise God.

She picked up her old Bible from the corner of her desk. Loose papers slipped out and she sorted through them. Her grandmother had taught her how to develop prayers from scriptures, and she'd written many down. She read through several, basking in the words. After a few minutes, she closed her Bible.

"Lord," she said out loud, "I would drop to my knees if I didn't have on these stockings and this short skirt." She chuckled and lifted her eyes. "You are so awesome, and I bless your Holy Name. I thank you, Heavenly Father, for this tremendous blessing. Thank you for your faithfulness. Thank you for your grace. I pray and thank you in the name of your son, Jesus, Amen."

Braxton's fingers continued their dance across the keyboard until he clicked on his speakerphone. "Hello," he answered impatiently, and once again vowed to get caller ID.

"Braxton, we got it!" Anya screamed.

His fingers froze and his eyes moved from the computer to the phone. "You actually *got* the Linden account?

That's great," he said, forcing enthusiasm into his voice. He paused. "Well, there's no doubt now that you'll keep the business."

He heard her sigh. Several weeks had passed since they last discussed closing her agency once they married.

"Even without Linden, I would have kept my company, Braxton. I've worked too hard to get here."

"I know, honey. It's just that I want to take care of you."

"I can take care of myself."

"I know you can," he said quickly. "It's just my way of saying that I love you. Listen, I think this calls for a celebration."

"That's why I'm calling," Anya said, cheering up again. "We're having a party tonight—nothing fancy. I'm just taking them to Crossroads. We'll have hors d'oeuvres in one of their private rooms."

"What time?" Braxton asked, trying to sound interested.

"Between five and six."

Braxton hesitated. "I don't know, sweetie . . ."

It was a moment before Anya spoke. "I thought you wanted to celebrate."

"Uh, yes, but I have to e-mail this chapter to my editor in the morning," he lied.

"And you can't find a couple of hours to spend with me?"

He waited a few beats. "All I want to do is spend time with you. Let's get together afterward. You can come by here."

Silence. Then, she asked, "Are you sure you can't make it to *my* party?"

Braxton could hear Anya's fingers tapping against her desk. "It'll be better if we meet later."

"Okay." Her voice was as sharp as a jagged rock.

"So, you'll come here?" he asked.

"Whatever."

"Now you have an attitude."

"No I don't."

"I can hear it."

"Whatever."

"Anya, I don't feel like going to a party with your office. I'll end up sitting in some corner while you go off and do your thing."

"I'll call you when I get home."

The dial tone droned in his ear. Braxton leaned back and tapped his fingertips together. That Linden account was going to impede his plans. How would he get her to sell her business now? He sighed. There was no way he could celebrate when he wasn't happy.

He picked up the phone and punched one of the speed-dial numbers. It was answered on the first ring.

"Hey, Carlos, what do you guys have planned for tonight?"

"My amigo, como estás?" Carlos sang out. Carlos was as Black as anyone, but since their childhood days in Oakland he'd told people he was Puerto Rican. To keep his story going, he always sprinkled his conversation with a few Spanish words.

"Just wondering if you guys were doing anything tonight."

"Are you telling me that Anya is letting you off the leash?" Carlos asked, laughing.

"You know it's not like that."

"Yeah, right. That's why an entire month has passed since we've heard from you."

"That's why I'm calling. So what's up?"

"Well, William and I are going to the Sports Bar in Hermosa. The Lakers are playing the Warriors."

"Sounds good. What time?"

"I have a client at five, and I'll be heading over after that. The game doesn't begin until seven-thirty, but we plan on hanging out until then. So are we finally going to see you on a Friday night?"

"I'll be there."

Carlos laughed again. "Either Anya is out of town or she finally dumped your sorry behind."

"Just get your wallet ready. I'm going to take all your money when the Warriors beat the Lakers," Braxton said, reminding Carlos that he'd never forgotten his home team.

They both laughed as they hung up. Braxton tapped his fingers on the desk. It was time for him to show Anya what he really thought of Mitchell & Associates. When she called him after her little party, she'd discover that he wasn't sitting around waiting, and maybe she would finally get the message.

Anya had wanted to be the first to arrive at the restaurant, but she lingered in her office, shuffling papers and waiting for the phone to ring. By six, she'd realized that Braxton was not going to share her joy.

"Hi, Anya." Dianna rushed to her side. "How does it look? I hope you like it. We didn't have a lot of time."

Anya took Dianna's hand. "It's fine," she said, smiling, taking in the festively decorated room already filled with most of her team.

The room was dimly lit, getting much of its light

from the lampposts that shone through the large windows. There were red and white balloons hovering near the ceiling, and the small tables throughout were covered with alternating red and white tablecloths. Anya's heels clicked against the wooden planks on the floor as she walked to the center. "You've outdone yourself, Ms. Macy."

Dianna beamed. "I'm glad you're pleased, Ms. Mitchell."

"Aren't we on a first-name basis yet?" David laughed as he joined them.

"Hello, Mr. Montgomery." Anya chuckled, as Dianna excused herself.

David grinned, a kind of crooked half-smile that highlighted the dimple in his left cheek. He took a sip of the drink he was holding. "Can I get you something?"

"I'll have a soda."

David casually placed his hand on her lower back and guided her to the bar.

"Only a soda? I think you deserve a little celebration yourself."

"I'm celebrating, but I don't drink." She smiled at the bartender and requested a Sprite.

David arched his eyebrow. "I didn't know that."

"There's a lot you don't know, Mr. Montgomery. Because every time I've asked you to join Braxton and me for dinner, you've declined. I'm beginning to take it personally."

David led Anya to the only empty table, in the back corner, next to a window that looked onto a crowded Melrose Boulevard. "Believe me, I don't have anything against you. I don't go out much. Speaking of your fiancé, where is Braxton?"

Anya paused. "He couldn't make it."

"Ah, the busy writer."

"Busy, busy." Her words dripped with sarcasm.

David frowned but didn't respond.

"So," Anya started, as she leaned toward him, "Mr. Boy Wonder, did you get all your business savvy from American Express, or did business school have something to do with it?"

David smirked. "It was more your savvy than mine that got this account."

She ignored his implication. "But your expertise certainly helped. If I didn't know better, I would think you were one of those high-powered New York–Wall Street types."

His face clouded, but he managed to keep his smile. He made a gesture with his head that Anya couldn't decipher. "Have you lived in Los Angeles your entire life?" he asked.

"Umm-hmm. Except for when I went to school in New York. I went to Columbia."

"I didn't know that. I saw your degree from USC and assumed—"

"That was for graduate school. But I lived in New York for four years. Quite an experience. Where are you from?"

The smile left his face. "A little bit of everywhere. Did you like New York?"

She nodded. "It's different from Los Angeles. Have you ever been there?"

It took a moment for him to nod. "I was born in New York. You've built quite a business here. You've got to be proud."

"I am." She paused. "I wouldn't have guessed that you were from New York. How long did you live there?"

He lowered his eyes. "Until I was a teenager." He raised his hand, signaling a waiter.

Anya watched him closely as he ordered another Midori Sour. By the time he turned back to her, he was smiling. He raised his glass in a toast and Anya followed. "To our winning team. May things with us just get better and better."

He held her eyes as he took a sip of his drink, then smiled when he placed his glass on the table. "So what inspired you to start your own company?"

"One day I got tired of working for other folks and was convinced I could do this."

"You've done good. It had to take a lot of courage."

She noticed his dimple again and resisted the urge to reach out and touch his cheek. She cleared her throat. "It wasn't courage as much as faith."

"Sounds like you're a religious person."

She chuckled. "I don't know what that means."

"Religious," he said, as if he was about to give her a definition. "A person who goes to church and believes in God."

"I go to church and I believe in God. But if you were to ask me about my spirituality, I would say that I have a personal relationship with Jesus."

David ran his hand through his beard. "I see."

Anya laughed. "That's all you can say?"

"That's all I *should* say."

She smiled. "Now that you know all about me, tell me something about you that I don't know from your resume."

David looked past Anya and raised his hand.

"Melissa, come over here a second," he said to one of the senior associates.

"Hi, David, Anya." Melissa's long auburn hair swung over her shoulder as she looked around the room. "This is really nice."

"You deserve it—we all do," Anya said. "I'm going to refill my drink, do either one of you want anything?"

"Nothing for me. I want to catch my breath first," Melissa said.

David shook his head.

As Melissa sat with David, Anya stood at the bar. Her eyes swept the room, but she kept returning to David. She sipped her soda and watched as he laughed with Melissa. "What's your story, Mr. Montgomery?" she muttered.

"Anya, thanks for a great party." A few of the associates came over to chat with their boss.

"You're welcome, but beware—it's my way of bribing you for the long hours ahead."

They laughed as she strolled away, to talk to Alaister who was standing alone by the door.

"I hope you're having a good time, because this celebration would have never happened without you," she said.

He looked at her and smiled slightly. "Thanks, I did work hard on getting this account." Then he lowered his eyes. "I wasn't sure if you knew that."

"Alaister, I'm very aware of how hard you work." She paused. "I had hoped we cleared up everything a few months ago."

He took a sip from the wineglass he held. "It's all clear, Anya."

She squinted slightly. "I hope so, because you are a valuable asset to the team. The only reason I brought David in is because he has more experience. But I expect you to grow with me, Alaister. Although you weren't ready for the position six months ago, you'll be ready soon."

He twirled the glass in his hand. "Whatever you say."

He walked away without saying another word, and Anya sighed. She knew he had been disappointed when she announced David's addition to the team. And even though they'd discussed the reasons, she still had the feeling that Alaister didn't accept her decision. But at least he's professional, she thought. He didn't let his personal feelings get in the way of his performance. The Linden account was proof of that.

The group started spilling into the restaurant for the Friday night jazz ensemble. Anya scanned the room and found David alone at the bar. She emptied her glass and walked over to him.

"The troops were happy," she said, as she motioned for the bartender to pour her another soda.

"Yeah, Boss, thanks again." He grinned.

She couldn't resist. "How do you do that?" He frowned, confused. "You only smile with half of your mouth, kind of to one side. It looks . . . rugged, mischievous."

His smile disappeared, and he looked into his glass.

"That was a compliment."

When he looked up, he stared into her eyes for a long moment, and Anya held her breath. The faint sound of music was coming from the next room.

"My mother used to say the same thing." He leaned his head back and emptied his glass in one swallow. "She— she passed away a few years ago, and you reminded me of her."

"I'm sorry. I didn't know."

"It's not something I like to talk about."

She nodded slightly. "I understand. I lost both of my parents a while ago."

His eyes widened, and he lightly touched her shoulder. "Now I'm sorry."

"It's all right," she said, waving her hand. "Though it's not something you ever get over, I've found a way to live with it. And I know they're with the Lord."

His smile returned. "Let's not end such a fabulous day this way." He hesitated before he added, "Why don't we go somewhere so we can talk?"

"Ah . . . I can't," she faltered, surprised by his invitation. "I have to be at the airport early tomorrow."

"Running away just as things are starting to get good?"

She shook her head. "I'm picking up my cousin." Anya pulled her valet ticket from her purse.

"Let me walk you out."

"No, you should stay. The music is good, and who knows who you might meet," Anya teased.

"I'm too much of a gentleman to let a lady go into the night alone. Anything can happen in the dark."

Anya bit her lip, but she allowed him to lead her into the main restaurant, which was still filled with customers.

Before they could make it to the valet, one of the young men ran to them. "Hello, Ms. Mitchell."

"Michael, you're always working."

The valet grinned. "It seems that way. I'll get your car." He trotted off before she could give him the ticket.

"Now I am impressed." David grinned. "Even the valet knows your name."

"I come here a lot, don't be impressed."

"Too late, I already am."

Anya looked at him and froze. There was that dimpled, crooked smile again and his eyes seemed to hold her hostage. She forced herself to look away and poked through her purse, pretending to look for something. The squealing tires from the underground parking lot were a welcome relief.

"Good night, David. Thanks again for a great job."

He held the car door open for her. "That's why you pay me the big bucks, right?"

She laughed. "You earned your dollars today."

He bowed. "Thankyouverymuch." He closed the door and his eyes drilled into her again as he leaned into the car window. "Have a good evening." Their eyes held for a long moment before he headed back into the restaurant.

Anya fumbled with her keys, giving herself time to watch him stroll away. "Mr. Montgomery," she said aloud, "you are a man of mystery." She waited until he disappeared, then laid her foot on the accelerator and screeched her car into the night.

nya made a sharp turn, maneuvered her car into the LAX parking lot, and sang hallelujah when she found a space on the first level. She'd planned to arrive a bit earlier, giving herself a chance to grab a Starbucks vente mocha and find the right gate, without having to rush. But when the alarm had chirped this morning, she slapped the clock and turned over, yielding to the comfort of her satin sheets.

It took her just a few minutes to run from the car to the terminal. The blinking numbers on the schedule board indicated the Chicago flight had already arrived. With her leather backpack bouncing against her, Anya sprinted to Gate 49A and made it just as the first passengers began exiting. She stepped from the crowd, eagerly awaiting the arrival of her cousin, Sasha.

Although they were first cousins, they were not as close as Anya would have liked. Before Sasha was two and when Anya was just nine, her uncle Jake had relocated his family, accepting a teaching position at the University of Chicago. Her father's brother and his family had visited them almost every Christmas and

Sasha had come for many summers, but they hadn't spent much time together as adults. This was their first real chance.

"Hey, cuz!" Sasha yelled, waving both hands in a frenzy. She strutted toward Anya like a runway model, her long limbs swinging with a cool confidence that Anya didn't remember. Sasha tossed her head as if flinging back her hair, only her shoulder-length curls were gone. Her hair was cropped so close to her head that Sasha was almost bald. It was a shocking hairstyle, but Sasha carried it off. It made her look younger than her twenty-nine years.

Sasha's black-leather jumpsuit hugged every curve of her body, flaunting her one-hundred-and-twenty-five-pound statuesque form. Fellow passengers stepped aside, allowing Sasha to flow through the crowd and Anya could hear their whispers—who is she? This woman was somebody, for sure.

Anya's smile widened. She didn't know what she expected, but clearly Sasha had landed solidly on two very shapely legs. "I am so glad to see you!" Anya said as they hugged.

Sasha held her cousin for a moment, then pulled back suddenly. "Come on, Anya. Let's go to baggage claim." She took Anya's hand and started a slow trot.

"What's wrong?" Even though she was almost as tall as Sasha, Anya had difficulty keeping up with her leggy cousin.

"Nothing." The heels of Sasha's boots clicked against the newly waxed floor as they scampered past shops in the United terminal. "I just want to get my bag so that we can get going."

At baggage claim, Sasha hovered close to the carousel as her eyes searched the crowd.

Anya surveyed her cousin from head to toe. "Well, you look great. All the havoc you were causing in Chicago hasn't seemed to affect you."

"I wasn't burning down the city. All I did was appear on a television show."

"*Jerry Springer* is not just a TV show."

She shrugged. "Gordon deserved it. But it was no big deal."

Anya couldn't believe her cousin's nonchalance. From the way she'd heard the story, Gordon, Sasha's ex-husband, had threatened to do everything except put a contract out on her. And, with his connections, Sasha's parents were terrified. "No big deal? Then why did you hightail it out of Chicago?"

"Because Gordon *is* crazy. And my parents believed his threats."

"You knew he wouldn't sit back after you told the world his business."

"What was I supposed to do? Take everything he was throwing at me?"

Anya shook her head. After seven volatile years of marriage, a turbulent divorce, and discovering that Gordon's wife-in-waiting was pregnant, Sasha had exhibited the fury of the scorned ex. The producers of *The Jerry Springer Show* had eagerly given Sasha her forum to dish the dirt on Chicago's most successful real-estate developer. Her tactics were dubious, but effective. When the show aired last week, Gordon had been appropriately humiliated—and furious.

"Your parents didn't deserve this drama."

"Maybe it wasn't one of my best moves." She paused as a wide grin broke across her face. "But, girl, it was fun. And everyone knows that Gordon barks like a toothless Rottweiler. He's not going to do anything. I came here to give my parents room and take a vacation from those crumb-snatchers," Sasha said, referring to the second-grade students she'd left behind while she took this sabbatical. "And I knew this would please Madear. She didn't give my parents a break. Calling every day to give her opinion on how they should handle me. I'm grown. No one can *handle* me."

Anya rolled her eyes as Sasha droned on.

"Where is Grandmother Dearest anyway? I was sure she would be at the gate waiting with her usual look of disdain."

Before Anya could object to Sasha's statement, a portly gentleman interrupted them. "Ah, excuse me, Sasha." The man grasped his briefcase handle tightly and shifted his feet. "Sasha, ah, I wanted to get your telephone number."

Anya's eyebrows arched as she watched her cousin move closer to the man.

"I don't have a number where I can be reached," Sasha said throatily. "So give me your number." She towered over the man and her breath flickered the few wisps of hair atop his head. "I'll call you this evening and we can do *all* those things we talked about."

The man licked his lips and stared into her eyes, then suddenly broke eye contact. He swallowed hard, disappointment etched on his face. "Uh . . . ." The man looked down and spoke to his shoes. "Maybe we'll see each other . . . some other time . . . soon, I hope." He turned and walked away quickly.

"What was that all about?"

"Just a married man who conjured up some chocolate fantasy," Sasha said. "And don't look so shocked. I've decided to live a little differently. Instead of being walked on and tossed away, I'm going to do the walking and tossing. It's all about me. If it feels good, I'm going to do it."

Anya sighed. Maybe she should drop Sasha off at Madear's and let her grandmother handle this rebel.

"Do you have any other bags?" Anya asked, as Sasha pulled the garment bag from the carousel.

"Nope, just one. I'm gonna do some serious shopping while I'm here." She slapped her sunglasses on her face. "Let's go. I'm ready to become a California girl!"

Anya followed her cousin who acted as if she knew where she was going. When they got to the car, Sasha threw her bag into the trunk.

"Well, you go, cuz." Sasha pranced around the BMW. "I knew things were going good, but I didn't realize how well. Madear said your business is thriving."

"I have been blessed and give all the glory to God."

Sasha glanced sideways as she wiggled into the seat. "Madear has finally gotten to you, huh? Got you talking all that God stuff and she probably has you going to church."

Anya paused. One reason she'd insisted that Sasha stay with her was so she could share her faith with her cousin. She knew that Madear would witness to Sasha but Madear pushed, and that would shut Sasha down. "I go to church, although I don't go to Madear's church," Anya finally responded. "But I do love the Lord."

"You haven't become a Jesus freak, have you?" When Anya frowned, Sasha continued. "You know, one of those people on the corner who yells that everyone is going to hell?"

"I haven't stood on a corner in a long time." Anya chuckled. "I just rededicated my life to the Lord many years ago, and everything has been different since then."

"How?"

"I have a peace and joy in my life that I can't fully explain. All I know is that I'm saved and I'm happy."

Sasha was silent for a moment. "I never understood that God stuff. And in Madear's church, I didn't stand a chance. I never got beyond all that whooping and hollering."

"So you don't go to church at home?"

Sasha shook her head. "Only for the normal things— weddings and funerals."

"I'm surprised. The way Uncle Jake and Dad were raised."

"Maybe that has something to do with it."

They were silent as Anya paid the parking attendant, then maneuvered through the crowd of cars that filled the airport.

"It's not that I don't believe in God," Sasha said suddenly. "It's all of that other stuff that I can't deal with. Like praying to someone that you can't see and believing that God controls everything. It doesn't make sense to me."

"It will never make sense if you try to understand God with your mind. You can't do that. God is a Spirit and has to be approached on that level. The Bible says, *God is a Spirit and they that worship him must worship him in spirit and in truth.*"

The cackle of Sasha's laughter startled Anya.

"Do you actually go around quoting scripture to people?" Sasha laughed.

Anya's shoulders tightened, but she kept her tone

light. "Only if they need to hear it. I was trying to explain it to you."

"I didn't mean to laugh." Sasha was still chuckling. "I just didn't realize. What made you so religious?"

Anya hated when people called her that. They didn't understand that she wasn't practicing rituals, she had a personal relationship with God.

"I went through a tough time and it brought me to the Lord in a real way."

"Something *bad* happened to *you*? What happened?"

They were at a stoplight and Anya tapped her fingers on the steering wheel. Should she tell Sasha? Only Maria Covington, her college roommate, and Braxton knew her secret.

"It was something that made me rethink my life."

Sasha nodded her head slowly. "I understand. That's what's going on with me. I'm changing everything in my life."

Anya picked up speed as she turned onto LaCienega. "Well, any time you want, we can talk about what I found in my life with God."

"You're sounding like a street-preacher. Can we talk about something else?"

"Sure." Anya backed down. "Are you hungry?"

"Yeah, but take me to one of those famous L.A. restaurants where I can see and be seen. I'm dying to see someone famous."

Anya chuckled. The request of every L.A. visitor—to see a celebrity. As if they hung out on every corner. "Well, cuz," Anya said, mimicking Sasha, "I know just the place."

Serendipity's parking lot was only half-full with the usual Mercedes, Jaguars, and Lexuses. Anya expected a larger Saturday crowd, and was relieved when they didn't have to endure the normal thirty-minute wait. They both squinted in the dim light as they followed the hostess past the mirrored bar to the back of the room. The low lights and the oak furniture always made Serendipity seem darker than it was.

Customers were sprinkled throughout the restaurant, but the bar was completely surrounded by people chatting and drinking, even at this early hour.

"The food is good, and you'll probably see someone . . ." Anya leaned across the table so that she could be heard above the din.

Sasha fanned her face. "I already did! Didn't you see Rick Fox and Vanessa Williams?" Anya picked up the menu, making Sasha frown. "Don't you want to see them?"

Anya looked up. "No, I *want* to eat." She returned to the menu. "Unless Rick and Vanessa are going to pay for our lunch."

"Well, if they won't, I will," a masculine voice said.

Anya didn't even have to look up. She recognized the deep, hoarse voice. Hunter Blaine. Hollywood's African-American flavor-of-the-month. He kissed Anya's cheek.

Hunter had just completed his first major film, *Secret Lovers*. The audience had swooned, panted, and then demanded to see more of Mr. Blaine. The surprise box-office hit led to a bigger surprise: Hunter's Academy Award nomination. And although he didn't win, mainstays like Denzel, Wesley, and Will were already being pushed aside by the name of Hunter Blaine.

"How are you?" Hunter asked in his bedroom voice.

"Hunter, good to see you." Anya forced a smile to her face. "I heard you were in London working on a film."

"Baby, I'm back." His eyes wandered to Sasha. "And *who* is this vision?"

As Sasha stood, Hunter scrutinized her body and his grin told Anya that he liked what he saw. Anya knew that Hunter had been with a lot of beautiful women—he fancied himself a Hollywood player. She didn't want her cousin added to his list.

"Whatever you want me to do, I'll do it," Hunter said as he lifted Sasha's hand and kissed it.

Anya wanted to stick her fingers down her throat. She hoped her cousin felt the same way, but the giddy grin on Sasha's face told Anya that Hunter's magical powers were in full force. "Hunter, this is my cousin, Sasha Clarke. Sasha, this is Hunter Blaine."

Still holding his hand, she gushed, "I am such a big fan. By the way, my name is Sasha Mitchell now. I'm *divorced*."

"Ah, the first thing we have in common."

Anya closed her eyes and said a quick prayer.

"I knew you were related. You are as beautiful as your cousin. Has she told you that she broke my heart?"

"What did she do?" Sasha sat down and looked from Anya to Hunter.

Anya waved her hand in the air. "Don't listen to a word he says."

Hunter leaned over Sasha as if he were about to divulge a top secret. His lips were close to her ears. "After my divorce, I tried to get your cousin to go out with me, but she always refused. And now"—he lifted Anya's left hand—"she has given herself to another man. Have you seen this rock?"

Sasha laughed. "That was the first thing I noticed at the airport."

"You're from out of town?" Hunter took a chair from the next table, then straddled it.

As Anya watched Hunter, she tried to determine why she'd never liked him. Maybe it was because he was just a little too smooth.

But Sasha seemed to be taken with this man who had been calculatingly designed by his agent; from the sheen of his bald head to his perfectly capped teeth that hid a gap in front. Many people mistook him for the model Tyson, and Anya could definitely see the resemblance.

Anya watched Sasha fall further into Hunter's web, and she had to stop it. "Hunter, I'm so sorry you won't be able to join us."

Hunter chuckled. "You're so subtle, Anya." He took Sasha's hand again. "Your cousin doesn't like me."

"That's not true, you're one of my best clients." Anya smiled.

He chuckled again. "One of these days, Anya . . ." He stood and turned to Sasha. "Since you're new in town, I'd love to show you off—I mean, show you around." Staring at Sasha, he reached into his jeans and then handed her a card. "Give me a call. I'll make sure you have good times while you're here."

He was barely out of hearing range, when Sasha slouched in her chair. "Girlfriend, I am im-pressed! I didn't know you knew *him*. Did he really ask you to go out? Did you really turn him down? Are you crazy?"

"Which question do you want me to answer first?"

"How do you know him?"

"I met his wife at church and became their financial

planner when he was on that sitcom. He wasn't anybody then."

"He's somebody now. Did he really ask you to go out?"

"He asks every woman he meets to go out. That's why Cynthia divorced him."

"He'll only have to ask me once." Sasha flicked the business card against the tablecloth, then tucked it inside her purse.

The waitress told them the specials, and they agreed to share the crab cakes and then the barbecue pasta.

Sasha took a sip of water. "If Hunter Blaine doesn't fan your flames, tell me about the man who does."

Anya glanced at her hand. Even in the dull light, the diamond's colors danced. "Braxton. He's wonderful," she said flatly, her eyes still on her finger.

Sasha frowned. "Mom and Madear told me you had this incredible man and were totally in love."

"I am." Anya finally looked up from her ring.

"So what's wrong? And don't bother to tell me that everything is fine. I just escaped from a nightmarish relationship and know the signs."

Anya leaned her elbows on the table. "Recently I've been feeling like this may not be right."

Sasha frowned. "He's not suffering from the Gordon Clarke syndrome, is he?"

"I'm afraid to ask . . ."

"A man with a hyperactive zipper. You know, a zipper that constantly goes down around other women."

Anya laughed so hard she had to take a sip of water. Finally she said, "Another woman is not the problem."

The waitress placed the crab cakes in front of them and, just as Sasha was ready to dive in, Anya took her hand.

"Would you mind if I blessed the food?"

Sasha's brows knitted together, but she shrugged. "Fine with me."

Anya bowed her head, and Sasha followed suit. When Anya finished, she heard Sasha sigh. "Thank you," she said as she patted Sasha's hand.

They ate in silence for a few moments, before Sasha returned to her questioning. "So what is going on with you and Braxton?"

"I have a feeling that we're not going to make it, we may be too different."

"That should be a good thing," Sasha said, swinging her fork in the air.

"Differences are good as long as they're not fundamental differences."

Sasha's eyes narrowed, then opened wide in understanding. "Oh, *fundamental* differences. He's not into God like you are."

"That's not it at all," Anya snapped.

"Hey, girl!" Sasha put her hands up as if to block an attack. "Don't go to war with me. I'm not the enemy."

"Braxton's not the enemy either."

"I never said he was."

"And Braxton *is* a Christian."

Sasha raised her eyebrows. "Who are you trying to convince?"

Anya pursed her lips and picked at her crab cake. But her favorite dish had lost its savor.

The waitress returned with the pasta. With downcast eyes, they both silently swirled the fettucine through the red sauce.

After a few minutes, Sasha dropped her fork. "Anya,

I'm sorry. I've been here for less than an hour and you're ready to ship me back. But I can't go back to that lion's den with Gordon and his new wife, and their new baby— please forgive me and let me stay, pretty-please?" She contorted her face, like a lost puppy.

Anya couldn't hold back her laughter. She didn't blame Sasha. All she'd done was ask good questions. "You can stay," Anya said playfully.

Sasha exhaled, feigning relief. "Thank goodness. I couldn't face the new Mrs. Clarke."

"Isn't it too late to say that? How did they get her on *Jerry Springer*?"

"I have no idea." Sasha shook her head fiercely. "I couldn't believe it when she walked onto the stage. That woman is lying-down-horizontal-on-the-couch-telling-all-of-your-thoughts-to-a-man-in-a-white-jacket crazy! Showing up pregnant and getting all in my face when *she* got pregnant while I was still married to Gordon. She's lucky I didn't beat her down on national TV. With her eighteen-year-old self."

Anya's mouth opened into a wide O. "Isn't Gordon my age?"

"He wishes. He saw forty a long time ago. Maybe I'm exaggerating—but she's barely twenty-one. Her mother probably had to sign the papers."

Anya pursed her lips. "Weren't you twenty-one when you married Gordon?"

"Yeah and he was ten years older than me. So now he's old enough to be this hussy's grandfather," she said. "His child won't know whether to call him Pappy or Granddaddy."

"Well, I'm glad you're away from that madness."

"I'm not thinking about Gordon. I got my money," she said, holding one finger in the air and moving her neck in her best sistergirl imitation. "And that will keep me happy for quite a while."

They laughed and chatted while the waitress removed their plates. For the first time in days, Anya took flight from what weighed heavily on her. For now, she was going to enjoy these harmonic moments, before she faced the real music.

Chapter 7

*T*he plush white towel fell and, as Braxton leaned over, he caught his naked reflection in the mirrored wall. He stood, flexed his muscles, then turned sideways, focusing on his legs. Time to hit the bike again.

He tucked the towel around his waist, then, with his electric shaver in one hand, he brushed the other across his facial stubble. Good thing the summer months are coming, he thought. He needed some color. Maybe for the honeymoon, he and Anya could jet off to someplace warm where he could revel in the sun and roast his tan skin to a deeper brown.

The razor's whirring snapped his daydream. He opened the bathroom door and glanced at the answering machine on the nightstand. No blinking light—no calls, no messages.

He wanted to check anyway. One push of the button: "The time is two twenty-seven. You have . . . no messages," the mechanical voice announced.

Braxton threw a pillow across the room, then sank into the bed. "How could she not call? She can't still be mad." But, even as he spoke, he knew she was.

Last night, he had stayed out as late as possible. It didn't matter that he'd been thinking about Anya all night—the point was to teach her a lesson. She was supposed to return home, call him repeatedly, and be overcome with worry . . . or jealousy. Either would have worked.

But when the taxi dropped him home after four this morning, there were no calls from his fiancée. Growling, he had crawled into bed. With all the wine he'd consumed, he'd fallen asleep instantaneously.

This morning, he'd awakened to the percussion symphony in his head, and he'd spent the last few hours in the soothing, bubbling heat of his Jacuzzi. He had taken his time, knowing that, once he'd finished, Anya's call would be waiting.

Braxton sighed. This was not the time to let pride get in the way. His plan would never come to fruition if they weren't speaking.

Still clad only in the towel, he shivered as he traipsed down the hall to his office, his toes gripping the warmth of the deep pile carpet. Before he entered, he heard the clicking of his fax machine. He knew it was from his agent; his latest contract. As the machine spewed forth pages, he sat back in the chair and smiled. Seven years since his first book—his third contract—his first seven-figure advance. He looked at the pages and whispered, "Thank you, Lord."

When he was growing up in Oakland, moving from one foster home to the next, he never imagined this. This was a long way from Oakland, and from his first advance of thirty-five hundred dollars. He couldn't buy a believer in those lean years. Even his wife, Roxanne, had walked away. When she'd told him she was returning to Oakland, Braxton had strongly protested and seriously considered giving up his dream. But he'd stayed his ground, birthed his novel, and never looked back. Success was bitter-sweet, though. It cost him his family; but that was going to change.

He tossed the contract aside and searched his desk. Within minutes, he had the information. It took a few phone calls and more money than he'd expected, but finally everything was arranged.

Braxton leaned into his chair and his towel fell open, but he made no moves to cover himself. Instead, he allowed his mind to drift. After Roxanne, he was sure he would never expose himself to love again. And having a traditional family—he'd given up on that too. But like a blessing from God, Anya had changed all that. Not only did he love her more than he thought possible, but she was the key to building his future.

He rubbed his hands along his face. Anya had to understand what he needed to do and tonight would be a start. Tonight, Anya Mitchell would be like clay, and he would be the master sculptor.

Chapter 8

$\mathcal{T}$*he man was parked a few feet away, but when he saw her car, he slouched into his seat. Only the top of his head, covered with a New York Yankees cap, was visible. He watched as she pulled into the garage and closed the door. Then, he lifted himself up. It seemed that she had company and this might take a bit longer. But that didn't bother him. It was the chase that had always thrilled him.*

From the first time until now, he'd always enjoyed the hunt. Stalking the prey was exhilarating, though he knew his teacher would disagree.

"You're such a sissy," he could hear Sean saying.

His friend had never thought much of him. From his first day in school, Sean had taunted him, first with his words, then with his fists.

"Mama's boy, mama's boy!" Sean had chased the six-year-old around the playground.

He had been horrified. "Why are you doing this to me?" he cried.

"Because you're nothin' but a mama's boy."

He hadn't known what to do. It was the first time he'd

been away from home and his mother at the same time. They had both shed inconsolable tears as she dressed him for school that morning. As he cried, "Why?" his mother had explained that it wasn't her choice, the law made her do it. Their tears had continued as they left the house, and his mother walked him down the blocks, past aban-doned buildings to the school that looked as if it should have long ago been condemned.

From the moment his mother left him, the taunting began. He'd endured countless days of terror as he ducked and dodged, trying to escape the wrath of Sean. He was no contest for the older, bigger boy and went home daily with bloody lips and fresh cuts. It didn't help when his mother went to school to complain. He would never identify his assailant, fearing that the beatings would worsen.

Desperate, he finally found his own way to make peace.

"If you leave me alone, I'll do your homework." His lips had trembled as he spoke.

Sean's fist stopped mid-air. "You'll do my homework . . . every day?"

He'd nodded quickly.

"But, I'm in the fourth grade. You're only in the second."

"That's okay, I'm very smart." The words quivered from his mouth.

A slow smile came across Sean's face. "What about mathematics?"

"That's my best subject," he'd replied, his confidence suddenly building.

His life changed that day. No longer did he live with the fear that had consumed him for over a year. Instead, the seven-year-old became "the scholar" in one of the most notorious neighborhood gangs, led by Sean Thomas's sixteen-year-old brother—the Bedford Boys. "The scholar" now had an automatic ticket for protection from anyone in one of the toughest areas of the city.

A car pulled up next to him, and honked. "Are you coming out, buddy?"

The man quickly turned on the ignition and pulled the car away from the curb. Careless, he thought as he shook his head. No one should see him outside of her home.

He slowly drove up the street and looked at her townhouse in his rearview mirror. It didn't matter that he had to leave—if today wasn't the day, so be it. Patience was what he had to practice. Everyone said that was a virtue.

"How poor are they that have not patience," he recited Shakespeare's line aloud.

His favorite writer was correct. It didn't matter if he showed her today, tomorrow, the next day, or the next. He would have his chance, and when he finished, she would know for sure that he was a man.

Chapter 9

irl, this place is laid!" Sasha exclaimed, as she bounded up the stairs to the living room of Anya's tri-level townhouse. She dropped her bag, and raised her head, looking up at the fifteen-foot ceiling. "Wow!"

"This is the main level. The family room is downstairs," Anya said, as Sasha followed her through the dining room and kitchen, which were decorated in the same black-and-white décor as the living room.

"The bedrooms are up here." Anya led Sasha upstairs. "There are three of them. One I use as an office, and this one"—Anya swung open the double doors—"is your room."

"You have got it going on." Sasha tossed her garment bag onto the wrought-iron bed, then went to the window and pushed aside the sheer white curtains, allowing the late afternoon sun to shine freely into the room. Sasha looked onto the patio, which was trimmed with colorful mums and impatiens that bloomed even in the middle of the California winter. "I love this. I could stay for a year!"

"How long do you plan on staying?" Anya asked.

Sasha shrugged. "I haven't decided. But don't worry, if I get in your way I'll go to Madear's. She'd love to have me stay with her so she could lecture me on all the things I've done wrong."

"You should call Madear and let her know you arrived safely. We could go over there this evening."

Sasha sat in the cotton-damask chair that faced the window. "Not today. Give me a chance to get settled."

"Okay . . ." Anya dragged the word out. "You sound like you're mad at Madear."

"Our grandmother doesn't like me." She put up her hands before Anya could protest. "Save your breath, it's true. You just don't know the whole story."

"What story?"

Sasha went to the window and stared at the blooming flowers. "You remember Miss Mattie?"

Anya nodded. "She's still Madear's best friend."

"One summer when I was visiting, Miss Mattie brought some pictures that she'd taken of us to Madear." Sasha took a deep breath. "Madear looked at a picture of me and said, 'That chil' sure is black and ugly.'" Sasha paused, shaking her head. "My own grandmother said that."

Anya frowned. "I can't imagine Madear saying anything like that."

"I heard her. I had just walked into the kitchen. There was Madear holding the picture, and shaking her head like she was disgusted."

Anya was silent for a moment. "Do you think you could have misunderstood?"

Sasha shook her head strongly. "I understand English."

"It doesn't make sense. You look more like Madear than any of us."

"Only ten shades darker. That's the part she hates." When Sasha turned to Anya she was smiling. "For a lot of years, it hurt. But I don't trip anymore. Haven't you heard, Black is beautiful. And I am *so* comfortable in my skin now. My dark-chocolate lovely skin," Sasha said, with her hand on her hip.

Anya hugged her cousin. "I love the way that sounds." She leaned away from Sasha and playfully rubbed her head. "So it's only your hair that's a challenge now, huh?" Anya teased, anxious to change the subject.

Sasha turned to the mirror and smiled at her reflection. "Do you like it?"

"It looks good on you."

"It was the final page of my life with Gordon. He liked my hair long, so when I cut it, it was my sign of complete freedom. I cut that man right out of my hair!"

Anya giggled. "Why don't we go out to celebrate the new Sasha Mitchell Clarke Mitchell?"

Sasha sighed. "I'd rather stay in tonight."

"I thought you were eager to become part of the L.A. scenery. You've got to experience L.A. on a Saturday night."

"Tonight I'd love to crash."

Anya shrugged. "Okay, I just want you to have a good time." She turned to the window and let her eyes drift along the parked cars. There wasn't a person in sight. Still, she pulled the curtains closed.

"Don't worry about me," Sasha said, as she looked at the business card she'd just taken from her purse. She stared at the name—HUNTER BLAINE—printed in bright red on the white linen paper. "I plan on nothing but good times. Anyway, what about you and the writer? Don't you have plans?"

"I haven't spoken to him today," Anya said, and resisted the urge to run and check her messages.

"Call him. I can't wait to meet the world-famous author."

Before she could respond, chimes echoed through the house.

Sasha's eyes scatted around the room. "What's that?"

Through the curtains, Anya saw the cream-colored Land Cruiser in the visitor's spot. "That's Braxton."

"Whoa, this man is strange. What other sounds does he make?"

Anya laughed. "That's the door." She bounded down the stairs and tried to hold her smile when she opened the door.

"Hey, you."

"You cut quite a dashing figure," she said, holding the door open wider. Braxton was decked out in the Armani tuxedo she'd helped him select for the Image Awards.

He smiled. "So do you."

Anya glanced down at her jeans and T-shirt, then smiled back. "I can't compete with you right now."

He moved so close to her that there was barely space for the air between them. "If I have my way, that'll change. I'm going to seduce you into going with me."

"Where?" Anya asked softly as his light brown eyes held hers.

He leaned forward, set his lips upon hers, then jerked back when he heard the coughing. "Oh" was all he said, as his eyes moved from Anya to Sasha.

Anya grabbed Braxton's hand. "This is my cousin, Sasha. Remember I told you she was coming?"

"Yeah." He held out his hand to Sasha, who was leaning against the banister. "It's nice to finally meet you."

She slapped his hand playfully. "Give me a hug. From the look of the ring on my cousin's finger, we're family." As they hugged, Sasha said, "I've heard great things about you."

"I guess she didn't tell you about last night." He lifted Anya's hand and kissed it. "I'm sorry, honey."

"Maybe I should go to my room and unpack," Sasha said, as she sank into a chair across from them. "Seems like this might become a private moment."

"You don't have to leave." Braxton led Anya to the couch. "Apologies should only be in private if you don't mean them." When they sat down, Braxton lifted Anya's hands to his lips. "Forgive me for last night. When the woman I love has success like that, I should have been right by her side."

Sasha sighed. "How sweet!"

"You're going to have to give up your front-row seat, cousin dear," Anya said. "I need to talk to Braxton."

"Sure," Sasha said, and started up the stairs. "Pretend like I'm not even here!" she yelled down to them. "Just do whatever you would if I weren't here."

When Braxton heard the bedroom door close, he said, "I'm really sorry I wasn't there for you. Sometimes it's just hard being engaged to a superwoman."

Anya raised her eyebrows. "What about you? I can't open a magazine without seeing your face." She squeezed his hand. "And that makes me proud."

"I'm proud of you too, but it's different. You're comfortable in all situations. I'm not like that. But," he said, taking her face into his hands, "that's no excuse, because last night was your night. I should have been there." His fingers glided down the side of her face. "I want to make it up to you. Get into your most dazzling dress."

Her eyes gleamed. "Where are we going?"

"I'm not telling."

She hesitated. "This is Sasha's first night. I can't leave her alone."

"You'd better go with your man!" Sasha shouted from upstairs.

"Sasha!"

"It wasn't like I was up here listening." Sasha was still not in their sight. "I was just . . . coming down . . . to get something to . . . drink. I'm thirsty." She finally bounced down the stairs and sat on the arm of the couch. "It sounds so romantic and from the looks of your man here," she paused, motioning toward Braxton, "umph, umph, umph. Anya, he looks like he's ready to take care of some serious business."

After a moment Anya said, "If it's really okay with you."

Sasha nodded.

"But what should I wear? Something long or short? Give me *some* idea of where we're going."

Braxton's smile widened. "Long might be better, but it doesn't matter. Just wear your mink."

"Hey, now," Sasha exclaimed, pushing the palms of her hands toward the ceiling.

Anya stood and started toward the stairs.

Sasha said, "So tell me, Braxton, what happened last night?"

Anya glanced over her shoulder and saw Sasha sliding

onto the couch. "None of your business, Sasha," Anya scolded. "Don't ask any questions. Just keep Braxton company while I get ready."

Sasha grinned widely. "It'll be my pleasure. You just take your time, cuz!"

Chapter 10

$\mathcal{A}$nya read the name: *Obsession*. With a slight frown, she took Braxton's hand and followed him up the metal stairs. At the top, six white-gloved men dressed in black uniforms greeted them. Although Anya wasn't sure who they were, she could tell one was the captain and the one with the large white hat was obviously a chef.

"Good evening, Mr. Vance." The captain shook Braxton's hand.

"Captain Norris, nice to meet you. This is my fiancée, Anya Mitchell."

The captain bowed. "Welcome aboard the *Obsession*. We are here to provide you with every pleasure you desire. Would you like some Dom Perignon?"

Braxton shook his head. "No thank you. I ordered sparkling cider."

Anya smiled casually and pulled her mink tighter. She glanced around the deck as if she frequented ninety-foot yachts all the time. She didn't want to give any hint to the crew, who remained standing in place, that she was trembling with excitement.

"Would you like a tour, Miss Mitchell?" the captain asked.

"That would be nice," she said in her most casual voice.

She took Braxton's hand, as they followed the captain up the brass-railed staircase. "What is this?" she whispered.

He responded only with a smile as they stepped through sliding glass doors.

"This is the Ocean Room," the captain said, with a sweeping gesture. "The main chamber on this yacht."

This time, Anya could not hide how impressed she was. The spacious room resembled a lounge in Trump Tower. Everything was ash-white, from the deep-piled carpet to the Queen Anne–style couch, matching chairs, and English lamps—even the oak coffee table had been stained to match. An ash-white baby grand piano at the far end added to the grandeur. Fine crystal glasses lined the wenge-wood bar and matched the vases filled with fresh-cut flowers that were throughout the room. The last of the day's light peeked through the full picture windows, but overhead recessed lights provided most of the light in the room.

"This is beautiful," Anya whispered.

They stopped next in the master stateroom. The Royal Suite was filled with more luxuries than she had at home. The king-sized platform bed was trimmed in gold and matching cabinets were built in along the walls.

The captain opened the double-door armoire. "Should you want to use this room," the captain said without a hint of judgment, "everything you need is in here." He pointed out the large-screen television, along with the entertainment center. The captain led them into the full-sized bathroom with two gilded-faucet pedestal sinks.

"This is a whirlpool tub and if you should have need of them"—he opened the walk-in closet—"there are complimentary bathrobes."

In awe, Anya and Braxton followed the captain throughout the rest of the yacht, each room more luxurious than the last. There were two other staterooms, a library that was reminiscent of an English study, lounges throughout, and a spacious galley.

Finally, the captain took them by a small elevator to the top deck. "This is the Solarium." Both Anya's and Braxton's eyes opened wide as they looked around the glass-enclosed pool area with a panoramic view of the sea. The captain pushed a button, and Anya and Braxton raised their heads and watched as the ceiling retracted. "As you can see, this area is perfect for all kinds of weather."

Shaking their heads in amazement, they followed the captain back to the Ocean Room, which was now bathed with the flickering light of candles. One of the staff was standing behind the bar holding fluted glasses filled with sparkling cider.

"Mr. Vance, we have dinner set for nineteen hundred hours. Is that all right with you?"

Braxton calculated the time and looked at his watch. That would give them an hour. "Yes." He nodded and passed a glass to Anya.

The captain showed them the button that would summon any one of them. Then, they were left alone.

Anya slipped out of her coat, revealing the garnet slip dress she was wearing. The ankle-length dress had a front slit ending a few inches above her knee. The velvet hugged her healthy curves and revealed her toned arms. A single strand of pearls graced her neck.

Braxton whistled. "You are gorgeous, my love."

"Thank you," she smiled, sipping her cider. She was glad she hadn't let him see what she was wearing before they'd left. Moving to the couch, she snuggled into the generous cushions. "Honey, this is incredible."

His grin showed that he was pleased and he sat down next to her. "I would do anything to make you happy." He caressed her bare arms and kissed her gently. She leaned back into him.

They silently sipped their drinks and watched the Marina homes slowly pass by, as the yacht slipped into the Pacific Ocean.

Braxton sighed. "When I was growing up, I could never imagine something like this," he said. Anya nodded, but remained silent. At times like these, he was talking as much to himself as her. "I couldn't see beyond the next foster home. But I knew one day things would be different." He was quiet for a moment, and she felt his arms tighten around her. "That's why I thank God for you, Anya. We are going to have the family I never had."

His hands were clasped around her middle and she lifted them to her lips. But still, she remained quiet, letting Braxton reflect on all he'd accomplished. After a few minutes, she said, "I am so proud of you."

He kissed the top of her head. "Thank you."

For the next hour, they chatted, making wedding plans and enjoying the starlight twinkling on the sea.

At exactly seven o'clock, the captain led them to the dining room. The mahogany-paneled chamber was lit by candlelight. The table, designed to seat twelve, had been set with Waterford crystal and silver cutlery. After blessing the food, Braxton motioned to the waiter.

They began with lobster bisque so smooth, it barely touched Anya's tongue before it slid down her throat. A crabmeat cannelloni followed, then roast duck with wild rice for the main course. The waiters hovered nearby, though out of sight—until Anya or Braxton's plate was empty or a glass only half-filled. By the time they were shown the dessert tray, Anya was sure she'd burst from just looking. But Braxton chose the double-chocolate mousse cake.

After dinner, Anya and Braxton roamed through the yacht, revisiting every room. They finally settled on the aft deck, where they sat in a full-sized leather-cushioned deck chair and enjoyed the peace of the cool winter night.

"Braxton, I have had an incredible time."

He caressed her hands. "It's not over yet."

The sliding glass doors opened and a waiter stepped onto the deck, balancing china on a silver tray. Braxton took one of the steaming cups and gingerly passed it to Anya. She wrapped her hands around its smooth warmth, savoring the sweet pungent aroma of the hot apple cider. The rising vapor flitted over her, forming a slight mist that felt wonderful against the sea air. She took tiny sips, relishing each one.

"Will there be anything else, Mr. Vance?"

Braxton turned to Anya and she shook her head. "No thank you." The waiter disappeared into the cabin.

Holding the cup carefully, Anya leaned back into Braxton. He tightened his arms around her and snuggled against her coat. "Are you sure you don't want to go inside?" he asked.

"I know it's cold, but it's so beautiful out here. I'm fine if you are."

"Well, this night is for you, so whatever you want."

They sat silently, as shades of darkness rolled past. The ocean's wind whirled around them.

"Braxton, I can't remember when I've had a better time. I don't want tonight to end."

As if on cue, the nocturnal air was suddenly filled with a soft melodic sound.

I thought that I was through, trying to find someone exciting and new . . .

Anya sat up and looked around the deck. "What's that?"

Braxton stood and took Anya's hands, lifting her. He snuggled her against his chest. "That's for you. Something I want you to listen to."

You taught me how to love.
Showed me how simple things could mean so much . . .

"Who's singing?" Anya asked. "It sounds like Phyllis Hyman."

"That's Dawnn Lewis."

"She's not a singer, she's an actress."

"Don't tell her that. Ssshhh now, I want you to hear all the words."

I'd cry, I'd cry if you left my side
I place no one above you . . .
My love . . . is so good to me
It's your love I need

The music continued, but Braxton pulled back slightly. "I'm supposed to be so good with words. But when it comes to telling you how I feel . . . sometimes that's difficult. This song—this is what I want you to know. I feel so blessed to have you in my life. I will always love you."

She was full with emotion and this time, she pulled him close.

As the *Obsession* coasted past the southern California beach cities, the words of the song continued to replay and echo into the night. They swayed to the music, though they barely moved, holding each other tightly.

Finally, the music ended and the whirring of the yacht's motor faded.

Anya looked over the railing. "We're not back yet, are we?"

"I think we still have about fifteen minutes. We're going to just drift in now."

The wind blew relentlessly through the channel and Anya shuddered.

"Are you sure you're not cold?" she asked Braxton.

"No, I'm fine."

"Too bad." She opened her coat and spread her arms wide. "I was going to invite you under this with me."

When he joined her, he brought his lips to hers, their fervor taking only seconds to build. Minutes passed before they stepped apart.

Anya sighed. "How can I ever thank you for such a beautiful evening?"

He stared into her eyes and kissed her deeply, running his hands along her back. "Does this give you any ideas?"

She smiled.

Darkness became illumined from the homes lining the Marina's coast. The ocean's motion enticed them and they explored each other, touching, feeling, connecting, as the boat drifted to its destination. When the boat's rocking finally ceased, they pulled away breathless.

"It's time for us to go down." His voice was husky.

"I don't want to," Anya whined softly.

He pulled her toward the glass doors leading to the Ocean Room. "We'll have many nights like this."

"I don't think you'll be able to top this."

"Maybe I'll surprise you with your own yacht."

"Braxton, you don't have to buy me a yacht."

"Why not? We can afford it. I was looking for an investment and this might be a good idea. Our yacht may not be as big as this one, and we might have to call it a boat—"

They laughed together.

As the ship anchored, they held each other and looked out the window, taking in the last moments of the night.

"I love the Marina," Anya said, as she peered at the beach houses across the channel.

"Then I'll buy you a house here."

"You just bought a house."

"I'll sell it. If you want to live here, that's what we'll do."

"Why are you always talking about buying me things? You don't have to—I love *you*."

"That's why I want to give you the world."

They heard footsteps and then the captain appeared. "Mr. Vance, Ms. Mitchell," the Captain said, "I hope you had a good evening."

They nodded. "Thank you, Captain Norris."

The captain bowed slightly and started down the stairs. Their heels clicked rhythmically over the steel floor as they followed him to the lower deck. On the pier, Anya stood to the side as Braxton talked with the captain.

When Braxton came back to her, she said, "You're amazing."

"So I've been told."

"By whom?" She poked him.

"No one that matters . . . except for you."

"Good answer!"

They stopped in front of his car and Anya put her hands around his waist. "I have to find a way to thank you."

He smiled. "If you can't think of anything, I have a few ideas."

"I'm sure you do," Anya said, just before she covered his lips with hers. The whispering wind stirred and whipped around them, although they hardly noticed.

"You said you didn't want this night to end," Braxton said softly. "It doesn't have to." The words hung gently in the air and mixed with the song on the CD: *A love so fine is finally mine . . .*

Anya said nothing and Braxton matched her silence. He guided the Land Cruiser onto Admiralty Way. A few minutes later, he said, "Let's go to my place."

Her eyes lingered on him for a long moment before she responded with a slight smile. "I don't think so. It's late, and we have church in the morning."

"Well . . ." He paused, searching for words. "We can get up early and I can take you home before we go to church."

"Braxton." Anya closed her eyes and shook her head.

He touched her with one hand as he continued steering. "I don't want this night to end either."

Anya twisted in her seat, facing him. "But I don't want it to end in a way that we'll regret tomorrow."

Braxton snatched his hand from her and banged the steering wheel. Anya jumped at the sound. "Don't say *we*, Anya. *I* won't regret anything. The only thing I regret is making this stupid deal with you."

"I don't believe this!" Anya slammed into her seat. "We had a wonderful evening and you're ruining it!"

He inhaled deeply, filling his cheeks with air. *It's your love I need—* He clicked off the CD.

The ten-minute ride dragged longer, and before Braxton stopped in front of her house, Anya was poised to flee.

Braxton reached for her before she could move. "Wait."

"Braxton, I'm not going to argue with you."

Using his fingers, he turned her face toward him, then brushed a stray curl from her forehead. "I love you. That's the reason I keep bringing this up. I want to love you in every way. We made this commitment, but I don't think it's necessary now."

"I'm going in—"

"Anya, just listen to me." His words came faster. "When I agreed to stop having sex until our wedding, I thought we'd be married by now. We haven't been to-gether in almost six months." He took her hand. "Don't you remember how good we were?"

She squeezed her legs together but remained silent.

"We've set a date, Anya. There's no reason to keep this up."

"Except for the reason that God gives us," she said in a low voice.

He dropped her hand. "Be real, God isn't talking about us."

She folded her arms across her chest. "Exactly what book of the Bible says that Braxton Vance and Anya Mitchell are excluded?"

"You know what I mean. God has already ordained this relationship."

She sat listless, unable to come up with any words to make him understand.

After several minutes, she looked into his eyes and she saw love. She unfolded her arms and brushed her hand across his cheek. "Don't you realize that I feel the same way about you? Don't you know that I love you and want you to love me fully?"

He nodded slightly. "It's just hard."

"For me too, but this is the right way."

He looked at her, opened his mouth, but then said nothing.

She said, "We're getting married in a few months . . ."

"I'm trying to understand, Anya . . ." His voice trailed off as if there were more he wanted to say.

She forced herself to smile and squeezed his hand, hoping to encourage a truce. When he turned to her and smiled, she knew she'd accomplished her mission. But she still wondered how many days would pass before he complained about their abstinence again.

"I'd better go in now."

He opened the door for her, taking her hand as she stood from the car. "Anya, no matter what you think, I do love you."

At her front door, he kissed her deeply. Then he walked away.

The SUV's engine purred as Braxton took off into the light middle-of-the-night traffic. He was too wound up to go home, so he headed toward the freeway. His tie felt like a noose around his neck and he loosened it. After all the effort and money he put into this evening, the day had almost ended the way it started.

The night had been so perfect. She had given so many signals and, at one point, he thought they would make love right on the yacht. But she was still using God as an excuse.

He couldn't understand it. He was a man of God and since they'd become a couple, his relationship with the Lord was as strong as it had ever been. But he was a grown man, tired of acting like a chaste teenager.

He sighed as he turned the car onto the freeway, unconcerned with which direction he was going. Didn't she understand how tough it was for a man to abstain? He loved her, but he wasn't going to allow himself to be denied much longer.

Anya stepped quietly through the darkened house. She was grateful that Sasha hadn't waited up. Her cousin would want a report, and she didn't have the energy. She leaned against her closed bedroom door and breathed deeply. Tonight had been one of the most beautiful times she and Braxton had ever spent together. How had it metamorphosed into a nightmare?

She undressed quickly, dropping her clothes on the chaise, then climbed into her queen-sized bed. She spread her arms across her sheets and thought of the times she and Braxton had made love in her bed.

In the beginning, she found ways to justify it, ignoring the feelings of guilt that filled her afterward. But, once they'd become engaged, she knew they had to change. Maybe it was the way he had asked her to marry him—in church, in front of God. Maybe that's what made her want to do this right. But this wasn't right, according to Braxton.

It had been difficult from the first time they discussed a celibate relationship. It was a Sunday, after church, and they were sitting at M&M's on Manchester Boulevard.

"What's wrong?" Braxton had asked, noticing the frown that had been on her face since they'd left the service.

Anya glanced over her shoulder, making sure no one would hear her words. "Did you hear what Pastor Ford said today?"

It was his turn to frown. "We were in church for three hours. She said a lot of things."

Anya stared past Braxton, remembering the pastor's exact words. "She said that when she became a Christian, she was still fornicating. She was only able to stop after someone told her to practice the presence of God."

"So?"

"She said that once she was aware of God's presence, it became almost impossible for her to sin purposefully. When you're really in God's presence, you can't continue—"

"Hey, hey." He stopped her. "You're not talking about *us*?"

Anya paused for a few moments. "Braxton, doesn't it bother you?"

"No it doesn't." His words were quick and strong.

"It bothers me," she said, her voice still low. "I can't stand spreading my legs on Saturday and then, on Sunday, sitting primly in the pews."

Braxton guffawed. "Pastor is *not* talking about people like us. We're in a committed relationship."

Anya had shaken her head in doubt, but ended the conversation when the waitress arrived with their catfish and eggs.

The next Sunday, while they were sitting in Roscoe's Chicken and Waffles, Anya said, "I can't get Pastor's words out of my mind." She hadn't begun to eat the waffle and chicken wings that were on her plate.

Braxton had just placed a spoonful of grits into his mouth. He waited until he swallowed before he spoke. "What is it this time?" he sighed.

Anya ignored his tone. "She said that if you're truly saved, God has to come first. It's like she was talking to us."

"Anya, she doesn't know we're sleeping together."

"But *we* know and *God* knows. That's what I think Pastor Ford means when she said we can't be part-time Christians."

"So what are you saying?" Braxton didn't hide his irritation. "That two healthy thirty-somethings should abstain from sex? Are you saying that we shouldn't sleep together?"

She paused for a moment. "I think we should *think* about it."

Those were the last words they spoke. Braxton dropped Anya off at home and sped off, leaving her standing on the curb, confused and angry.

The next Sunday, Braxton proposed. "Honey, I love you and I should've proposed a long time ago," he had reassured her.

They continued their physical relationship, but Anya didn't feel the same. Her desire to walk in God's light became greater than her desire for Braxton. Within weeks, after being bombarded by conversation, Braxton had reluctantly agreed to abstain from sex until they married.

It had not been easy. The physical struggle was obvious. But what Anya had not expected was the emotional turmoil. Since they'd stopped having sex, it had been one disagreement after another, some so serious that Anya doubted whether their relationship would survive.

She lifted her hand. Even in the dark, the diamond sparkled. Twisting it, she wondered what was happening. Was this just the devil tempting her?

Sighing, she turned onto her stomach. She had waited so long to be with a man of God. And she'd found him, when she met Braxton. But, she wondered, when in the last few months had she lost him?

"Please, God," she said aloud. "Please make this work. Make everything all right with Braxton and me."

But even with her prayers it was hours before she fell asleep.

Chapter 11

The first rays of new morning light filtered through the soiled window, and the man shielded his face, protecting his sensitive eyes. He snatched the towel from the clock. It wasn't yet six. He'd been asleep for less than two hours.

He sat up, but stiffness caused him to pause and stretch. A piece of paper crumpled under his feet, and he picked up the three-day notice that had been tacked on the door when he'd arrived in the early hours of the morning. Taking short, sluggish steps, he meandered to the barred window and peered onto the deserted street below.

Everything about this place reminded him of where he'd grown up. Then, he'd been so eager to escape his desolate surroundings, that he'd taken that first job as a bookkeeper outside of the city when he was just seventeen. But somehow, he had returned to his past. What was he doing here when he had his own home?

He sighed. He knew what he was doing—living two lives like he'd done when he was growing up. After he joined the Bedford Boys, he'd had to wear two faces. It wasn't difficult to fool his mother. As long as he brought home progress reports filled with A's, she still looked at him as the perfect son—no matter what others told her.

But it wasn't as easy to fool Sean.

"Have you gone from being mama's boy to teacher's pet?" Sean sneered one day, as he snatched his progress report from his hands.

He shook his head. He'd been part of the gang for two years, had been doing Sean's homework for all of that time, still to Sean he was suspect.

"I'm not the teacher's pet," he objected. "I'm doing what you taught me—not to bring too much attention to myself. Besides your progress report was good this time too," he said, referring to the two A's and two B's that he'd helped Sean to receive.

"I don't care nothin' 'bout school." Sean scowled.

But he hadn't missed the slight smile that crossed Sean's face.

He smiled too, wondering if Sean had known what he knew, even at nine years old—that grades would be their ticket away from this place. And he'd been right. He'd been away for thirteen years, but he wished his friends could see him now, especially Sean. They'd be surprised at how well he'd done.

But as he looked around this apartment, he felt himself moving backward. He'd been doing this for so long, not realizing that there was no need to lead a double life anymore. He didn't need this apartment. He could do this from his own home.

His eyes roamed the room, pausing, reflecting, soaking up every image of her. Finally, he snatched her photos from the walls, tearing some in the process. It took him only fourteen minutes to gather what he needed and fill a box with his belongings. Surveying the room, he appraised what remained. They could keep it all. He chuckled. Sell it for the rent.

He took thirteen steps to the door and left it wide open, the ticks of the clock following him into the hallway. He bounded down the two flights of stairs, moving into the dawning light of Sunday morning. Relieved that his car was still where he'd parked it, he clicked the remote, deactivating the alarm, and tossed the carton inside. He looked at his watch. There was still time to get a few hours' sleep in his own bed before he went to her. And he knew just where she'd be—church.

Chapter 12

Anya's eyes were closed as her hand grappled over the nightstand until she felt the ringing telephone. She clicked it on, cradled it to her ear, and waited.

"Baby?"

Even with sleep still filling her body, she smiled at her grandmother's voice. "Madear."

"Baby, did I wake you?"

"Uh-huh," Anya groaned, finally opening her eyes. She squinted at the clock. "But it's time for me to get up."

"I was waiting for you children to call me last night. Did Sasha get in?"

"Yes, didn't she call you?"

"No."

Her grandmother's tone told her an explanation was expected. "I'm sorry, Madear. Braxton and I went out. I guess she was tired and fell asleep."

"Well, how is she?" Madear lowered her voice, as if Sasha could somehow hear.

"She's fine, Madear. It was a good idea for her to come."

"I still wish she was with me. That child can be wild and I don't want her getting in your way."

Anya leaned against her headboard. "Madear, we'll handle everything."

"Umph. We'll see. Is she going to church?"

She hadn't discussed it with Sasha, but she knew what her grandmother wanted to hear. "I think so. I'm going to wake her now. We'll come over right after church." Anya swung her legs over the side of the bed.

"Oh, no, baby. We have our ushers' brunch today."

"What time will you be home?" she asked. Then, she crossed her fingers, closed her eyes tightly, and added, "I know Sasha is anxious to see you."

"Around four. I already started cooking. I wanted to get some of the food done before I left for church."

"We'll see you then. Braxton will probably be with us." A flash of last night accompanied her words.

"How is my favorite grandson-in-law?" Madear's voice lightened.

Anya bit her lip. Her grandmother loved Braxton already, and Madear had a good sense about people. So why should she have any doubts? "He's fine."

"I hope you're going to tell me some news about the wedding soon."

"I'll talk to you about it later, Madear."

"You know, Anya, you can't keep that boy waiting too long. You know how men are."

"Madear . . ."

"I know you love your business and believe me, I couldn't be prouder. But that business is not going to hold you at night, or be by your side as you grow old, or get on its knees and pray for you—"

"Madear, don't you have to get ready for church?"

There was a pause. "Chil', look at the time! Now make

sure Sasha goes to church, and I'll see you later. Your brother is coming to dinner too. He wants us to meet someone."

Anya smiled. She hadn't seen Donovan in a few weeks. "Great, we'll see you later, Madear."

"I love you, baby."

Anya ran her fingertips over her face trying to massage away her tiredness. She wrapped herself in her robe and walked barefoot to Sasha's bedroom. With her ear to the door, she tapped lightly. "Sasha," she said after a few taps, then she opened the door enough to peek into the darkened room. "We have to get ready for church; service begins at eight."

Sasha rolled over and removed the satin blindfold from her eyes. "Are you talking about eight in the morning?"

"Yeah, and we only have an hour."

Sasha moaned. "I'm not going anywhere."

Anya could hear Madear's voice: I told you. I told you she should have stayed with me.

"Okay . . ." she said hesitantly. "I was hoping that you would come. I think you'll enjoy my pastor."

"Anya, not today, I'm tired."

Anya nodded. No pressure. That was the best way to reach her. "Okay, maybe we'll make Bible Study this week."

Sasha covered her eyes with the blindfold. "Whatever." She rolled over, dismissing Anya.

Anya stared at her cousin, sprawled across the bed in pajamas matching the material covering her eyes. She closed the door softly. Sasha had to be exhausted—turmoil did that. I should know, she thought, as she dragged herself into her bathroom. She could use extra rest herself. But no matter what she was going through, she rarely missed church.

She let hot water run into the tub for several minutes and thought about filling it so that she could soak her tired bones. But there was not enough time. She'd overslept, probably because she had tossed all night, finally falling into a restless sleep sometime after four.

Her weary skin welcomed the shower's warm mist and she relegated thoughts of Sasha and Braxton to the back of her mind. Instead she thought about her business and her thoughts wandered to David.

"David Montgomery." She didn't know why she said his name aloud, and was even more surprised when her mouth curled into a wide smile. But just as quickly she shook her head, scolding herself. What are you thinking, Anya?

She stepped from the shower, and in a short time was ready to leave. With her Bible in hand, she knocked on Sasha's bedroom door once again. There was no answer, but she stepped into the room anyway.

Sasha was hiding under a pillow.

"You can answer the phone if it rings," she said, knowing her cousin heard her. "I'll call you when I get out of church. We can go to brunch, if you'd like."

"I'd like to sleep," Sasha grumbled.

"You wake up cranky, don't you?"

Sasha didn't respond.

"Well, get some rest, because we're going to Madear's later."

She could hear Sasha's groan, even after she closed the door.

Anya sighed deeply. Her life was filled with complicated people and she wondered if that said something about her. It was a good thing she was on her way to church. She needed to talk to God.

Chapter 13

"This is not just a book." Pastor Ford strutted across the platform in a black knit suit. She held her leather-bound Bible in one hand and the wireless microphone in the other. "This is the Word of God talking to *you*." Echoes of Amens swirled through the air. "And you need to hear what God is saying every day."

A single bead of perspiration ran slowly down her back and Anya leaned forward, hoping it wouldn't seep into her knit dress. She glanced around and wondered why no one else seemed to be melting in this sweltering air. Fanning herself with the bulletin, she tried to soak up a bit of the thin breeze flowing from the vents above.

Braxton placed his hand on hers and she stiffened. He smiled and cupped her hand into his. She didn't pull away, but kept her gaze focused straight ahead. She tried to follow the pastor's words, but her mind kept drifting to what had happened last night.

The tug of Braxton's hand brought her back to the present, and when she looked around, everyone was standing for the benediction. She stood, and then, as if on automatic pilot, she hugged the person standing next to her, like she did at the end of service every week.

As the congregation dispersed, Anya stepped into the aisle, barely stopping to greet the other parishioners. Once outside, she quickened her step.

"Hey, why are you walking so fast?" Braxton trotted to keep up with her.

"I'm just—" She stopped in front of her car and fumbled with her keys.

"I was hoping that we would go to Madear's." Braxton stuffed his hands into his pockets. "And tell her about . . . our wedding date." He sounded tentative.

"Madear said for us to come over this evening."

Braxton exhaled with relief. "That's good. Do you want to go somewhere now so that we can talk?"

She turned to him with angry eyes. "I'm not going through this anymore, Braxton."

He held up his hands. "Not to rehash last night. I want to . . . explain some things."

She fidgeted with the key in her car lock, but it didn't seem to fit. "Nothing for you to explain. I understand exactly where you're coming from."

The beeper clipped to his belt vibrated and Braxton checked the message. "It's Junior. Wait while I get my phone."

"No, call him. I'll see you later."

Braxton hesitated and looked at his beeper once again. "Okay," he said reluctantly. "What about meeting me in an hour?"

"I'm going to the office, so I'll meet you at Madear's at six."

His eyes narrowed and he stared at her for a long moment. "I'll see you later," he said tersely as he walked away.

"Thank God for beepers," she sighed, looking to the heavens. This time, when she put her car key into the door it opened immediately. She sat inside for a moment, reflecting.

"When are you going to admit that this is not going to work?"

The voice was so clear that, for a moment, she thought there was someone else in the car. It took a few seconds for her to realize it was coming from deep inside of her.

"The bad times will pass," she said aloud, starting a conversation with herself. "When we're married, all of these issues will disappear."

"What planet are you living on?" her inner voice argued back.

"We'll be fine. I want to marry Braxton."

"At what price?"

She popped a cassette from a previous sermon into the player and listened to her pastor's comforting words. She was not going to allow doubt to overtake her. With counseling, all of their problems would be gone.

The street was almost empty of cars by the time she pulled away from the church. As she turned onto Prairie, she clicked on her cell phone.

It took several rings for Sasha to answer.

"You wanna grab something to eat?"

"Anya, I just want to rest," she whined.

"I thought you might be hungry."

"I know I'm cranky, but I'm tired."

"No problem," Anya said quickly, wanting to end the

conversation. "But remember, we *have* to see Madear this evening, no matter how tired you are."

She hung up before Sasha could offer another complaint. She needed to be alone anyway and ran her mind through the places she could go—to the beach, up the coast, to the Beverly Center. But she cast all those away and turned her car onto LaBrea, heading toward her office. That was one place she knew she could find some peace.

Chapter 14

D avid had seen dawn break but, even though he was exhausted, he couldn't sleep. Now, as noon approaches, he decided to get out of bed and go outside.

He dressed quickly and walked the two blocks to the ocean. Clouds hung low, shrouding the sun's light, and the ocean breeze blew cool. For the first time in days, David felt calm. He kicked off his shoes and enjoyed the tugging sand under his feet, as the tide threatened to pull him into the ocean's arms. But minutes later, peace disappeared, and once again, the voice swirled around him.

In the past, he'd only heard his mother. But, over this weekend, his father had relentlessly taken him back to that night.

Barefoot, David sprinted down the coast, but he could not outrun the voice. Stopping suddenly, he threw his shoes onto the ground, took off his sweater, and leapt into the water, swimming to the caution buoys. He turned south, taking stroke after stroke, until fatigue took him. He treaded for a while, his head bobbing in the waves, and then he swam back, using the tide to propel him.

Totally spent, he sat on the sand until his breathing

steadied. When he stood, his jeans were heavy with the ocean's water. He started down the shore, shivering as he walked back to where he'd left his clothes.

After he put on his shoes and sweater, he stared into the Pacific. The bombarding waves of the afternoon surf, and a few muffled voices, were welcome sounds to his ears. He had drowned his father's voice in the depths of the Pacific. It was safe to go home.

In his condo, he stepped from his wet clothes, leaving them dripping in the living room. It didn't take long for him to shower and dress. He moved hurriedly, eager to get to his next task. Grabbing his wallet and cell phone, he sprinted from his apartment, jumped into his car, and headed into the city.

Anya sighed when the phone rang. She'd come to the office for peace, but apparently someone had another idea.

"Hello."

Through the silence on the other end, she could hear slight breathing. She waited for a few seconds, then dropped the phone into its cradle, and returned to the computer. A moment later, the ringing interrupted her again.

This time when she picked up, she listened. Hearing nothing, she slammed the phone down.

"Just some kid playing games," she muttered, as she punched numbers into the computer.

But minutes later, when she heard a key in the front door, her fingers froze above the keyboard. She remained still as she heard the door open, then close.

"Who's there?" she called out.

There was no response.

She listened for footsteps but the only sound was the hum of the computer. She stood and walked around her desk, peering into the hallway. "Hello," she said, trying to control the slight shaking in her voice.

Finally he appeared through the vestibule.

"Why didn't you say anything? I am not into playing games," Anya snapped, holding her hand over her heart.

"I'm sorry." David followed Anya into her office. "I thought I'd be here alone and, when I heard you, I thought about turning around."

"Gee, thanks." Anya sat behind her desk. "Don't worry, I won't get in your way."

"That's not what I meant. I'm just not good company today."

"Join the club."

David saw the deep frown on her face. "Is there something I can help you with?"

She lifted her eyes and, for the first time, took a good look at him. She'd never seen him without one of his tailored suits, and she approved of this casual attire. The tight black short-sleeved turtleneck and very well-fitting jeans revealed his daily workouts.

"If it's one of the accounts," David continued, "I can give my input. I'm looking for something to take my mind off . . . some things." He sat across from her.

She smiled. "Look at us pitiful souls. What's your problem?"

He shook his head. "I was just bored and thought I'd get a head start on the week."

Anya didn't miss the way his eyes had darkened. "Same here," she said. "What are you going to work on?"

"I'm not sure." He folded his arms. "I need to get those monthly reports to you. I have Alaister's; he's so quick with his numbers. I'll have the rest by tomorrow." He stood. "I'll be in my office if you need me."

Anya returned to the computer screen and watched her screensaver scatter across it—LET GO, LET GOD. She hit the mouse, returning to the invoices. Twenty minutes later, she was staring at her blank computer screen.

She walked to the window, her mind mingling thoughts of her business and Braxton.

Sighing, she turned back to her desk and jumped. "Oh, my God! What is with you? You keep scaring me half to death!"

"Anya—" David started, then stopped.

"Yes?" When he said nothing, she took a step toward him. "What is it?"

They both turned as the front door opened, then Alaister appeared at her door.

"Oh. Hi," he said, surprise in his voice.

"Is *everyone* having a bad day?" Anya asked irritably.

Alaister frowned. "Why are you asking me that?"

Anya waved her hand. "You came in to get some work done too?"

"Ah, no." He hesitated and took off his cap, running his hands through his hair. "I . . . I had to pick up a few things." He turned to David and spoke quickly. "You need the numbers and the final paperwork for Linden in the morning, right?"

David nodded, his eyes still fixed on Anya.

"I came to pick up the reports. I forgot to take them with me on Friday," Alaister explained.

Seconds of strained silence slipped by, and Anya watched Alaister's eyes dart from her to David.

"I'll go to my office and be on my way." Alaister disappeared down the hall.

Anya turned back to David. "What is wrong with you? Why were you just standing in my door?"

"I was going to ask if you wanted to get something to eat. I'm not being productive, and I thought I'd go out." His gaze was intense.

She frowned. What did she see in his eyes? There was something dark, maybe dangerous, something that she couldn't figure out. But then, she smiled, thinking she'd seen too many movies lately. "Sure, I'm not getting much done either."

The front door opened again, and Anya and David were silent until the footsteps stopped outside her door.

"Oh, hi, Anya." James, one of the junior associates, came into her office. "I came to pick up a few things. I'm going to be at that seminar next week."

"How did you get in?" Anya tried to keep her voice casual.

"Melissa gave me her key. I picked it up because she couldn't leave her house today. I'm going to take it right back. I hope it's okay." James looked down at his feet.

"It's fine."

As James walked away, Anya whispered, "Talk to Melissa." She grabbed her purse. "I don't want everyone having access to the office outside of business hours."

David nodded. "Come on, we'd better get out of here before the entire office comes in."

As Anya walked around her desk, she once again noticed the way his shirt hugged his chest. "Where should we go?" she asked, working hard to keep her eyes on his face.

"Not Crossroads. You're too much of a celebrity there and no one will even notice me," he kidded.

"I doubt that." The words were out before she realized it, and her face became hot.

He smiled. "If that was a compliment, I'll take it. I have an idea. And I'll drive if you don't mind trading down to a Jeep."

She was acutely aware of his hand, lightly holding her elbow, as he guided her from the office. "Don't mind at all."

In the elevator, they chatted, and Anya smiled when he said, "My day is looking up."

"So is mine," she said, feeling relaxed for the first time that afternoon.

When the Jeep turned into Speedy's, Anya smiled. It had been a year since she'd last been here.

Since the February afternoon was warming, they sat outside. Anya placed her purse atop the red-and-white checkered tablecloth, then scooted her iron chair closer.

Even though the sun was beating down on them, David removed his sunglasses.

"I thought only us natives knew about this place." Anya smiled.

"I discovered it a few days after I started working for you."

"This is one of my favorite places, although I haven't been here in a while. It's too casual for Braxton."

They scanned the menus and gave their hot-dog orders to the waitress.

"I thought I was taking you someplace you'd never been." David laughed, squinting as the sun beamed into his eyes. "Tell me, if I ever want to surprise you, is there anywhere that you haven't eaten?"

She laughed with him. "I can't think of any."

"You're a social butterfly, huh?"

"No, I just love to eat."

He paused, as his eyes moved from her face, roving down as far as he could see. Then he stared straight at her. "The way you look, I would've thought you counted every calorie."

"You're kind." She lowered her eyes a bit. "I *do* try to stay in shape."

"I can tell."

She took a sip of water and narrowed her eyes. "I can tell you work out too," she said, continuing the flirtation.

He leaned toward her, then lifted and flexed his arm, showing his bicep.

Anya laughed.

"I want to make sure you *really* notice. I put in too many hours not to show off every once in a while."

"So what do you do when you're not working out?" she asked.

"Work for you." When she frowned slightly, he said, "And I love every minute of it. It's great being part of a smaller business where I know I'm needed."

The waitress brought their hot dogs and fries, but before Anya could say anything, David popped a french fry into his mouth. She bowed her head and said a silent grace.

"Sorry." He raised his voice a bit, over the blaring

motor of a passing bus. "I usually do that . . . but I forget sometimes."

Anya answered him with a smile.

He shook his head. "It just doesn't fit you." She raised her eyebrows, and he continued. "You don't look like a God person."

She snickered. "How does a God person look?"

He dunked a fry into the ketchup he had poured on the side of his plate, chewed for a moment. "Not like you."

Anya couldn't hold her laugh. "That's because being a Christian is more inside than out."

"But what I see on the outside doesn't match. You have a successful business, make quite a bit of money, drive an expensive car, live in a nice home, I'm sure. From what I remember, that's not the Christian lifestyle."

"Christians are supposed to be poor?"

He nodded. "Everyone in the church I went to was poor and happy about it. I thought that was how you served God. I never understood why God wanted it that way, but that's why I never had much to do with church after I left home."

She wiped her mouth before she said, "You should visit my church so that you can hear the truth. What are you doing next Sunday?"

"You don't waste any time." He laughed.

"That's because you don't know how much time you have. The truth will change your life in ways you never thought possible."

His head bobbed as he smiled at her conviction. "Not this Sunday, but one day soon."

"That's all I can ask. The church you're talking about—was that in New York?"

He nodded but his smile disappeared.

"Which church?"

David waved his hand in the air. "It was in Harlem, but there's a church on every corner there."

"Did you grow up in Harlem?"

She watched him stiffen and, now, curiosity made her press on.

"I spent some time there . . ."

"Do you have any brothers or sisters?" Her tone was casual.

"Do you?"

"I have a younger brother, Donovan."

"Does he live here?"

"In Woodland Hills, so I don't see him much. But we're still very close. Always have been—especially since our parents died. What about you? I asked if you had any brothers and sisters and you turned the question around to me."

He pushed his plate away, still filled with a few fries and a half-eaten hot dog. "I'm an only child."

"Why *do* you do that?"

He looked at her blankly.

Anya said, "Whenever we're talking about you, you change the subject."

"I didn't realize I did that." He pushed back his chair slightly and put on his sunglasses.

She leaned forward. "Well, let's see if we can change that. I'll ask you questions and you answer them."

David picked up his plastic knife and tapped it lightly on the table. Even through the tinted glasses, Anya could see his eyes darting around the restaurant's patio. "I don't like to talk about myself." He put down the knife, but his eyes still wouldn't meet hers.

She studied him. "Okay, I'll buy that . . . for now."

A few moments passed before he smiled. "We're too serious. Let's have some fun."

Laughter rose from the next table, and Anya glanced at the couple holding hands. She brought her eyes back to David. "I'm having a good time. Aren't you?"

"Are you kidding? I've been dreaming about taking you out."

She crinkled her eyes and began twisting the ring on her finger.

His eyes dropped to her hand. "When are you getting married?"

"I thought personal questions were off limits."

"For you, not for me." His dimple winked at her.

She hesitated for a moment. "In June."

"That soon?" he asked with raised eyebrows.

"We've been engaged for a while."

"Oh." He paused. "If we were engaged, I'd marry you right away."

Anya crossed her legs, trying to shift from the sun that baked her back. "We've been busy."

"Too busy to marry the man you love?"

It was her turn to avert her eyes. She glanced at her watch. "I can't believe the time."

"You know what they say about time flying when you're with the right person."

She hid her blush by shuffling through her purse. "I've got to go. My cousin has been home alone all day."

David signaled for the waitress and, when she brought the check, Anya took a twenty-dollar bill from her wallet.

David shook his head as he handed the waitress his credit card. "I don't know what kind of men you're used to dating, but when I take someone out, I pay."

When I take someone out! She had to set him straight. "Okay, but next time, lunch is on me."

He smiled his half-smile. "Next time?"

"Of course." She tried to sound casual. "We're business partners. You're stuck with me."

He laid his hand on top of hers and smiled. "That's exactly how I want it."

Chapter 15

Anya picked up her keys, and glanced at Sasha slouched on the couch. She was dressed in a long gray sweatsuit skirt with a matching jacket tied around her neck. Her feet, in white platform Keds, moved to a beat that only Sasha could hear through her headphones. At the same time the television blasted, as football players ran over each other on the large screen.

Anya wished she could just stay home, but missing one of Madear's family gatherings was a major offense. "I'm ready," Anya yelled over the television.

Sasha clicked off the TV. "The Bears are losing big time anyway." She jumped up and wrapped the earphones around her neck.

As they got into the car, Sasha sighed. "I'm not looking forward to this."

"It'll be fine. Madear loves you. She just has her ways."

"And her ways include wishing I wasn't part of her family. Watch the way she treats me. She'll have something to say about my clothes, my hair, anything to bring me down. I know it's hard for you to believe since you're her favorite." Sasha paused, and held up her hand. "Don't protest, it's true."

Anya turned onto the street and headed toward Carson. There was no way to change Sasha's mind. In just the few hours that she had spent with her cousin, Anya knew that Sasha had *her* ways. She punched a CD into the player and the sounds of her church's choir filled the car.

> *Perpetual Praise and continual prayer*
> *Take the joy of the Lord with you everywhere*
> *Perpetual Prayer and continual praise,*
> *Acknowledge him in all of your ways.*

"You are sprung, aren't you?"

Anya laughed. "God'll do that to you."

"Umph!"

They rode silently down the 110 Freeway and when Anya exited at Carson Boulevard, in less than three minutes, they parked in front of their grandmother's home.

The Spanish-style house, built in the 1930s, still had all of its original detail. Beige with a red-rust trim, the one-story home was the largest on the block.

As they approached the porch, Anya took Sasha's hand. "Donovan's already here," Anya said, lightheartedly.

Pouting like a teenager, Sasha did not respond.

With the same key that she'd had since she'd lived with her grandparents, Anya opened the door. Before they stepped into the enclosed foyer, a voice boomed from the living room.

"Hey, hey, hey! Is that my big sis?" Donovan jumped from the brown leather recliner they'd bought their grandmother last Christmas. He hugged his sister, almost lifting her from the floor. At six-five, with a linebacker frame that was put to good use at UCLA, he enveloped his five-eleven sister.

"Hey, bro," she said, running her hand over his head. "You got a Kobe Bryant hairdo going here, huh?"

He threw his head back and laughed heartily and, as he often did, he reminded Anya of their father. Donovan had inherited more than just his father's physical characteristics.

"Hey, how do you know Kobe didn't get this from me?" He laughed again as he tapped his hands on his head. A second later, he turned to his cousin. "Come here, girl." He grabbed Sasha and she disappeared inside his arms. "What's up?"

"Just you." She grinned, looking her cousin up and down. "You look good."

Donovan sucked in his stomach and patted his middle. "I've been trying to keep it together. It's not easy as you get older." His laugh filled the room again. "But, look at you. The way Madear's been talking, I thought you'd walk in here with two heads. But, you lookin' good, girl!"

Sasha's smile was wide and, for a few seconds, she forgot that she was standing in her grandmother's house, until her eyes flitted around the room. It had been a few years since she'd been here, but she felt as if little time had passed. Even with lamps lit throughout, the room was as dark as she remembered. The living room was somber—from the dark wood furniture, to the gold brocade drapes, trimmed in brown, that hung heavily at the windows. The walls were covered with tall, weighty bookcases that overflowed with old textbooks and past issues of *Ebony* and *Jet* magazines. The only brightness was the colorful picture frames that provided a pictorial history of the Mitchell family.

Nothing had changed, and Sasha knew that probably included her grandmother. "Where's Madear?" Her smile disappeared.

"In the kitchen, doing her thing. My stomach has been growling louder than I talk," Donovan said.

They all laughed.

"Madear said you were bringing someone for us to meet?" Anya settled onto the couch.

"Cecilé couldn't make it. She had an emergency at the hospital." When Anya's eyes questioned him, he said, "She's a surgeon."

Anya raised her eyebrows. "How did you finagle your way into a doctor's life?" she teased.

"I'm her lawyer."

"Maybe you'll have a Cosby thing going." Sasha playfully poked Donovan, then sat on the couch next to Anya.

As Sasha and Donovan laughed, Anya sat back. Childhood memories were as much a part of the room as the furniture. She remembered the summers they'd spent together. The three of them would play all day, spending most of their time laughing at Donovan's silly jokes.

"His mother was so stupid, she got hit by a parked car."

Even now, the memories made her smile. As the oldest, she was always put in charge, but often found herself right in the middle of their capers. Her parents would come into the room, admonishing them to keep the noise down. But Madear was always two steps behind, saying that the sound of laughing children was God's blessing.

"Just leave my grandchildren alone," Madear would always say.

Those were some of the last recollections Anya held of her parents.

"If Jesus called me home now, I would be ready to go! This is what makes an old woman feel wonderful. All of my grands here with me."

Madear stood with her hands folded, her green eyes sparkling against her pale skin. Petite in every way, Mabel Mitchell was still a beautiful woman. Often said to be a Lena Horne look-alike, she could do little to hide her attractiveness.

Today, her shoulder-length, wavy hair (that had long ago turned silver) was pulled into her favorite style, a twisted bun high on her head. Beneath her apron, she still had on the sky-blue knit dress she'd worn to church. Even at seventy-four, her body was toned from her daily six A.M., thirty-minute walks, and occasional yoga sessions at the Los Angeles Senior Citizen Center.

Madear went to Sasha first and hugged her tightly. "How are you doing, baby?" she asked, concern blanketing her face and voice.

"I'm fine, Madear. How are you?"

"Fine, now that I can see for myself that you're in one piece. Chil', what were you doing in Chicago? I told you a long time ago that Gordon was no good. He was much too old and—"

"Madear, what about me? I didn't get my hug today," Anya said, interrupting the pending rampage.

"Oh, I didn't forget about my baby." She hugged Anya. "You know how I feel about you."

From the corner of her eye, Anya saw Sasha's head drop. She leaned away from her grandmother. "Madear, doesn't Sasha look great?"

"Oh, yes." Madear took Sasha's hand and led her to the brown floral couch. Sasha squirmed against the rough plastic that covered the couch until she found a spot that gave some relief from the hard corners that stuck her legs. "You do look good, Chil'," Madear said, through squinted eyes. "Except . . ." She ran her slender manicured hand over Sasha's head. "What did you do to your hair? You look like a boy."

Sasha twisted her mouth, but before she said anything, Anya intervened. "I was just teasing Donovan about *his* hair." Anya forced a chuckle. "Look how long he's let it grow, Madear."

"Yeah, Madear," Donovan said, joining his sister's rescue attempt. "My hair is long and Sasha's short. That's the way it is these days."

"I know that," Madear snapped in her grandmotherly tone—not angry, just making her point. "But Don still looks the way he's supposed to. You—" She turned Sasha's face from side to side. "This messes up your pretty face."

"Madear, even my hair is short," Anya said, a bit too quickly.

"You have curls, it's not nappy like this," Madear tisked.

Sasha lowered her eyes. "I'm sorry if you don't like it. I can't seem to do anything to please you," Sasha said softly.

"What are you talking about, Chil'?"

Before Sasha could respond, Donovan coughed. "You know, Madear, it's been weeks since we've had some of your good cooking. Can't I get a sneak peek?" he playfully begged.

Madear's smile was wide. "Absolutely not! And, it's not my fault that it's been a few weeks. I keep telling you to come over any time. I don't see you enough anyway." She lifted herself from the couch. "Let me check on things."

"Do you need any help, Madear?" Anya asked, the way she always did, though she already knew her grandmother's answer.

"No, dear." She patted Anya's hand. "By the way, where is my future grandson?"

At that moment, the doorbell rang and Anya jumped up. "That's probably him now." When she opened the door, she hugged Braxton tightly, relieved for the refuge he provided.

While Madear worked in the kitchen, her grandchildren remained in the living room watching the thirteen-inch television placed on top of the larger television console that hadn't worked in years. No matter how many times Anya and Donovan offered to buy Madear a new one, she refused, saying that her little TV worked just fine. And when Donovan came by to have the console moved to a junkyard, Madear complained. "This is the perfect television stand," she stated, as if she had made a major discovery.

"So how was last night?" Sasha asked.

"What happened?" Donovan leaned back in the recliner. It had been his idea to buy the chair for Madear, and Anya often wondered if it had been his way of making sure he had a comfortable place when he came to visit.

Braxton took Anya's hand, but they remained silent.

"They didn't tell me anything," Sasha said to Donovan, tucking her feet under her. "But when these two left, he was dressed in a tuxedo and she was wearing a dress that stopped traffic."

"I couldn't have described my lady any better," Braxton laughed and squeezed Anya's hand.

Anya forced a smile. The time on the yacht was almost all but forgotten. It was what followed that played in her mind.

"What did you guys do?"

"It's a secret, but we do have some news to share," Braxton smiled.

"Now there's my other grandson," Madear said, as she ambled back into the living room. Braxton returned her generous hug.

"He was just about to tell us some news," Donovan said.

"Well, you're already getting married," Sasha said gaily. "So you must be pregnant!"

Quiet fell as Madear stared at Sasha.

"Hush your mouth," Madear said, as if she were speaking to a two-year-old.

"No, I'm *not* pregnant." Anya rolled her eyes at her cousin.

"What's the big deal?" Sasha looked around the room.

"We've set a date," Braxton said hurriedly. "We're getting married in June."

"Praise the Lord!" Madear exclaimed, as she took both Anya and Braxton into her arms. "I have been praying that you would jump the broom before the Lord called me home."

"Madear, you ain't going nowhere. You'll be here to see even Donovan get married," Anya teased.

Donovan held up his hands and laughed. "Don't cast those words toward me. I'm not getting anywhere near marriage, at least not for a few years."

With a slight smile, Madear tisked and shook her head.

"I don't blame you," Sasha huffed. "Marriage stinks!"

"Thanks for the support, cuz," Anya kidded Sasha, while she eyed Madear.

"Sasha, nothing's wrong with marriage," Madear said. "Not everyone will mess up the way you did." Before anyone could respond, Madear lightly slapped Donovan on his arm. "Don't listen to Sasha. You need to settle down with a good Christian woman, and have those Mitchell babies. Anyway, I am so happy. Let's celebrate—it's time for us to eat!"

As Braxton and Donovan followed Madear down the narrow hallway into the dining room, Sasha lingered behind and grabbed Anya's arm.

"See how she treats me?" Sasha whispered.

Anya shrugged, but remained silent. There was something wrong; she'd talk to her grandmother later. Anya put her arm around Sasha's shoulder and led her down the corridor, lined with more photos of the Mitchell grandchildren.

The aroma of the Sunday dinner had wafted a bit into the living room, but once they stepped into the dining room, it hit them full force. Laid out on the long antique buffet was a spread that would make any Black family proud—fried catfish and chicken, macaroni and cheese, collard greens, candied yams, rice with brown gravy, and, of course, corn muffins. Moans of pleasure filled the room, and none of them had yet seen the peach cobbler and sweet potato pie hidden in the kitchen.

Anya shook her head. "Madear, I don't know how you do it."

"I've been doing this all my life."

"I'm going to pack on those pounds I just got rid of," Donovan said, patting his stomach.

Madear beamed. These weekly dinners had become more like monthly ones, but she was always thrilled when her grandchildren came by, and she would cook as much as they wanted. "Stop talking and eat," she admonished them. "Remember, we're celebrating the upcoming wedding."

The room filled with the clatter of silverware hitting plates, as everyone worked to get their fill. They laughed as they compared dishes, teasing Donovan whose plate was piled high. But by the time they sat down, it was decided that there was a tie between Braxton and Donovan.

"You leave my grandsons alone," Madear scolded Anya and Sasha, as they teased Braxton and Donovan. "They're growing boys. By the way, Carlos called to check on me and I invited him, but he and Michele had other plans."

"That means more for us!" Braxton chuckled and Donovan high-fived him.

When they settled at the table, they waited for Madear to take her place. Madear rested her arms on her chair, and took her time, looking at each of them. Anya and Braxton sat to one side and Sasha and Donovan sat at the other. Then, she spoke like she did every time they got together.

"After God, my family is the most important thing in the world to me. It fills my heart to be here when there are so many in this world who have nothing. I thank God for every blessing, including each of you." She took Anya and Sasha's hands, a signal for the others to do the same. "Now, let's bow our heads."

As Madear said the grace, Anya wondered if her grandmother realized that she spoke the same words each time. And every time, fresh tears came to Anya's eyes.

When Madear lifted her head, they attacked their plates as if they hadn't eaten in days.

"Madear, I asked Anya to marry me so that I could ensure my place at these dinners," Braxton said, just before he put a spoonful of macaroni and cheese in his mouth and shook his head in delight.

Madear smiled, stood, and with a serving spoon, packed another heap of macaroni and cheese on Braxton's plate. "I don't want any food left. You all hear me?"

They nodded, though everyone knew that would be impossible. Even after forcing care packages on them, Madear would be eating leftovers for a week.

Conversation flowed as the food on the plates dwindled, then filled up again. Everyone talked about what they had done since they'd last been together, and Braxton filled them in on the completion of his latest book, *Kiss and Say Goodbye.*

"Man, I love that title," Donovan said, before he started a falsetto rendition of the 1970s Manhattans song.

"Oh, please, brother dear. We're trying to eat."

They laughed and Madear turned to Sasha. "I am so happy you're here, honey." She put her hand on top of Sasha's. "I don't see you often enough. I've never forgiven your father for moving to Chicago." Madear chuckled, but everyone knew she meant what she said. "Anyway, did you enjoy church this morning?"

"I didn't go."

The fork, filled with yams, was halfway to Madear's mouth but stopped in mid-air, as her eyes fluttered.

"Madear, I suggested that Sasha rest this morning," Anya said quickly.

Sasha pointed her fork at Anya. "Don't lie," she said boldly. "*I* decided not to go to church this morning."

Madear glared at Anya. "This is what I was worried about. You lied to me," Madear said indignantly. "Is this what I can expect now? You acting just like her?"

Sasha's eyes flared. "What is that supposed to mean? I didn't tell Anya to lie!"

"But she felt she had to."

"So it's *my* fault?" Sasha dropped her fork onto her plate and looked directly at Anya. "I told you, I can't win with this lady."

"Who are you calling 'this lady'?"

Anya held up her hands. "Wait!"

Sasha slammed back in her chair, while Madear tapped her fingers along the table. Both Donovan and Braxton sat quietly, neither sure of what to say.

"Madear." Anya looked at her grandmother. "I'm sorry I lied, but I knew telling you would lead to something like this."

"And she knew that if you thought it was her idea, it would be fine," Sasha added, her voice raised slightly. "But as soon as I said that *I* decided not to go, it's a major sin. What is it about me that ticks you off so much?"

"First of all, young lady," Madear said through clenched teeth. "Don't speak to me that way. I am your grandmother."

"And I am your grandchild! Why do you hate me?" Sasha cried.

"Sasha!" Madear slammed her hand on the table and stood. Her petite frame loomed much larger than she was.

Sasha lowered her eyes, but kept her arms across her chest. Silence had replaced their joyful noise.

Madear's cheeks were flushed with fury and, holding her head high, she stared at Sasha. "I don't know how you can say that I hate you." Her words were tight. "I love you, but I don't like your ways. You've been trouble since you were little. You wouldn't mind your parents, you played around in school. Nothing was serious to you. And nothing has changed. You're not even thirty years old, and you've destroyed your marriage . . ."

Sasha's head snapped up. "I should have stayed with a man who cheated on me?"

"Well," Madear paused and sat back in her chair, "if you had been taking care of business at home—"

"I told you it was a mistake for me to come here, Anya," Sasha said, her eyes now filled with tears. She threw her napkin across the table, then ran from the room.

Donovan pushed his chair back, but Anya put up her hands. "I'll get her." She turned to her grandmother. "How could you say those things?"

Madear's chin jutted forward. "We told her not to marry that man."

Anya shook her head. She stood and said to Braxton, "I'm going to take Sasha home."

He nodded solemnly. "But we need to talk," he whispered.

"Not tonight, Braxton." She kissed him. "I'll call you tomorrow."

She glared at Madear, who sat stiffly in her chair with her eyes straightforward. "Good night, Grandmother." Anya turned away before Madear could respond.

They were sprawled across the bed in Anya's bed-room. The Sunday night soulful sounds from KJLH softly floated through the room.

"What is it about me?" Sasha asked for at least the fiftieth time.

"It's not you," Anya repeated what she'd been saying for the last hour. "Madear said that she loved you and was happy to have her grandchildren with her."

Sasha pulled the last tissue from the box sitting in the middle of the bed.

Anya continued. "I'm going to call her tomorrow and find out what is the problem."

Sasha shook her head. "I don't want her blaming me for coming between you two."

Anya didn't respond, already knowing what she was going to do.

Sasha rolled over and put her feet on the floor. "I don't want to keep you up all night with this."

"Why don't you drive me to the office in the morning; then you can have the car and go shopping? That always does it for me."

Sasha smiled for the first time since they had left Madear's. "That sounds good."

They hugged.

When Sasha left the room, Anya reached for the phone, then pulled her hand away. She would have that talk with her grandmother but it had to be face to face.

Sasha looked at the clock and wondered if it was too late. Probably not, he was an actor and didn't they keep late hours? Before she could change her mind, she reached for the card in the corner of the mirror. She curled up on the bed, then dialed the number quickly.

"Hi, Hunter? This is Sasha." The pause on the other end told her that he didn't recognize the name. "Anya's cousin. We met yesterday."

"Hey, Sasha. How are you?"

Madear's words flashed through her mind. "I'm doing great."

"I hope you're calling to take me up on my offer."

"Your offer for what?" she said in the most seductive voice she could gather.

"To show you . . . the city," he chuckled. "But, I don't have to stop there."

Sasha leaned back against the bedpost and smiled. Her husband left her for a younger woman, and her grandmother didn't love her, but now, she was on the telephone with the hottest man in Hollywood. She was not a failure and Hunter Blaine was just the man to help her prove it.

Chapter 16

*T*he man squeezed his vehicle into the small space that blocked a driveway. His eyes darted up and down the street, then back to the two-story duplex. He trotted up the steps and, before he raised his hand, the door opened.

She leaned against the doorframe, one hand above her head, the short red negligee barely covering her curves. "I've been waiting for you," she said huskily. Her voice was deep for a woman. "What took you so long?"

He walked past her without a word, and moved through the darkened apartment, until he stood at her bedroom door.

She swaggered toward him. "You're in a hurry tonight." They were standing so close that he could feel her breath.

He grunted, and she moved into him, forcing his body into the room. With a gentle push, she lowered his body onto the brass bed. "Since you're in such a hurry." She remained standing with her hands on her hips and a wide smile on her face.

His eyes roamed over her, from the brown curls that

framed her face, past the curve of her neck, down to her legs that were spread wide, arched in stiletto heels.

Slowly she brought the spaghetti straps of her gown from her shoulders, pushing the thin material past her hips, until it slid down her legs and fluttered around her ankles. She kicked the material away. In the bright light, she stood, totally naked. He closed his eyes.

"What's wrong?" he heard her say.

He opened his eyes. "Put that back on," he whispered, motioning with his head toward her gown.

She smiled. She loved hearing his voice, but he'd been quiet tonight.

Before she had the gown completely on, he closed his eyes and brought forth his vision. Then, he pulled the woman into him and moved his hands to her chest, squeezing as tight as he could.

"Ouch!" She swung around, facing him, her face twisted in pain. But, then, she licked her lips. "It's going to be like that, huh?" She kissed him, softly at first, then pushed her tongue into his mouth. A moment later, he pulled away and pushed her onto the bed.

She laughed, too loud. "Come on, baby, come to Mama." She uttered the words that he had taught her to say.

In one move, he unzipped his pants and fell on top of her. She began to gyrate beneath him, but he stopped her—holding her still. Then he pounded away, causing her to moan. The louder she became, the harder he pushed into her. His eyes were closed tightly and he could see her. It was Anya holding him. Anya moaning for him. Anya wanting him.

Within minutes, he was standing, straightening his clothes.

"That was different," she said, as she stretched on the bed. "Now you'll have to take off your clothes."

"I'm not staying the night," he said simply.

Her disappointment showed on her face, then she forced a smile. "It's your party."

He took three twenties from his wallet and threw them toward her. They floated in the air, finally resting on the sheet next to her.

"Hey—"

He turned and left, leaving her front door wide open. As he jogged to his car, he shook his head in disgust. For six months, he had wasted his time coming here. Well, he wouldn't anymore. It was time for him to be with her.

Chapter 17

*D*avid caught his reflection in the glass top of his desk, held the somber gaze, then watched his lips curl into a smile. Since his bonding with the Pacific Ocean yesterday, he hadn't heard any voices. Even the visions were gone—except for the one of Anya.

The clock chimed and David looked up. It was still early; he could get some work done. He pulled papers from his fax machine, resumes from the headhunting firm. Spreading the dozen sheets across his desk, he glanced over them casually. He would select the best, then review those with Anya.

His eyes wandered when he thought of her. He had never spent time with her before, knowing that his secrets were safer in the office. He smiled as he thought about the day before and his rewards for casting caution aside. He couldn't get her out of his mind.

He shook his head sharply. It didn't matter where his imagination drifted at home but at the office, he had to thrust all thoughts of her away—except the most professional ones.

He closed his eyes and remembered the plum-colored

dress she'd worn. It fit her perfectly, providing a flawless silhouette of her shapely form. He liked that she wasn't model-thin. She was a real Black woman, with all of the parts that came with that genetic blessing. Just the way he liked them—

"Stop it!" he scolded himself. He returned to the dozen names staring from the resumes but, minutes later, his thoughts reverted to Anya. He sighed. The woman monopolizing his brain space was his engaged boss. In all his working years, he'd never mingled with anyone from the office. So why was he thinking about Anya this way?

The creak of the front door tugged him from his fantasies. Good thing; he couldn't spend the day daydreaming like a forlorn teenager.

"Good morning, David." Alaister and Geena stood at his door.

This was the third time he noticed the two coming in together, and he wondered if there was something going on. Big problem—Geena reported to Alaister. He'd talk to Alaister later.

"How was your weekend?" David asked them.

"Fabulous!" Geena's grin at Alaister aggravated David's suspicions.

"Great." David smiled back at them. "There's a lot to do before we go to Linden. Alaister, do you have those numbers?"

"Ah, no. Last night . . . I got busy."

"We'll need them as soon as possible." David smiled, but the message was received and Alaister moved with urgency toward his office.

Turning back to the resumes, David sorted through the pile. But before he got past the first one, the front door opened and, this time, the voice made him stop. For several moments, he listened to the chatter. Then he stood and walked to his door. He would just say good morning.

He casually strolled to her opened door and tapped lightly. She was standing behind her desk and, when she looked up, David was pleased by her immediate smile. "Good morning."

He bowed his head, suddenly feeling like a shy schoolboy. But he'd only taken two steps into her office, when he stopped abruptly.

"Oh, excuse me." He hesitated, taking in the woman sitting on the couch. "I'll come back." He retreated toward the door.

"David, I want you to meet someone." Moving to him, she took his hand. "This is Sasha, my cousin."

David's eyes assessed the woman expertly, the way a man who truly appreciates the female form would. His wandering gaze drank in her attire, and he noted her skirt was as short as her legs were long.

"Nice to meet you." Her voice was strong as she held out her hand.

"Ah, David Montgomery." He realized he was still holding Anya's hand. He dropped hers and took Sasha's. "Nice to meet you."

Anya watched the exchange. David reacted to Sasha the same way Hunter had, but this pleased her. "David, Sasha's visiting from Chicago."

He forced his glance from Sasha and took in Anya's wide grin. "I don't want to disturb you," he said. "I wanted to say good morning and let you know we're ready to go with Linden."

"Great, set up a time and let Dianna know."

"And we received some resumes—"

She waved her hand in the air. "I'll leave that to you."

He couldn't stop the smile that lit his face. He gave Sasha another long glance. "I hope I'll get to see you before you leave."

Not uttering a word, Sasha sat down and crossed her legs, allowing her skirt hem to ease high up her thigh. "I'll make *sure* we see each other again." Her words were a husky whisper.

David cleared his throat, then smiled at Anya before he left the office.

When Anya was sure David was out of hearing range, she turned to Sasha. "He's nice. Did you like him?"

Sasha raised her eyebrows. "Are you trying to hook me up with David?"

"No."

"Liar."

"I am not!" Anya said, crossing her arms in front of her.

Sasha raised her eyebrows. "You're right. You're a *big* liar."

Anya dropped her arms and smiled. "I just wanted you to meet someone nice. And I could tell you liked him, especially the way your eyes moved up and down his body."

"Well, boyfriend does raise your temperature a degree or two." She pulled a nail file from her purse.

"And I can vouch for his other assets."

Sasha raised her eyebrows. "And what *are* they?"

Anya ignored Sasha's tone. "He's smart, personable, successful. He hasn't been here long and he just landed the biggest account of my career. You two would have a good time together. Didn't you see the way he looked at you?"

Sasha sighed. "He's a man, men look at me that way."

"Just admit that you'd like to go out with him."

Sasha waved the nail file in the air. "Girl, I'm not going anywhere with that man. David only has eyes for you!"

Anya was stunned into silence.

"I know there's something going on between the two of you." Sasha stood, and closed the door. She settled on the edge of the desk and leaned over toward Anya. "Tell me the real scoop!"

Anya sat behind her desk. "Sasha, you have lost your mind. If there was something going on between me and David, would I introduce you to him?"

"Good point," Sasha said thoughtfully. "Well, there's nothing yet, but something'll happen soon. Girl, that man wants you!"

"I don't even know him. Yesterday was the first time we were together outside of business."

"Then let the games begin." Sasha snapped her fingers in the air. "I don't know your history, but let me tell you your future. There were more sparks flying around this office than you can legally set off on the fourth of July."

Anya jumped from her chair and tripped on the edge of the Persian rug that covered the carpet around her desk. When she regained her balance, she smoothed her skirt and stood straight. "You've forgotten one thing. I'm engaged."

"I know you're betrothed to the great author, but that's what makes this so exciting. David will be your last fling before you promise to love, honor, and cherish forever."

"I am not like that!"

Sasha shrugged. "Whatever you say."

"And David is not interested in me."

"I said, what-ever."

"I am in love with Braxton."

Sasha sucked her teeth. "I ain't thinking about Braxton and, if you were being honest, neither are you."

"This is ridiculous."

"Okay, don't get your Fruit of the Looms in a snit." She bounced from the desk, and adjusted her skirt. "Well, I've got to go. Find some trouble of my own. I'm meeting Hunter this morning."

Anya crossed her arms. "Be careful, Sasha. Hunter's just looking to add another notch to his belt. He's not interested in anything else."

"Then, we're perfect; it's about how many notches I can put on *my* belt."

She picked up her purse and took a long look in the mirror on the back of the door. Nodding, she waved at Anya. "See ya! I'll call."

Anya leaned her head against the window and looked onto the street below. Cars darted around slow-moving trucks, and buses merged from the curb. It was confusion—exactly the way she felt right now. What was she going to do about Sasha? First, there were these delusions about David, and now Hunter Blaine. If Sasha thought she had escaped madness in Chicago, there was no telling what kind of psychiatric assistance she would need after Hunter. She needed to keep Sasha away from him, and if she had to, she would tell Sasha what she knew—she should never be alone with that man.

Anya returned to her desk, and did the only thing she knew how to do at disturbing times like these. She prayed.

"I'm sorry, Anya, but I can't go along with this. We should take as few people as possible to Linden. Just David, Geena, and me. Any more people will just bring confusion."

David leaned forward to say something, but Anya held up her hand. "The only way there'll be confusion is if our people are not trained. And everyone in this agency is very well trained. I'm making the decision, Alaister. Melissa's team will join you."

His blue eyes became darker as he twisted his face in disgust. "It's not fair, Anya. I did all the work and now I have to share it with another manager. Where was Melissa when I was crunching numbers every weekend for the last four weeks?"

Anya's eyes moved to the motivational poster just behind Alaister's head. It showed a group of men and women rowing a boat. The words above the picture read: TOGETHER EVERYONE ACHIEVES MORE: TEAM. It was her favorite poster—a concept she promoted in her business. Alaister had been with her long enough to know how she would feel about this, and she wondered why he was pushing.

After a long pause, Anya said, "Alaister, this is no different from the time your team went with Melissa to the city of Inglewood. I didn't hear you complaining then."

Alaister slumped in his chair.

"Let's move on," she said emphatically, looking directly at Alaister, who kept his gaze down on the table. "Okay, guys"—she turned to the others who had sat silently during the exchange—"you've done a great job on this. Let's deliver more to Linden than we promised."

There was a knock on the door. Dianna stepped in tentatively. "Anya, is this meeting almost over?"

"What is it?" Anya's tone was impatient.

"I'm sorry, but you have a call."

Anya frowned. Dianna was instructed to interrupt only in an emergency. "Who is it?"

Dianna clutched the door as her eyes searched the room for an ally. "It's Braxton and it must be important, because he's called several times. And now, he's been holding for almost ten minutes."

Anya picked up her folders from the conference table. "Tell him I'll be right there." Turning to David she said, "Can we meet in five minutes?"

She stomped down the hall to her office, steam building with every step.

"This is Anya," she said into the phone.

"I've been trying to reach you since yesterday."

"I was in a meeting, Braxton." Her voice was tight. "And I'm upset that Dianna interrupted me." Anya raised her voice so that her assistant could hear.

"I told her this was important. I called you last night till midnight and there was no answer."

She had turned the telephone ringer off the moment she and Sasha had gone into the house to avoid Madear. But it wasn't until this moment that she realized it was probably to keep Braxton away too. "Sasha needed to talk and I didn't want to be interrupted."

"I need to talk to you, too."

"I can't talk, Braxton, I'm at work."

"Why are you mad now? I thought we fixed everything yesterday."

"I'm mad because I'm at work and you're interrupting me with something I can't handle right now." She heard coughing behind her and turned. She shook her head and David left her office. "Braxton," she said in a lower voice, "I've got to go. I have another meeting."

"We still have to talk. Pastor Ford told us that in counseling, and since counseling was *your* idea, I think you should follow the rules."

Anya was tempted to hang up the phone, but she knew that would only incite him. "I'll call you later."

"What time?"

"I'm going to hang up now, Braxton."

But before Anya could hang up, she heard the drone of the dial tone. Shaking her head, she fell into her chair. "Should I come back later?"

Anya looked up. "No, now's fine." She closed her eyes for a moment and took a deep breath.

David closed the door. "Anything you want to talk about?"

She shook her head. "Do you have the group reviews?" she asked wearily.

"I do, but I can be a friend if you need an ear."

"I don't need a friend," she snapped, then she softened her voice and tried to flash a smile. "I'm sorry, it's just that the best thing for me right now is to get back to work."

He nodded in understanding and laid the papers across her desk. David started summarizing each report but, like yesterday in church, Anya's ears clogged.

Everything is going to be all right—she repeated the mantra in her head. My business is fine, my relationship is fine, and anything negative that I'm feeling is going to go away.

But the mantra in her head did not match the words hidden in her heart.

Chapter 18

ome home with me. There's something"—
Hunter licked a chocolate-covered strawberry—
"I want to show you." He nuzzled against Sasha's neck.

They had come to the Arena Club in the Staples Center after a whirlwind afternoon. First, an early lunch at Serendipity, then they returned Anya's car and were taken by limousine into Beverly Hills, where they strolled Rodeo Drive and the surrounding streets. All afternoon, she tried on clothes and modeled for Hunter, loving the way his eyes devoured her. When they stopped at the St. John's boutique and she strutted across the floor in a cream tank dress that hugged her, Hunter pulled out his platinum card. Sasha protested; he insisted, saying that he knew just the way she could repay him.

Now, they were surrounded by Hollywood types—actors, talk-show hosts, music stars—all waiting for the Lakers game to begin. But their surroundings didn't stop Hunter from his public display of affection.

As his tongue tickled her neck, Sasha pulled back. Though she had attended endless posh affairs with Gordon, she'd never been around so many celebrities. For the past hour, she and Hunter had chatted with Tyra Banks, Dyan Cannon, and Christopher Darden. She even glimpsed Cookie and Magic Johnson as they passed through the Club on their way to their seats.

Sasha chatted, sipped Chardonnay, sampled the endless supply of hors d'oeuvres, and did a good job of hiding the fact that she was star-struck.

Hunter intertwined his fingers with hers. "I bet you taste a lot better than these strawberries," he whispered.

She simply smiled and brought her glass to her lips. Her eyes wandered around the dimly lit room. The Lakers' history was scattered on the walls. There were pictures of past championship teams, Paula Abdul's framed "Laker Girl" uniform, and photos of stars in concert.

She was drunk with awe but not blind to Hunter. Their conversation had been sprinkled with sexual innuendoes the entire day. To her, it was playful banter. She had no intentions of sleeping with him—not tonight.

But this is Hunter Blaine, her inside voice spoke. This man has been with every beautiful woman yet, today, he was with her. Sasha had to admit she got high on the envious looks and regal treatment she'd received all afternoon because she was on Hunter's arm. But she wasn't going to be just another one of his conquests. He was taken with her and, if she played right, she could end up with far more than just a one-time romp.

"Hey, Hunter." Three women, each barely covered in black spandex, sauntered over to them. Sasha thought she recognized the tallest, with bushy red hair and the longest legs. As the three kissed Hunter familiarly on the lips, Sasha pushed her chin higher, and clasped the glass of wine tighter, but her smile remained in place.

"So, Hunter," one of the women started, as she looked Sasha up and down, "what are you doing after the game?"

The question seemed to remind Hunter that Sasha was there. He put his arm around Sasha's waist.

"I have plans." He grinned at Sasha.

"Well, if your plans *change*," the redhead said, nudging herself between Sasha and Hunter, "we have something you might enjoy." The woman whispered into Hunter's ear. When Hunter and the women laughed, Sasha resisted the urge to throw what remained in her glass into all of their faces.

"See you, Hunter," the roving ménage à trois said in unison, as they meandered to their next prey.

Hunter cleared his throat, then forced his eyes from the swaying hips. "It's time to go to our seats. Are you ready?" he asked, taking her hand.

She had made up her mind. "I'm ready for everything with you, Hunter." She leaned into him.

He smiled knowingly and led her into the elevator that would take them to the beginning of the game.

During the limousine ride from the Staples Center, Sasha had visions of Hunter's home. But nothing in her imagination prepared her for this. As she stood in the middle of the living room, Sasha fought to keep her mouth from dropping in shock. If she hadn't seen the building's concierge, or the lobby's crystal chandelier, or the hallway's marble floors, she would have thought she was in a college dormitory.

As Hunter strolled the room, turning on the small

mismatched table lights, she hoped her curious confusion wasn't obvious. She could see most of the apartment from where she stood. It appeared to be a one-bedroom—just barely. The tan carpet was industrial, the kind designed for high-traffic corporate offices. Not what you'd expect in a high-rent building.

It looked like Hunter had done most of his shopping at a discount warehouse. At least the brown futon couch matched the pine-veneer end tables and bookcases that overflowed with books.

She moved toward a stack piled high in the corner: Richard Wright, James Baldwin, William Shakespeare, Zora Neale Hurston. "You like to read."

"Every chance I get, I love the classics." Then, sweeping his arm, he asked, "What do you think of my place?"

"It's nice."

He laughed. "This is just a pit-stop. I gave Cynthia the house."

"Looks like you gave her a lot more than that," Sasha said lightly.

He laughed again. "I'll be looking for a new place soon. I just have to take care of a few things first. But I have to admit I'm comfortable here. It's better than where I grew up."

Sasha frowned. She'd read about his pauper-to-prince transformation, which was why she'd expected more palatial surroundings.

"So." Sasha walked to him. "What do you use this for?" She pointed to the high-powered telescope that was directed toward the dim lights in the hill.

He swung the instrument east, leveling at the Hollywood sign. "To see things." He put his eye to the lens.

When he stood straight, he saw Sasha's frown. "But I'd much rather participate in the act than watch."

He put his arm around her waist, and drew her to him. His tongue parted her lips and Sasha closed her eyes, trying to fall into the feeling. She brought her hands around his neck and pulled him closer, pushing away the resistance that stirred inside. This was not who she was nor who she wanted to be. She would never settle for a one-time romp.

Hunter pulled back and, as his eyes held hers, he slipped her jacket from her shoulders, letting it drop to the floor. When she didn't resist, he kissed her again, more urgently.

An alarm rang in her head. This is not right, she said over and over inside.

But what was right? Was it right that Gordon had thrown her aside, even though she loved him? Was it right that her grandmother couldn't love her? Was it right that, no matter where she searched, there was no one for her?

Hunter Blaine could have any woman, yet he was unbuttoning her blouse. His moans showed how much he wanted her. Goosebumps rose on her, as his fingertips gently traced her bare skin. Her moans mimicked his as his tongue followed his fingers.

Suddenly he stopped. His eyes were thin slits. He took her hand and pulled her with him. She followed, but before she stepped into the bedroom, she glanced over her shoulder, focusing on the telescope. She was going to do this. It was time for her to stop being a voyeur and live life on her terms.

Chapter 19

*A*nya sighed as she hung up the phone. Madear hated answering machines, but she was suddenly using hers. Over the past few days, it had come on every time Anya called. She knew her grandmother was fine—Miss Mattie told her so when Anya had checked on Madear through her best friend.

"It's time for me to camp out on the porch, Madear," Anya whispered. "You *will* talk to me."

"I think this should do it." Dianna dropped files on Anya's desk.

Anya looked at the clock. "Perfect timing. I have to leave in an hour."

She and Braxton were going downtown to select wedding bands. It had been her idea—a peace pact. For the past few days, an unspoken truce had kept them on an even keel, and Anya had jumped full-force into the wedding plans, not leaving time for doubts.

But her wedding was not the only thing keeping her preoccupied. Her family was doing their share. Madear wouldn't return calls, Sasha was spending all of her time with Hunter; Anya was more than a bit concerned.

"Okay, Dianna. After I go over these files, I'll be out of here. I'm not even going to answer the phone."

The shrill of the ringing phone shocked them for a moment, then they laughed.

Dianna answered it at Anya's desk. "Oh, yes, Mr. Greene."

Anya nodded and took the phone from Dianna. Still standing in the office, Dianna sighed as she watched her boss's face.

"I can answer any questions you have now." Anya twisted the ring on her finger. "Okay, we'll see you in a little while." She hung up.

"It doesn't sound good," Dianna said.

"Mr. Greene said that some of his employees had questions that he hadn't thought about. He wants to come over now." She slammed her hand against the desk. "Sometimes I think this man makes up excuses for meetings. What am I going to do?"

"Do you want me to try to reach Braxton?"

Anya glanced at the clock again. Braxton was probably already on his way. "No, I'll do it. Buzz David and tell him I need to see him in five minutes."

When Dianna left, Anya sighed loudly. This would probably end their truce.

She dialed Braxton's cell phone, only to hear his voice mail. She knew it would be worse now.

Just as she put down the phone, there was a knock on her door.

Braxton stepped into the office with a wide grin. "Hey, honey. Ready?"

"Braxton—"

He searched her face. "Oh, don't tell me . . ."

Her gaze broke from his. "Braxton, the people from

Linden just called. They have some questions—I tried to reach you."

"You can't go." His words were flat.

"I am so sorry."

"I rearranged my whole afternoon." He stepped away from the desk and jammed his hands into his pockets. "Ohh-kay." It was a long, low groan. "Will it take the rest of the afternoon?"

"No!" she spoke quickly. "They'll be here in less than an hour, and it won't take more than an hour or two, depending on—"

"Why don't we say three hours?" He looked at his watch. "I'll give you a call at four. The stores don't close until seven."

With a relieved step, Anya went to him and put her arms around his waist. "Thank you for understanding. I'll be finished by four, I promise."

He kissed her forehead. "We can't have lunch, but maybe I can plan something for dinner."

"That would be great." She hugged him.

There was a knock on her open door. "Excuse me."

Anya broke their embrace. "Braxton, you remember David?"

Braxton held out his hand. "Nice to see you again. Congratulations on the Linden account. My fiancée tells me she got it because of you."

"Anya is generous, but thank you. Speaking of Linden, Dianna said that we're having a special meeting?" David asked Anya.

Braxton held up his hands. "Let me get out of here. Honey, I'll call around four."

She squeezed his hand. "Thank you," she said softly.

She smiled as she watched him leave. This was a sign—her prayers were being answered.

David's cough interrupted her short reverie.

"Okay, let's get to work," she said with renewed energy. "I have to get out of here by four!"

Braxton slapped his hand against the wall, missing the elevator button. It had taken every bit of control to hold back. With Anya, there was always something that took precedence over him. When was their relationship going to become a priority?

In the elevator, he flexed his hands, willing himself not to slam his fist against the wall. When the doors opened, he jogged to his car and sat motionless inside.

The entire afternoon had been planned. First, a romantic lunch, then to the diamond district. And tonight, he would have finally broken the news. Carlos told him that Anya had to be brought in if he was to have any chance of getting his son by the first of the year.

Braxton knew that Carlos didn't approve. But he was doing what he had to do.

"This is going to be a tough one, Braxton," Carlos had said to him this morning.

They were sitting in the lavish offices of Beekman, Joseph, and Stone. Carlos was a partner in the prestigious firm he'd joined over ten years ago.

"Judges always favor the mother, and Roxanne is a good mother."

"I don't care." Braxton had shaken his head stubbornly. "Just tell me what I have to do to get my son."

Carlos had sighed and leaned across the large mahogany desk. They'd been friends since childhood. As Braxton had been moved from one foster home to another, Carlos and his family provided Braxton with the only stability he'd known.

Now, as Carlos held his best friend's stare, he knew there was little he could do to change Braxton's mind. "Well," Carlos began, "you're right about needing things stacked in your favor. And Anya being at home full-time *may* help, but, Braxton, I can't see Anya giving up her business."

"She doesn't need the business. I have more than enough money."

"It's not about money with Anya. I think—"

"I don't care what you think!" Braxton snapped.

With a surprised look, Carlos moved back in his chair and held up his hands.

"I'm sorry," Braxton said, "but I want my son with me, Carlos. Junior is on the verge of being a man, and he needs his father." Braxton began pacing the floor. "Do you know what's wrong with this picture? The news is full of stories about Black men who don't want to take care of their babies. I'm dying to take care of my son and you're telling me that it's going to be just about impossible for me to win."

"Braxton, you are taking care of your son."

"I want to be more than the monthly check."

Carlos nodded. He couldn't find fault with that. "Okay, man. I'll do what I can. I've alerted Benjamin Stein. He handled the McLeod case, remember that one?"

Braxton had nodded solemnly.

"Against all odds, he got the father custody there, so if you have any chance, it'll be with Benjamin."

Braxton sat silently as Carlos buzzed his secretary. Benjamin was in his office. Braxton followed Carlos down the dark-oak hallway, lined with pictures of all the partners.

In a meeting that took almost an hour, Benjamin had expressed the same concerns as Carlos. But he agreed to accept the case.

"The only chance we have, Mr. Vance," Benjamin Stein had said as he accepted the five-thousand-dollar retainer, "is to bring out anything against your ex-wife that will work in our favor."

Braxton had grimaced, but remained silent. He had no intention of going after Roxanne. He would wait until they began planning, then he would tell the lawyer how to do this. All he needed to do was prove that his home would be better and with Anya as a full-time mother, there would be nothing that he wouldn't be able to provide his son.

Braxton sighed now as he remembered the looks on Carlos's and Benjamin's faces. They didn't have much hope, but he had enough for all of them.

Finally, he turned on the ignition and maneuvered his car from the parking structure. He shook his head in disgust. This was the type of thing that had to end. Well, tonight, he would tell her she had to sell her business and with Junior in her plans, he knew she'd never say no.

It was exactly four, and Anya snapped her briefcase with a flourish. The knock on the door made her smile. She put her purse on her shoulder, ready to impress her fiancé.

When the door opened, Anya's smile disappeared. "David, don't even think about it! I don't want to hear anything." She put her hands over her ears. "Whatever it is, handle it."

David laughed. "I wanted to tell you that I scheduled a meeting with Bleu Foods for an annual review."

"Good idea. Have Dianna put it on my calendar."

"Already done."

Her smile returned. "You really do have everything under control." She sat in the chair in front of her desk.

He grinned with that crooked half-smile and sat next to her. "That's why you hired me."

"You're doing quite a job. We have a great future."

"That's what I was thinking," David said.

To her, it seemed his voice dropped an octave, and Anya felt the warm rush of heat rise to her face. She was grateful when, a second later, the ringing phone broke the silence.

Dianna tapped on her door. "Anya, it's Braxton."

As she reached for the phone, David asked, "Do you want me to leave?"

"No, this will only take a moment." She picked up the phone. "Hi, honey. You won't believe this, but I'm ready."

"And you won't believe this. I have to do a conference call with New York."

"It must be important." Anya frowned, looking at her watch. "It's already after seven in New York. Is everything all right?"

"Oh, yeah. Carolyn said they want to talk through some points on the contract. But I don't know how long it will take. I'm sorry, babe."

"That's okay. No one understands better than I do. Do you want me to come over there and wait for you?"

Braxton was tempted to say yes. Then he would know for sure she was away from that business. But there was no need for that. In just twenty-four hours, Mitchell & Associates would be on its way to being a bad memory. "No, why don't we plan a late dinner for tomorrow after counseling," he said, thinking that Anya was always in a better mood after meeting with Pastor Ford. "There's something we have to talk about."

"That works. I'll see you then."

"I love you."

Anya glanced over her shoulder at David, who was flicking invisible lint from his jacket. "Me too," she whispered.

She hung up and leaned back in her chair. "Looks like I'm free."

"Great! Have dinner with me."

She looked at him for a long moment, then dropped her eyes. "No, I have some work to do."

"I'm talking about a *working* dinner. We can go over some of the upcoming account meetings and"—David glanced at his watch—"we'll finish early enough for you to come back to the office and impress me with your workaholic ways." When Anya twisted her lips in doubt, David continued. "We can accomplish a lot together."

She smiled and wondered if he was flirting. Probably not. She picked up her purse. "Where do you want to go?"

"Doesn't matter. I'll follow you anywhere."

There it was again, she thought.

He stood and put his hand out. "After you." He smiled and his dark eyes bore into her once again. This time, Anya stared back, refusing to break away. When he finally took a step forward, she exhaled and followed, walking past Dianna and into the hallway, never noticing the raised eyebrows that Dianna sent her way.

Chapter 20

$\mathcal{T}$here was a light knock on her door. "Anya, may I talk to you for a moment?"

She swerved around in her chair. Her lips tightened slightly when she saw Alaister standing stiffly in the doorway, but she maintained her smile. "Come on in."

She wasn't surprised when he closed the door; from the look on his face, this wasn't going to be quick. A glance at the clock made her sigh. She needed to leave in fifteen minutes if she were going to make it to church on time.

Alaister shifted his feet, keeping his eyes lowered as he approached her desk. His hands were stuffed deep inside his pockets.

Anya leaned back in her chair, never taking her eyes from him. As she had done many times before, she noted his resemblance to Prince William, and wondered again if Alaister was related to the royal family. He acted as if blue blood were furiously pumping through his veins.

Alaister continued his silent stance and Anya motioned for him to have a seat. "What can I help you with, Alaister?"

When he lifted his head, his eyes flashed at her. "I

don't agree with you on the Linden case, Anya. It's not fair that I have to split commissions with Melissa. I did all the work, all the strategic planning," he said forcefully, pointing to his chest. "It was my lead."

Anya placed her elbows on the arms of her chair and waited a moment before she spoke. "I thought David brought in this business."

Alaister stood and walked behind the chair he'd been sitting in. "You know what I mean," he said, his British accent thick with agitation. "I was with David when he made the contact. This is *my* case!"

Keeping emotion from her face, she folded her hands. "First of all, Alaister, we'll talk about this, but only on a professional level. Calm down." His gaze, once again, dropped to the floor as he sat.

Anya allowed a few long seconds to pass before she continued. "I'm really surprised by your attitude."

His thick blond eyebrows rose in question and she leaned forward on her desk. "I know how hard you worked, but I also know that you're the first one to consider what's best for the client."

"I am thinking about Linden and—"

She held up her hand. "What's best for Linden is having a full team to enroll the employees. There are over two hundred fifty people we have to handle."

"My team can handle it. It might take a day or two longer."

"There's no need for that." Anya stood and went to the other side of her desk. She perched herself on the edge. "Alaister, you've always been a team player, so I know you understand my position on this. What's *really* bothering you?"

His shoulders slumped as he leaned forward, and Anya watched silently as Alaister breathed deeply. Finally he said, "I've worked really hard and now Melissa is about to make as much money on this as I am."

"But Alaister, we've always shared accounts and you've made money from Melissa's leads. So why do you care how much money she'll make?" Anya frowned and crossed her arms in front of her.

He looked up at her, his eyes again flashing. His lips parted, then he paused and turned away.

With the patience that had come from managing sales people for ten years, Anya waited.

Suddenly Alaister stood. "If that's your final decision . . ." He sounded defeated.

"It is." She smiled, but her tone was firm.

Without another word, he moved toward the door. Before he opened the door, he turned back. "You're not being fair."

Before she could respond, he stepped from her office.

Anya covered her face with her hands. It's a good thing I love this business, she thought. She dropped her hands and picked up her purse. She didn't have time to ponder. She had a pastor and fiancé waiting.

This had to be the longest freight train in the country. Anya tapped her fingers against the steering wheel and stopped herself from looking at her watch. She knew the time—just a minute past the last time she'd checked. She sighed as the train's whistle blew, the slow-passing cable cars showing no signs of coming to an end.

She tried to block the image of Braxton from her mind. It didn't help that she hadn't spoken to him since he canceled their dinner yesterday. She had stayed out with David much longer than she planned. They talked for almost four hours at the restaurant. Then for another hour when he'd taken her back to her car. Business had taken a backseat to the playful banter they exchanged about everything from politics to who was *really* the best WNBA team. By the time she got home, there were three messages from Braxton. The tone of the last one made her once again turn off the phone's ringer.

She was surprised that he hadn't called her at the office today and now guilt eased its way into her conscience. Maybe things had not gone well with his phone call. "I should have called him back," she said aloud.

As she uttered those words, the last of the train's cars passed. Anya sighed. Please, God, make this all right.

It took just a few minutes for her to pull into the church's parking lot and run from her car, into the church and down the hall to the pastor's office.

She knocked once. "Hi. Sorry I'm late."

Pastor Ford grinned and tapped her long manicured fingernail against her watch. She was sitting on the couch and Braxton sat across from her in one of the two matching wingback chairs.

Braxton mumbled as Anya scooted next to him. She ignored his unsmiling stare, and brushed her lips against his.

"Okay, let's get started." Pastor Ford bowed her head and prayed. "Heavenly Father, we come before you this evening with praise and thanksgiving . . ."

Anya opened one eye, trying to sneak a glance at Braxton. He was tapping his right hand against his shaking knee.

Oh God, she started in her own silent prayer, please let us get through this.

"Amen," Pastor Ford said. "Okay, let's look over the assignment. Did you both complete it?"

They nodded.

"Who wants to go first?"

Anya turned to Braxton and, when he didn't return her gaze, she reached into her briefcase. "I will," she volunteered.

Pastor Ford skimmed the notepad balanced on her lap. "I want you to read the list of why you're marrying Braxton. Then, before we discuss it, we'll have Braxton"— Pastor Ford turned to him—"read his list, okay?"

Braxton shrugged and rolled his eyes. The pastor frowned, but nodded toward Anya to begin.

She took a deep breath. "The five reasons for me are, I love him and I know he loves me. He loves the Lord. We enjoy being with each other and I trust him." Anya stopped and the pastor lifted her eyes from the notes she was taking.

"That's four reasons." The pastor looked at her list. "Did I miss one?"

Anya studied her sheets. "I counted I love him and he loves me as separate points. Is that okay?"

"It's okay if you can't think of anything else to say," Braxton muttered.

Hushing stares descended upon him.

In a slow move, Pastor Ford laid her pad on the table. "There's something you two need to clear up." Pastor Ford stood. "So I'm going to step out for a few minutes and then we'll begin again."

They were silent as the pastor picked up her mug and

closed the door behind her. For several minutes, Anya kept her head lowered. When she finally looked up, Braxton had turned away, his attention on the darkened street outside.

"This is embarrassing, Braxton." He turned to her with a blank face. "What is wrong with you?"

"You tell me," he grunted.

"You're acting like a child and I don't know why."

He jumped from his seat. "Oh, I'm a child now."

She stood in front of him, eye-to-eye. "You're acting like one."

"Then I should leave. This counseling isn't for children, is it?" His voice was raised and he had turned his back to her.

Anya held up her hands. "I shouldn't have said that. But you're angry and I don't know why."

He swung around. "You want to know what's wrong? I don't want to be here," he hissed. "This was your idea, but, it's not important enough for you to make the effort to get here on time."

"I'm sorry I was late. I got caught in a meeting and—"

"There's always something that keeps you from *us*, isn't there?"

"I was only a few minutes late."

"If I counted up all the minutes I had to sit and wait for you." He shook his head. "Never mind. You don't even try to understand."

Anya raised her hands and massaged her temples as she spoke. "I said I was sorry—"

"And that's supposed to be enough? See, you don't even get it!" he exclaimed, pointing his finger at her.

She brought her hands to her sides and balled them into fists. "You better take your finger out of my face."

He stood glaring, but only for a moment before he backed away. Anya fell into her seat, keeping her eyes glued on him. He stood at the window, his back to her. Almost five minutes of silence hung in the room before there was a knock, and the pastor entered.

"Are we ready now?"

"Pastor Ford, we can't finish this tonight," Anya said, her eyes burrowing into Braxton's back. "We'll be better next week."

Pastor Ford brushed her dark brown hair away from her face. "That is one way to handle this: Leave, ignore it, and hope that it will pass. Or you can do what you would do in a good marriage—and face it now."

The room stayed silent.

"This is relationship counseling," the pastor said, then paused. "Braxton, please join us." She smiled, but her serious tone made Braxton drag himself to his chair.

The pastor's eyes darted between the two. "So what's the unsolved opportunity?"

"Well—" Anya began.

The pastor held up her hand. "Braxton, why don't you tell me?"

His face was twisted with anger, and it was a moment before he began. "I don't know, Pastor Ford. I'm frustrated, overwhelmed, and—" He stopped.

"Is it about the wedding?" Anya jumped in.

"Anya, let Braxton finish everything he has to say."

Sighing, Braxton continued. "I was fine when I got here, but then when we had to wait for her . . ." His breathing seemed labored, as if his fury were building. "Anya's business always comes first, no matter what else is going on in her life." He paused. "But I *always* put her first."

"Always?" the pastor asked.

"Always! She is my priority. Just ask her," he said, pointing toward Anya.

"This is ridiculous. I am not going to allow you to disrespect me like this," Anya snapped.

"I'm just telling you how I see it."

Anya plopped back in her seat and folded her arms.

The pastor smiled. "At least we're making progress."

"Progress?" they said simultaneously.

"Yes, there are issues here that we can now address. Braxton," the pastor continued, "what is it about Anya's business that agitates you?"

"It's not her business, Pastor. It's that her business is more important than anything else in her life, especially me."

"What are you talking about?" Anya interrupted.

"Anya!" the pastor said strongly. "You'll have your turn."

"Thank you, Pastor." Braxton cleared his throat. "She throws everything aside for that business."

Anya gritted her teeth. "I own the business."

"Anya, please step outside for a few minutes," the pastor said.

Anya pursed her lips and sat back. "I'm sorry, Pastor. I won't say anything else."

"That's true because you're going to be outside." Pastor Ford gestured toward the door.

No! Anya yelled in her head. But there was no way she would say that to her pastor. She grabbed her briefcase, and stomped toward the door, then took softer steps as the pastor caught her eye. Anya took her time closing the door behind her.

She threw her briefcase down and began to pace the small anteroom. As she passed the door, she stopped a few times but could hear nothing. Finally, she sat down and flipped through an issue of *Christian Life Today*. She started reading, but then turned to a new article before she finished the last. She repeated this pattern before she gave up and slammed the magazine shut.

I should just get in my car and go home, she thought, though she knew there was no way she'd leave.

She stood and went to Pastor Ford's door, this time flushing her ear against the wood. But the sounds were muffled. She tried to push her body closer, then heard movement and scurried back to the chair. Anya picked up the magazine just as the door opened.

The pastor opened the door. "Anya, join us now."

Anya gingerly placed the magazine on the table, hoping Pastor Ford hadn't noticed that she'd been holding it upside-down. With as much grace as she could gather, she picked up her briefcase and walked back into the office. She took her seat, crossing her legs and arms at the same time.

"This has been a bit unorthodox, but you know how I feel about these things—let the Holy Spirit have His way. But we have discovered something that is crucial to this relationship. It can be worked out, but only if it's talked out. But, I'm going to require two things." The pastor turned to Anya. "Remember, that the same letters that spell *listen* make up the word *silent*." She paused. "Secondly, remain calm. You cannot listen when you're emotional."

Anya raised her eyebrows. Surely the pastor wasn't talking about her. Braxton was the one who loved drama.

"Okay, Braxton, tell Anya what you just told me."

Braxton faced Anya and leaned toward her, their knees almost touching. "I don't feel like I'm important to you, Anya. I feel that you would give up on me, give up on our marriage, if it interfered in any way with Mitchell & Associates."

With her arms folded, Anya pursed her lips, willing her mouth to remain closed. She was still fuming over being expelled from the room. And this accusation made it worse.

"I'm concerned," Braxton continued, "that your business will interfere in our marriage."

That's it! There wasn't that much patience in her. She'd just have to get kicked out again. "Braxton, you're jealous of my business, and for no reason. I would never put my company in front of my family."

Braxton looked at the pastor for assistance, but Pastor Ford remained silent.

"That's not true, Anya. You do it all the time."

"Braxton, tell Anya how you see your future together."

Braxton took a deep breath and took Anya's hand. "Anya, I love you so much." His voice shook with emotion. "I want to have a family and build a life with you."

"That's exactly what I want," she said, softening to Braxton's words.

Braxton nodded. "I don't think you realize the toll your business takes." He paused. "I wonder, what is going to happen when we have children?"

"Of course, I won't be able to work the same way, I'll make adjustments." She rubbed her hands against his. "That's why I work so hard now. I want everything in place so that when we have children the business will run itself."

"Braxton," the pastor interrupted, "you and Anya are still not talking about the same things."

Anya's heart started to pound. There was something

ominous in Pastor Ford's words. What was Braxton hiding? Jumbled thoughts formed their own conclusions in her mind. "What is it, Braxton?"

The ticking of the clock on Pastor's Ford desk was all that could be heard for an eternal moment.

"I want to have a family now."

Anya released a relieved sigh. But when she turned to Pastor Ford, the pastor's eyes were urging Braxton to continue.

"Anya, I've filed for custody of Junior. I want him to live with us. He needs his father and you would make a much better mother than Roxanne."

Her mouth dropped as she leaned back in her chair, pulling her hands away from him. Just a moment before, she felt as if her heart was beating through her chest. Now she wasn't sure if it was beating at all.

"I didn't mean to spring this on you." His words came quickly. "I've tried to tell you a few times, but something . . . always got in the way."

"How long have you been thinking about this?" she whispered without looking at him.

"A while."

She looked at him as if she couldn't believe his words.

"That's why you have to sell your business. We have to have something over Roxanne if the courts are going to give us custody. I figured with my income and you as his full-time mother, we have a good chance."

She swallowed hard. With few words, he took away her career and relegated her to a housewife at home with his son. "What about me?" She wondered if she had shrunk to the size of her voice.

Braxton took her hands again. "I can give you the kind of life that you want."

"I have the life I want."

His hands tightened around hers. They stared at each other, saying nothing.

Pastor Ford said, "The tension you've been feeling has been built around this. Now that it's out, you can *talk*. Talk and listen. You'll be able to resolve this."

Pastor Ford turned directly to Anya. "I know you love that boy. I'm not telling you what to do, but listen to Braxton and hear his desire to have his son in his life so that he can raise him to be a man. And Braxton," she said, looking pointedly at him, "be very careful about asking anyone to give up anything for you. That's dangerous and would change the dynamics of any relationship."

Anya couldn't move. Just one hour before, she had come into this room to discuss marriage, not an instant family. She listened as Pastor Ford gave them instructions and told them what they would discuss next week. She accepted the papers the pastor handed to her and, without looking at them, dumped the pages into her briefcase.

When the pastor stood, Anya followed, grateful for the direction. She bowed her head as Pastor Ford said a final prayer.

"I'll be available if you need me before next week."

Anya nodded, her head moving in slow motion. She started toward the door, when Braxton picked up her briefcase and handed it to her. They followed the pastor to the front doors of the church where she left them.

The moment Pastor Ford walked away, Anya stared at Braxton for a second, then whipped around him and out the door, rushing down the stairs.

"Anya, wait!" He caught up to her at the car. "Honey, it was Pastor Ford's idea to talk about this. I wanted to wait."

"Wait for what?" she snapped. "Our wedding night, so that it would be too late to turn back?" Braxton winced. "I am grateful for Pastor Ford because only God knows when you would have told me. Your son would have already moved in before you said anything."

"I was trying to find the right time!"

She got in the car and slammed the door, refusing to roll down the window when Braxton tapped on it. When she started the ignition, then floored the accelerator, Braxton hurriedly backed away, a tint of fear in his eyes.

She watched in her rearview mirror as he walked slowly to his car. He drove off, and once he was far from her sight, she turned off the car. Alone on the darkened street, she held her face in her hands. What am I going to do? She looked back at the church and thought about going back to talk to Pastor Ford. She needed some help. Some scriptures, some prayers—something.

Through the windshield, Anya gazed at the blue-black sky. How could she be angry with any man who wanted to raise his son? But why hadn't he shared this with her? What about Roxanne? This could turn into a nasty fight. Why should Roxanne lose her child? What if Junior blamed her for this? And did Braxton really expect her to give up her business? There were too many questions.

She started her car and drove through the streets of Inglewood. These were the same streets she'd taken to the church, but nothing was the same. The homes that were alive with lights on her way over were now mere shadows. Only the churning in her stomach was familiar.

Her eyes filled with huge tears that blinded her as she

drove. She was surprised when she finally turned into her garage, barely remembering how she got there. She didn't have enough energy to close the garage door, or even move. So, she sat—waiting for some divine intervention to give her direction. While she sat in her car, sobbing and praying, she never noticed the car that drove up and down the street watching her.

*a*nya wanted to sleep. It had been emotionally draining getting through work on Friday. Now she wanted to sleep away her Saturday, but someone had a different idea. Even her oversized pillow couldn't drown out the sound. The bell rang incessantly and, finally, Anya surrendered.

With slumber-heavy eyelids, she rolled from her bed and grabbed her bathrobe. By the time she stumbled down the stairs, the ringing had ceased and Sasha was sitting with her feet kicked up on the couch.

"Good morning!" Sasha exclaimed brightly. "You sure slept late."

Anya squinted, screening her eyes from the sun's brightness that flooded the room, then grunted as her morning radar propelled her toward the brewing coffee. "I thought I heard the doorbell." Her voice was still filled with sleep.

"It was a delivery boy with these." Sasha lifted the oblong box from the table.

Anya peeked over the kitchen counter and frowned. "Oh."

"Don't you want to know who they're from?"

"There's not a whole lot of people who send me flowers."

Sasha settled on the couch. "Oh, I don't know. It could be Braxton or . . . it could be David professing his undying love."

Anya slouched into the chair facing Sasha. "I already told you—"

"I know. They're from Braxton anyway."

Anya arched her eyebrows in question.

"I checked."

"Sasha! Stay out of my business."

"Okaaay." She paused. "Since you're already in a snit, I should probably tell you that I read the card."

Anya shook her head as she brought the hot cup to her lips. "You're incorrigible."

"And you're old and cranky. But I love you anyway." She handed the box to Anya and sighed. "Your man is quite the romantic. I never got letters like this from Gordon."

Anya rolled her eyes. She opened the box overflowing with yellow roses. Anya searched through the bundle.

"Sorry, I forgot to put this back." Sasha grinned, as she pulled the note from her nightshirt pocket.

Shaking her head, Anya read the note silently.

I am so sorry that I hurt you. I should have told you, and I apologize with all my heart. My prayer is that you will forgive me. We need another chance.

Forever, Braxton

"Isn't that wonderful?" Sasha gushed.

Anya grunted.

Sasha leaned over Anya. "So what did he do this time?"

Anya returned to her coffee.

"Does silence mean that you're not going to answer me?"

"Exactly."

"Why not?" Sasha whined. "I know how to handle difficult men."

Anya continued to sip her now-cooling drink.

"At least call Braxton. I told you he called a few short of a million times yesterday."

"I'll call him," Anya said flatly.

"Call him now." After a couple of seconds Sasha said, "Stop acting like someone with a bad case of hemorrhoids." Another beat. "Well?"

Anya almost licked the last drop of coffee from the cup. Finally, she took the cordless phone and sank back into the overstuffed chair, while Sasha curled on the couch with the newspaper in hand. Anya eyed Sasha, hoping telepathic waves would jolt Sasha into her room or some other place in the house. But Sasha continued to fake interest in the real-estate section.

She breathed deeply, and pressed the memory button.

"Hi, Braxton." She put as much cheer in her voice as she could gather.

"Anya!"

"I wanted to let you know that I got the flowers. This morning and the ones you sent yesterday." She watched Sasha drop the newspaper and raise her eyebrows, all pretense of not listening tossed aside.

"I meant everything I said," Braxton said softly. "I am so sorry, Anya. I didn't mean for it to go down this way."

"There's a lot for us to settle."

Anya heard Braxton's sigh of relief. "I'll come right over."

"Not today."

The tightness returned to his voice. "We can't avoid this."

"I'm not doing that. It's just that . . ." She paused.

"Sasha's not feeling well." Anya had to hold back her giggle as she watched Sasha feel her forehead.

"I could come over there so you won't have to leave Sasha."

"No, she's been sick a couple of days and has been stuck in her room. Today is the first day she's gotten up, but if you come over, she'll just go back to bed. She should be fine by tomorrow though. I've been giving her some of that over-the-counter stuff."

Sasha laughed out loud and Anya made a face for her to keep quiet.

"What was that?"

"Sasha . . . sneezing. I need to go. I have to . . . fix Sasha something to eat."

"*You're* going to cook?"

"Just soup . . . or something," Anya stuttered.

"What about tonight?"

"Maybe. We'll see how Sasha is feeling."

"Anya—"

"I promise I'll call. If not tonight, definitely tomorrow. After church."

"Anya, I want to work this out."

"Me too," she responded simply. She clicked off the phone and placed it gently on the table. She could feel Sasha staring at her.

"Why did you lie to him?"

"Because we're going through something, and he wouldn't have accepted anything else. But don't worry, he didn't believe me anyway."

Sasha giggled. "What happened to the perfect little Christian?"

In that second, words from Pastor Ford's recent sermon

echoed in Anya's mind. "You're a living example. People are watching every move you make." Anya groaned and rolled her eyes. "Unfortunately, being a Christian doesn't make me perfect."

"At least you know it. The Christians I've met think they're above us mere mortals. That's why I was so surprised to hear that *you* were a Christian. You seem so different from the ones I know."

"How so?"

Sasha bit her lip in thought. "Well, you're cranky, but you're not judgmental. You're all in my Kool-Aid because you're my cousin, but you're not judging me on some religious level. The Christians I know aren't like that. Their lives are so perfect that they spend all their time telling other people what to do and how to live."

"How do you know these people are Christians?"

"Because they act like Christians. They act . . . holy. They don't drink or smoke or anything like that."

Anya had to stop herself from chuckling. "Do you drink?"

"Just a little wine now and then."

"Do you smoke?"

"No, but it's my choice. I don't want some old fogey dictating to me what I can do."

"Neither would I. You know how old fogies can be."

Sasha glanced sideways at Anya. "Are you making fun of me?"

"No, it's just funny what people believe about being a Christian. All it means is that you've confessed with your mouth that Jesus is Lord and you believe in your heart that God raised Him from the dead."

"Sounds like you're just quoting the Bible."

"Romans 10:9. Do you want me to show you?" Anya asked casually.

"No." Sasha paused. "And what else do you have to do?"

"That's it."

"What about all those other things?"

"There are things I try to do because I'm saved and I want to please God. But as far as *being* saved, that's all there is to it."

Sasha shook her head. "You make it sound simple, but I know this religious stuff is confusing."

"It is hard to understand. There're a lot of things that don't make sense in my mind. But it makes all the sense in the world . . . in my heart. That's because it's all inside— it's about having a personal relationship with God."

Sasha, silent, was thoughtful.

"Do you want me to show you what I'm talking about?" Anya asked again, this time reaching for the brown leather, gilt-edged Bible that she kept on her coffee table.

"No, not right now. I'm starving. Wanna get something to eat? My treat."

Anya felt the opportunity slip away. "Sure." She hoped she hid her disappointment. "We can go to Santa Barbara. There are some great places to eat up there."

"Great. Where's Santa Barbara?"

"Almost two hours up the coast."

"Girl, I will die from starvation! Let's go somewhere closer. Remember, I'm sick." Sasha dramatically touched the back of her hand to her forehead.

Anya tossed a pillow at her cousin. "We're going to Santa Barbara. It'll keep you away from Hunter for at least one afternoon. You're spending too much time with him."

"I surrender," she said, tossing the pillow back and ignoring Anya's commentary. "But what if Braxton calls?"

"I'll call him when we get back."

Sasha was the first to stand. "Let's go then." Sasha started up the stairs and Anya followed.

"It might take me a few minutes longer to get ready," Anya said. "I have some things I need to pray about."

Sasha turned around and looked at Anya questioningly.

"That's the thing about being a Christian. When I sin, I pray and God forgives me. Now you, on the other hand . . ." Anya casually strolled into her bedroom and closed the door softly, leaving her sentence unfinished and Sasha standing in the middle of the hallway, with her hands on her hips and a deep frown on her face.

"Sasha, please take your foot out of the window!"

She sighed and pulled back, readjusting her seat. "You are so uptight." Sasha looked at Anya out of the corner of her eye. "I hope you're not going to be like this all day."

Anya smirked. "No, I'm determined to have a good time, no matter how much you try to upset me."

Sasha laughed. "Now that we have that settled."

They proceeded in comfortable silence up the coastal highway with the ocean's mist hanging in the air. Although it was almost the middle of February, it was warm and they drove with the top down. At speeds a bit over seventy, the trip took just two hours. Anya turned into a sparsely filled lot along the beach.

"This is pretty cool," Sasha said, eyeing the main street over the top of her sunglasses. "We'd better get to a restaurant soon or else there'll be a corpse sitting in the seat next to you on the ride back."

Anya laughed. "What do you want to eat?"

"Food!"

They went into Whaler's and were seated along the windowed wall. They took a moment to enjoy the ocean view, marveling at how the high surf came almost to the restaurant's edge. One of the blond, tanned, muscular waiters brought water glasses to their table and stood impatiently as their eyes roamed the menu. They placed their orders and watched the waiter sulk away, as if this were the last place he wanted to be.

"Anya, thank you for letting me stay with you. I'm having a great time."

"I'm glad." She smiled. "I just wish you weren't spending all of your time with Hunter."

"Why are you so against him?" Her question sounded like pleading.

"I'm not. He's just not right for you, especially with what you've been through."

"Don't you think I'm too old for this advice? Plus Hunter is helping me. I feel good when I'm with him."

Anya twirled the water glass in her hand. "Do you know his . . . history?"

Sasha leaned back in her chair and sighed. "I was wondering when you were going to bring that up. Anya, Hunter was cleared of all of those charges. That woman admitted that she was lying."

Anya thought back to two years before, when Hunter had been accused of assault by an extra on his sitcom. The police had taken her statement, but a few days later the young woman recanted and charges had never been filed.

But the tabloids continued the story as if Hunter were on trial. It wasn't until Hunter hired Melvin Johnson, a Johnnie Cochran protégé, that the story miraculously disappeared and before long was forgotten.

In her head, Anya knew that Hunter had been falsely accused, but doubts still lingered. She hated that her brain kept repeating that cliché: Where there's smoke . . .

Anya said, "I'm just concerned because Hunter is not serious about any relationship. Since his divorce, he's been linked with every single woman in Hollywood."

"And after all those women, now he's with me." Sasha put her hand on top of her cousin's. "I'm not looking for a relationship. That's what makes this so special. We're not trying to be like you and Braxton. And, speaking of Mr. Author, why are you avoiding him?" Sasha asked, purposely changing the subject.

The waiter returned and, in one swoop, set their plates in front of them. Sasha knew the routine now, and she waited for Anya to say grace. But before Anya could pronounce the second syllable in "Amen," Sasha had dug full force into her lobster omelet. After a few bites, she eyed Anya's salmon pasta.

Anya laughed and waved her fork in her cousin's direction. "Don't even think about it."

Sasha returned her laugh. "So, why are you doggin' Braxton?"

Anya shrugged her shoulders nonchalantly. "We're just going through some . . . things that I'm sure are normal for any couple."

"Is it the pressure of the wedding?"

Anya sighed. "No, we're just trying to find a comfortable place in our relationship. It's not like it was in the beginning."

"Thank God for that," Sasha said, her mouth stuffed with lobster and eggs. "Let's hope that you've both grown. The only thing that matters is that you're still in love."

Sasha's statement sounded like a question, and Anya felt the need to affirm it. "I *do* love Braxton. I just don't know if that's enough. We're always arguing. Everything in our lives is an issue. We're not pleased with each other."

Sasha shrugged. "Then don't marry him."

She said the words so casually that Anya wondered if she had heard her correctly. "I can't do that."

"Why not?"

"Because . . ." Anya stopped and put down her fork.

Sasha's mouth opened wide. "I was only kidding, but if you can't answer that question—you don't need to get married."

"I really do love Braxton."

"Girl, I loved Gordon. But, like you said, sometimes that's not enough."

"If I'd known you were going to try to talk me out of getting married, I would have left you in L.A. with Hunter." Anya laughed, but she shifted uncomfortably in her seat.

"I'm just responding to what I've seen. You haven't been happy since I got here. Except for that night on the boat and, even then, you said you guys had a fight. You should call the marriage off."

"I'm not prepared to do that . . . just yet." Anya twirled the ring on her finger.

"You're afraid of being alone."

"That's not true! I've been alone all these years."

"My point exactly. I think you feel that you're getting

older and this might be your last chance. And," Sasha lowered her voice, "I think you missed having a family and now you want one of your own."

Anya shook her head. "Madear and Donovan are my family. You and your parents were there for me too. I never felt I was missing anything."

"You missed your parents more than you'd ever admit," Sasha said softly. "And you want to create that family unit in your own life now."

"That's not true." Anya was still shaking her head.

"Then how do you explain an independent, successful woman like you going through all of these changes? I know you. If something's not right, you get rid of it."

"This is a relationship, not a pair of shoes. I can't throw it away because of a few little problems."

"Your problems have suddenly been downgraded. A minute ago, they were big issues."

"We're in counseling," Anya protested. "I have to at least see the counseling through."

"You think counseling will change anything?"

"I think counseling will *reveal* everything. We'll understand each other better."

Sasha nodded, but then another thought came to her mind. "How are you going to handle the fact that Braxton isn't a Christian?"

Anya pushed her plate aside and sat up stiffly in her chair. "I never said Braxton wasn't a Christian."

Sasha squinted at her cousin for a long moment. "Then you're all set."

"Yes, I . . . am."

Sasha smiled. "I'm glad to hear that, because I think Braxton Vance is one fine catch."

Anya blinked rapidly. "A moment ago, you said that I should get rid of him."

"Just testing you. But I think you should marry the man. He obviously worships you. Sure, he doesn't do everything right, but he's a man—and it's not like you're perfect. You guys are going to make a great team. There are women who would offer up their well-managed stock portfolios for that man, not to mention their first-borns."

"Funny you should mention children."

Sasha's eyes opened wide. "I knew it! You're pregnant!"

"Almost."

"You're going to have to explain that."

"I'm about to give birth to a ten-year-old, Braxton's son."

"He's coming for a visit?"

"A permanent one, if Braxton has his way."

"Oooh! An instant family. How do you feel about that?"

"I don't know. I just found out and I'm stunned more than anything. Braxton's a good father, but I didn't know he wanted *this* much of a role."

"I can't imagine you with a grown boy."

"He's only ten."

"Honey, you haven't been around a lot of ten-year-olds. They are grown and it is not a pleasant sight."

"Maybe I'll hire you to help me," Anya joked but she was only half-kidding. The idea of having Junior was beginning to settle in, making her feel unsettled.

"Oh, no! I'll sell Amway before I'm ever locked in a room with kids again."

They both laughed.

"But having that kid is going to be no joke. How are you going to do it with your business and everything else in your life?" Sasha asked.

"You're getting ahead of things," Anya said, holding up her hands. "Braxton and I have to talk first, not to mention winning a custody battle that I think is a long shot."

"I don't envy you, but is this why you're mad at Braxton?"

"I'm mad because he didn't tell me."

"Come on, Anya. You said you guys have been having some issues—translation: fights. What was Braxton supposed to do? In the middle of a battle say, 'Hold it. I have something to tell you'?"

"He should be able to talk to me about anything."

"That's only if he can catch you. Between you dodging his calls and telling him lies, what's the man supposed to do?"

Anya remained silent but smiled.

Sasha licked her finger and held it in the air. "One point for me. You wanna know what I think? We should get in the car, break the speed of light, so that you can get to Braxton." She leaned forward and looked Anya straight in her face. "That man loves you."

Anya swallowed a piece of ice, then motioned for the waiter.

When he brought the check, Sasha tried to grab it. "I told you, this was my treat."

"No, this is mine. Call it a fee for service—for all of your advice. And don't argue with me. That will just slow me down. I have a fiancé that I have to see."

Sasha smiled and raised her glass in a toast. "Now *that's* what I'm talking about."

Anya jammed her hands deep into the pockets of her leather swing jacket and pulled it tightly around her waist. A cool night had descended upon Santa Monica. Looking at the stained-glass window in the front door of the two-story Colonial, she took a deep breath before she pressed the doorbell. Almost a minute passed before the entryway light came on, then the door opened immediately. He was covered by just tan silk pajama bottoms, totally naked to his navel.

"Hey," she said softly.

"Anya." His voice matched hers.

Seconds ticked by.

"May I come in?" She was shivering on the front steps.

"I'm sorry. I'm just surprised to see you. I've been calling all day." He reached for her, but she kept her hands hidden.

After he closed the door, they stood in the vast foyer, not daring to make eye contact.

"Anya—"

"Braxton—"

They chuckled nervously.

"You first," Anya said, her eyes darting between his face and the mosaic-marble tiled floor. She didn't dare look at his chest.

Braxton took a step toward her, then stopped when she lowered her head. He cleared his throat. "I feel so bad. I should have told you what I was thinking and it was wrong the way it came out."

She met his eyes. "You never talked about wanting Junior," she said softly. "Why didn't you tell me?"

"I don't know. As soon as it came to me, I should have

told you." He took another tentative step forward. "But I promise there are no other surprises."

She forced a smile. "There's a lot we have to talk about."

"I know! Let's go in," he motioned toward the sunken living room.

She kept her feet planted. "No, it's getting late. I only came by because I couldn't sleep without seeing you."

He smiled. "I'm glad to hear that."

"I want you to know, I'm not *against* having Junior with us."

Braxton let out an audible sigh. "Thank you, baby. We'll work this out, I promise."

An easy quietness fell between them.

"I'd better go."

This time his step brought him so close, she could smell the mintiness of his freshly brushed teeth. "I wouldn't mind if you stayed. Even if you don't want to talk. I just want to hold you." His eyes pleaded with her.

She reached for him and they held each other in silence, feeling the need to hold on to the moment. It was Anya who pulled away first.

"I'd better get out of here if we're going to make it to church in the morning."

"Want me to pick you up?" His voice was filled with hope.

She hugged him again, her palms lingering for a moment on the hardness of his back. "I'd like that."

"Let me get my robe so that I can walk you out."

Her eyes followed him as he ran up the winding staircase and then, when he disappeared down the hall, she looked around the formal entryway. In a few months, this would be her home. Her eyes scanned the open, sparsely furnished space. He was waiting for her to move in so they could shop together.

He trotted down the stairs and tied his robe around his waist. They walked to her car with their arms entwined. "Maybe I should drive you home."

"No you shouldn't. I'll be all right."

"I want to always protect you." He kissed her forehead. "Call me when you get home."

"As soon as I walk in the door."

They kissed.

"I love you, Anya" was the last thing he said before she got into her car.

Another battle had passed. Anya still didn't know how she felt about this—she couldn't imagine Junior living with them. It was too much to think about right now. She popped the CD that Braxton had given her into the player.

My love . . . is so good to me
It's your love that I need

She smiled. She did need Braxton's love. They would find a way to work through this.

She was in automatic mode, driving the familiar route without taking much notice of anything around her. She never saw the car that followed her all the way to her front door.

The second time Anya called, the phone only rang once. "I'm home."

"I was worried—you didn't call right away."

"I did but your phone just rang. I thought you had stepped out to 7-Eleven or something."

"Oh. I don't know what happened. I'm just happy to hear your voice now."

"We'd better get some sleep."

"I'll be there at seven-thirty."

"I'll be ready."

"Good night, Anya."

"Good night. And Braxton—"

"Yes?"

"I love you too."

Chapter 22

David's hands trembled as he gave the cab driver a twenty. "Keep the change," he said, his voice matching the quivering of his hands.

"Thanks, pal," the New York driver responded. "Hey buddy, are you sure this is where you want to go?"

David nodded, making eye contact with the driver through the rearview mirror.

"Okay, pal. Just be careful, 'kay?"

"Thanks," David said flatly. He wasn't afraid—the neighborhood gangs and wandering thugs didn't pose the greatest danger.

As the cab rolled away, David fought the sweeping desire to run after the car. But he remained steadfast, being drawn by forces refusing to relinquish their hold on him.

He looked up at the elderly building. The bricks had weathered the years well, but many of the windows had not and were boarded up with various shades and sizes of plywood, making the building look like a strange patchwork quilt.

David shivered and started toward the building. He kicked the overturned garbage can that barred his path and jumped as two squealing rats sprang from their habitat.

Taking forced steps, he moved toward the building and fleetingly glanced at a little boy coming out with a bicycle.

The boy crinkled his eyes at David. "You comin' ta see my mama?"

"No."

The boy maintained his stare, putting a finger in one of the holes of his tattered shirt and moving it around, making the hole larger. "Someone else up there wit' her right now."

"I'm not going to see your mother." David tried to push past the boy, but the bicycle blocked the path.

"You the po-lice?" The boy stood firm.

David understood the young boy's suspicions. He'd been the same way, enforcing the neighborhood rule: No strangers allowed. David picked up the bicycle and stepped around the boy.

"Hey, get yo' hands off my stuff!" the boy yelled.

David entered the five-story building and covered his face as the dank air hit him like a right uppercut. Urine, marijuana, and other indistinguishable elements mixed to cast a pungent odor that convinced him the building hadn't been cleaned since he moved away.

He took the steps, two at a time, not stopping until he reached the third floor. Breathing heavily, he leaned against the railing. The Flintstones blended with reggae, yet both were outdone by screaming voices that pushed their way into the corridor.

He hadn't raised his eyes yet, unable to find the courage to face what he'd come to see. As his breathing steadied, he forced his eyes to travel upward until he saw the number on the door. 3A.

His heart thumped with a force that shoved him back against the banister. He closed his eyes, trying to combat the images that flooded him. Then he heard it. *Bang! Bang! Bang!*

Startled, he opened his eyes and whirled around in the hall, crouching low as his eyes shot from corner to corner. Suddenly, the hallway was threateningly silent. The music, the television, the voices had all disappeared.

Bang! Bang! The shots came again. He covered his ears, but the gunfire continued.

David bolted down the stairs and out of the building, running past the young boy and the garbage cans that lined the street. He ran faster, but the sounds came louder. *Bang! Bang! Bang! Bang!*

David screamed and sprang up in his bed. He held his chest and felt the pounding against his hand. It wasn't until he turned on the light and surveyed the room that he realized he was at home, in Los Angeles.

His fingers grasped the damp sheets tightly and he lay back, inhaling deeply until his breathing became even. Finally, he turned on his side and glanced at the clock. He'd only been asleep for two hours, yet in a few more Sunday's dawn would be peeking through his window. Dragging the heavy quilt over him, he reached for the switch on the bedside lamp. But suddenly, he pulled his hand back, leaving the light shining.

Sasha twisted under the sheets and gently removed Hunter's hand from her waist. He rolled over and Sasha remained still, until she heard his low, smooth snore. She wiggled from the bed and stood by the edge, searching in the darkness for her clothes, and then she remembered—her shirt and pants were by the front door, right where Hunter peeled them from her body last night.

"Baby, you are a sight to wake up to," Hunter crooned, his voice still full of sleep. "Come back to bed."

He could only see her naked silhouette, but Sasha still felt his smile. "I didn't plan on spending the night, and I don't want Anya to worry."

He pulled her down onto the bed. His lips nuzzled against her neck. "You're grown. You don't have to answer to Anya."

Her head fell back as she let herself enjoy the sensation of his tongue gliding up to her face. "Anya wouldn't approve of this."

Hunter leaned back suddenly and clicked on the nightstand lamp. "You mean she wouldn't approve of me." Hunter's eyes narrowed and he pouted slightly. "Anya doesn't like me because I don't fit her image of how a man should behave. Sometimes, I just want to put her in her place."

Sasha frowned. "What kind of threat is that?"

Hunter's eyes opened wide. "It's not a threat, baby. I just want her to give me a chance because I don't want her to affect us."

She relaxed and kissed him, eager to end the conversation.

He pulled her back against his chest, resting her head on his shoulder, stroking her until bumps rose on her arm.

"Are you cold?" he asked, as he wrapped the sheet around her.

"No, it's just your touch." She rolled over onto him. "I have to go."

"I *want* you to stay. I enjoy being with you, Sasha."

His eyes told her he meant what he said, and she was filled with joy. She loved being with him too, although this was not what she'd planned. Falling for Hunter Blaine was like stepping into a minefield knowing where all the explosives were. But she couldn't stop where her heart was going.

"I've had the best time with you," he said.

She laid her head on his chest. Maybe something real could happen with Hunter and me, she thought.

He kissed the top of her head and said, "We're going to have some great times together."

She burrowed herself deeper. Maybe he was ready for a serious relationship again. She sighed deeply, relishing her thoughts of the life she could have.

"It's hard for me," Hunter continued. "Women always say they don't want any strings, but fifteen minutes into the first date, they're talking about marriage." He pulled her closer. "But not you. You're different."

Her smile widened. What would Gordon think the first time he saw her with Hunter? And what about Madear? Her grandmother would see that she *could* do something right.

"What I love about you, Sasha, is that you know this is just about sex. Some good old-fashioned, rock-my-world kind of sex. You don't mind just kicking it for a while, and I really appreciate that about you."

The smile on her face remained, stuck in place, while every muscle inside tightened.

"So, how about some of that good sex?" he asked, as his hands moved from her shoulders, caressing and kneading the rest of her.

Sasha could feel the heat of him as he pushed her against the mattress and laid his weight on top of her. Desire shined through his eyes. Moments ago, she would have mistaken his stare for love. But now she knew he wanted nothing more than the pleasure her body could bring. She held back the tears—she would never let him see her cry.

"You are so beautiful." The tips of his fingers brushed against her face.

Her plastic smile remained.

"You know, I've never dated anyone as dark as you."

Her mask disappeared.

"That's a compliment." His words came quickly as he felt her stiffen. "You know how American standards are. 'The lighter the skin . . .' I have to admit, I have gone for the fair-skinned beauties in the past. But you," he said, moving his hand along her body. "You are my Black beauty."

She waited a beat, then raised her hand, holding it next

to his face. The coffee-glaze polish on her fingertips almost matched her skin tone. And both the nail polish and her skin perfectly matched his complexion.

"Just checking. I thought maybe you were a *different* color," she said.

He frowned and the muscles in his jaw pulsed through his skin. But when she smiled, he chuckled. "You're pretty funny, Sasha. That's another thing I like about you." He kissed her neck, then moved his mouth down her body. "That's what you are," he said, pausing for a moment. "You are my Black beauty." He reached for the box of condoms he had on the table next to the bed.

Sasha closed her eyes, willing herself to block out his remarks. But what his lips and hands had been able to do before, couldn't be managed this morning. She was wounded under the assault of his words.

However, as Gordon's wife, she had been well trained in the art of removing herself. She responded to Hunter, doing with her body what he had come to expect. And when he finally collapsed on top of her with a loud grunt, a fake groan escaped from her lips.

Finally, Hunter rolled over and ran his hands over her head. "You know what I'm going to do?" He sat up in the bed. "I'm going to find a good hairstylist for you."

For the first time in what seemed like hours, Sasha heard her own voice. "For what?" she said shakily, running her hand over her hair.

He stood and walked across the room, then stopped at the bathroom door like he was posing for a scene in a movie. Sasha's eyes washed over his naked body. He really was a beautiful specimen, with runner's legs and a weight-lifter's torso. There were muscles and bulges everywhere a woman expected.

But, it was his mouth that held her attention. She watched his full lips move. "You would look so much better with longer hair. You're gorgeous now, but what would happen if you had braids or a weave? Either one is fine with me." He shook his head. "I can't even imagine how much better you'll look when I get through with you."

It wasn't until he had closed the bathroom door and Sasha heard him relieving himself that she was able to close her mouth. He was out of his mind. Or maybe, she thought, I'm out of mine.

Morning had not yet revealed its light, still the townhouse was warm with yesterday's heat. Anya opened the French doors that led to the balcony, and inhaled the morning air as a soft breeze whispered across her face. The street was still dark and desolate. Even the earliest of churchgoers were just stirring from their sleep.

She was wide awake though, having slept soundly for the first time in several days. She smiled, recalling her conversation with Braxton last night. "Thank you, Lord," she whispered. There was still a lot they had to work through, but she had hope.

In the kitchen, she set the coffee machine. Within minutes, the Colombian brew filled her nostrils, rousing her even more. She loved this time of day—a head start before the world began.

There were still a couple of hours before Braxton arrived. Maybe if she woke Sasha and filled her belly with a few eggs, strips of bacon, and sourdough toast, she'd be able to talk her cousin into going to church.

Anya scurried up the steps, then tapped on Sasha's door. No answer. She tapped again, this time a bit harder. Still no answer.

Anya tiptoed inside. Empty. There were no signs that Sasha had been home at all. She crept to the closet; Sasha's clothes hung the way they had since she arrived.

She slammed the door and strode into her bedroom. Maybe there was a message. But the red light on the answering machine stared back at her, unblinking.

Anya paced the floor. There was no doubt in her mind: Sasha was with Hunter Blaine. She trooped back and forth, mumbling, threatening Sasha, then Hunter. She stopped. What would her grandmother think?

"This is ridiculous," she said aloud. "Sasha is grown. She can do whatever she wants." But, even as she said those words, she shivered. If only Sasha weren't with Hunter. She shook her head, trying to rid her mind of those thoughts.

Back downstairs, she got her coffee and curled onto the couch with yesterday's newspaper in her hand. She rummaged through the paper, tossing segments onto the floor, until she was left with the business section. Maybe checking on her stocks would improve her mood.

Less than a minute later, the front door lock clicked. Sasha stepped silently inside, and closed the door gently behind her.

"Good morning."

Sasha jumped, holding her hand to her chest. "You scared me. I thought you'd still be asleep."

Anya placed the newspaper on the floor. "Most people *are* asleep or just getting up. Not just getting in," she said sharply.

Sasha winced inside, wishing she'd come in a few hours earlier. But to Anya she said, "Come on, cuz. I'm grown."

"Too grown to call?"

"I'm sorry." Sasha threw her purse onto the chair. "I'll call next time."

"So, you're going to make this a habit—hanging out with Hunter until the sun rises?"

Sasha's eyes hardened as she remembered Hunter's words.

Anya misunderstood Sasha's silence. "I told you, Sasha, that man will just use you up, then spit you out. You're just another one of his conquests."

This is just about sex . . . Sasha fought to keep Hunter's words from her mind. No matter what he said, he was still with her. And, as he dropped her off just now, they had made plans to meet again tonight. Obviously, he couldn't get enough of her. Maybe . . . "Why do I have to be one of *his* conquests?" She sat down on the couch, leaned back, and dramatically crossed her legs. "Maybe I was the one who conquered him."

Anya rolled her eyes.

"Girl, why are you trippin'? Hunter and I are just friends having a good time."

"Please don't tell me you're sleeping with him."

Sasha leaned forward and looked directly at Anya. "Don't be naïve. What do you think I was doing all night?" She crossed her arms. "And, not that it's any of your business, but you should know I plan on going back for more."

"Listen to you." Anya stomped across the room. "You sound like some kind of slut."

"You say that like it's a bad thing."

Anya glared at her cousin.

After a few moments, Sasha went to Anya's side. "Come on, I'm just having fun and I can take care of myself."

Anya slumped onto the couch. "Fine!" She picked up a few pages of the newspaper and held it in front of her face.

Sasha sighed. By the way her cousin was hiding behind the paper, she knew this was not over. "So what are you *really* angry about?"

Anya was silent.

"You don't have to say anything, but I know you're not mad because I stayed with Hunter. Did you have another fight with Braxton?"

"No." Anya didn't lower the paper from in front of her face.

"Something must be wrong. You're here and Braxton's not."

"Nothing's wrong. Braxton and I talked last night and then I came home." Her voice was still muffled by the paper.

"Ah, so you're mad because you didn't get any?"

The paper dropped slowly from in front of Anya's face. "'Get any'?" she said sarcastically. "I'm impressed with your command of the English language."

"Girl, I know what it's like when you're not being satisfied—"

"Not that it's any of *your* business," Anya interrupted her, "but Braxton and I are celibate."

"Celibate?" Sasha repeated the word as if she didn't know what it meant. "Why?"

"Because we're building a relationship on something more than sex."

"People do that and still sleep together. You're not sleeping together at all?"

"Not anymore," Anya said, softening since they weren't talking about Hunter. "Once we became engaged, we decided to try to do this right."

"But you've been engaged for over six months!"

"Sasha, you sound like a woman can't live without sex."

"Maybe by some miracle a woman could do it but *not* a man. What about Braxton?"

In seconds, a dozen of their arguments went through Anya's mind. "It's hard for both of us. But it's important that we try to do this."

Sasha shook her head in surprise. "I didn't think there were people like you in the world."

"There're a lot of single men and women struggling with this—because it is a struggle—but we're handling it because we think it's right."

"Is this another one of those God things? Are you trying to follow some rule?"

"It's not a rule. This is about parameters and protection that I think God has set for me so that I won't get hurt."

"I can't imagine that God thinks you'll get hurt by being with someone you love."

"He doesn't. That's why there's marriage."

Sasha was thoughtful for a moment. "But . . . what do you do when you get an urge?" She lowered her voice to almost a whisper.

Anya laughed. "There're other things besides sex. But when everything fails, I pray."

"Oh, please! You say that like prayer is the answer."

"It is for me."

"Wow, life without sex," Sasha said, shaking her head.

"You're a better woman than me." She stood and stretched her arms overhead. "I think I'll go to bed," she yawned. "I didn't get much rest last night."

Anya forced a smile, ignoring Sasha's remark. "Since you're already up, why don't you go to church with me?"

Sasha's arms dropped, dangling at her sides like a rag doll's. "Anya, I'm so tired, my bones hurt. I promise, I will go one of these Sundays, just not today."

Anya kept her voice upbeat. "Okay."

Sasha frowned. "Hey, that was a little too easy. You're not mad?"

"No, just remember, you promised." Anya smiled. She raised the newspaper, returning to the article she'd been reading. When she heard the door to Sasha's room close, she sighed. "Lord, please help me to keep planting the right seeds."

The living room was now alight, as the morning's rays engulfed the space. Anya went to her bedroom, dropped her robe in the middle of the floor, then stepped into her bathroom. She had one foot in the tub when Sasha called through the door.

"Anya, I wanted to know—does it matter what I wear to church?"

Anya smiled. "No, girl. My pastor believes that if God doesn't care about stuff like that, then neither should she. People wear everything from jeans to their Sunday best."

"Okay."

"Braxton will be here in about thirty minutes."

"I'll be ready."

The shower was on full blast and Anya stepped in, enjoying the sensation as it pulsed against her body. Her

smile was bright as she raised her face to the ceiling.
"Lord, you are so awesome."

Sasha couldn't help it. The music was moving, and finally she stood, joining the parishioners surrounding her.
Suddenly she wasn't so tired and she swayed to the beat.

My Jesus, my Savior
Lord, there is none like you

Anya tried to pass her a sheet with the words to the song, but Sasha shook her head. She didn't want to sing; she wanted to get inside the words, feel each one.

She closed her eyes, releasing herself into the words of the song that talked about God being comfort, and shelter, and refuge and strength.

Maybe there really was strength in God. And if He could provide strength, He could help her get Hunter.

Her eyes snapped open. Why was she still thinking about him? She let out a deep sigh, then felt a hand on her shoulder.

"What's wrong?" Anya said, her voice raised so she could be heard above the singing.

"Ssshhh. I'm trying to concentrate." Now Sasha found herself tapping her feet as the people around her sang about shouting to the Lord, because he could make mountains bow and seas roar. She loved these words. If God had that much power, certainly He could make Hunter want her.

It had been a long time since she'd been in church, but

all of a sudden, she was glad to be here. Hope floated through this room and faith thickened the air. She could feel it.

In an instant, everything changed. Hunter had already fallen for her, she knew that. With time, he could fall in love. He was Hunter Blaine. So he was worth extra effort.

Then suddenly, she began to sway a little less. What am I thinking? she wondered. These are not the kinds of things I'm supposed to talk to God about. Anyway, this would be too hard—even for God. Not even He could help me with that man.

The choir continued to sing, but Sasha sat down and ignored Anya's questioning glance. She didn't know why she'd come to church. There was nothing for her here. She crossed her legs and waited for the service to be over.

Anya tried to keep her attention on the pastor's words but, instead, she kept sneaking glances at Sasha. But Sasha stared straight ahead, even when Anya hit her gently in her side.

"Turn to Genesis 18:14," Pastor Ford said.

The rippling sound of turning pages filled the sanctuary. When Anya found the page, she placed her Bible on Sasha's lap so that she could follow along.

"The scripture says *Is anything too hard for the Lord?*" Pastor Ford looked up.

"No." The word was hummed in unison.

Pastor Ford continued her sermon and Anya sneaked another look at Sasha. Her cousin was watching intently, as if she were suddenly interested.

Anya let out her breath. Obviously, Pastor Ford had said something to get Sasha's attention. She smiled. One goal accomplished. Now, if only everything would go as smoothly with Braxton. She took her left hand and placed it over his. She could feel his smile, but she kept her eyes on Pastor Ford.

"Hebrews 10:23 says *Let us hold fast the profession of our faith without wavering, for he is faithful that promised.*" Pastor Ford paused, letting God's Word melt into her congregation. "To get all of God's promises, you have to hold on to what you believe. What you know is true with God. That is what He wants from us. Our faith."

Anya nodded, looking down at her Bible again. She wanted to commit that scripture to memory. That's what I have to do, she thought. Hold on to the fact that God wants Braxton and me together. This time, she looked at Braxton and smiled. He squeezed her hand, and Anya knew everything would be all right.

Braxton wrapped his hand around Anya's and the last lingering doubts melted away. This morning, when he picked her up, he hadn't been sure. Anya had smiled, they had kissed, and even held hands as they walked into church.

But now, as their fingers were intertwined, they had silently made up. It didn't surprise him.

He stood for the benediction but, suddenly, nausea washed over him. His hand tightened around Anya's, but she didn't seem to notice. But then, just as quickly as the feeling had befallen him, it disappeared. Still holding onto

Anya, he took his handkerchief from his inside jacket pocket and wiped his brow. What was that? he wondered.

He shook it off. There were other things to think about—their wedding, for one. In a few months, he and Anya would be married, permanently relegating their engagement challenges to the past. They had a wonderful future together.

Just as he thought those words, Anya's hand dropped from his.

Anya and Braxton strolled the Marina boardwalk, past the shops and trendy eateries, then stopped and leaned against the railing, as they watched a few boats drifting into the channel. They were silent, both trying to imagine the words of the conversation they had to have.

Anya gazed across the Marina to the homes that sat ensconced in the hills of Playa del Rey, and sighed.

"I'd love to buy you a home here," Braxton said as if reading her mind.

She smiled, but didn't respond to his statement. "Let's talk." She took his hand and was surprised that it was as sweaty as her own.

She motioned toward a bench and, before they'd even sat down, Braxton said, "Anya, I am so sorry."

"I know you are." She took a breath. "But, now, we have to talk about Junior."

His eyes turned from her, gazing into the blue of the water. "I should've never agreed to Roxanne and Junior moving back to Oakland, but Roxanne convinced me that she needed her family and it would be best for our son."

He paused as if remembering. "I thought it could work, but I want Junior with me."

"Have you considered moving back to Oakland?"

His eyes stretched wide with surprise. He should have thought of that. Anya would have to close her business and he would be closer to his son. "You'd *do* that?"

She shook her head so hard that the tight curls on her head bounced from side to side. "No—no," Anya stuttered, and stuffed her hands into her pockets. "Did you ever consider it *before*—before we met?"

"I didn't want to go back that way. Plus, I'd made a life here. I was writing . . ."

"You could write anywhere."

"Why are we talking about this?" He was agitated. "That's not an option now, is it?"

"So, what are your options, Braxton?" she asked, matching his tone.

He lowered his eyes. "I see only one. I want Junior. I want to go to his football games. I want to go to his school plays. I want to fight with him over his homework. I want it all." He pushed himself off the bench and went to the rail where they'd been standing. When he turned to face her again, he said, "I want to be his father."

Anya went to him. "You *are* his father. Nothing can change that."

"It's not enough for me." He took her hand. "So what do you think about this?"

She shrugged slightly. "You're talking about taking Junior away from everything he knows, especially his mother."

"He needs his father now." He stared into the water.

"Have you played this tape all the way through? What

kind of custody battle are we going to have to fight?" Braxton remained quiet, so Anya continued. "Braxton, you're great with Junior, under the circumstances."

"I want better circumstances." A few moments passed. "Are you with me, Anya?"

She took her sunglasses from her purse and, with deliberate movements, slipped them on. "I haven't been able to think that far ahead, because I'm thinking about how Junior will be affected by this." When she heard him groan, she faced him. "Braxton, I'm going to be your wife and I will support you." She clasped her hands together. "But I want you to think this through. What about Roxanne?"

"She'll fight, but we can win this. Especially if . . ."

She held her breath, knowing what was coming.

"You're willing to do *anything* to help me?"

She stared at the ring on her finger. "I can't give up my career."

He sighed. "I thought we'd have a better shot if you were home."

"I don't think the courts are going to care about that."

"But if you *were* going to be home with Junior, we'd have something over Roxanne."

She took in a quick breath. "Braxton, we should only get Junior if that is truly best for him, not because we arranged it so that we would look better."

"I want my son any way I can get him."

She recoiled at his tone and the way his eyes had glazed cold. He stared, silently challenging her, and at that moment she realized Junior was his mission; she was his tool.

She shook her head to rid her mind of the thought. "I will help you."

"You'll support me?" His voice had softened, although his eyes had not.

"In whatever way . . . I . . . can."

His face returned to the Braxton she knew. "You don't know how much this means to me." He pulled her close. "I need this chance." He kissed her, then said, "Have I ever told you that I love you?"

She stared into his eyes, searching for the words she needed to say. "Me too."

He grinned. "Let's get something to eat."

"Actually, I want to go home." She pulled her jacket tighter around her. "I need to speak to Madear."

He frowned. "We're all right, aren't we?"

"Of course." She smiled.

He hugged her again. "I know we're going to win now."

Holding hands, they returned to the car. Anya was grateful for the glasses she was wearing that protected her from the bright afternoon sun and hid the single tear that had formed in the corner of her eye.

Braxton parked, then took Anya's hand, bringing her palm to his lips.

"I'm glad we had a chance to talk," Anya said hurriedly, wanting to get away.

"Call me later?"

She nodded and opened the door.

"Hey." He grabbed her arm. "What do you want to do on Tuesday for Valentine's Day?"

"That time already?" She tried to pump enthusiasm into her voice.

He nodded. "We have a lot to celebrate. Why don't I plan something?"

"Okay."

"The big question: Are you sure you'll be able to get out of your office?"

He smiled, but his tone didn't.

"Let me know what time and I promise, I'll be there," Anya said.

His smile widened. "With bells on?"

"With bells that I hope are still ringing."

Braxton didn't seem to notice that he laughed alone.

By the time Carlos answered the phone, Braxton was beaming. "What's up, my brother? You weren't asleep, were you?" Braxton raised his voice, speaking over the traffic around him.

"No, man," Carlos yawned. "I was watching the game. You sound like you're in a good mood. Where are you?"

Braxton pushed the button raising his car window, blocking the outside from coming in. "I'm running over to the Tar Pits. Need to check out something for a scene. But I called to tell you that Anya is a go."

Even through the pocket-sized phone, Braxton could tell that his statement suddenly had his friend wide awake. "You're kidding. She's going to sell her business?"

The ends of Braxton's smile turned down and his brows knitted together. "We haven't worked out that part, but we're almost there. The most important thing is that she agrees with me about getting custody of Junior. Once we start, I know Anya'll do whatever she has to for us to win."

It sounded like Carlos was blowing air from his cheeks. "Well, you've gotten past the first hurdle, mi amigo."

Braxton's full smile returned. "I think this is even going to improve things with us."

"I didn't know you guys were having problems."

"We're not." Braxton's words came quickly. He thought of Anya's sunglassed face as she stood against the rail at the Marina and told him she would support him. At that moment, he couldn't have loved her more. "I'm just saying this kind of thing always brings a couple closer. I told you before, Carlos, don't worry. All I need is Anya and my friends in my corner."

"Well, you got that part, buddy." Braxton could almost hear Carlos smiling again. "Make sure you let Benjamin know. He'll need to talk to you and Anya."

"I'll call him in the morning," Braxton said, turning onto Wilshire. "It is time for me; I'm going to have a real family."

Carlos chuckled. "Okay. Hasta mañana, man."

Chapter 24

$\mathcal{A}$nya rang the doorbell. No answer. She waited a few minutes, then let herself in.

"Madear," she called out. There was only silence when she closed the door and walked into the living room. Anya sighed. She had called, but when the answering machine had come on, she thought her grandmother was still avoiding her. But it looked like Madear was still at church, or spending time with friends.

With a shrug of her shoulders, she removed her coat and laid it across the couch. Then she sat in the recliner and closed her eyes, but, within minutes, the silence was too loud and she clicked on the television, raising the volume just enough to erase the quietness.

She wrapped herself in her arms and strolled the room, stopping in front of the fireplace. The mantel and the wall above it were covered with photos. Her eyes scanned the frames that told the story of her life. Not only hers, but Donovan's and Sasha's. Mixed among the grandchildren were pictures of Madear's children.

Anya picked up one of the photos. The ceramic yellow frame was heavy in her hands, and it overpowered the small image inside. But this was still her favorite picture of her parents. It had been taken only four days before they died.

The tears that had overwhelmed her as a teenager were long gone. Now, there was only the desire to hold on to fading memories.

She ran her fingers along the outline of her mother. "Mama." She sighed. "I could really use some advice."

She returned the frame to the mantel and said a silent Amen, like she always did. Her eyes continued to scan the room. This home smelled of memories—even now, the roasted chicken mixed with the fresh-cut flowers from the farmer's market that Madear filled her house with every Saturday. Just standing there, Anya was taken back to a time when she always felt safe and loved.

The sound of a car motor disrupted her reverie, and she peeked through the side window. Her grandmother maneuvered her Lincoln Continental into the long, narrow driveway along the side of the house.

It fascinated Anya, the way her grandmother wielded that nine-year-old car. The black vehicle swallowed her petite frame; you could barely see Madear over the steering wheel. But she handled that car like it was a toy, breezing through the streets, whizzing around corners, and zipping through traffic.

Anya watched as Madear gathered her Bible and a shopping bag from the car, then drew back from the window. Her grandmother had seen her car out front. Anya drew in her breath until Madear, with her hands full, stepped into the living room.

"Hi, Madear." Anya rushed to her side. She took the Bible and the shopping bag from Madear's hands.

"I didn't expect to see you." Madear kissed Anya's cheek, although her voice was tight. She shrugged her long sweater from her shoulders and went to hang it in the front closet.

"I've left you quite a few messages." Anya dropped the bag on the coffee table, then handed the Bible to Madear.

"I've been busy," Madear said, without raising her eyes. She reached for the Bible from Anya and put it on one of the bookcases, then straightened some of the magazines hanging from the shelves. She returned to the couch, and began folding the crocheted comforter that hung over the edge.

Anya softened as she watched her grandmother flitting around the room. This was the woman who loved her, raised her, and taught her how to become a strong Black woman of God. And Madear's teachings weren't just words. Mabel White Mitchell was a living example. Anya recalled what she knew of her grandmother's past.

Mabel White married Herman Mitchell at the age of sixteen—he was seventeen—on the same day Pearl Harbor was bombed. Not much later, she left behind the only home she'd known, in Emory, Texas, to move to Los Angeles. Mabel had been horrified at the thought of living in a huge city without her mother, father, brothers, and sisters, and the other relatives who populated Emory. But Herman was set on the golden opportunities that awaited them in the golden state.

With a stiff upper lip and daily prayers, Mabel and Herman settled into a one-bedroom apartment in Watts, a neighborhood overflowing with transplants from Texas, Oklahoma, Louisiana, and other states too numerous for Mabel to count.

Herman worked as an auto mechanic and, at night, attended college at Southwestern University. Mabel took a job in downtown Los Angeles, laboring as many as fourteen hours a day, as a pieceworker.

Just as Mabel was becoming used to her life, World War II touched them personally when Herman was called to serve. If Mabel had been horrified before, there weren't words to depict what she felt now. Her new husband would be leaving in eight weeks to fly to parts of the world she'd never heard of. To add to her fears, she was five months pregnant.

Herman trained in Fort Sam Houston, then went to Norfolk, Virginia, where he received his orders. Burma was his final destination. He became part of an all-Negro unit responsible for building airstrips and guarding American aircraft and airmen on the British airfields.

Mabel fought her urges to go home, and stayed in California where her husband really wanted her to be. With few friends and no family, Mabel stayed on her knees, keeping her husband and herself lifted before God.

Eighteen months later, Herman returned, unharmed and ecstatic to set his eyes on fourteen-month-old Herman, Jr. Ten months later, Jake joined the family.

Herman returned to his ritual of work and school, and Mabel stayed home with their sons. But between changing diapers, cooking, feedings, cleaning, potty training, and naps, she secretly studied through correspondence courses to earn her high-school diploma.

On the day Herman graduated from college, Mabel presented her husband with *her* certificate and an announcement that she was going to college.

He was proud, but concerned. "What about the boys?" he asked.

Mabel gave him her plan. "I promise neither you nor the boys will even miss me."

Herman was filled with doubt but loved his wife. He went along with Mabel, comforted knowing that somehow she'd make it.

So they stayed in that one-bedroom apartment and Mabel enrolled in L.A. State College. The civil rights movement was brewing all around her, but Mabel hardly noticed. With Jake just six, and Herman, Jr., eight, Mabel worked a schedule that would have made Wonder Woman tired: taking the boys to school, going to her part-time job, picking the boys up from school, helping with homework, serving dinner, and getting them ready for bed, before she went off to her classes three nights a week. Herman, Sr., was usually home by six, after leaving Jefferson High School where he taught, to go to the Community Center to tutor college students for extra money. When Herman came home he took over, letting Mabel go to class or spend time studying. On Saturdays, Mabel washed clothes, cooked meals, cleaned house, did homework, and anything else her family needed. On Sundays, together they walked two blocks to the Church of the Solid Rock to worship and praise God. When they returned home, Mabel rested.

Eight years later, she received her degree on the lawn of the college, with one man and two teenagers in the audience cheering until their throats throbbed. She was one of twenty-two Negro students. When she got that diploma in her hand, she looked up to the sky and yelled,

"Thank you, Jesus!" to the surprise of everyone—except her family.

Mabel taught in the Los Angeles Unified School District for more than thirty years—recognized as Teacher of the Year seventeen times. She finally retired at sixty-five.

Madear had rejoiced in her victories, and endured heart-breaking tragedies. Almost twenty years ago she buried her older son and daughter-in-law, after a loose boulder had fallen onto Pacific Coast Highway and crushed the car Herman and his wife, Alice, were in. Then, just four years ago, Mabel buried her dear husband of fifty-four years, after a long battle with prostate cancer. In the last year of his life, Herman had been completely bedridden, but Mabel declined all offers of help. She took care of her husband herself, morning and night, until the day she tearfully released him to the Lord.

"Go on, baby," she had said, taking his feeble hands into hers. "The Lord wants you. It's His time now. We'll be together again."

Within an hour of her uttering those words, Herman had passed.

People marveled at how Mabel White Mitchell handled life. But it was no marvel to her. Her faith kept her lifted and helped her to remember there'd been more blessings than burdens.

"God is holding me up and pushing me on," she was fond of saying. As the Mitchell matriarch, Mabel showed how to stand. She was an example for her family.

That was why Anya was so confused with Madear's attitude toward Sasha now. Nowhere in her memory could she conjure up the image of Madear behaving this way toward anyone—although Madear was one for snide comments. When Anya thought about it, there really wasn't anything special about what Madear said to Sasha; it was the way she said it.

Her grandmother had finished folding the comforter, and reached for the coat that Anya had tossed onto the couch.

"I'll hang this up." Madear still had not looked at Anya.

Anya reached for her grandmother, stopping her. "I want to talk to you." Her voice was softly polite but stern.

Their eyes met for a long second.

Anya took her grandmother's hand and gently led her to the couch.

Madear sat with her hands tightly clasped, and her legs crossed at her ankles. "Go ahead," she said curtly. Her gaze remained toward the window.

Anya took a breath. "What's up with you and Sasha?"

Madear's head turned slowly and when she finally looked at Anya, her eyebrows were raised. "What's up?" she repeated in the teacher's drawl that Anya knew well. Anya had learned many things from her grandmother— one of them being that when Madear spoke in that tone, Anya had to find another way to ask the question.

"I mean, there's something going on with you . . . and Sasha. Why are you angry with her?"

Madear's head whipped away from Anya, her gaze turned back to the window. "I am not angry with Sasha!" Her chin jutted forward. "Except for the fact that she's been here all this time and hasn't even called."

It was Anya's turn to raise her eyebrows. "Madear, she's hurt. You expect her to call after the way you treated her?"

Even with Madear's head turned, Anya could see her eyes narrow. "I didn't do anything. I'm her grandmother, her elder. *She* should come to me."

Anya moved to the chair directly across from the couch. She shifted against the plastic that pushed against her legs. Finally, she leaned forward and looked into her grandmother's eyes. "Madear, she can't come to you. She thinks you don't like her." Anya took another breath and said, "She thinks it's a skin-color thing." Anya had lowered her voice slightly.

There was a pause. "How dare you say that to me!" Her volume built as she spoke. "That is not true!" By the time Madear said the last words, her voice was trembling.

Anya reared back, away from her grandmother's wrath. Another thing she'd learned from Madear: Truth could ignite fury.

She waited a few seconds before she spoke. "Madear, *do* you have a problem?"

Madear slumped back onto the couch. "No." Her head moved back and forth in denial. But her voice was so soft, Anya had to strain to hear. "I swear, I don't."

"Madear?" All kinds of thoughts veered through her mind. Could her grandmother be prejudiced that way? Against her own granddaughter?

Madear's head had been lowered, but now she looked directly at Anya. "My grandmother's mother was a slave."

Anya nodded. Of course she knew that. Madear was still looking in her direction, but Anya felt like her grandmother saw beyond the living room. "My great-grandmother told stories of living on that plantation and just how horrible her life really was."

"You've told me that before," Anya said, shrugging her shoulders in confusion.

Madear continued as if Anya hadn't spoken. "But it was still better for her, because she was a house-slave." Madear paused. "The Massah kept all of his bastard children in the house." Madear spat those words through the air.

"My grandmother told me that her mother thought shoes was special. Imagine that? But shoes were unheard of for slaves—unless you were in the house."

"Madear, I don't mean any disrespect, but we're a long way from slavery and the big house—"

Madear sucked her teeth. "We're not! That's the misconception," she said, pointing her finger at Anya. "If you were really honest, you'd admit that it is easier for colored people today if . . ."

Anya's eyes opened wide. This was a God-fearing, educated woman. Yet she sounded as ignorant as people who went on talk shows saying these things.

It took a few minutes for Anya to respond. "Madear, if we participate in that myth, we're continuing something that we blame white people for." Anya paused, recalling incidents where her grandmother had said someone's hair was nappy or commented on the dark knees of one of the neighborhood children.

"Madear, is Sasha right? Is this why you don't like her?"

Madear's eyes were glassy. "I *love* Sasha. I don't know why she thinks I don't like her. It's just that I always knew it was going to be harder for her because of . . . the way she looks. And I was right," Madear said, her voice strong again. "Look at her life and the way things have turned out for her."

"Madear!" Anya exclaimed, suddenly standing. "Sasha could have been as yellow as the bananas on your kitchen table and she would be exactly where she is now, because of who she is."

"And she is who she is because of the color of her skin."

Minutes passed without either saying a word. Finally Anya picked up her coat. "I have to go, Madear," she said, looking away from her grandmother.

"You don't understand. My grandmother taught me how important it was to preserve—"

Anya resisted the urge to cover her ears. Instead she bent down and kissed Madear before she could finish her sentence. "I'll call you—"

Madear grabbed her hand and Anya noticed how small and soft her hand felt. "I want you to understand what I'm saying. I love Sasha."

Anya longed to give her grandmother comfort, but she couldn't pass along anything that she didn't feel. She was overwhelmed. In her own family, there was this prejudice that she so despised—from the woman she so loved.

Anya wanted to get away—from Madear, from her beliefs, and from her own internal fears, as she thought about how people said she was so much like her grandmother.

When Anya walked to the door, she heard her grandmother catch her breath. But she continued quickly through the door, not wanting to hear anything else.

If Anya had stayed, it wouldn't have been Madear's words that she heard. As Anya ran to her car, Madear stood at the window, watching her granddaughter flee and trying to battle the sobs that rose like bile inside of her.

Hunter's and Sasha's arms were hooked as they strolled. At the front door, Hunter kissed her gently, allowing their lips to linger for a few moments.

"Come in, please," she pleaded.

"No way. I can't handle Anya right now."

"You can handle anything," she said coquettishly.

There was no way she was going to give up now. After the pastor told her in church that nothing was too big for God, she'd said two prayers. One was that Hunter would grow to love her, and two, that Hunter and Anya would get along. Well, God had answered her first prayer in a big way. So she knew in a short time Hunter and Anya would find a way to at least be cordial.

Hunter frowned but Sasha tugged, and he followed when she opened the door.

Anya was on the couch, covered with a blue chenille throw. Her Bible lay in her lap, and she smiled when she looked up.

"Hey, cuz," Sasha said, pulling Hunter inside. "Hunter wanted to come in and say hello."

"I can tell by the way you're dragging him," Anya said.

Only Sasha laughed.

"Hey, Anya," Hunter said. Seeing the Bible she held, he wanted to turn and run. There was no telling what kinds of things she was saying to God about him.

Anya returned his greeting.

"Anya, guess what?" Sasha sounded like a breathless child. "Hunter's taking me to the Victory Awards."

That made Anya sit up and Hunter smiled. If Anya hadn't acted like she was too good for him when he had asked her out, she could be the one on his arm.

"That's great," Anya said, looking between the two.

The Victory Awards recognized African-Americans for achievement in various categories, including entertainment. Though not as prestigious as the NAACP

Image Awards, they still received celebrity attendance and press coverage.

Sasha sat next to Anya, leaving Hunter standing by the door. "I am so excited!"

Anya glanced at Hunter. Her eyes squinted slightly, but she kept her smile. "Hunter, it's so nice of you to invite Sasha. I didn't realize you had been nominated."

Hunter's jaw was tight. "I wasn't, but I *was* invited."

Anya turned from Hunter and smiled at Sasha. "You'll have a great time." She stood. "Well, I'll leave you two alone—"

"You don't have to do that, Anya," Hunter said, taking a step toward her.

"It's okay. I have something to do anyway. Like . . . go into the kitchen . . . and . . . sharpen some knives."

Hunter barely waited for Anya to leave the room. "See, she just doesn't like me. What was that knives thing all about?" he hissed.

"She was kidding." Sasha chuckled. "Give her a break, she's not as funny as I am."

"It's time for me to go." He looked toward the kitchen. "There's something that *I* have to do."

Sasha put her arms around his neck. "Thank you, for making my day, my week, my year!"

He smiled. "You're worth it. I'll call you tomorrow so that we can go shopping."

The moment Sasha closed the door, Anya came back.

"Can you believe I'm going to the Victory Awards with Hunter Blaine?" Sasha fell back on the couch and kicked her legs in the air. "You know what's so incredible to me? You're onto something with this God thing."

Anya frowned deeply. "What are you talking about?"

"Well, at church this morning, I really felt something happening." She stopped, trying to find the words. "Like God was talking to me. So I prayed."

"That's a good thing," Anya said tentatively.

"I told God that I really wanted to be with Hunter. Then I go over to Hunter's apartment, and he invites me to the Victory Awards. I'll be back at church next week for sure." She stood and started up the stairs. "I have to get my nails done and a pedicure—my God, I have so much to do." She had disappeared but Anya could still hear her voice. "Where should I shop? I wonder what Hunter is going to wear."

Sasha had probably been in her room a few minutes before Anya closed her mouth. She should have said something to her cousin, but what?

"Father," Anya whispered, "Sasha has no idea who You are or what You have done. Please give her the desire to truly know you. Deal with her, according to your grace and mercy. And, help me, Lord, to plant the right seeds, through my words and actions so she will come to know you."

Anya leaned back onto the couch. Her head was beginning to ache again, just like it had when she first came home from Madear's. While her conversation with Madear was still heavy on her, she had listened to the answering machine and heard Braxton asking her to come over so they could plan Junior's case. Her head had throbbed so badly then, even her eyeballs were sore.

She had lain down, finding comfort in her Bible. It was her favorite chapter—John 14—that she read, and her favorite scripture, John 14:27, that she read over and over. *Peace I leave with you, my peace I give unto you:*

not as the world giveth, give I unto you. Let not your heart be troubled, neither let it be afraid.

That's what she was searching for—peace. She had prayed for it and had prayed that she would lose this overwhelming feeling that troubled her heart. Then Sasha had walked in with Hunter.

Anya sighed deeply. Braxton. Madear. Sasha. Their drama filled her head.

After a few minutes she rose, turned off the lights, and slowly went up the stairs. She couldn't take on the weight of her family's problems. Everyone would have to find their own way. Sasha—eventually she'd learn the truth. And Madear—her beliefs were her challenge. The only thing Anya could do for them was pray.

She was going to focus on herself and Braxton; that alone was more than she could handle.

Chapter 25

$\mathscr{T}$he man wrote the last line on the yellow legal pad, then sat the sheet next to the other five pages laid neatly across the table. It had taken a few hours, but his strategy was complete.

He liked writing out his plan, although Sean had never agreed.

"You have to plan this carefully," Sean had explained the first time he was included in the game. "We don't pick just any girl. It has to be one who deserves this. One of those snobs who walks around thinking she's better than we are."

He had wanted to tell Sean that there were no snobs in their neighborhood. But he had ended up with a black eye the last time he ignited his friend's fury.

Sean continued. "And it's best to choose a girl who doesn't have any brothers who could come after us."

He had nodded and reached for a notebook from his bag.

"What are you doing?" Sean had frowned his disapproval.

They were sitting in their clubhouse, the basement of one of the abandoned buildings. Years ago, when he was *first initiated into the gang and was brought into the first clubhouse, he had almost puked over the stench. But in the seven years that he'd been a member of the Bedford boys, he'd gradually become used to it.*

"You said we had to plan," he'd replied weakly as he pulled out a pen with the paper.

Sean snatched the paper from his hand. "You can't write anything down!" he had screamed. "That's evidence."

"But planning is important—"

"Don't be stupid." Sean had sneered as the others joined in. "You're supposed to be the scholar. Why are you so dumb?"

He had fought to keep the hurt from his face and leaned back against the cold wall. The only thing that kept the tears from squeezing through his eyes was that he knew he was smarter than Sean—much smarter. But Sean was the leader and older and bigger. So he sat and listened as Sean laid out the plan.

It had taken them a week to follow the girl—measure her patterns and determine the best place to take her. As the days progressed, he found himself becoming more excited. He had never been with a girl before and Sean knew it.

"We're going to give her to you first." Sean patted him on the back the night before the big game. The others nodded because that's what they always did.

He had shaken with excitement. When they'd finally taken the girl, he hated that he had to be with her in front of the three other boys Sean had chosen to participate. But, he'd gone along, that time and the other times, knowing that one day he'd be able to do this alone.

Now, as he remembered that first time, he clasped his hands together to stop the trembling. His shaking had nothing to do with fear. He was too careful for anything to go wrong. But, he could never be overly confident—only a fool would do that.

That's why he carefully planned his strategy. The only reason they were never caught was because their attacks had only been reported to the police once. In their neighborhood, these crimes had been accepted. People sighed, shook their heads, then went about the business of taking care of their families with the little they had.

But in today's times, he had to be more careful. That called for perfect planning.

He pulled out a bottle of Merlot that he had been saving for a special occasion. There wouldn't be a time more appropriate than this. With surprisingly steady hands, he poured a small glass. Just enough to calm him.

As he sipped the wine, he wondered what had ever happened to his childhood friend, although he only called Sean a friend because he couldn't think of another word. He had despised the boy and he remembered every taunt, every sneer, every ridicule. But he could never hate him for what he'd taught him. He'd always be grateful for this.

He raised his glass in a salute. He had no idea where Sean lived today. Probably in the same place or maybe he even ended up in jail. That's how it turned out for most of the kids in his neighborhood. He knew he'd been one of the lucky ones.

He drank the last of the wine in one swallow and returned to his notes, reading through them one last time. Then he folded them neatly four times before he took the pages into the extra room, tucking them inside one of the photo albums that held her pictures. He wouldn't look at the notes again. They were already a part of his mind.

Chapter 26

Anya blew out the two candles in the silver holders and watched as dark smoke spiraled into the air, twirling to the bass of the music. Braxton stood and removed the last crystal platter from the coffee table.

"Do you want me to help?" Anya asked.

"No, this is your night. Relax."

Braxton put the dishes inside the insulated carton the caterer had left.

When he returned to the living room, he paused at the arched entryway. Anya was still on the floor, in the same place where they'd eaten dinner. With her legs crossed, her eyes closed, and her head thrown back, she seemed hypnotized by Luther's words.

Here and now, I promise to love faithfully

Feeling his presence, she opened her eyes. He stretched forth his hand, pulling her from the floor.

She kissed his nose. "Thank you for a wonderful Valentine's."

He returned her kiss.

They swayed, with locked lips, until the song ended.

Braxton led her to the couch in front of the bay window. The sun had long ago retreated into the Pacific, and only the rose-scented candles that flickered around them lit the massive room. Anya sat down and Braxton knelt in front of her, slipping off her left shoe.

"Sit back," he whispered.

She eagerly obeyed, anticipating the coming pleasures. Braxton rested on his knees and began lightly massaging her foot. "You're tight." He pressed a little harder. "Relax."

As Braxton kneaded, pushed and pressed, Anya felt her tension waning. He took off her other shoe and resumed his pursuit to please her.

After a wonderful eternity, he placed both of her feet on the floor. He joined her on the couch and she reclined into his arms. He pressed the remote for the CD.

A love so fine is finally mine

"Braxton, we have some of the best times together." Anya squeezed his hand, wishing it were true all the time.

He tightened his arms around her. "We have a lot to celebrate. I can't tell you how much it means to have you in my corner with Junior—"

She flinched.

"What's wrong?" he asked.

"Nothing." She paused. "Tonight, let's just think about us."

He lifted her from the couch and brushed his lips against hers. "To us," he said. He pulled her to him and they began swaying.

I'd cry, I'd cry if you left my side

She leaned in, running her hands from his neck, down over the tightness of his back. He kissed her head, her ear, then his tongue grazed her cheek, finally finding her lips. As they kissed, they backed their way to the couch, falling and continuing to explore each other.

He leaned back slightly. "Anya," he breathlessly whispered. "Please . . ."

She was panting as she pulled his face back to hers, their lips once again meeting. Their passion deepened, and they were falling, falling . . . His breathing became more rapid. Moans from inside him matched hers.

"Tonight." His voice sounded like something was caught in his throat.

She was lost in her own urges, as she shuddered against his touch. She allowed herself to drift, giving herself in the only way she could.

It wasn't until her blouse was unbuttoned that she came rushing back.

"Braxton," she panted his name.

He squinted at her through thin slits. Then he leaned forward and covered her mouth once again.

She pushed him away. "Braxton." She was still trying to catch her breath.

He moved in again, this time forcing his lips against hers. Anya used both hands to push him and he fell back.

"Braxton, no!"

Confusion covered his face. He leaned forward, trying to reinstate their bond, but Anya shifted on the couch, turning her head away from him. "We have to stop."

"I don't want to," he nuzzled against her neck, trying to put his full body weight over her. She could feel his desire and for a solid moment she responded, wanting to yield to all that she had been keeping inside. She wanted him.

But no! She pushed him again, forced herself to sit up, and closed her blouse.

He took her face in his hands. "I want to make love to you," he breathed heavily. He kissed her cheek, letting short, wet kisses cover her skin.

When he went for her blouse, she stood. "Braxton, I'm going home," she said, buttoning her blouse.

"I don't want you to." His voice pleaded and he kissed her again.

She tried to resist. "Braxton . . ." she called through his kisses. With all of her emotional strength, she pulled back. "We won't be able to stop."

Through the candlelight, she saw her shoes under the coffee table. After she slipped into her pumps, she turned to him. In his eyes, she saw desire that matched her own, and she stopped. Why am I putting myself through this? she wondered. We're getting married. We won't be judged for this.

But she knew that wasn't true. "I have to go," she said again. "For both of us." She prayed he would understand.

"But . . . okay, let's just talk." When she looked at him doubtfully, he repeated, "Just talk." He reached for her and she took his hand.

Braxton went toward the couch. Anya hesitated, then followed. But the moment she sat down, he was over her. She pushed him away and stood. Before she could move, he grabbed her, pulling down. The thump, then her scream, froze them both.

Their bodies remained tangled, but their eyes were clear, as they stared at each other.

It's your love I need

"Oh, my God! Are you all right?" Braxton stood still looking down at Anya. Fear kept him from doing anything else.

Anya held the part of her head where it hit the wall. Her scalp throbbed excruciatingly. She squeezed her eyes hoping that would stop some of the pulsating, but the pain stubbornly continued.

With her hand still on her head, she stomped across the room.

"Anya, are you okay?" Braxton came after her. "Let me take a look at that." He reached for her, his fingers grazing her arm.

Anya whipped around, eyes flaring. "Don't you touch me!" she warned through clenched teeth.

Braxton took two steps back.

"What did you think you were doing?" she screamed. "I told you to stop!"

Braxton's eyes widened. "Anya, I'm sorry. I just got caught up . . ."

She grabbed her purse and jacket. She was holding her head again, when she faced him. "I'm leaving now." She spoke the words slowly, then walked into the foyer.

He followed her. "Anya—"

The door slammed against the wall as she jerked it open and fled down the steps.

"Anya, I'm sorry!" he shouted. He made a move toward her car, but when she turned and glared, he backed away. All he could do was watch her get into the car, roar the engine, then screech into the night.

Braxton closed the door. "What was I thinking?" he said aloud. He opened the door again, then closed it slowly. There was no way she would let him get close.

He walked into the living room and turned off the stereo. With great effort, he moved around the room and blew out the candles, one by one, until he was surrounded by darkness. He gazed out the window into the blackened sky for several minutes before he reached for the phone. He gripped the receiver tighter when he heard her voice on the answering machine.

"Anya, please," he spoke to the machine, "call me. I have to know that you're all right. Please. I'm so sorry and I love—"

Beep!

He held the phone away from his ear and stared at the receiver, then shook his head as he turned off the phone.

His legs felt like weights as he climbed the stairs. At his bedroom door he stopped, staring at the candles around the room. Preparations to welcome her back into his bed.

He closed his eyes. Tonight was supposed to be another one of those times that Anya would have never forgotten.

But now, as he lay on the bed, he knew the look in her eyes was something *he'd* never forget. He had only wanted to show her how much he loved her.

"Braxton, I'm going to be your wife," Anya had said. "I will support you in any way I can."

Everything was planned to show her how much he loved and appreciated what she was willing to do.

But instead of seeing how he felt, she'd left believing he had attacked her. "Anya, I would never do anything to hurt you!" he said, closing his eyes tightly to fight against the memory of the look in her eyes.

He curled his body into a small ball. Then he prayed. Prayed that, somehow, he would gain Anya's forgiveness and find a way to make up for this. But the peace that normally accompanied his prayers did not come tonight. Still clothed, he tossed on his bed for hours, before he finally succumbed to a fitful sleep.

Anya had cried all the way home. She was still crying when she heard Sasha come in after one A.M., and now, as the clock showed 3:40, tears still filled her eyes.

Her head continued to throb; but it wasn't the bump that caused her pain. Images harassed her: Braxton pulling her, hitting the wall, the thump that silenced them both. Why would Braxton do that to her?

But he hadn't done anything. It was an accident. Maybe it was her fault for going too far. She had wanted him too, more than she had in a long time.

She shook her head. When she said stop, that's what he should have done.

She tried to turn over, but something tugged at her hand. She pulled, but her ring was caught in the quilt. It took a few minutes to untangle it. When she held her hand up against the dark, she could barely see the sparkle of the diamond. Sobs were still rising in her when she removed the ring from her finger, placing it gently on top of her Bible on her nightstand.

She curled her knees into her chest and cried deeply, pushing her head into her pillow to soften the sounds. She cried until there was nothing left. Then she rolled over and looked at the clock. It was 6:01.

Chapter 27

The limousine crawled, but Sasha's heart raced. "I'm so excited." She squeezed Hunter's hand.

He rubbed his hand against her face and smiled.

It had been three days since he'd invited her to the Victory Awards and, with each passing minute, her excitement had grown. Now, at its peak, she hoped she'd be able to walk without trembling.

Hunter peered through the tinted window. "We're next."

She opened her mouth, but could only nod.

This entire day felt like it had been designed in heaven. The gold Vera Wang dress that she and Hunter had picked out had been delivered with perfect alterations. For an hour, she strutted in front of the full mirror, amazed at the image that stared back.

A stray hair brushed against her face, and her smile turned down just a little. The long brown hair hung beyond her shoulders, and she sighed. Hunter had called before eight that morning, bursting with a surprise. Within thirty minutes, he had arrived—with this wig and a stylist.

Sasha had been shocked, but didn't protest. Maybe

Hunter knew best, she reasoned. Maybe the dress called for a wig.

The limousine stopped and Hunter squeezed her hand, bringing her back to the moment. The door opened and Hunter stepped out first, then reached for Sasha.

The moment she stepped from the car, she knew Cinderella was not a fairy tale. There was a softness under her foot and, when she looked down, she saw it—the red carpet. She shuddered as they moved forward, trying to take in as much as she could. But flashing bulbs and the bright afternoon sun mixed to blind her. She could have worn sunglasses; in fact, she'd thought of it. But she wanted her face to be clearly seen.

Above, network helicopters hovered low. Their engines roared and mixed with the crowd that lined the carpet on both sides.

"Hunter, Hunter, Hunter, over here!" women with cameras screamed. "We love you, Hunter!"

Hunter waved, and hooked his arm through Sasha's. As they made their way toward the front, Sasha was grateful for the time she'd spent prancing and practicing. She knew she looked good. The slinky gold dress glittered against her dark skin, and the train attached to the back brought attention to the dangerously low cut that stopped just above the small of her back. She could hear the oohs and aahs as she passed, and her chin rose even higher.

"Hunter, can we talk?" Lyza Easton, a television anchor for *The Hollywood Rumor,* stuck a microphone in Hunter's face. "You look fabulous, Hunter. Do you have a few words for our viewers?"

"I feel great tonight," Hunter said in his actor's voice that was a few octaves deeper. "I don't have to worry about whether they're going to call my name. I can sit back and enjoy."

Lyza's laugh came from her throat and Sasha frowned. "Are you upset that you weren't nominated this year?" Lyza moved her microphone and body closer to Hunter.

"Not at all." Hunter grinned. "I didn't have a film this year. But my next movie, *Tears on My Pillow,* which just finished filming in London, will be released by the end of the year."

"So you were in London—how was it?" Lyza stood so close to Hunter, Sasha was sure there was not enough room for him to breathe.

Hunter kept his smile wide. "London is now one of my favorite places. I can't wait to return."

"Umm. Maybe we'll end up there together, someday." Sasha held Hunter's hand tighter.

"So who is this with you tonight, Hunter?" Lyza's eyes scanned Sasha from head to toe. "Your sister?"

Hunter laughed, Sasha didn't.

"This is a friend, Sasha Mitchell."

Sasha flashed a smile, parting her lips enough to show her top teeth. That was her best smile. As the camera turned to her, thoughts of Lyza were replaced with ones of Gordon. Was he watching?

They finally continued past the cameras and numerous reporters, into the Shrine Auditorium. But, even inside, the excitement was high pitched. Celebrities surrounded them. Some smiled, some waved, a few stopped to chat. Almost a half hour passed before they finally took their seats.

Sasha nodded nonchalantly as she sat next to Will and Jada, but she screamed inside. The night got better with each passing hour.

She counted the rows in front of them—five, six, seven, only eight rows from the front. Her eyes wandered around the room and stopped when she saw Janet Jackson. She watched Janet walk down the aisle and take a seat several rows behind them. She twisted in her seat.

Hunter took her hand. "It's about to begin."

When the auditorium darkened and Whoopi Goldberg came onto the stage, Sasha finally relaxed. She laughed at Whoopi's jokes, stood and clapped as Whitney Houston performed, and cheered as each recipient accepted their award. The four-hour show passed quicker than Sasha expected, but when it ended, she was anxious to move on with the rest of the night.

It was the after-parties that had her so excited. She'd heard about the celebrations, and she wondered where they would go—maybe to Magic's or Denzel's? Surely Hunter could choose any that he wanted.

The crowd moved slowly from the auditorium and, when they reached the lobby, the limousine line was backed up.

"They told me we'd have to wait at least an hour," a blonde woman in front of them complained.

It didn't matter to Sasha. That gave her more time to bask in the evening's glory.

"I need to make a call," Hunter said, after they'd been in line for about five minutes. "Wait here for me." He led her to a row of chairs outside the ladies' room.

Sasha frowned a little. She knew Hunter had his cell phone, but she said nothing.

Her eyes roamed the room. This was an elegant bunch; women donned in long, black dresses, with diamond and gold ornaments on almost every neck and wrist. The men were equally refined, in both traditional and unconventional tuxedos. Sasha grinned widely. She was officially part of the Hollywood set.

The crowd was beginning to thin and Sasha checked her watch—fifteen minutes. Where was Hunter? She finally spotted him on the other side of the vast lobby and she began to walk toward him.

Before she was halfway across, she stopped. Hunter was hovering over Lyza Easton, standing so close that Sasha couldn't tell where Hunter's body ended and Lyza's began. His lips were pressed against her ears. He was either whispering or nibbling—she couldn't tell which. In that moment, in Sasha's eyes, Hunter was gone; Gordon had taken his place.

Lyza was running her hand along Hunter's face, when she looked up and her soft eyes met Sasha's moist ones. Hunter followed Lyza's gaze and when he faced Sasha, his face hardened into a deep frown.

Hunter coughed, then straightened his body. "Are you ready?" Hunter asked, as if nothing had happened.

She wanted to say no, and make him give an explanation. She wanted to know why he would do this on such a special night. But she only nodded.

By the time they waited at the curb for their car, Sasha's breathing had steadied. Lyza and Hunter were probably discussing business. There couldn't be any more to it. Hunter was leaving with her. She would still have a good time tonight.

Once they were settled in the car, she snuggled against his chest. "So where are we going now?" She fought to put enthusiasm into her voice.

He shook his head. "I've gotta make a run. I'm taking you home."

Stunned, she couldn't hold back her next words. "Are you making that run with Lyza Easton?"

He frowned. "What does she have to do with this?"

"I don't know," Sasha whispered. Why had she asked him that? Why had she come tonight? Why had she fallen for Hunter Blaine? This is just about sex.

During the silent ride, Sasha prayed that Anya was not home. One look at her and Anya would know that she had been right.

When Hunter tried to kiss her at the front door, she turned, forcing his lips to her cheek. She ran into the darkened house before he could say anything. As his footsteps faded from the door, she peeked through the window and watched the black limousine zip into the night. Then she turned.

She was still standing with her back against the door when the clock on the mantel chimed eight times. Her chin dropped to her chest.

With slow steps, she went into the downstairs bathroom. It was several minutes before she turned on the light. When she did, the reflection in the mirror gave no indication of what had happened. The woman who stared back was model-beautiful. Every speck of her make-up was perfectly placed. She examined the graceful line of her neck, which gave way to toned shoulders. The brown-haired wig brushed the top of her dress.

She stared at the elegant, flawless reflection, until a single tear streaked down the side of her face. In horror, she watched the quivering lips of the reflection move.

"This is what you deserve. Look at you. Nobody wants you. You have to settle for anything you get."

Her body slid down the tiled wall, until she sat on the floor with her knees to her chest. The gown was bunched around her waist. She dropped her head and cried, letting the tears fall for Madear, Gordon, and Hunter. Then, finally, the tears came for Sasha.

Chapter 28

The streets were illuminated with the red, white, and yellow glow of car lights. Anya stared from her window, watching the clustered cars make the evening exodus to their suburban homes. The city lights held her hypnotized gaze.

The view gave her a reprieve from the scene that played repeatedly in her mind all day. How could Braxton have done that? she questioned again and again. After two years and countless situations, she knew everything there was to know about him. The man she knew would never force himself on her.

"Just goes to show you," she said aloud.

"It's come to that, huh?"

Anya felt the blood warm her face. I should have closed my door, she thought. It was almost seven and everyone had gone home—except for David.

He grinned. "I didn't mean to interrupt your conversation," he teased, then sat in front of her desk.

"What do you want, David?" Her tone was sharper than she expected.

His eyes widened a bit. "I didn't mean to intrude. I

thought you were just thinking out loud. Is it one of the accounts?"

Anya stared at David. He was such a private person, but was becoming a friend.

Maybe another male could help her understand. Maybe David could give her the explanation that she was desperate to hear.

"I'm sorry, I didn't mean to snap at you. I have a lot on my mind."

"Anything I can help with?" he persisted.

She could see his concern. Maybe . . . "No." She sat at her desk and toyed with a message slip Dianna had left— another call from Mr. Greene requesting a meeting with her. She shook her head. "Is there something I can help *you* with, David?"

"Uh, no." He twisted in his seat. "I came to tell you that I'm going to get out of here, unless you need me."

"Oh, no." Anya smiled for the first time that day. "You never leave this early. I'm glad to see you come up for air." Anya looked away from him before she asked, "You have . . . plans?"

He dropped his gaze. "No, just going home." His words were as quick and sharp as hers were before.

Anya nodded. They both had secrets.

David cleared his throat. "Are you going to be here much longer?"

"Not much. I just want to clear my desk."

"Don't work too late."

Anya sat motionless, as she listened to David return to his office, then come back down the corridor and through the front door. When the lock clicked, she returned to the haven of her window.

There was really no reason for her to stay, but she had nowhere to go. Knowing Braxton, her house was staked out and the only reason he hadn't shown up at the office was because Dianna had told him that she hadn't come in today. Touching her head, she could feel the small lump that remained. In her mind, she went over the scenario again. He hadn't meant to throw her down that way; it was an accident. Anya shook her head—that's how it started. First a shove, then a push.

She looked at her ring. She had surprised herself when she put it on. When she'd taken it off last night, she believed that was the end. But the light of day brought clarity—at least that's what she thought this morning.

Now, as she twisted the ring, her mind was a potpourri of thoughts. One thing she knew, she couldn't hide in her office forever. She sighed. It was time for her to face what had been building for weeks.

She started to put on her jacket, then paused. She needed to go to the bathroom. Maybe I should just try to make it home, she thought, but then decided against it.

When she got to the front door and unbolted the lock, she realized she'd left her keys on her desk. She looked toward her office, and wondered if she should go back so that she could lock the door while she went to the rest room. But, it would only take a minute. She stepped into the main hallway and scurried down the hall.

The moment she opened the office door, Anya shuddered; a body-tingling chill ran through her. She stood, listening to the silence. After a few moments, she stepped completely through the doorway, locking the door behind her.

"This thing with Braxton is really getting to me," she said aloud.

Still, she quickened her step, determined to leave immediately. The instant Anya grabbed her jacket and purse, the office darkened.

It took a moment, but Anya's mind finally caught up with the pounding in her chest. She peered into the darkened hallway; the lights were out throughout the entire office. Then her glance moved to the window. The city lights continued to glow. That was when fear totally gripped her.

She sought to collect her thoughts. Using her palms, she groped along the top of her desk until she felt the cold tip of the scissors. As she picked them up, her hand hit the telephone. It didn't take a second for her to decide. She moved quickly through the dangerously dark room. She would lock herself in, call the police and pray.

The force hit her so fast, so fiercely, that she was knocked across the room, back against her desk. She tasted blood instantly. Her scream lifted from inside her belly but locked in her throat. She looked up to see the faint outline of a figure that blended with the darkness.

Still against the desk, her fingers felt the scissors that had dropped. Fear mixed with survival, and she gripped the scissors tightly. She could barely see the outline, but she listened for movement. When she felt him move, she held her breath, then lunged forward, the pointed ends of the scissors directed toward his face.

He screamed and, for a split second, Anya hesitated. There was something familiar. Regaining her wits, she ran for the door.

He grabbed her, hooking his arm around her neck. When her hands reached for him, the scissors dropped. The scream that had been bolted inside her throat finally released itself, filling the office with her fear. She moved all her limbs—kicking, waving, scratching, grasping at the nothingness in front of her.

"Shut up or I'll kill you."

Anya quieted to whimpers, believing the voice. "Please, don't hurt me."

Without warning, he turned and threw Anya face down on her desk. Her stomach hit the edge hard, sending pain screeching through her limbs. Fear became secondary to rage. She swung around prepared for battle, when she heard the click an instant before she saw the glimmer.

The gleaming blade made her freeze. "Please, please," she whimpered.

"I should kill you." The voice was filled with such hatred, she knew she would not survive the night.

He tossed her onto the floor, then slipped the knife to her neck as he straddled her. He leaned into her, his hot breath seeping into her skin.

"One word—you're dead." He carefully murmured the words, but to Anya, it sounded like he screamed.

They were so close that, through the darkness, under the knit ski cap, his eyes seared through her, singeing her, and she knew he spoke the truth.

Soundlessly, he slid the knife against her blouse, then with a smooth stroke, ripped through the silk. He lingered for a moment, rubbing the cold metal against her skin.

She cringed, but remained still as she stared into his eyes. Sick eyes, crazed eyes, familiar eyes, she thought, but only for a moment. She knew no one like this.

His eyes smiled as he lifted her skirt and with, another switch of the blade, tore her stockings and panties from her body. The knife moved back to her neck and his eyes spoke. "Don't move," they said.

He unzipped his pants and Anya trembled. She squeezed her eyes tightly as he entered her. The man grunted; she drifted away—to Braxton. He was probably at home now, waiting for her. And Sasha—she was at the Victory Awards. Maybe she was home by now, bursting with excitement, waiting to tell Anya about her night.

Animalistic whimpers brought her back and she realized the sounds were coming from her. As the man stabbed into her, the cold blade remained against her throat.

She wondered why it hurt so much. She wondered how she was able to keep breathing. She wondered why she had never taken a self-defense class. She wondered what to-morrow would be like—if it would be sunny or raining.

When she squirmed under the pressure of his weight, the blade pressed harder against her neck. Oh, God, she thought. Oh, God.

It was then that she made her decision. She would not remain silent as he had told her to. If she were to die tonight, she knew there was something she had to say. As the man released his seed, she began to utter what she knew could be the final words of her life. *Our Father, who art in Heaven. Hallowed be thy name. Thy kingdom come, thy will be done on earth as it is in heaven . . .*

Chapter 29

David quickened his step. He opened the front doors and his eyes skimmed the marble-floored lobby. It was too late for anyone to be there. When he pushed the button for the elevator, the doors opened instantly, and he waited until the doors closed before he pressed the number 17. He watched the floor numbers and counted silently along as he tried to calm his breathing.

At the seventeenth floor, he walked to the huge double doors with the gold M&A embossed in the walnut panels.

"Mr. Montgomery. What are you doing here?"

Gina struggled toward him, her cleaning cart rolling slowly over the carpeted hallway.

His hands shook and he returned the key to his pocket. "Gina . . . what . . . you're still here?" He glanced at his watch. The cleaning crew should have been long gone.

Gina grinned. "I know, we are very late tonight," she started in her deliberate cadence. "Five people called in sick. It's that flu," she tisked. "So, it's just me and Tony on the top floors." Gina leaned against the cart and used her arm to wipe the sweat from her brow. Then eyeing him, she asked, "Why are you here so late?"

"I . . ." David swallowed hard. "I forgot . . . something."

"I will open the door for you." She tried to push herself between David and the door. "I have to clean your office next."

"I have it." David steadied his hand as he put the key in the door. He turned on the lights, as Gina's cart squeaked through the reception area.

"I will start on the other side, Mr. Montgomery. So that you can do whatever you came to do. Don't work too late, Mr. Montgomery."

She continued to mumble as she meandered down the hall. David sighed, grateful for the few moments he would have alone. He passed Dianna's desk and the uniform cubicles that lined the office.

Suddenly he stopped, hearing something, but in seconds, it disappeared. The moment he began toward his office, it started again—a low moaning. He stepped toward the moan, and stopped in front of Anya's office. The door was slightly ajar and David walked in.

His eyes widened in shock. He picked up the overturned chair blocking his path, and stepped over papers that seemed to have been thrown from the desk. Stumbling forward, he moved through the wide office until he heard it again, this time louder and clearer.

"Anya!" he screamed.

She was sprawled on her stomach on the floor, her face buried in the pile of the carpet. He knelt, turned her over and drew back at the sight of the blood.

"Anya," he whispered.

She moaned.

He jumped up, reaching for the desk. Where was the phone? His eyes bounced around until he located it in the corner. He picked it up, tapping the receiver button furiously. Nothing. He clicked it again; that's when he saw the ripped cord.

"Gina! Please, come quickly!" he screamed through the offices.

He ran back to Anya and held her head, mumbling softly, trying to propel her into consciousness.

"Mr. Montgomery, where are you?"

"In Ms. Mitchell's office," he yelled.

Gina shrieked. "Oh, my God!" she said, then reverted to her native tongue, making the sign of the cross over her body. She fell to her knees.

David took his arms from around Anya and leaned toward the cleaning woman. "Gina. Call 911," he said, pointing to Dianna's desk.

Gina cried through her screams. He shook her shoulders. "Call the police!"

"Yes, yes," she whimpered. She struggled to raise herself from the floor and ran to Dianna's desk.

He knelt again, resting Anya's head in his lap. He stroked her face and softly called her name.

David struggled to pull Anya's skirt over her nakedness, then tried to tug her shredded blouse together. When she moaned faintly, he removed his jacket to cover her.

As he stared at her, memories rushed to him, taking him to another place, a different time. He shook his head to rid himself of the thoughts. He couldn't allow the past into the present.

Blood seeped from the corner of her mouth, and he used his shirtsleeve to wipe it away. He hoped his touch soothed her, letting her know she was no longer in danger.

"Mr. Montgomery, they are on their way." Gina's

voice was still quavering as she returned to the office. "I told them to hurry, that a lady had been shot!"

"Okay, Gina." David tried to keep his voice calm. "Go downstairs and wait for the paramedics."

"I want to stay with you." She knelt and touched Anya's forehead, then muttered words that David could not understand.

"Gina, this is a big building and we need to lead the paramedics right here."

She hesitated, then stood. "Yes . . . yes."

David's small sigh was one of relief. He held on to Anya, and continued to call her name. A few minutes later, he realized her moans had stopped.

"Oh, God," he said aloud. He had to do something, but what? He looked at Anya, and knew what he had to do. But how could he pray? He hadn't spoken to God in such a long time. He closed his eyes, willing words from long-ago Sunday school classes to come forth. The first words that came to his mind he spoke aloud. *"The Lord is my shepherd. I shall not want. He maketh me to lie down in green pastures. He leadeth me besides the still waters. He restoreth my soul."*

The front doors banged as the paramedics rushed in. David was kneeling beside Anya as they pulled the stretcher into the office. Gina followed the medics, trailed by a train of other cleaning people.

"What do we have here?" one of the paramedics asked David, moving him aside.

"I . . . found her . . . like this," David stammered. "She

hasn't spoken, just made a few sounds—" David stopped, realizing they weren't listening.

"Do us a favor, please?"

Even though he never looked up, David knew the man was speaking to him. He crouched down next to the medic, eager to get instructions.

"Get those folks out of here," the paramedic said, jerking his head over his shoulder.

David looked toward the door where the cleaning crew was crammed into the opening. As he approached them he heard their whispers, although he didn't understand their words. Gina, in front, held a shredded tissue in her hand.

"Gina, the medics have asked that we get everyone out of the way. You should go home." He spoke to the group.

"But Mr. Montgomery. We are not finished, and we will not get our money," Gina sniffed.

"I'll take care of that," David responded, speaking to the others as well. "Go home. I'll make sure that everyone gets paid."

Following his instructions, they began to back away. All except Gina.

"Mr. Montgomery, I want to stay and help Ms. Mitchell," she sobbed.

He forced a smile, hoping it would calm her. "It would be better if you went home. She's going to be fine."

As Gina walked away, moving even slower than normal, David turned back to the medics.

A chill filled the room and David looked around for his jacket. It was on the floor, tossed aside by the paramedics. As he put it on, the front door opened. The sight of the two men made him freeze. Neither was dressed in uniform, but David knew who they were.

The men nodded in David's direction as they entered and surveyed the office. The white detective hunched down, as the paramedics gingerly moved Anya from the floor to the stretcher. As the police and the medic talked, David strained to hear their words.

"What is it, Don?"

"We're stabilizing her, still not sure."

"The call came in that there was a shooting—" the policeman started.

"She was beaten. And raped."

Both policemen turned toward the words. The detective standing walked toward David.

"Who are you?"

"David Montgomery." He extended his hand, but the policeman reached inside his gray tweed jacket and pulled out a pad and a pencil. David glanced at the shield pinned on his jacket: DETECTIVE ROBINSON.

"Mr. Montgomery," Detective Robinson started, as he flipped through the pages of his pad, "how do you know she was beaten and raped?"

David twisted his face, as if he had been asked a ridiculous question. "I found her."

The detective made a note. When he looked up, he was squinting. "But how do you know specifically what happened?"

David realized what the detective meant by his question, and he wondered how he would answer. "All you have to do is look at her and you can tell she's been beaten!" David's hands waved in Anya's direction.

"That's fair," the detective responded. He took a piece of gum from his pocket and stuck it in his mouth, letting the seconds tick by. "The part that interests me is that you said she was raped. How did you know that? Just by *looking* at her?"

David folded his arms in front of him. "Look," he said strongly, "when I found her, her clothes were torn, she was almost naked from the waist down. And bleeding—"

"You have blood on your shirt," the policeman interrupted him.

David looked at his cuff that peeked from under his jacket. It was specked with drops of red. He unfolded his arms. "It must have gotten on me . . . when I lifted her."

"Uh-huh." The policeman allowed the silence to return. "What were you doing here?" he finally asked.

"I came back to the office . . ."

"So you work here?"

"Yes, I'm the vice president."

The detective raised one eyebrow and made a sound that was something like a cough. "And the victim, what's her name?"

The policeman's words made David shudder. He glanced over the officer's shoulder. The paramedics were still working on Anya.

"Her name is Anya Mitchell. She owns this business."

This time the detective raised both eyebrows. His eyes scanned the office quickly. "What kind of place is this?"

David told him and the detective grunted, continuing to scratch on his pad. Detective Robinson asked David to spell his last name, then resumed his questioning. With as much patience as he could gather, David answered but kept his eyes glued to the medics.

When the paramedics began wheeling the stretcher, David interrupted the detective. "I'm going to ride with

Ms. Mitchell." He took a step around the policeman, but Detective Robinson grabbed his arm.

"I still have a few more questions."

David gently but sternly pulled away. "I will answer your questions, after I make sure she's all right."

"That's fine," the officer said, surrendering surprisingly easily. "Just make sure you're accessible."

David shook his head, then rushed into the hallway behind the stretcher.

"How is she?" David questioned, his eyes fixed on Anya. But the medics didn't respond. One was talking into a cell phone; the other was still working on Anya. After they secured Anya into the ambulance, they reluctantly allowed David into the back, although he was still too far away to touch her.

His back was pressed against the doors, as the medical vehicle, with sirens blaring, sped through the darkened streets. He loosened his tie and glanced at his watch. It was hard to believe that only thirty minutes had passed since he'd found Anya. It seemed so much longer.

Suddenly it occurred to him that he had to let someone know. Braxton—but how could he contact him? Sasha—he could call Anya's number.

He pulled his cell phone from his jacket, then searched his wallet for the card Anya'd given him when he first came to Los Angeles. The phone was answered immediately.

"Sasha? This is David Montgomery."

"Hi, David." Her voice sounded stuffy. "I don't think Anya is home yet."

He bit his lip. "Anya is with me, Sasha." When the ambulance swerved slightly, David looked out the window. They were entering the hospital's parking lot. "She's been hurt."

"Oh, my God! What happened?"

David jumped from the ambulance and ran behind the stretcher. "We just got to Cedars Sinai," he responded, purposely not answering her question. "Can you call Braxton?"

"Yes," Sasha said, her voice trembling. "Tell Anya I'll be right there."

He hung up the phone, and ran behind the medics. Other medical personnel met the gurney, and pushed Anya through the swinging double doors of the emergency room. David tried to follow, but one of the nurses stopped him.

"Sorry, staff only." Her words were short and static. "You have to wait out here."

David opened his mouth, but the nurse raised her hand, anticipating his protest. Disgust from a long day was on her face. "The doctors will tell you something shortly. Check with that nurse," she said, pointing to a white round desk that had an ADMITTING sign hanging above. "And fill out the papers."

The nurse entered the emergency ward and the doors swung closed behind her. He tried to peek through the small windows, but finally turned away.

He went into the waiting room. One man was watching a repeat of the late-night news and another was lying across several of the blue plastic chairs that lined the wall.

David chose the chair closest to the entrance, and leaned back against the cold walls. How could this happen in his life again?

For the second time that night, he prayed. "Dear God,"

he whispered, not having the strength to talk louder. "Dear God, please, please . . ." He didn't know what else to say, but, for some reason he was sure that God would fill in the blanks.

First their footsteps clicked along the tile of the hospital hallway, then David heard their demanding, anxious voices. "We're looking for Anya Mitchell."

David called out and they ran in his direction. "Where is Anya? What happened? Was it a car accident? How is she?" Braxton and Sasha bombarded him with questions.

The last thing he wanted was to give this news. His eyes searched the empty lobby and, on cue, a brown-haired man in a white jacket came from the emergency room and went to the Admittance Desk. The nurse pointed in their direction and David exhaled.

"I think this is the doctor now," David said, pointing toward the man.

"Braxton Vance?" The doctor asked the question to no one in particular.

Braxton stepped forward. "I'm Braxton . . ." David and Sasha crowded behind him.

The doctor reached out his hand. "I'm Dr. Covey. Ms. Mitchell has been asking for you." The doctor turned around and Braxton followed, leaving David and Sasha standing in the middle of the stark white lobby.

David swallowed hard. Maybe he should have told Braxton. It would be horrible for him to see her—

"David?" Sasha said, as if she had been calling his name a few times.

He took her hand, and they walked slowly to the waiting room. Only the blaring television and the man lying against the wall remained.

"What happened?" Sasha's voice quavered, and David could tell she'd been crying.

The chair scraped the floor as he pulled it from the wall so that he could face her.

"I don't know everything . . . but she was beaten and . . ."

Sasha gasped. Even with her hand covering her mouth, she could not silence her sobs. "Who would do this?"

David told her what he knew—how he found her, the police—everything, except for the rape.

"Why would anyone attack her?"

"I don't know . . . maybe robbery. Maybe they saw that it was a financial services company and they thought there was money in the office . . ." He stood and began pacing.

Sasha nodded and took a deep breath. "Okay. We have to be strong for her." She joined David, walking back and forth along the length of the waiting room. "Oh, my God!" she exclaimed, stopping suddenly. "I have to call Madear. Our grandmother has to know."

"We should wait until Braxton comes out before we call anyone else."

"That makes sense," she said, sounding like she was out of breath. Sasha sank into the chair and began sobbing again.

"Anya's going to be fine." David put his arm around her shoulder.

"She has to be." When Sasha looked at him, her swollen eyes tried to smile. "Thank you for helping her."

David squeezed Sasha's hand, then laid her head on his shoulder. He held her and they silently waited. And, without knowing what the other was doing, they both closed their eyes and prayed.

"Attacked? What does that mean?"

"That's all we have for now, Mr. Vance," Dr. Covey said as he led Braxton through the large emergency unit, passing smaller rooms along the perimeter. Even though it was after midnight, medical personnel still bustled around.

Braxton's eyes frantically searched the area until the doctor turned into the last room. And his eyes stopped moving when he saw her. But he had to hold his fist over his mouth to hold back his gasp.

She was propped up in the bed and a nurse was removing a blood-pressure band from her arm.

"Ms. Mitchell," Dr. Covey called to her.

Her head slowly turned. She grunted, a soft sound, but Braxton knew she was beckoning him. Deliberately she lifted her hand and reached toward him.

He blinked rapidly to fight the instant tears that stung his eyelids. As gently as he could, he touched her, though he feared he'd cause her more pain.

Her face was covered with scratches, turned to welts. A large white bandage covered the left half of her face. But it was her clothes that shocked him most. Her skirt and blouse were shredded, like they had been ripped methodically with a sharp blade.

He pressed his lips together, fighting his urge to cry out. Who would do this to his woman? Instantly, his brain filled with thoughts of revenge, images of what he would do when he hunted down the attacker and tortured him until he asked for death.

"Are you starting to feel better, Ms. Mitchell?" Dr.

Covey asked, although he didn't look up from the chart in his hand.

Anya started to nod, then grimaced. "Fine," her voice squeaked.

Dr. Covey looked at her with a smile. "It looks like you're doing a lot better."

At that moment, a cinnamon-skinned, tall woman entered. She wore a white jacket over her navy dress, as if she'd been on the verge of leaving the hospital. Her hair was twisted high on her head in a French roll, fixed in place with jeweled combs, and her makeup was freshly applied.

"Dr. Young, looks like you were on your way out."

She nodded and glanced at Anya. "I was, but I'd rather be here." She picked up the chart. "Is everything here?" she asked Dr. Covey.

He nodded. "We were going to keep Ms. Mitchell overnight," the doctor said, looking between Anya and Dr. Young. "But I don't think that's necessary now." He made a note on the chart and handed it to Dr. Young. "There were no signs of any head trauma."

The female doctor moved closer to the bed. "I'm Dr. Young," she said, gently taking Anya's hand. "I'm going to be working with you from this point."

Anya took a deep breath and squeezed Braxton's hand.

Dr. Young noticed the gesture and nodded reassuringly. "You'll be all right."

Braxton extended his hand. "I'm Braxton Vance, Anya's fiancé."

By the time they completed the exchange, Dr. Covey was gone.

Dr. Young rolled a stool close to the bed. "How are you feeling?"

Her gentle voice reminded Anya of Madear. On one hand, the voice soothed her. But as the doctor's eyes smiled at her, Anya thought of what her grandmother's eyes would look like when she received this news. "I'm fine," Anya whispered, hoping that if she said those words, she'd feel them.

The nurse handed Dr. Young a clipboard with loose papers attached. "Anya, let me explain what we're going to be doing." She spoke softly. "I specialize in taking care of women who've been attacked this way." The doctor paused and squeezed her hand. "First, I'm going to ask some questions, then we'll do a physical. We're going to use something called a rape kit, have you ever heard of that?"

Anya pressed her lips together. She'd hoped that somehow it hadn't happened. But to hear the doctor say the word aloud made it a terrible reality. She shook her head.

"A rape kit?" Braxton whispered. He gripped Anya's hand tighter.

Dr. Young frowned. "I'm sorry," she said, looking from Anya to Braxton. "You didn't know?"

Braxton shook his head, and hoped not to hear details. He couldn't know—not right now. The veins in his head pulsed.

The doctor sent him a reassuring smile, then turned back to Anya. "Dr. Covey says you're going to be fine. The bruises are superficial and will heal in a few days. So, we want to focus on getting information for the police." Dr. Young squeezed Anya's hand again, then continued, "The more you give us, the better chance the police have. You understand?"

Anya breathed again and nodded.

As the nurse assisted Anya in sitting up, Dr. Young said to Braxton, "Mr. Vance, I have to ask you to wait in the lounge. You can go right out there," she pointed. "You don't have to go to the waiting room."

Braxton shook his head. "I need to stay with Anya."

"I'm sorry." The doctor's soft eyes told him she understood. "It's procedure. We have to ask Anya some questions, but that's why we have the lounge," she said gently. "You'll be close by and I'll get you as soon as we're finished here."

This time, it was Anya who squeezed his hand. In the next second, their fingers slipped apart.

Braxton left the room and walked straight to the desk in the center. "Is there a rest room I can use?" he asked no one in particular.

A nurse pointed toward the opposite corner.

He walked with surprisingly steady steps even though his mind screamed, "Rape!" He entered the bathroom with images cannonading his mind. Who? Where? How?

A man stood at one of the three urinals and Braxton stumbled past him. He barely made it to the last stall before he fell to his knees and retched into the bowl.

"Hey, man," a voice behind him called. "Do you want me to get a doctor?"

Using the back of his hand, Braxton wiped his mouth. "No," he finally responded. "I don't need a doctor."

When the sounds of footsteps receded, he stood. He flushed the toilet, then washed his face at the sink, before he went to the lounge.

He leaned back in the chair, letting his eyes focus on the picture across from him. There was a man, woman, and child holding hands with the caption: FAMILY FIRST. He clenched his hands into tight fists.

"Please, God, help me to find a way to get through this without—" He stopped, and his shoulders slumped. He was afraid to think, afraid of where his thoughts would take him.

Anya was groggy—like she was wakening from a dream that she couldn't quite remember.

Dr. Young handed the clipboard to the nurse and sat back down on the stool.

"We're finished with the questions, now we'll do the physical. I'll explain each step, Anya, and we'll continue only as you feel comfortable." The doctor paused. "The first thing you have to do is take off your clothes. You can use that screen," the doctor said, pointing to a thin partition. "There's a large sheet of paper that you'll stand on as you're disrobing. That's part of the package that we'll send to Forensics. Okay?"

The doctor helped her from the bed. It took a moment for her to begin, but then she quickly stripped the remnants from her body.

"Doctor, is there a robe I can put on?" Anya peeked from behind the screen. She was surprised that her voice sounded like she was just going through a routine exam.

The doctor's voice was low. "There's a robe, Anya, but first I have to conduct a visual exam and Kathy will take photos of any bruises. Is that okay?"

She closed her eyes and cringed. Photos? She knew she had to do this, but all she wanted to do was go home. She opened her eyes when the doctor called her name.

Anya stepped from behind the screen with her arms crossed in front of her chest.

Dr. Young said, "I promise, this won't take long."

As the doctor looked over her body, and made notes, Anya's gaze roved through the room, from the stark white walls to the removable ceiling tiles. She shivered and the doctor tried to soothe her, but Anya found no comfort in her words. When the nurse picked up the Polaroid, and the camera's shutters clicked, Anya squeezed her eyes so tightly, they began to burn.

"Okay, Anya," Dr. Young said after an eternity. "Put this on."

Anya hated the paper robes that she wore during gynecological exams, but now she grabbed the thin blue paper as if it were a gift from God. She lay back with her feet in the stirrups and tried to focus on what Dr. Young was saying.

"This won't hurt at all. It'll be a lot like the exams you're used to. I'll be checking for blood and fluids and . . ."

Anya shut her ears but she couldn't close her mind and she remembered another time when she lay on a hard table, with her legs spread, as she stared at the ceiling.

Back then, the red-faced, bald-headed man had uttered almost the same words Dr. Young was saying now. "You'll feel some discomfort, but it will feel a lot like the exams you're used to."

Both doctors had been wrong. This wasn't what she was used to.

Dr. Young occasionally pierced the block Anya had around her.

"Checking for semen . . ." She felt the cold metal of the speculum being inserted.

"Need a saline swab . . ." The nurse handed Dr. Young a small package.

"Pubic hair . . . sexually transmitted diseases."

Anya began to hum silently.

"The blood we're taking is for an AIDS test . . ."

She hummed a little louder as the nurse tapped her arm for a vein. She kept her eyes on the ceiling and imagined that it was heaven.

It seemed like long hours had passed before the doctor finally said, "We're finished. Are you all right?" The doctor helped Anya sit up.

Anya couldn't bring herself to look into the doctor's face, so she simply nodded.

Dr. Young scooted the stool to the edge of the bed and began showing Anya brochures about rape counseling.

Anya shook her head. "I won't be needing that. I'm fine." She paused. "I'm strong," she added faintly.

Dr. Young frowned. "Anya, everyone needs help with this."

Anya was still shaking her head. She wasn't about to sit in a room with ten other women, *sharing* this experience. That was not the way to handle this. All she needed was God and prayer. She folded her arms in front of her.

"Counseling will help you cope with this trauma and deal with things like flashbacks or feelings of shame . . ."

"Dr. Young, I'm a Christian," Anya said, holding her chin high. In her mind, words finally came together to form the question that filled her. Why did God let this happen?

"Anya, I'm a Christian too."

Anya's face softened in surprise, but she kept her

arms folded. "Then you know that I don't need anything but God."

Dr. Young looked directly at Anya. "There is no doubt God will get you through. But he has provided other vessels to help with healing."

"I'm sure that counseling is good for some women, but it's not necessary for me. I don't feel ashamed; I know that I didn't do anything wrong."

"That's true," Dr. Young said, as she nodded and patted Anya's hand. "But feelings may come up later and counseling prepares you."

Anya stared at the doctor and said nothing.

Dr. Young sighed. "All right. There is one other thing. Pregnancy—"

Pregnancy! Anya exclaimed to herself. Dr. Young rambled about the chances being minuscule, but there was a pill they advised all victims to take.

She nodded, then interrupted the doctor. "I'd like to see Braxton now."

The doctor nodded knowingly. "I'll get him." But before Dr. Young left, she dropped brochures on the bed. "These are for you. Think about it." She patted Anya's arm.

All energy had been ripped from her and she lay back down. The room had become smaller and Anya prayed that Braxton would come quickly and take her home.

The door squeaked and she turned. Braxton was standing with his hands stuffed in his pockets. The rims of his eyes were swollen red, and Anya knew he'd been crying.

She forced herself up and he rushed to her. They held each other for long minutes before the tears that had been clogged inside of her were released.

"I am so sorry," Anya sobbed into Braxton's shoulder.

Braxton shook his head, but kept his arms around her. He wanted to tell her that she had nothing to be sorry about. He wanted to tell her how sorry he was that he hadn't protected her. He wanted to tell her how much he loved her. But the words were choked in his throat. So he held her tightly and hoped that she felt safe.

They held each other until the nurse assisting Dr. Young returned to let them know that she'd delivered Braxton's note to Sasha and David.

Within an hour, Sasha returned with a sweatsuit for Anya. While Anya dressed, Braxton noticed her hand, but said nothing at first. He watched her as she signed the release papers and took medicine from Dr. Young. As they waited for a wheelchair, Braxton took her hand and kissed it.

She smiled.

Then he said softly, "Anya, baby, where's your ring?"

Chapter 30

The pitch-blackness of the middle of the night was beginning to fade by the time Sasha and Braxton led Anya into the house.

"Do you want me to take you upstairs?" Braxton asked, as Anya held onto his neck.

Anya nodded. She was already feeling groggy from the sedatives. Sleep would be a relief. If she could sleep, she could forget.

It was a slow trek up the stairs and, when Anya finally lay in her bed, the clock on her nightstand blinked 4:07. She tried to calculate how much time had passed since this all began. But her eyes closed before she could begin to count the hours.

Braxton covered her with the quilt and sat on the edge of the bed.

"Do you want me to stay?" he whispered.

Anya shook her head. "No, go home," she said, her eyes still closed. "You've been up all night."

Braxton stroked her arm until her steadied breathing told him she'd fallen asleep. Then, he tiptoed from the room, leaving the door opened to hear any signs of her waking up.

As soon as he got to the bottom of the stairs, Sasha asked, "Did the doctors say that she was going to be all right?"

Braxton squeezed his tight shoulders and sighed. "She'll recover from the beating. It's the rape that I'm worried about."

Sasha's eyes widened and immediately filled with tears. "She was raped?"

"I thought David told you."

"No, maybe he didn't know."

"Well, that's good. The fewer people who know, the better."

She nodded. "But we have to tell Madear. She'll call Donovan." Sasha reached for the phone.

Braxton glanced at his watch. "Let's not wake her up. We'll call in a few hours."

Sasha nodded, then tried to stifle a yawn.

"Go up to bed," he said.

She shook her head resolutely. "I can't, suppose Anya needs something."

"I'm going to stay until Anya wakes up."

With a wide smile, Sasha hugged him. "Anya is lucky to have you."

He followed Sasha up the stairs and took a blanket from the linen closet, then tiptoed into Anya's room.

He sat on the bed and gently stroked her face. She stirred in her sleep and he paused until she was still again. Even with the scratches and bandages, Anya had never looked more beautiful to him.

"I will take care of you for the rest of my life," Braxton whispered. "Forever."

He took her hand and kissed her bare fingers. He'd report the missing ring in the morning, but it really didn't matter to him. He'd buy her one hundred more, if that's what she wanted.

Finally, he stood and rolled the chaise across the carpet so that he had an unobstructed view of her. He pulled the blanket over his body, though he had no intentions of sleeping. He was just going to watch her. Watch her, protect her, and pray for both of them.

In her head, it was completely dark. Anya tried to grasp the air, needing something to hold on to. She tried to lift her legs, but they were bolted to the floor. Scream, she thought. But her lips wouldn't move and she could feel him coming . . .

Anya's eyes fluttered, then slowly opened. She blinked in confusion. She was in her bedroom, but how did she get here? The last thing she remembered was being in her office—she had to go to the bathroom.

Her eyes followed the soft snoring and she saw Braxton, twisted like a pretzel in the chair that was too small for his frame. What was he doing here? She lifted her head, but felt heavy and bounced back onto the pillows.

"Ouch," she wheezed. She glanced back at Braxton; his snoring continued.

What time is it? she wondered. Her neck hurt too much to turn toward the clock, but she could tell by the sunlight pouring into the room that it was mid-morning.

"I've got to get to the office," she said. As she lifted herself, a pain shot through her stomach. "Ouch," she grunted, this time waking Braxton.

He jumped from the chair. "Are you okay?"

Anya pulled her mouth into a smile. "I feel like I've been in a fight with Mike Tyson." Then she remembered, and her smile disappeared.

"What do you need?"

"Nothing." She tried to stretch, but her body wouldn't move without pain. "Did you sleep here all night?"

Braxton sat at the edge of the bed. He nodded.

She reached for his hand. "I wish you hadn't done that. It couldn't have been comfortable in that chair."

Tears burned behind his eyes. "I couldn't leave. I'm just so sorry about—"

"Braxton, there was nothing you could do."

Braxton lowered his head. He was apologizing for much more than last night, but maybe this wasn't the time. "Nothing bad will ever happen to you again."

He hugged her, then pulled away when he felt her flinch.

"I think you need to take another pill."

In the bathroom, he filled a paper cup with water, then gave her two of the small red pills that the doctor said would make her more comfortable.

She grabbed the pills eagerly. Slumber was safer.

Within minutes, she was sleeping again. This time, Braxton lay next to her and gently put his head on her chest.

"Oh, God," he breathed softly. "How am I ever going to deal with this?"

His dreams had been packed with visions of a facelsss man and what had happened in that office. Now he squeezed his eyes, trying to erase the horrid pictures.

The minutes passed, and he began to feel calmer as his head lifted and fell against Anya's chest. But, he still knew he needed help. It was the only way he'd make it through. He would call Pastor Ford the first chance he got. She would know what to do.

At the sound of the bell, Sasha ran to the door. Madear stood stolidly in place, her purse clutched to her chest. With her chocolate tailored pants suit and silver hair tied back in her trademark bun, she looked like she was just going to spend a leisurely day with friends. But what pulled at Sasha's heart was her grandmother's mournful eyes. Her make-up couldn't hide the swelling of her lower lids, which looked like they had tripled in size.

She hadn't seen Madear since that Sunday dinner, but all of that anger was forgotten. Wordlessly, Sasha pulled her grandmother into her arms.

"Thank you for calling me, baby." Madear's words were muffled into Sasha's chest.

"Of course, Madear."

Madear held on to Sasha even after they sat down. "Who would do this to my baby?"

"We don't know anything yet, Madear. The doctors said that the police would be in touch."

Madear was silent for a moment. "Is she asleep?"

Sasha nodded. "Braxton stayed with her last night."

"Hey, Madear." Braxton came down the stairs and all three hugged.

"Has Anya said anything about what happened?" Madear whispered.

He shook his head. "She's been asleep most of the time. The doctor said that she had to get some rest because they weren't sure why she was unconscious when she was first found. They're sure it's not a problem. The doctor said that the body goes into shock to protect itself . . ." His voice trailed off.

Madear and Sasha nodded, not knowing what else to say.

"You know," Braxton started, his voice quavering, "I don't think I have it in me to talk . . . about it." The image of the faceless man seeped into his mind again. "Though I have to talk to this man." He pulled a card that Dr. Young had given him. "Detective Bush has been assigned to this case." Braxton shook his head.

Madear took Braxton's hand. "You are not going to go through this by yourself." Madear's voice was suddenly stronger. "We'll get through this with each other and—" she squeezed their hands—"we'll get through this with God." Still holding their hands, Madear bowed her head and they followed.

Madear prayed, "Heavenly Father, in this time of distress, we come to you with thanksgiving and praises. We thank you for keeping us, and for keeping Anya, and for being by our sides during this time of need . . ."

As Madear prayed, Sasha opened her eyes but kept her head lowered. How could Madear turn to God, when He had allowed this to happen? God had let her down in so many ways—with Gordon, Hunter, and now this.

But she wasn't going to say anything to Madear. If her grandmother needed her faith, so be it. But *she* was beyond God. She would rely on herself, and make sure Anya could rely on her.

As Madear said, "Amen," Braxton joined in with his own. Sasha raised her head and said nothing.

Sasha closed the door behind Braxton, just as Madear came from the kitchen.

"Braxton went home to get some clothes, and then he's going to stop by the police station."

Madear nodded and lifted her purse from the couch. "You children don't have any food. I'll pick up a few things."

Sasha smiled. "I don't think Anya would want you to do that."

"Okay." Madear looked at Sasha for only a moment. Then her eyes turned away as she walked along the couch, fluffing the pillows.

Sasha stood with her back against the door, as Madear moved past the couch over to the plants. She inhaled, taking in their fragrance, then began picking at the leaves.

"Madear, do you want me to turn on some music or do you want to go downstairs and watch television?" Sasha was desperate to end the quiet.

"No, baby," Madear said, as she leaned over the plants. Her back was still toward Sasha.

Sasha tugged at her sweatshirt and took a deep breath. "Madear, I've been meaning to call . . ."

Madear straightened and stiffened but didn't turn around.

"I wanted to apologize for . . . when we were at your house . . ."

When Madear turned around, a tear was already rolling down her cheek. She brushed a stray hair from her face, and with the slowest steps, moved toward her granddaughter.

She placed a soft palm on Sasha's face. "I'm the one who's sorry, baby."

Sasha shifted from one foot to the other, opened her mouth, then closed it.

"I love you with everything in me." Madear's eyes were thin slits, but remained pasted on Sasha. "You know that, don't you?"

It was a weak nod. Sasha barely moved, even when Madear put her arm around her neck and hugged her for what seemed like minutes.

"I love you, baby," Madear repeated.

Sasha trembled as she thought of how long she had wanted to hear those words from her grandmother.

They were still holding each other when they heard the creak of the stairs. They turned around, and Anya was standing at the bottom.

"Hey," was all she said.

Madear hesitated, then pulled Anya into her arms.

"How're you, baby?" Madear stepped back and tried not to focus on the scratches on her granddaughter's face.

"I'm fine," she said. Those words were becoming easier to say. She moved toward the couch.

Madear followed, sitting down next to her.

"Are you hungry, Anya?" Sasha asked.

Anya smiled, then grimaced as the cut on her lip felt like it was going to rip open. She held her hand at the side of her face, then looked at Madear and Sasha who were staring at her. "I don't want you guys waiting on me."

Madear frowned in doubt. "Braxton said the doctors were still wondering why you were unconscious."

Anya waved her hand in the air. "Dr. Young said that sometimes our brain will shut down—a protective something-or-other." She stopped, as the morning's sun shadows on the patio caught her eye. She had wondered last night if she would even see this day and she wanted to drop to her knees right there.

"Well, I don't care what you say," Madear interrupted her thoughts. "I'm going to take care of you."

"Me too." Sasha sounded like she was going to cry.

Anya rubbed Madear's hands, but inside, she wanted to scream. Asleep, she'd been haunted by hollow dreams, but here with Madear and Sasha, reality made her want to flee. Didn't they understand that she needed to pretend this never happened?

She smiled at Sasha. "So tell me about the Victory Awards. I want to hear every detail."

Sasha sat back, seeming startled.

"You went to the Victory Awards?" Madear asked. "With who?"

"It's a long story," Sasha said quickly, before Anya could respond. "I don't want to talk about it now." She turned back to Anya. "I'm just concerned about you."

Anya shook her head. No matter how much she wanted to forget, all they wanted was for her to remember.

Madear stood. "I'm gonna run home and get some of that chicken I cooked last night. I don't know why I didn't bring it." She made a face at Sasha. You stay, she mouthed silently.

Madear kissed Anya's cheek, then hugged Sasha before she went out the door.

The moment Madear was gone, Anya reached for the phone. "I need to call my office."

Sasha frowned. "David said he'd handle things for the next couple of days."

"He won't have to do that. I'm going in tomorrow."

Sasha's frown deepened, but she said nothing, as she listened to Anya talk to Dianna. From her end, she could tell that Dianna was asking Anya how she was feeling.

But Anya was abrupt, and within minutes, she hung up the phone.

"That's odd," Anya said, "The police were in my office this morning and then right after they left, David left. Dianna has no idea where he went." She paused. "I guess I will go back tomorrow."

Sasha shrugged. "I think David will have things under control for you. But for now, is there anything you want to do?" Sasha asked.

Anya shook her head. "I'm just going to sit down here for a while. I'm tired of laying down," she said. I'm tired of the dreams, was what she didn't say.

Sasha almost sucked her teeth when Anya picked up the Bible from the table. She bit her lip, fighting to keep the words to herself. There had to be something she could do—get Anya to talk instead of reading that Bible. "Anya, do you want to talk about it?" she asked softly.

When Anya looked up, Sasha noticed that the scars on Anya's face seemed to be fading already.

"Not yet."

Sasha scooted closer to her cousin. "Okay, just know that I'm here when you're ready."

"That means a lot to me." Anya smiled, then returned to the Bible.

Sasha glared at Anya as minutes passed, then suddenly she said, "I have one question, Anya. How can you read the Bible after . . . what happened?"

Anya raised an eyebrow. "That's all I *can* do right now."

"But—" Sasha stomped across the room. "But how could God let this happen to you?" she almost screamed, finally releasing the question that had been gnawing at her.

Anya nodded. She'd asked herself the same question.

"That's why I don't know if I believe in God," Sasha continued. "With this kind of stuff going on," she said, waving her hands in the air, "how can there be a God?"

"Sasha, no matter what happened to me, one thing you can be sure of is that God exists. All you have to do is look around and His creation bombards you from every angle."

"Well, if he can make all of this, why did he let you get hurt?"

"Being a Christian doesn't mean bad things won't happen," she said slowly, knowing these would be some of the most important words she would ever say to Sasha. "The only thing that God promised is that He would always be with us."

"Well, where was He when you were being raped?" Angry tears bit at Sasha's eyes as she fired the words at Anya.

Anya waited a beat. "He was right there—that's why I'm not dead."

Sasha stared at Anya, as if she couldn't understand what she was saying. "You really believe that?"

"I know it. Sasha, God was there the entire time. He tried to warn me, to get me out of there before—" When Sasha continued her stare, Anya motioned for Sasha to sit down. "When I walked into my office last night, I knew that man was there."

Sasha's eyes opened wide.

"It was that voice inside of me, God tried to warn me."

"Well, why didn't God tell you to run?"

"He did. *I* didn't listen. That's how I hold on now. Because even through that darkness, God was there." Anya took Sasha's hand. "All I have is the Lord and I'm not

going to let some . . . man take away what I know."
Anya's voice shook as she spoke.

Sasha shook her head. "You're unbelievable. You've
been through the worst thing that could ever happen, and
except for a few scratches, no one would ever know.
You're acting normal, like nothing's happened."

Anya's thoughts returned to the dreams that she knew
weren't normal. But that wouldn't help Sasha. "How do
you think I should act?" she asked.

Sasha shrugged her shoulders like she was frustrated.
"I don't know. It's not like I want you to fall apart, but
you should at least be mad!"

Anya held her head. How could she let her cousin know
that the fury inside of her was so strong she thought she'd
explode? "I feel like I'm being held together by paper clips,
Sasha. So give me time; I still might fall apart."

"That's not what I mean. I just think it would be more
natural if you were doing something instead of just picking up your Bible." Her voice was filled with disdain
when she uttered the last words.

A few moments passed. "Sasha, when I woke up this
morning, I didn't know whether I should cry or jump with
joy. So I did a bit of both. But what I need now is to move
forward and I will only be able to do that if I have peace.
And my peace always comes from the Lord."

Sasha was thoughtful. "Do you really think that God
was with you?"

"If I were to tell you all that happened, you would
know that God was there. And that's all I want to remember from last night." Anya walked to the French doors
leading to the patio. She opened them and took a deep
breath. "All I'm thinking about right now is that I can see

these flowers and that I can smell that grass." She turned around and faced her cousin. "And that I can talk to you."

Sasha hugged her. "You make it sound so easy."

"It's not, but I can't let go now, Sasha," Anya shuddered into her cousin's shoulder. "Because if I do, I might never come back."

Sasha tightened her arms around Anya. "Your faith is incredible."

"Even my faith comes from God. I just have to practice it a little and there's no better time than now."

Sasha shook her head. "Go back to your Bible. I want to take a shower before Madear gets back."

Anya smiled as Sasha trotted up the stairs. She couldn't explain it, but she knew that today, she'd reached her cousin. Maybe now it would just take time.

Words that Pastor Ford repeated over the years came to her mind now. "Sometimes, the only Jesus that people will see, is the Jesus that is in you."

Anya nodded her head. Just another reason for her to hold on.

Chapter 31

He could hear Sean's words clearly. "Never leave scars—that's evidence."

He sat on the edge of his bed, staring at his shaking hands. Hours had passed and nothing would stop his trembling. He took six steps to the window, then closed the miniblinds, bringing semi-darkness into the room. He returned to his bed, holding his head in his hands. His headache, like the quivering of his hands, would not go away.

The surrounding quiet disturbed him, but it was better than the screams that had taken over his mind. He couldn't get rid of the screams.

The sheets felt cool as he slid under the blanket. He pulled the cover over his body, and took deep breaths meant to calm. But his shivering quickened.

He never planned to hit her, but when she started talking to God . . . He had told her to be quiet. But she kept praying. She prayed until he'd beaten her into silence.

He had only done that once before—the time he'd nearly been caught in New York. It had been the first time he returned to the game. In his excitement, he'd beaten the *woman. That had cost him and he'd had to leave the city. He had promised himself that he'd never do that again.*

He took a deep breath. There was no need to worry. He'd been so careful, this was so perfectly planned. There was nothing to link him to what had happened.

The sparkle of the ring came into his view and he picked it up from the nightstand. That was never part of his plan. It wasn't like he needed it for money. But when he noticed it, he knew taking it would be the final degradation. He hadn't decided yet what to do with it. Maybe he'd give it back. Tell her he found it, then become the hero. He shook his head. He'd have to think about that.

At least he had taught her who was really in control. She wouldn't be bouncing around anymore like she was the only one in charge. He couldn't wait until the next time he saw her. That smirk of arrogance would be totally gone, and though he could tell no one, everyone would have him to thank for it.

Chapter 32

$\mathcal{D}$avid held his fingers to his temples as he listened to the murmurs in the hallway. Even though the meeting had ended almost thirty minutes before, the associates were still hovering and sharing their disbelief.

It had been tougher than he thought to tell everyone about the attack on Anya. As he spoke, images of her swept through his mind—the same ones that had kept him up all night.

At least his prayers had been answered. Sasha told him this morning that Anya was going to be fine. He wished he could see her with his own eyes, but for now, all he could do was run the business for her. And it was time to get the team back to work.

He stood, and just as he was about to move into the hall, a man knocked on his door. This one is smiling, David thought, as he remembered the officer from last night.

"I'm Detective Bush." The man held out his hand. "I've been assigned to the Anya Mitchell case."

David nodded, but stood silently.

"I understand that you're in charge." Even though

David was standing, the detective sat in a chair in front of the desk.

David followed the detective's lead. "Yes, I'll be running the office."

Detective Bush smiled. "I wanted to go over some things with you. We're finished with Ms. Mitchell's office, but I need to arrange a way to talk to the people who work here."

David frowned. "You don't think it was anyone here, do you?"

The detective waited a beat, and peered at David with hard eyes. "We don't rule *anyone* out." He paused, letting his words hang in the air. "But," he said, softening his tone, "I want to do some preliminary interviews. You never know what information people may be holding."

David swallowed, trying to dislodge the lump in his throat.

The detective stood. "I'll give you a call this afternoon after we put together a plan. Is that okay?"

David nodded again, and silently walked the detective to the door.

"By the way"— Detective Bush stopped suddenly — "I understand you found Ms. Mitchell."

"Yes," David breathed.

"When you came back to the office last night was the door locked?"

David blinked, trying to remember. "Yes, I think so."

The detective stared at him for a moment, then walked away.

David returned to his office and closed the door. Sitting at his desk, his trembling fingers flipped through his

Rolodex. He dialed the number, and was surprised when he was directly connected.

"This is David Montgomery."

He exchanged pleasantries before he got to the reason for his call. "I need some help." He paused, taking a breath. "I may need you to tell the police that I was with you last night. Would you be able to do that for me?"

Braxton zipped the small weekend bag and darted for the door, when the telephone rang.

He had barely picked up the receiver when Carlos's voice boomed through.

"Man, I heard what happened—"

Braxton's jaw tightened. "How did you find out?"

"You know Cia, William's wife. She works at the police station and saw some paperwork. I couldn't believe it. How's Anya?"

"As well as you'd expect."

"Does she know who . . . Have they arrested anyone?"

Braxton slumped onto his bed. "No."

"Man, if there is anything we can do. We were over here talking and couldn't decide if we should get together and try to find this bum or just get on our knees."

Braxton closed his eyes, hoping that when he opened them, this would all be over. "I was on my way back to Anya—"

"Okay, I won't hold you. One thing, do you want me to cancel your meeting with Benjamin this afternoon?"

Braxton opened his eyes. He'd forgotten. But he had to

move forward with the custody suit. He paused for only a moment. "Cancel the meeting. I'll call you tomorrow."

Braxton didn't even say good-bye. He dropped the phone into the cradle and while he sat with his head in his hands, the face appeared in his mind. The face without color or features or shape. The face that had taken his woman in the way that she had been preserving, saving, only for him. In his mind, he aimed for the face, and with one shot, the image would disappear forever.

Suddenly, he stood and ran into his bathroom. He spent five minutes over the toilet releasing his anguish. When he returned to his bedroom, he once again picked up the phone. His breathing was heavy as he waited to be connected.

"Hello, Detective Bush. My name is Braxton Vance and I understand you're working on the case for Anya Mitchell—she was . . . attacked last night." He paused. "I need to see you right away."

This was the first time Braxton had ever been inside a police station, and as he waited, he knew why. Uniformed officers with weapons casually strolled the brightly lit halls and, occasionally, he heard laughter from the enclosed offices. But he shared none of their cheer. He was only here to speak about Anya's case, yet Braxton shifted with nervousness. Strange, he thought. Must be a Black man's thing.

"Mr. Vance, I'm Detective Bush." The red-faced detective reached out his hand and smiled.

The gesture didn't make Braxton feel any better. He

nodded and followed the detective into a small office made tinier by the stacks of paper piled high on the desk.

"Thank you for taking the time to see me." Braxton sat in one of the metal chairs and crossed his legs.

The detective pulled a file from the top of one of the piles. "No problem," he responded, as he made a note, then peered at Braxton over his glasses. "I'm glad you called. I wanted to speak with you anyway."

Braxton folded his arms across his chest and waited for the detective to continue.

"I want to get a statement from Ms. Mitchell when she's up to it."

Braxton exhaled. "Of course. The reason I'm here is I wanted to know how this is going to work. How are you going to find the man who did this?"

The detective leaned back. "It's a process," Detective Bush explained patiently. "One thing we know is that in most rapes, the victim knows her attacker." He paused.

Braxton twisted in his seat.

"So we're going to speak to a lot of people."

Braxton coughed. "What about fingerprints?"

The detective frowned at the question, then looked down at the papers in front of him. "According to Ms. Mitchell, the man was gloved. But even if he wasn't, it wouldn't do much good. There are a lot of fingerprints in that office." The detective looked up. "Even yours, I'm sure."

Braxton stood. "Thank you for seeing me, Detective." He moved quickly toward the door.

"Mr. Vance?"

Braxton turned around.

"Where can I reach you if I need any more information?"

Braxton stared at the detective for a long moment. "I'll be staying with Ms. Mitchell."

The detective nodded and Braxton didn't breathe until he was in his car. It wasn't until then that he realized he hadn't told the detective about Anya's ring.

Too bad, he thought. I'm not going back in there. I'll call him.

As he pulled out of the parking lot, he sighed. Nothing about this was going to be easy.

Chapter 33

Darkness completely blanketed the room and Anya was sure that not even the moon shined tonight. She rolled over, and grimaced as a spark of pain shot through her. The red numerals on the clock screamed 3:17 and not one hour of sleep had relieved her.

She could hear Braxton's soft snore over her shoulder. He had insisted on staying and she hadn't tried to stop him. Dr. Young said that not only did she have to recover but everyone who loved her, especially Braxton, would have some healing to do too.

So at dinner, when Braxton had announced his plans to stay, Anya didn't protest. Especially not when all of them—Sasha, Madear, and Donovan—had insisted that it was a good idea. Madear and Donovan had left early, saying that she needed rest. But hours later, she still hadn't had one hour of sleep.

"Hold on, Anya," she whispered. "God is good and He is faithful." She repeated that thought over and over in her head.

But even through those words, she could see the silver

glitter of the blade pressed against her throat. And then she felt him. All over her.

She eased from the bed and walked softly to her bathroom. The faucet squeaked when she turned on the water, and within moments, there was a light tap on the door.

"I'm okay, Braxton," she said, through the closed door. "I just want to take a shower."

"Another one?"

She opened the door. "I thought it might help me sleep." She smiled to reassure him.

Creases of doubt wrinkled his face and she squeezed his hand. "I won't be long. Would you wait up for me?" she asked, already knowing that he would.

They hugged, then he left her alone. As she turned, she caught a glimpse of herself in the mirror, but instantly looked away. Swiftly, she tossed the XXL Hampton University T-shirt over her head, then stepped under the shower's tepid water. After a few minutes, she turned the hot knob, raising the temperature until her skin screamed. She stood under the spigot, keeping her face away from the rushing water, and closed her eyes. Her prayer was that somehow the water would cleanse her insides too.

"God is good and He is faithful."

It wasn't until she heard the tap on the door that she knew she had been in there too long. The fogged mirror hid her image, but she still turned away, while she dabbed at her body with the towel. Her fingertips had crinkled like an elderly woman's, and the bandage on her face was wet. But she was clean.

"God is good and He is faithful."

Braxton, dressed in a gray sweatsuit, was pacing the floor when she entered the bedroom.

"I'm fine," she said, running her hand along his anxious face. The spiky hairs of a new beard tickled her palm. He hadn't even taken the time to shave. Everything had become secondary to taking care of her. She smiled. "Let's go to bed."

He took her hand, but before she lay down, she picked up her Bible, then leaned back into his arms, sinking into his warmth.

Silently she said, "Speak to my heart, Lord." Then she opened the book. It fell to the Book of Psalms, and with Braxton's arms still around her, she slowly skimmed the scriptures until she got to Psalm 4, eighth verse. She smiled. She read the verse again and again. *I will both lay me down in peace, and sleep: for thou, Lord, only make me dwell in safety.*

"Braxton," she said finally. "Turn off the light, please. I'm ready to go to sleep."

Anya's eyelids fluttered. The bedroom was dark, and through the stillness, she felt Braxton next to her. She lay still, trying to remember what visions had invaded her dreams. But there was nothing to remember. God had promised her peace.

As she turned over, the gauze on her cheek rubbed against the pillow. She brushed her hand against the rough fabric. Yesterday afternoon, Braxton had changed the dressing for her. She had searched his face for a reaction—a grimace or something that would give her some indication of what the scar looked like. But he had been unreadable. Since then, she'd been adept at avoiding anything that would give her a reflection of her image. But now, she needed to see.

Gently she removed Braxton's arm from around her waist. He stirred in his sleep, but did not awaken. As she'd done a few hours before, she rose from the bed and tiptoed to the bathroom. She hoped this time Braxton would remain asleep.

The brightness of the fluorescent lights made her squint and it took a few moments for her eyes to adjust. But soon, she was able to stare at her reflection in the mirror.

There seemed to be nothing wrong with the woman who stared back—just slight swelling and scratches under her left eye. The bandage that covered most of the side of her face was really the only sign.

She took a deep breath before she lifted her hand and gently peeled back the tip of the gauze, pulling slowly until her entire face was exposed. A red-purple welt began under her eye and ended at the corner of her mouth. Her fingers traced the line. The doctors had asked her about the laceration, but she couldn't remember.

She closed her eyes, trying to bring back the memory, but all she saw was the glimmer of the blade.

She snapped opened her eyes. There was no need to return to the place she was trying so hard to escape.

She gently patted the bandage back in place. Then she returned to the bed as silently as she left it. It was 5:47. In less than an hour, sunlight would be seeping through the window—her signal to rise for work.

She closed her eyes. Everything inside told her to return to work when her scars had faded a bit more. Return when she was stronger. That's what she would do. Wait to regain all of her strength. In every way that she knew.

The heat of the morning sunlight awakened him; Braxton sat up with a start. It was Anya's face that made him remember. He glanced at the clock. How could it be almost ten? He had to wake up Anya, but the second before his hand touched her shoulder, he pulled back.

I'll just let her sleep, he thought. Braxton turned onto his stomach, resting on his elbows, and stared at Anya. She was sleeping on her side, her hands under her head. With the bandage hidden, there were few signs of her trauma.

He tried to imagine what she was dreaming about. Her face didn't show any signs of anguish, in fact, she looked like peace covered her.

He sighed and wondered if he would be able to put this behind him as easily as she seemed able to do. He didn't know how he would do it. His night had been filled with images of a faceless man, touching Anya, hurting her . . .

"Good morning." She smiled.

He hadn't noticed her opened eyes. "I was just going to wake you. You're late for work." He held his breath.

The ends of her lips turned down a bit. "I've decided not to go in today."

He couldn't hide his pleasure as he kissed her. "Good. I think you should rest." With energy that surprised him, he jumped from the bed. "I'm going to run home to get my laptop. Is there something you want to do?"

She sat up and pulled her T-shirt over her bent knees. "Actually, I was thinking about giving Pastor Ford a call."

When he remained silent, Anya continued. "I want to talk to her."

Braxton hesitated, then said, "That's a good idea." He had been standing at the foot of the bed, but now he sat next to her. "You can talk to me," he said softly.

She lowered her eyes. Braxton had been a blessing from the moment he rushed into the hospital. But this was one thing he couldn't solve for her. "I want to talk to her first," she said without lifting her eyes.

He hugged her. "Give her a call while I take a shower. I'll take you over there."

Anya smiled as Braxton walked into the bathroom. Funny, she thought, how this situation was actually bringing them closer. "Just God's way of turning something bad into good."

She reached for the phone to call her pastor.

Pastor Ford was waiting on the steps when Braxton stopped in front of the church. Anya was barely out of her car before the pastor wrapped her in her arms.

The sadness in Pastor Ford's eyes belied the smile on her face. "How are you, sweetie?" she asked softly.

Anya smiled. "I'm doing all right."

Braxton honked and they waved as he pulled away. In the pastor's office, Anya moved toward the chairs, but Pastor Ford took her hand and led her to the couch. There were tea cups and croissants set up on the table. They sipped and chatted for a few minutes before Anya said, "Thank you for seeing me right away, Pastor."

"I wanted to see you yesterday, but I thought you needed to rest." She pulled Anya into her arms. "You're going to make it through this."

Anya nodded. "I'm better than I ever thought I would be."

The pastor smiled. "That's because you're strong. Have you had a chance to talk to a counselor?"

Anya stood and walked to one of the bookcases overflowing with Bibles in every translation. Her eyes focused on one of the burgundy covers: *The Living Bible*.

"No," Anya finally responded. "I don't think I need counseling as long as I stay fixed on the Lord."

The pastor tilted her head. "That sounds like a pat answer, Anya."

Anya raised her eyebrows in surprise.

"There's no doubt God will get you through, but He puts all kinds of assistance vehicles on the road to bless us. In the case of rape, I think counseling is necessary."

Anya shook her head.

"Did you know that I used to be a rape counselor?"

Anya looked at the pastor with surprise. "I didn't know."

"It was some of the best times in my life—helping women through one of their most difficult times. But one thing I found was that it was especially hard to get Black women to accept counseling." The pastor stood and took Anya's hand. "We've been taught to hold in our feelings, keep a stiff upper lip and just move on. But, it doesn't have to be that way. You can scream, you can yell, you can kick, you can break down—do anything that you have to do. You have people who want to help you through this."

"I know that, Pastor. And I'm so grateful for you and Braxton and my grandmother. Everyone around me has been incredible. But while I know counseling can help, it's not what I need right now." Anya glanced away from the pastor. "My questions can't be answered by a counselor."

Pastor Ford nodded. "Okay." Her tone encouraged Anya to continue.

Anya turned toward the window, her back to Pastor Ford. "Pastor, have you ever been mad at God?" Her voice was barely a murmur.

The pastor chuckled slightly. "Plenty of times. Though as I've grown in Him I haven't experienced that because I know He's in charge of everything."

Still looking out the window, Anya said, "I'm not really mad. I just want to know why did . . . God let this happen?" Her shoulders tightened as she breathed the words.

"That's a good question, Anya."

Relieved, Anya faced the pastor. "I don't want to question God at all. I want to stand strong."

"Seems like you're doing a good job to me."

"I don't feel strong." The glitter of the blade flashed through her mind. She closed her eyes and tried to squeeze back tears. "Pastor, I have never been so scared in my life."

Pastor Ford took Anya's hand, trying to hold back her own tears, as she led Anya back to the chairs.

"I'm confused about how I'm supposed to feel. I don't want to feel sorry for myself and I don't want to question God, but I feel all of that. One moment, I'm having flashbacks and asking why me, and then the next, I'm in the shower, trying to find a way to praise God."

"This is normal, Anya," Pastor Ford began. "What you experienced *wasn't* normal. It is going to take quite a bit of time and a lot of prayer. You wouldn't believe the number of women I've had to counsel through this. And everyone reacts differently, so don't beat yourself up with what you're feeling."

Anya nodded. "I've even asked is God checking me or disciplining me for something?"

"Get that out of your mind!" Pastor Ford's eyes widened. "God doesn't operate that way."

"I know that in my head, but it's hard for me to reconcile this in my heart." Anya sighed. "I feel like a weak Christian."

"Anya, you were raped two days ago and you're acting as if you were supposed to walk around like nothing happened. Yes, you love the Lord, but that doesn't stop you from being human."

"I just want to know why this happened."

Pastor Ford took a Bible from her bookcase. "You're looking for answers and that's understandable. But God won't always give an explanation. He tells us that in Isaiah." The pastor turned to the scripture and read, "*For my thoughts are not your thoughts, neither are your ways my ways, saith the Lord. For as the heavens are higher than the earth, so are my ways higher than your ways, and my thoughts than your thoughts.*

"Someday, God may reveal what this is all about," the pastor continued. "But you may never know. All you need to know is that there are promises in the Word," she tapped the Bible on her lap, "that God will always fulfill. He is always faithful."

"That's why I feel so guilty about—"

Pastor Ford held up her hands, stopping Anya mid-sentence. "*There is therefore no condemnation to them which are in Christ Jesus,*" Pastor Ford said. "Guilt doesn't come from God."

Anya nodded. "I know that," she said softly.

"Anya, I want you to reconsider counseling."

"Pastor, the brochures that I got from the doctor talked

about how this wasn't my fault and that I shouldn't feel responsible—I know all of that. My questions are about staying strong in God. I'll be honest—my faith has been shaken and I hate feeling that."

Pastor Ford was thoughtful for a moment. "Why don't we get together for the next few days? We can talk, we can pray, and then in a week or so, you can decide what you want to do."

Anya hugged her pastor.

"There are some scriptures I want you to go over." Pastor Ford flipped through the Bible. "I give these to people who are doubting God."

"I don't doubt Him."

"Well, you're just having a little trouble understanding His ways. Jot down Psalms 18:30 and Psalms 34:19. And never forget one of my favorite scriptures: *We know that all things work together for good to them that love God, to them who are called according to His purpose.* That is you, my dear."

The pastor closed her Bible, then took Anya's hand, lifting her from the couch. "I want to pray for you." Pastor Ford placed her hand on Anya's forehead and began, "Heavenly Father, our awesome and powerful God, I pray for strength for Anya. She knows that you are with her, Father, and you know her heart. We don't have the answer, Lord, but you do. And, we rejoice because you said in your Word that you would give strength to your people, that you would bless your people with peace. So, now I ask, Lord, that your power be released here. Give Anya the strength and the peace that you promised . . ."

As Pastor Ford continued her prayer, Anya's head fell back and she felt her blood run warm. The power of God was with her, and Anya knew that if she continued to believe, His power would always be there.

Braxton held Anya's arm as they walked up the stairs, steadying her as if she were disabled.

"Honey, I can walk by myself."

"I want you to be careful," he insisted. "This was your first time out."

She sighed but decided not to resist him, even though it was more difficult for them to move.

As they walked up the steps, they could hear Sasha's voice. "Wait, David, I hear them coming now."

Sasha covered the phone's mouthpiece with her hand. "Anya, it's David—"

Braxton shook his head before Sasha could finish. "No, she's not up to it yet."

Anya rolled her eyes. "Thanks, Sasha, give me the phone."

"Baby, you need to rest."

"As soon as I get off the phone."

He held his hand up and backed away.

"Anya, it is so good to speak to you," David said. "How are you?"

She smiled at the sound of his voice. "I'm doing great. How's everything in the office?"

"Everyone is very concerned, but I know they'll feel better once I tell them I spoke to you. I would love to see you."

Her hand grazed the bandage on her face. "Give me a few days."

His silence told her that he understood.

Anya could hear Braxton's whispers in the kitchen, and she took the phone into the bathroom. She closed the door, but didn't turn on the light. "David, everyone tells me that you . . . helped me. I can't tell you how much—"

"Anya, I really didn't do anything."

"But you found me, and got me to the hospital. Thank you."

There was silence before he said, "I would do anything for you, Anya."

She took a deep breath at his words, then turned on the light. "The Linden enrollment—how is that going?" she asked, needing to change the tone.

"Fine." Anya could tell he was a bit surprised by her question. "Alaister and his team are going over there this morning," David continued. "I have something to do. I'll join them later . . ." His voice trailed off as if he were searching for words to say. "Everything else is fine."

"Thank you for handling things. I should be back in a few days . . ."

"Take all the time you need. I will be here for you. There is one thing, though." He hesitated. "I've spoken to the leasing people. Anya, if you want to move the office, I can take care of that before you come back."

Anya frowned. She hadn't thought of that. She closed her eyes, trying to envision her office, but her mind's canvas was blank. How would she feel going back to that place? "No. We can't move everything now. I'll be fine . . . in a few days."

"Okay. The building is going to be adding security."

"That's good."

More silent seconds passed between them.

"David, thank you again—"

The knock startled her. "Anya, are you all right?" Braxton raised his voice through the door.

"David, I have to go," she spoke quickly. "I'll call you tomorrow." She clicked off the phone and leaned against the door.

"Anya?"

She took a deep breath. "Yes, Braxton. I'm fine." She turned off the light.

Chapter 34

It had been a few days, and he still hadn't seen her. As he straightened his tie in the mirror, the ring caught his eye. He lifted it from the table.

"Evidence."

It was time for him to do something with this. Although he was very careful with who he allowed in his space, the ring was incriminating. He was too smart to make any mistakes.

He held the ring in front of the window twisting and turning it, marveling at the way the sun's rays set off the jewel. He was sure that she was missing it.

"What am I going to do with you?" he said aloud. He tried to develop a plan to return it to her, but it would be too dangerous.

He looked at the clock, then stuffed the ring into his pocket. He had to hurry or he would be late for his appointment.

He drove seven miles away from his front door. His eyes searched the street until he found what he was looking for. He parked his car, leaving the engine running, *and trotted to the large blue Dumpster. Looking around, he pulled the ring from his pocket and tossed it inside.*

    He was surprised at the pounding of his heart as he drove away. No problem, it was probably just the excitement of completion. Now there was only one thing left and that was to see her again.

Chapter 35

A mist hovered in the bathroom. Anya used her palm to wipe a small space on the mirror. She stopped when she saw her left cheek.

With slow, steady hands, she gently pulled back the gauze. She stared at the wound for several minutes before she replaced the material. No, she thought. There was no way she could go to church without the bandage. But there was no way she could go to church with it.

For days, her anxiety over the facial bandage had limited her movements. Besides Pastor Ford's office, she had made only one quick trip through a Jack-in-the-Box drive-thru. Even she was surprised that she had stayed away from her office, talking only to David and deflecting all offers and efforts to see her. Staying close to home warded off the stares she was sure would come.

The bathroom door opened and Braxton walked in. "Good morning." He yawned. "You should have woken me up. We're going to be late for church."

When he put his arms around her, she tightened the towel around her mid-section. "I was thinking . . . maybe we don't have to go to church today."

The mist was beginning to dissipate and she saw his confused reflection in the mirror. Without words, he asked her why.

"I don't want to go, with this." She raised her hand to her face.

His eyes softened. With his arms still around her waist, he pulled her close. "There's nothing wrong with the way you look, Anya. You're beautiful."

His words comforted her. Though she had discussed a myriad of subjects with Pastor Ford—from how she felt at the time of the attack, to what her fears were for the future—she had thoroughly blocked out thoughts of the facial scar that would forever be a reminder of that night.

Braxton pulled away with a smile on his face and said, "I have an idea. Get dressed. And don't ask me any questions." Before she could say a word, he added, "Dress warmly, and take your Bible." He playfully pushed her from the bathroom. "It won't matter where we are, we're going to have church this morning."

Braxton wrapped the large blanket around Anya's shoulders. Then he laid the pillow against the rock and sat next to Anya. Less than twenty feet away, the morning surf crashed against the lower rocks on the Santa Monica shore and Anya shivered.

"Maybe it's too cold," Braxton said, as he joined Anya under the blanket.

Anya nodded. "But I don't want to be anywhere else." She scooted closer to him.

He put one gloved hand around her and, with the other hand, opened the Bible on his lap. "Is there anything you want to study this morning?"

She smiled. "I'm going to leave this all to you."

"Well, I've thought about it, but first, let's pray." Before they bowed their heads, Braxton took Anya's hand into his. "Heavenly Father, we come to you this morning, not in our usual place of worship, but to worship you nonetheless. We thank you, Lord, for all of the blessings that you continue to pour over us. We know, Father, that without you, we wouldn't have made it through this tough time. We love you, Lord, and we stand in awe of your power and glory."

As Braxton prayed, Anya squeezed his hand. She felt closer to Braxton now than she ever had, and she wondered if this were God's message.

"So today, Father, we just want to come before you and not think about ourselves or what we've been through. But we want to worship you for who you are and to give you praise for all you have done, in Jesus Christ's name. Amen."

She kissed him. "I love you," Anya said.

He lifted her hand and kissed it, then rubbed his finger along the place where her ring used to be. "We have to do something about this."

She shook her head. "This is not the time to think about that."

He nodded, pulled her back into his arms and opened his Bible.

Sasha was relieved when the garage door rose and Braxton's car was gone. She parked, then gathered her packages, putting the *Los Angeles Times* on top, and struggled into the house.

It was quiet when she entered the living room, and when she scurried upstairs, she confirmed that she was alone.

She let the bundle slip from her arms, onto the bed. Her intent was to find a suit or two—something appropriate for interviewing. But as usual, she skipped on moderation and drove away from Beverly Hills with five new outfits.

"One for each day of the week." She laughed as she shook the purple-and-red suit from the Escada garment bag.

After days of tears, today was her first good day. Anya was getting better and Hunter . . . well, it had been four days since the Victory Awards and no calls. But she didn't fault him; he told her it was just a sex thing. Obviously, a couple of weeks was long enough.

It was time for her to get over it. And that's what she planned to do. First a job, then a place of her own. Los Angeles was the perfect place to delve into this season of self-discovery. No one knew her. All she had was Anya and Madear.

Sasha smiled at the thought of her grandmother. They'd spoken every day, chatting like girlfriends. And although most of their conversations were about Anya, Sasha knew that Madear was calling to check on her too. Each day, Madear ended the calls with words that warmed her.

"I love you, baby," Madear always said. "I want you to know that I'm proud of you."

It was the new beginning with Madear that made Sasha realize she needed to clean up every aspect of her life—starting with the basics. And she'd leave men alone! At least for now.

She hung the last of the clothes, then picked up the newspaper. As her fingers skimmed the countless small squares of employment opportunities, Sasha mused, "Maybe I should start with an apartment."

Before she had a chance to turn to the real-estate section, the phone rang. With her eyes still plastered on the paper, she picked up the receiver.

"Anya?"

"No, this is Sasha, her cousin."

"Is Anya there? This is Pastor Ford."

The announcement made Sasha sit up straight. "Hello, Pastor. Anya's not here."

"Okay. Well, please tell her I called."

Sasha sighed when she clicked off the phone. Even though she had vowed to stay away, church had found its way to her. A moment later, the phone rang again, and Sasha wondered what the pastor had forgotten.

"Yes, Pastor Ford?"

"Sasha?"

A lump choked her vocal cords.

"This is Hunter."

She was silent as options ran through her mind. Should she go off, revisiting her best Jerry Springer personality? Or should she be a classy, I-couldn't-care-less kind of gal? Without time to decide, she simply said, "Hi," in a voice that didn't commit.

"How are you?" he asked, as if he'd seen her yesterday.

"Fine." She still had not made a commitment.

"Let's get together this afternoon."

It took a moment for his words to register. Without any

mention of what happened, she was supposed to just fall in line.

"Why would we want to do that?" She chose the casual, classy tone.

"'Cause I miss you, baby," he whined in the voice that a few days ago would have made her melt. "I've had a few things I had to take care of, but now it's time for me to get back to my life and that means seeing you."

"Hunter." She stated his name in the sweetest tone she could muster. "Remember when you said this was just about sex? Well, you were right. It was good, babe, but it's done. I've moved on to new territories." Sasha barely suppressed a giggle as she imagined Hunter's facial contortions. But a moment later, she stopped when he laughed.

"That's a good one, Sasha. Come on, what time should I pick you up?"

She stood and paced alongside her bed. "This is not a joke, Hunter." Her casualness was gone. "I don't want to see you."

Several beats went by before he said, "Oh, you're mad because we didn't hang out after the Victory Awards. I told you I had to take care of some business."

"Did that include Lyza Easton?" The question slipped before she could stop herself. She punched her fist against her thigh.

"I'm an actor, Sasha. There are things I have to do if I want to be successful."

Sasha shook her head at his gall. "It's time for us to say good-bye, Hunter."

"I can't believe you're angry about a little thing like that."

Sasha wondered if Hunter heard himself. Or was she so insignificant that it didn't matter how she felt?

When she remained silent, he said, "So you want to throw away everything we have just because of the other night?"

What they had left her curled up on the bathroom floor. Her shoulders slumped at the memory. "It's a lot more than just the other night, Hunter, but we don't need to go into it. So, adios, ciao, whatever language you speak, good-bye."

There was a long pause before he said, "Do you think I care if you walk away?" He spat the words like darts through the phone. "Let me tell you something, Sasha. After I hang up, I'll be able to dial any number and get any woman I want."

"Then you need to start dialing." This was the point where she knew she should slam the receiver down.

Hunter chuckled. "Do you think you're ever going to be with someone like me again?"

"I hope not!"

It was Hunter who slammed the phone in her ear.

"Argh!" Sasha screamed as she clicked off the phone. She swung around and almost bumped into Anya. "Oh, I'm sorry." Sasha tossed the cordless phone onto the nightstand. "I didn't hear you come in."

"I'm not surprised; you were screaming." Anya sat down next to Sasha. "Doesn't sound like things are going well with you and Hunter."

Sasha rolled her eyes. "Just say it. 'I told you so, Sasha,'" she said in a high-pitch tone, mimicking Anya. Sasha punched one of the pillows beside her. "You were right about him."

"I wish I wasn't. What happened?"

"Nothing—except the things you said would happen.

It was like I was disappearing under his spell. I was wearing certain clothes because of him and . . ." Sasha paused, and ran her hand over her head, remembering just how far she'd gone. She sighed deeply before she continued. "I feel like I'm a fly trap for dysfunctional, egomaniacal men. So, I'm changing my scent. I've had it with Hunter. In fact, I'm going to leave all men alone."

"That's hard to believe."

"At least until I decide what *I* need to do." She paused and grinned at Anya. "What would you think about your cousin becoming a native?"

Anya smiled widely. "You're going to stay? That's wonderful."

"This is a good place to start over. No one knows me, but I still have you and Madear." She paused. "Speaking of Madear—" Sasha scooted closer to Anya as if she were about to tell a secret. "She apologized to me. Not just for the other day, but it was almost like an apology that covered the years. I can't tell you how good it made me feel."

Anya thought about her conversation with Madear. "I told you she loved you."

Suddenly Sasha's face changed, her eyebrows knitted together. "I've been talking about me. How're you doing?"

"Pretty good," Anya said. She stood and walked to the dresser where Sasha had framed photographs lined in front of the mirror. There was one that had been taken over twenty-five years before, where she and Sasha stood between their mothers. Anya picked up the silver frame and ran her fingers along her mother's face. "Talking with Pastor Ford really helps. She's reminding me of who I am."

"I'll tell you who you are—you're unbelievable! I know I wouldn't be this strong if it happened to me."

Anya sighed. "Believe me, I have my moments. I feel like I'm in the middle of a tight circle surrounded by every emotion possible. Two steps in either direction, and I could become angry, or depressed or sad. But I'm hanging right there in the center. I'm keeping my focus on God."

"So, God is your solution, huh?"

"He's the only solution I got. I believe *in* God, and I *believe* God, no matter what I'm going through. He's going to make sure I get to the other side."

"I'm surprised you don't have a scripture for that." Sasha smirked.

"Isaiah 43:2."

They laughed.

"And I read that scripture every day, just to remind myself."

"You are amazing."

"It's God who's amazing. People say that God is good and He is, but what keeps me, is that God is God. He never lets me down."

Sasha crossed her legs under her and let her elbows rest on her knees. "I wish I could be more like you."

"There's nothing wrong with you, kiddo."

"I mean, the way God works for you. I wish He could do the same thing for me." Sasha raised her hand before Anya could open her mouth. "I know what you're going to say. But God doesn't work for me like He does for you."

"That's not true, Sasha. He's there for everyone. The Bible says that we all know Him in our hearts."

Sasha shook her head, then bounced from the bed. "I was looking through the newspaper before Hunter called." She ignored the disappointed look on Anya's face. "I'm going to have some interviews this week. You can count on that."

Anya opened her mouth, then bit her lip. She walked toward the door. "Sasha, I hope I can count on you joining me in church next Sunday. If you have questions, Pastor Ford can help you find the answers."

Sasha smiled but said nothing as Anya left the room. She didn't have the heart to tell her cousin that was one thing she couldn't count on.

Chapter 36

You know, Pastor Ford, the day that Braxton and I were here for counseling and he told me about his son, I thought I'd never face anything tougher."

Pastor Ford smiled and tapped her fingertips against her desk.

"I didn't think I'd laugh or be happy again," Anya continued. "But things are really good, Pastor."

Pastor Ford suddenly stopped tapping her fingers. "Anya, describe to me how you're feeling."

Anya laid her hands on the arms of the chair. "Well, I'm beginning to feel grounded. What happened doesn't occupy every space of my mind anymore. I think about other things and I'm thinking about going back to work."

"That's terrific, Anya." But the pastor lost her smile as she came from around her desk. The pastor sighed deeply before she said, "There is one thing I want to talk about." She took Anya's hands. "We've had three sessions now, and you've never said that you were raped."

Anya silently stared at the pastor.

Pastor Ford said, "Before you leave today, I want you to say it."

Anya opened her mouth, then closed it, shaking her head.

"Anya, once you say it aloud, you'll be free. The act of what happened will lose its control over you."

Anya folded her arms. "I've said it over and over, Pastor." She stood so quickly, her chair almost tipped over. "All we've talked about is that I was attacked. That's why I'm here."

Pastor Ford ignored Anya's anger. "I'm not talking about *attack*—I'm talking about *rape*. It worries me that you refuse to acknowledge what happened to you."

"I know what happened."

"Then say it."

After a few moments, Anya's shoulders slumped and Pastor Ford took her hand, leading her back to the chair. "I can't say it," she whispered. "If I say it, Pastor, then there'll be a lot of questions I'll have to answer. Like did I do everything I could that night?" Her voice trembled.

"Anya, you did what you were supposed to do—you survived!" She let her words settle in. "Rape is a terrible thing, and no one wants to be a part of it. But you already know that you didn't cause this. And, you know that you survived because of God. Now, you have to release it."

Silent minutes passed before the pastor shook her head and said, "All right, I just wanted to bring it to your attention."

Pastor Ford took Anya's hands, bowed her head and began to pray.

Anya closed her eyes and tried to stop the trembling that was beginning deep inside. Within seconds, the shaking reached her skin; every inch of her body quivered.

But Pastor Ford continued to pray, not stopping even when sobs heaved from Anya's chest.

"Let her feel your power, Father." Pastor Ford raised her voice and gripped Anya's hands tighter. "Free her from the hold that still controls her. You said in your word that *if the Son therefore shall make you free, ye shall be free indeed.* So I pray, in Jesus' name, that Anya be freed here, Lord."

The pastor began to pray in the spirit and Anya's sobs became louder.

"Oh, God. How could this happen to me?" Anya cried.

The pastor looked up.

"Pastor, how could I have been raped?"

Pastor Ford held Anya in her arms for the next hour, ignoring the knocks on her door and the ringing of the phone.

Finally when Anya was able to lift her head, Pastor Ford said, "This is a good day." She lifted Anya's chin with her finger. "I think you can go home now."

Chapter 37

From inside his car, Braxton waved at Anya, standing at the window as he pulled out of the garage. He took his time shifting gears from reverse to drive, watching her for a few moments longer, trying to decide if the smile on her face was genuine. He was still unsure when he drove away.

He didn't know what to think. Seven days had sped by since Anya's attack, yet she didn't seem to be recovering at the same speed. She hadn't returned to work, spending most of her mornings with Pastor Ford and her afternoons reading, resting, or running on Venice Beach. This was not what he expected from his high-powered fiancée.

How could he help her get past all of this? Though he craved answers, none were coming from her. They'd almost argued last night when he pushed.

"Anya, I'm really worried about you," he had said.

Anya had been stretched out on the chaise. She smiled before she said, "There's nothing for you to worry about. I keep telling you I'm fine."

"Okay," he said, joining her on the chair. "Then talk to

me. Tell me what you feel. Tell me what you talk to Pastor Ford about."

She closed the book on her lap and looked thoughtful. "We talk about how I feel better every day and how I'm finding a way to put this behind me. We talk about how I'm getting my life back to normal."

Normal! he wanted to scream. There was nothing normal about this.

He had chuckled bitterly at the irony. For months, he had done everything to get Anya away from her business. Now she'd done that, but it didn't make him happy. It was as if she had been raped of her will—she'd lost her volition to fight and he didn't like that at all.

"Why don't you watch the Lakers game?" That was her signal that the conversation was over and she returned to one of the novels he'd brought her from Zahra's Book Store that afternoon.

Pouting, he had returned to bed, turned off the television, and stared at Anya. But she never lifted her head, and he'd finally fallen asleep.

This morning, she had acted as if nothing had happened. They had jogged, then had brunch on Venice Beach. When they returned home, he'd worked for hours, while she slept. The only good news was that the bandage had been removed and Dr. Young had been pleased to hear that Anya was spending time with her pastor.

Braxton squirmed in his seat. "I need to do something!" he exclaimed, and picked up his cell phone. Pastor Ford could tell him what was going on. But he put the phone back in the holder before he even pressed the first button. Pastor Ford wouldn't tell him anything. But there was one place where he could go to get all the answers he needed.

"What are you doing here, baby?" Madear shouted from the opened screen door.

Braxton trotted across the bald lawn and up the three porch steps. He kissed Madear's cheek. "I wanted to check on you."

"Don't give me that." She chuckled. "I just hung up from Anya and she said you were going to get you guys something to eat. What am I? One of those fast-food places?"

"You got me. I wanted to speak to you."

"Well, come on in."

He followed her inside, and was immediately struck by a pleasant fragrance. Today it was one of Madear's multi-layered coconut cakes, overflowing with frosting, and Braxton had to stop himself from begging for a piece right then.

When they settled onto the couch, Madear asked, "So what do you want to know about Anya?"

Braxton forgot about the cake in the kitchen. "I didn't say this was about her." He shifted against the plastic cover.

"Boy, do you think you can fool me? What's bothering you, baby?"

Braxton placed his elbows on his knees. "I'm worried about her."

Madear frowned slightly. "She looked fine yesterday, and just now when I spoke to her, she was talking about the wedding and things. I think she's coming along nicely."

"How can you say that, Madear?" He paced the floor. "She's not herself. She won't go to work . . ."

Madear chuckled. "Isn't this something? All the grief you've given Anya about her business, I'd thought you'd be happy that she decided to rest awhile."

Braxton stopped in the middle of the floor.

Madear waved her hand at him. "Anya told me all about your . . . discussions."

"It's not that I don't want her to work," Braxton started to explain, but Madear held her hand up.

"That's between you and her. But you're thinking that since she hasn't jumped right back into everything, something's wrong. She's not reacting the way you expected."

"Madear, I thought Anya would have leapt into her work full-force. I thought that's what I would be complaining about."

"Has she told you why she hasn't gone back to work?" Madear asked.

"She said it's because of the bandage on her face."

Madear nodded. "That's what she told me. And it made sense to me, but it doesn't to you?"

"They took the bandage off yesterday and she still hasn't said anything."

Madear rubbed her hand along his back. "She is going to be fine, Braxton. I think she's doing the right thing for once. She's not putting that business first."

"I guess I didn't know what to expect. The first few days, I thought she'd cry or scream or want to talk about what happened constantly. But she won't talk to me about it at all."

"Give her time with that, sweetie. It took a mighty long time for me to talk when it happened to me."

Braxton leaned back and stared at Madear.

She shook her head. "The details don't matter. It was so many years ago, before I was married. I was a colored girl in Texas, working after school for the white man who owned the general store. So they certainly didn't call it rape."

Her words sounded matter-of-fact to Braxton. "Does Anya know?"

Madear squinted her eyes trying to remember. "I think so, but it doesn't matter. This is different. All you need to know is that it takes time. And everyone reacts in a different way; there is no textbook response. I shut down and couldn't go to school or work for weeks. Some people are so angry that they lash out at everyone around them. Anya is handling this her way and there are probably people who would look at her and say her reaction is not strong enough. As many women as there are in the world—that's how many reactions you'll get. Anya's fine. Just be grateful that she has Pastor Ford."

Braxton sighed deeply. "I just want her to know that I'm there for her too."

"She knows that, and she is grateful. But she also needs your patience."

"I'm trying . . ."

"Braxton, let me tell you something about the women in our family. From my grandmother to Anya, we are women who know how to triumph. Victory is in her genes—she's an overcomer. As much as I hate to think about what happened to my baby that night, I rejoice because I know who she is. She is reaching way down inside and pulling up what she has. Don't worry, she is leaning on you." Madear paused, and took Braxton's face in her hands. "But know one thing, Braxton. While Anya needs you, she needs the Lord more. And that's who is really getting her through. The Holy Spirit is ministering to her and counseling her."

Braxton allowed Madear's words to settle into him, then he hugged her. "Thank you, *Grandmother.*"

Tears filled her eyes. "Oh, baby, I love you like you were my own grandson."

He kissed her. "Let me get back to Anya." He stood, but Madear took his hand.

"Let me get you some cake, baby."

Braxton's grin was wide.

"You can eat it in the car. This way, Anya will never know that you were here checking up on her."

He smiled shyly, but eagerly followed Madear into the kitchen.

Anya stabbed at the chicken on her plate. She hadn't taken a bite of either the chicken or the potato salad. Without lifting her head, she peered at Braxton through lowered eyes. His eyes were downcast, as he read the newspaper spread out on the table in front of him.

She took a deep breath. "I'm going back to work tomorrow."

The chicken thigh was halfway to his mouth and he held it there, before he dropped in onto the plate. "Actually, I think that's good. But since tomorrow is Thursday, why don't you give yourself the weekend and go back on Monday?"

"No," she said firmly. "Tomorrow is better."

He nodded. "Okay. I'm just looking out for you."

"Well, there's no need for that." She walked behind him, and put her hands on his shoulders. "It's time for you to go home . . . tonight," she said, reaching down and putting her arms completely around him.

He pushed away from the table and turned to face her. "Anya, no, I don't—"

She kissed him before he could continue. "You have to go so that I can get back to normal."

"What does my being here have to do with that?"

"I need to be by myself now. Do you understand?"

Braxton moved away from her embrace. "*I* need to be here with you, Anya," he said with his back to her. "I wasn't there when . . ." He paused, then looked back at her.

"Braxton, nothing that happened is your fault. You've been with me through every part that counts and I thank God for you." She walked to him and took his hands again. "But the next steps, I have to take by myself."

When he began to protest, she gently covered his mouth with her hand.

"It's been a week and that's enough time for both of us. You were with me for all the right reasons, but if you stay any longer—"

"Please don't tell me this is because of God."

"It's because it's time." She smiled at him. "And Braxton, it's time for you to get back to your life—to writing, and figuring out what you're going to do with Junior." His eyes told her he was not convinced. "I'm not going to be talked out of this."

Braxton pursed his lips in anger, then paused. These had been emotion-packed days, and he didn't want to end with an argument. He sat back down and they finished dinner in silence.

After they cleared the table, Braxton took Anya's hand and they went up to her bedroom. He folded his clothes slowly, stuffing them inside his bag. As he packed, arguments raged through his mind, words to persuade Anya that he had to stay. But he kept it all to himself. The way Anya sat on the edge of the bed, with that stiff smile, let him know that her determination would win.

He took his time, wanting to hold onto each minute. It was more than just protecting her. It was the closeness they'd developed that he didn't want to slip away.

When it came to the point where he could no longer stall, he sat on the bed and pulled Anya into his arms. "Forgive me for loving you too much."

She squeezed him tighter. "I'll never forgive you for that. It makes me love you more."

He reached into the side pocket of his bag and pulled out a velvet box. "I was waiting for the right moment . . ." He looked at her with glassed eyes, then opened the box revealing a glittering diamond.

Anya gasped. "Oh, my God."

Braxton lifted the ring and held it in front of Anya. "I wanted to give you something really special this time because of all we've been through."

Slowly he slipped the ring onto her finger. The large round stone glistened, but it was the blue stones that surrounded the diamond that made her look at Braxton with tears in her eyes.

"I read somewhere that God gave Moses the Ten Commandments on sapphire tablets," Braxton said. "I don't know if that's true, but I wanted this ring to symbolize more than just our engagement." He took her hand into his. "These three sapphires represent our life together. Our past, present, and this larger one, that's our future."

"Braxton, this is beautiful," she whispered. "But what about—"

He smiled and held a finger to her lips. "I don't want my fiancée walking around without a ring. I'll get the insurance money for the other one. Don't worry."

She hugged him.

"Oh, there is one thing." He pulled away and looked into her eyes. "Anya Mitchell, will you marry me?"

She smiled. "The first chance we get."

He kissed her, then they held hands as they walked down the stairs.

"Braxton, I wouldn't have made it through this without you," Anya said, rubbing her lips against his.

"I will always take care of you."

"Promise?"

He nodded and kissed the top of her head. "I wouldn't live my life without you."

Anya let him tarry for a few minutes more, before she playfully shoved him through the door. She watched as he laggardly made his way to the car, then drove away.

She turned off the lights, then ran up the stairs, resisting the urge to knock on Sasha's door. It was time for her to face the night. As she lay on her bed, she held her hand in front of her, staring at the ring. And she knew then that her life was going to be fine.

She reached for her Bible, but exhaustion hung heavy over her. Instead she rolled from the bed, and fell to her knees.

"Father, all I can say is thank you. I thank you, for how

far you've brought me and for how you're going to take me all the way through. I thank you for blinding the negative images from my mind so that now, I can barely remember. I thank you for being Jehovah-Shalom, my peace." She lingered in the silence for a few moments, feeling the calming presence of the Lord surround her. "And tonight, Lord, for the first time I am alone physically, but you are here. I know there is nothing for me to fear, because you said you are always with me."

Even when she climbed into the bed and pulled the covers over her, she continued to meditate on the Lord. At first, she left the lights on but after only a few minutes, she turned them off. She lay back in the darkness and closed her eyes, knowing that God would answer her prayers. Just like He already had.

Chapter 38

The BMW's engine trembled as it sat idling, and finally Anya turned off the windshield wipers. A surprise storm had sneaked into the city in the middle of the night and continued, leaving the L.A. streets filled with chaos. Anya had crawled up LaBrea behind slow-moving cars and arrived at her office thirty minutes later than she planned.

Her hands shook when she turned off the ignition. She closed her eyes and whispered, "Lord, fill me with your strength."

Her heels on the concrete mixed with the rain that pelted against the building. When the elevator doors opened and she stepped inside, she let her eyes focus on the red numbers overhead as she rose alone to the seventeenth floor. I need your strength, she said silently.

She was still calling on God when the elevator doors opened. She soaked in the familiarity of the burgundy carpet and wood paneling. It seemed like a lifetime had passed since she walked down this hall. The corridor stretched long in front of her, and she moved like a robot until she stood in front of the doors of her business. This was a part

of her life that she had been proud of. But she wasn't sure
how she would feel once she was on the other side.

With a deep breath, she opened the door and stepped
into the reception area. She heard only the soft sound of
a computer printer's purr. Anya took slow steps, finally
entering the main part of the office.

"Anya!" Dianna jumped from her desk. "We didn't
know you were coming back today! I wanted to call you so
many times, but David said you were resting, and I'm so
sorry about what happened. I just couldn't believe it—"

In that moment, Anya felt normal. She held up her
hand and laughed. "Di-an-na!"

Dianna stopped and smiled. "Sorry."

"Thanks for making me feel like nothing's changed."
Anya hugged her, and then with a more confident step
headed to her office. The door was slightly ajar, and for a
moment, she stood at the edge of the entryway. Her eyes
darted from one corner of the room to the next.

"Who did this?" she said without turning around.

"The maintenance people, but it was Braxton's idea.
He had us do it just a few days after . . ."

The furniture had been completely turned around; the
desk now faced the window and the bookcases had been
moved to the opposite walls. Even her pictures and diplo-
mas and awards hung on a different wall. And the office
had been painted—a faint lavender.

She moved hesitantly; her eyes scanned the furniture and
carpet for telltale signs, but there were none. All evidence
had been erased—as if what happened, never happened.

She moved from her desk to the window and looked
down the seventeen floors to Wilshire Boulevard, where
cars as small as toys crept through the rain. The ghosts that

she feared were not here. She exhaled the deep breath that she didn't even realize she'd been holding inside.

"Welcome back."

She smiled before she turned around. David was standing in the doorway, leaning against the post, with his arms folded as if he had been watching her for a while. He moved toward her, and kissed her on the cheek. Anya closed her eyes and inhaled his scent. It felt good to be back.

"I'm glad to see you. How're you?" he asked softly.

"I'm fine." Without thinking, she brought her hand to her face and felt the gentle bump of the fading line.

His hand followed hers and rested gently on her cheek. "You look great."

Her face warmed at his words. She looked at him, as his hand remained on her face, and it was only when Dianna coughed that they remembered they were not alone. He dropped his hand.

"Do you like your office, Anya?" Dianna asked.

Anya stepped back, putting space between her and David. Her eyes roamed the room again. "It's great. Thank you for taking care of this for me."

Dianna grinned. "I'm going back to my desk. But let me know when you have a few moments. I have a ton of things to go over with you." Dianna paused. "It's so good to have you back," she gushed.

Anya smiled, and nodded. She and David were silent until Dianna closed the door.

"There was no one in this office more concerned about you than Dianna," David said. "Except for me."

The way his dark eyes bored into hers made her look away from his gaze.

"I really wanted to come by and see you," David continued as Anya settled into one of the chairs in front of her desk.

"I know, but it was better this way." She crossed her legs and looked around the office. "It is good to be back, though."

When David sat in the chair opposite her, he took her hand. "So you're doing all right?"

Anya shifted in her seat, but did not pull away. "I'm doing fine. David, I want to thank you. If you hadn't found me—"

He shook his head. "You've already thanked me and I told you I did nothing."

"You saved my life and I am so grateful."

He dropped his eyes, as he pulled away from her. "No, I didn't. If it wasn't me, someone else would have found you." He raised his eyes. "I'm glad I was there."

Anya tried to find a comfortable spot in her chair. "I'm anxious to get back to work. But are you sure you want me back?" Anya tried to make her voice sound light. "You've been in charge for so long, I might just get in the way."

David smiled. "You may be back, but nothing's going to change. I can handle things. So you can relax."

A few weeks ago his assured tone would have sounded patronizing. But she knew him better now.

She sorted through the messages Dianna had neatly lined on her desk. "It looks like I'll have little time to relax. There are a million messages from Mr. Greene."

David sighed. "He's been calling nonstop, insisting on speaking to you. He even tried to browbeat Dianna into giving up your home number."

"I'll give him a call later this morning."

"Maybe *I* should call him back. I really don't like the way he . . . badgers you."

"He's harmless. I'll call him."

David rested his hand on her arm. "I'm here for anything you need. I really don't want you to rush back."

His words were the same as Braxton's and Madear's, yet they were different.

"Work is the best thing for me." A door slammed and Anya flinched.

"Sounds like the troops are arriving," he said, ignoring her nervousness. "Everyone's going to want to come in and say hello."

Anya stood and walked to the window. The chill that was outside seemed to have made its way into her office.

"I could call a staff meeting," David said, following her. "That way, you can talk to everyone at once."

His voice made her feel safe. "Maybe we can do that later this morning. I need to spend some time with Dianna."

When she turned to face him, they were so close she could almost feel the movement of his chest. She shook her head and turned away.

He stepped back. "I'll be in my office." He coughed.

She took his hand, stopping him. "Thank you . . . for everything."

He looked down at their entwined hands, then raised his eyes to hers. "I would do anything for you, Anya." A long moment passed before he pulled away and left his words dangling in the charged air.

She stared at the door that he closed behind him, then shook her head. It had to be her imagination—the tension between them. He was just trying to be a friend.

Slowly she walked to her desk and let her eyes move

again through the room, soaking up every corner, angle, and crevice. Alone, she waited for the terror but felt only the comfort of silence. A smile came to her face. God always answered prayers.

She buzzed her intercom. "Dianna, give me five minutes, then come in. I need you to catch me up on everything."

The moment she released the buzzer, her phone rang. When Dianna buzzed and said it was Braxton, she immediately picked up the phone.

"Hey, honey." She spoke blithely, knowing that he would be listening to every nuance in her voice. She was surprised that it had taken him so long to call.

"I bet you think I'm checking on you."

They laughed together.

"I was reading my Bible and ran across something that I want to read to you."

Smiling, Anya reached for the Bible on the corner of her desk. She still suspected his motives, but she loved his methods.

He began reading the scripture. "*Do not be surprised at the painful trial you are suffering, as though something strange were happening to you. But rejoice that you participate in the sufferings of Christ so that you may be overjoyed when his glory is revealed.* Sweetheart, I've read this scripture a million times, but this morning, it was like God shined His light in my face. We can't be surprised at . . . what happened to you. We just have to know that there was a reason behind all of this."

She felt a heat in her eyes, like tears were going to come and she didn't know why. All she knew was that in the middle of that moment, she was filled with a fullness of joy that warmed even the soles of her feet. She was blessed with a man who knew God. A man who could pray for her and stand with her. A man that God could use to deliver His messages.

They chatted for a few minutes before Anya coaxed Braxton into hanging up. But not before reassuring him again that she was well.

Anya closed the Bible and smiled, knowing that something good was going to come of all of this. That's how God always worked—changing bad into good.

She buzzed Dianna again. "Di, if you're ready, I'm ready now, too."

"Oh, my gosh!" Dianna exclaimed. "It's lunchtime."

Dianna began gathering the papers from her side of the desk. "Do you think you'll need anything else?"

Anya didn't even look up from the files stacked in front of her. "No, just let me go through all of this. Could you order in something for me?" Anya asked. "I want to work through lunch."

"Do you need me to stay?"

Anya kept her eyes down, and shook her head. A moment after Dianna left the office, there was a knock on her door.

"Come on in, Dianna."

"Uh, Anya. I'm sorry to bother you."

She looked up; Alaister was standing in her doorway. His hands were stuffed into the pockets of his navy suit. She smiled. "Come in."

He closed the door. "David told us you were back. Actually, I saw your car in the garage. I've looked for it every day." He dropped his eyes. "I'm glad you're back." His voice was so low, Anya had to lean forward to hear him.

"Thank you, Alaister, it's good to be back." She paused, wondering if he had anything else to say. But he just stood stoically and stared at her. "Can I help you with something else?" she asked.

He exhaled. "I'm sorry," Alaister said, shaking his head as if he were in a trance. "David said we're having a staff meeting, but I wanted to speak to you personally because I know we've had some problems recently . . ."

She waved her hand in the air and smiled. "I wouldn't have it any other way. You're an asset because you're such a leader. Sometimes, leaders bump heads."

For the first time since he'd come into the office he smiled, and stuffed his hands back into his pockets.

There was a quick knock on the door.

"Here are our sandwiches. I'm staying in, just in case you need me." Dianna eyed Alaister.

"That's all I wanted, Anya," Alaister said, turned quickly and left.

"Was he complaining again?" Dianna sounded agitated.

"Oh, no." Anya shook her head. "He said he was glad I was back."

"Really?" Dianna said doubtfully.

Anya shook her head, then looked at the pile on her desk. "Well, let me get back to this." Anya's head was buried in her work before Dianna got back to her desk.

At five o'clock, Anya began collecting the folders she was going to take home. She was looking at the stack of messages growing on her desk, when David stepped into her office.

"Hey," he said, eyeing her briefcase.

"I know it's early, but I'm a little tired."

He held up his hands. "You don't have to explain." He screwed his face. "But there is one thing. Jon Greene is here."

Anya plopped down into her seat. "He just showed up?"

David nodded. "Said he was getting worried and he's threatening to pull his business unless he knows that you're here and still running things."

Anya blew a stream of air through her mouth.

"Are you up to it?" he asked.

She nodded.

When they entered the conference room, Anya's smile wasn't as warm as she wanted it to be. "Mr. Greene, how are you?"

He jumped from his chair, stumbling slightly on the carpet as he made his way to her. Anya noted that he was dressed up today, in a tailored brown suit that was different from the off-the-rack sports coats he usually wore.

"I apologize, Mr. Greene. I thought you knew that I was out on personal business." She motioned to his seat and she sat across from him. "What can I do for you?" She widened her smile.

"Reassure me that everything is all right. You know, I only went with this company because *you* sold me. Now, I feel like I'm being dumped on your peons." His head tilted slightly toward David who was leaning against the wall near the door.

Anya didn't have to see him to know that David's lips were probably turned into his cocky half-smile.

"Mr. Greene," she began, leaning forward with her palms planted flat on the conference table, "I can assure you that Linden Communications is very important to me. You are one of our largest accounts." Anya didn't miss the smirk that crossed Jon Greene's face. She was sure he knew that he was their largest piece of business. "I will do everything I can to make sure you are pleased."

He slapped his hand on the table, and Anya jumped, visibly shaken by the sudden move. "I didn't mean to scare you, little lady. I'm just pleased. That's what I've been waiting to hear. I want to know that you're in charge and I can get to you anytime I need to."

"Mr. Greene, even I have a personal life." She smiled, but her tone indicated her seriousness.

For a long moment, he gave her a hard stare and she leaned back into her seat. But then his lips parted into a wide grin. "Well, I got what I came for." He chuckled as he stood. He reached to shake her hand, then pulled back. "What happened to your face?" he pointed.

With her palm, she covered the scar. Through the all-day meetings and conferences, she'd held her breath waiting for the first comment. But by the end of the day when no one mentioned it, she'd almost forgotten her mark. "I . . . had an accident."

"An accident," he repeated, as if he didn't believe her. He shook his head as he reached for her hand. She took it, shaking it briefly, then stepped away from him.

David escorted Mr. Greene to the front door and Anya returned to her office. When David rejoined her, she was sitting at her desk, holding her head.

"Are you okay?"

With a deep sigh, she looked up. "I don't know what it

is about him, but that man makes me nervous." When she saw the concerned look on David's face, she said, "Ignore what I just said. It's just what I've been through."

"You should leave now. I'll walk you to your car."

Her first thought was to tell him not to bother, but instead, she nodded.

As he escorted her, they chatted about the presentation they would make next week to Zytec Computers. Both behaved as if it had been a regular day, like nothing had ever happened. But as Anya drove away and David returned to the office, both knew that normal would be different from now on.

Anya had barely put her briefcase down when her phone rang.

"Hey, honey. I'm glad you're home early."

She smiled. "Hi," she said, sighing, and immediately regretted the sound of her voice.

"What's wrong?"

"Nothing, just a long day." She kicked off her pumps, and glanced through the mail that Sasha had placed on the dining room table. "Please don't tell me that I should rest."

"I was just going to say—"

"But you don't have to say it, because I'm going to grab something to eat, take a shower, then hit the bed."

"Okay, I'll be right over. What do you want to eat?"

"Sweetie, not tonight," she said, then held her breath.

He hesitated. "Okay, just call me before you go to sleep."

Anya exhaled and smiled. A few weeks ago, that

would have led to an argument. "I'll call the moment I get into bed. I love you so much, Braxton."

In the silence that followed, she could hear his surprise. It had been a while since she'd said those words with such passion. But after what they'd been through, Anya couldn't say them enough.

"I love you more than you'll ever know, baby. Call me."

She was still smiling as she slowly climbed the stairs. But by the time she reached her bedroom, stress weighed down her shoulders. And by the time she undressed, she no longer wanted to eat. She lay down and closed her eyes.

"I'll just rest for a moment," she said wearily.

But her eyes didn't open until the morning's sun shone brightly through her window.

Chapter 39

_A_nya marched into her office. "Girl, I am ready for work today," she exclaimed to a smiling Dianna.

She closed her door behind her, but before she got to her desk, Dianna tiptoed in.

"You are not going to believe this—Hunter Blaine is out there," Dianna said breathlessly.

Anya sucked her teeth. "What does he want?"

Dianna's light brown eyes were shining. "He said he doesn't have an appointment, but he has to see you."

Anya sighed.

Dianna frowned. She wished Hunter Blaine were coming to see her. She said, "David's here. Do you want me to see if he'll handle him?"

"No, give me a moment, then tell Hunter to come in."

Anya put her elbows on the desk and bowed her head. With a deep breath, she buzzed Dianna. A moment later, Hunter strutted through the door.

Anya didn't try to smile when she stood. In the past, they'd always met at his home because Hunter wanted privacy when discussing his affairs. So she knew this had nothing to do with business. She hoped he wasn't coming to seek her help with Sasha. She'd lose his business before she'd do that.

"Hunter, what can I do for you?"

He gave her a half-grin. "I'm glad to see you, too, Anya." He sank into the chair and crossed his legs. "I wanted to talk about my trust."

Anya sat down. "Do you need me or the attorney?"

He chuckled. "I *need* you." He pulled papers from inside his jacket. "I've been doing some reading." He slid the pages across the desk. "I want to look into some new investments."

Anya stared at Hunter for a long moment before she shifted through the scribbled notes that covered the yellow sheets of paper. "Hunter, your investments are doing well. I'll pull a report for you." She turned toward the computer.

"No, I don't need that. I wanted you to be up on the new things."

Anya resisted the urge to turn around and look at her licenses that covered the wall. "I wouldn't recommend any changes right now. But I'll do whatever you want."

"What do you think about what I have there?" He motioned toward what he'd given her.

Anya squinted her eyes. Hunter was a smart man. She knew he didn't expect her to look over scrawled notes and make a recommendation. Not when she analyzed and scrutinized every item in his portfolio. "I'll need some time to look over this. I can get back to you in a few days."

"Well, no hurry." He uncrossed his legs. "Give me a call when you've done that. I think it's time for me to go over everything with you anyway." He paused. "When we meet, Cynthia may join us."

Anya's eyebrows raised slightly when he mentioned his ex-wife's name, but she said nothing. Could it be that they were getting back together? Was that why he'd come by—so that she would give the message to Sasha?

Anya smiled pleasantly, as she came around the desk. When she reached to shake his hand, he kissed her on the cheek. He pulled back and Anya could tell that he was staring at her face. She quickly turned away.

"By the way, I'm sorry about what happened to you."

She tried not to show her surprise. "How did you hear about . . . that?"

"I met with the police a few days ago in my lawyer's office. After what happened to me last time, I didn't want to take any chances. But it turned out that they only wanted to know if I knew anyone who wanted to hurt you." He paused. "I told them that you were one of the sweetest women I knew. I couldn't imagine *anyone* wanting to hurt you." He chuckled.

Anya stared at him, then said, "I'll call you sometime next week."

David was standing outside her door as Hunter left.

"What was that?" David asked. "An early meeting?"

"More like a morning nightmare."

"Sounds frightening. Anything I can help with?"

Anya shook her head. There was nothing David could do unless he could touch her temples and instantly halt the headache she felt coming on.

"I just found out that the Zytec execs are having an

open meeting this morning about their benefits program. I can handle this myself, but if you're up to it, I'm sure it would help to have the big boss there."

Anya picked up her briefcase. "I am more than up to it. Let's get going," she smiled, and suddenly the throb in her head didn't bother her as much.

Chapter 40

ours twisted into days and days blended to weeks. Anya threw herself into her business like she had when she first opened the doors. By the time a month passed, she'd forgotten that she'd ever been out of her office. And she made the rape a distant memory, pushing it into a small corner of her mind, only to be pulled out during times with Pastor Ford and discussions with Detective Bush.

"Anya," Dianna buzzed into her office, "Sasha's on the phone and she says it's important."

Anya picked up the phone. "Cuz!" Sasha exclaimed into the phone. "Let me take you out to dinner because I'm a working girl now!"

Anya smiled. "You got a job? Where?"

But Sasha refused to tell any news until they were together. They made plans to meet and by the time they were waiting to be seated at Eurochow, Sasha had poured out all the details. Even when they finally settled into their chairs in the bright-white restaurant, Sasha still could not contain her excitement.

"I am so happy."

"I can tell; you haven't stopped talking," Anya laughed, as her eyes scanned the menu for the glazed shrimp with walnuts. Seeing her favorite dish, she laid the menu aside. "Now, are you sure about this? You've never worked as a salesperson before."

Sasha waved her hand, dismissing Anya's question. "What's there to it? I put on the clothes, I look fabulous, people buy them. And obviously they think I can do it. I'm sure it's not easy to get hired at the St. John's boutique."

"Well, if you're happy, then I am too." Anya watched as Sasha's wide grin turned into a thin, tight line. Sasha pointed her chin toward the door. Anya had to turn completely around in the quilted chair to see what turned Sasha's face sour. A low moan stuck in her throat.

"Do you want to go someplace else?" she whispered.

Sasha tried to appear uninterested. "Why should I? You've been talking about this place and I can't wait to try their frog legs. I'm not afraid of Hunter." She slid down in the chair, picked up the menu and buried her face inside.

But Sasha and Anya could feel Hunter's steps, as he and Lyza Easton approached their table. "Well, if it isn't the Mitchell cousins. How're you two?"

Sasha lowered the menu, and looked at him with a plastic smile. The way he stood, clothed in his trademark black turtleneck and jeans, reminded her of the first time they'd met and how her heart jumped. Now months later, her heart was still jumping. Lyza looked like his twin in her black jeans, though her low-cut sweater barely covered her chest. "Hunter, how are you?" Sasha asked as sweetly as she could. "It's so good to see you."

The creases in his brow revealed that a cordial reaction

was not what he'd expected. And though Anya would have rather ignored him, she followed Sasha's lead.

"Hunter, I've been trying to reach you," Anya said pleasantly. "When are we going to get together? I'm ready to go over those numbers with you and your wife."

Hunter coughed. "Well, you guys take it easy," he said quickly. He put his arm behind Lyza trying to direct her to their table.

But Lyza would not be moved. "It's nice to see you again, Sasha." She batted her eyes and smiled through fuchsia lips. Then she stuck her hand in front of Anya. "Hello, I'm Lyza Easton."

Anya ignored her outstretched hand. "Hello, Lisa. I'm Anya Mitchell."

"Ly-za," she responded a little loudly. "*I'm* Lyza Easton."

Anya raised her eyebrows, giving Lyza a that-doesn't-mean-anything-to-me glance. Lyza bunched her lips together, and this time when Hunter nudged her, she didn't resist.

Anya and Sasha's eyes followed the two as they huffed up the stairs to their table on the second level. "What was she talking about—getting together with you and your wife?"

They could hear Lyza's hissing and Hunter's mumbling until they were out of sight.

Anya and Sasha shared a laugh.

"Hunter must've thought I would cower down." Sasha bit her lip. "Though seeing him with Lyza only reminds me of how he left me to be with her."

Anya's eyes opened wide. "When did that happen?"

Sasha forgot that she hadn't shared that with Anya, and she wasn't about to relive her bathroom experience.

"Don't want to talk about it. But—" she hesitated. "What does Lyza Easton have over me?" she murmured.

It took Anya less than a second to respond. "Absolutely nothing! At least you're real. Everything on that woman—from her hair to her inflated breasts—is fake."

"That doesn't matter to a man."

Anya laughed, but the look on Sasha's face made her stop. "Come on, girl. We're here to celebrate, remember?"

She nodded, but Anya saw tears beginning around the rim of Sasha's eyes. Through dinner, they chatted about Sasha's job and Anya's wedding plans. But Sasha couldn't hide her occasional glances toward the upper level, and Anya saw sadness deep in Sasha's eyes.

Anya's heart hurt. Her cousin was still searching for approval from men, when what she needed was the favor of God.

As the waiter brought their dessert, Anya said, "We should celebrate your job in church on Sunday and give thanks—"

"Anya, please," Sasha interrupted her. "That God thing is not for me."

Although Anya nodded silently, she knew she was going to have to become bold with her witness. For some reason, Anya felt like she was running out of time. She had to get the Lord's message to her cousin. Anya wasn't sure how, but somehow she would find a way.

Chapter 41

*T*he sheets were damp, as he lifted himself from the bed. It had been this way for the past few nights after he awakened from terror-filled dreams. In his mind, they were always in uniform, when they came and took him away.

It didn't make any sense for him to be thinking this way. He'd been questioned and eliminated as a suspect. He had outsmarted them all, just like he had before. There was nothing that would ever lead them to him. He held the only evidence.

But he couldn't get too cocky. Shakespeare said, "The fool doth think he is wise, but the wise man knows himself to be a fool."

Still, there was no need for him to be so worried.

He walked into his bathroom and stared at his reflection. Empty eyes stared back; he didn't even have the strength to smile. This was worse than the other times.

Seeing Anya didn't help. He didn't feel stronger and her words still cut beneath his skin.

Maybe it was time to leave this city. He had other options—New York, Chicago, even London. He'd make a *decision soon, knowing that these nightmares were warnings. Someone was getting close.*

    He turned off the lights and returned to his bed, shivering even though he covered himself with two blankets. He closed his eyes, although he knew he wouldn't sleep. All he could do was hope that daylight would soon give him relief from the horror of his dreams.

Chapter 42

$\mathcal{A}$nya massaged her temples, then her eyes. With only her desk light shining, her office had a soft, golden glow. She sighed.

"Long day, huh?" David asked, as he peeked into her office, then sauntered inside.

She nodded. "It never seems to end." She picked up her message slips, glancing at the notes from Braxton, Madear, Donovan, her wedding coordinator. "Between business and my family and . . . everything else, I'm feeling a bit overwhelmed."

"You've been working like a crazed woman for weeks."

"Is that your diagnosis, Doctor?"

"That's it." He settled on the edge of her desk. "And my recommendation is," he glanced at his watch, "go home."

Anya smiled at him. "You're the doctor. Give me a few minutes."

"Let me get my things. We'll walk out together."

Anya chuckled. David said that like it was a new idea. But he had walked her to her car every night since she'd returned to work.

As they descended in the elevator, they chatted like the

friends they'd become. In the garage, they leaned against her car, continuing their talk.

"Hey, instead of standing here, let's go get a drink," David suggested casually, the way he had almost every night. And she answered, the way she always did.

"David, we had lunch together. I don't want you to feel like you have to take care of me." She paused. "And, I'm sure there's a special lady that you want to be with."

"I want to be with you."

Her smile disappeared. "I'm kidding." He ran his hand across his mouth. "Anyway, let's have that drink tonight."

She hesitated, then said, "I'm too tired." She tossed her briefcase into her car.

"Anya, what I just said—I was joking. I'm sorry if I made you uncomfortable."

She lightly touched his arm. "I just have a lot to do." She looked into his eyes. "My wedding plans are keeping me really busy."

He lowered his head a bit and nodded. "I understand."

She slid into the car, then backed slowly from the space, past David and down the aisle, resisting the urge to look back at him through the mirror.

Shaking her head, she said, "David is not part of this plan, girl. Get over it!" Then she steered her car toward home.

At first, Anya thought she was dreaming, but she reached for the ringing phone.

"Hey, babe. You sound like you were asleep."

"No, not yet. I was just lying down. I think I've been

working too hard." She regretted the words as soon as they left her lips.

"I told you," Braxton started in. "You need to take it easy. I think you should take a few days off. I can stay over there or you can come here."

She sat up and turned on the light. "Braxton, stop huffing and puffing. I probably need to take some herbs or vitamins or something. Anyway—"

"I guess that means you want to go back to sleep."

"Yeah and this time, I'll get under the covers."

"Okay, do you want me to pick you up tomorrow for counseling?"

"No, I'll meet you there." In his silence, she heard his doubt. "I'll be on time."

He chuckled. "I love you."

She leaned back on the bed. "I love you too, Braxton." And, her eyes were closed the moment she put the phone back on the hook.

Chapter 48

$\mathcal{D}$avid traced his finger along the picture. He could barely see the image in the dim light of his living room. The light of dawn was still a half hour away. As he stared at the frame in his hands, hot tears rolled down his face. "Happy birthday, Mama," he whispered to the picture.

No matter what experts said, time did little for his wounds. His pain was as sharp as the day his grandmother called him.

"Mama, why?" Years later, he was still asking the question. The memory remained sharp—his grandmother's explanation about the gun, but his mother hadn't left anything behind to explain. Only, he didn't need an explanation. It was all because of him.

Gently, he returned the picture to its place on the mantel, and with the back of his hands, wiped his tears. He took several deep breaths, then zipped his sweatshirt up to his neck. He'd get to the gym a bit earlier this morning and still have time to see Detective Bush before he went into the office. Questions lingered that had to be answered. Especially today. Because it was his mother's birthday.

He grabbed his gym bag and keys. Enough reminiscing. It was time to take care of business.

Anya dropped her briefcase on the dining room table and looked at the clock. It wasn't even four. She kicked off her pumps and went to the kitchen.

"Hey, girl." Sasha bounced into the room. "I thought I heard something down here. I was getting ready to do my Kung Fu impersonation. What are you doing home so early?"

"I have a headache."

"Must be a whopper for you to come home. Anything I can get for you?"

"No," Anya said, closing the refrigerator. She'd been hungry, but the sight of food was making her sick. "I think I'll go upstairs," she said, picking up her briefcase, but stepping over her shoes. "Aren't you working today?"

"Nope, that's tomorrow. Right now, I'm on my way to the gym. In my search of the new me, I joined a few days ago, to improve on this fabulous body. Are you sure there's nothing you need before I leave?" Sasha had followed Anya upstairs.

Anya just moaned her answer. "Have a good time. I'll be here when you get back." She closed the door, leaving Sasha standing in the hallway with a deep frown.

Anya fell onto her bed, trying to understand the wave of warmth that suddenly washed over her. With quick steps, she moved to her bathroom and leaned over the toilet. After a few minutes of dry heaves, she straightened her head, then washed her mouth.

"What is wrong with me?" she asked her reflection. Her head was pounding so hard, she could feel her temple muscles beating against her skin. She stared at her dark eyes for a moment before she rushed to her bedroom.

Her hands trembled as she dialed Braxton's number and held her breath. She exhaled when his answering machine came on.

"Braxton, I'm so sorry, but I have to help Sasha with something tonight, so I won't make counseling." She paused, wishing she had planned her words better before she called. "I'll leave a message for Pastor Ford. Also," she hesitated again. "I forgot to tell you about my doctor's appointment. If you want, you can come with me." She closed her eyes and tried to keep her voice steady. "I'll call you in the morning and tell you what time, okay. And Braxton . . . I love you so much."

She hung up the phone and, before she had time to think, she called Dr. Moore. It took a few minutes to convince the receptionist that an emergency appointment was needed.

She finally put the phone into the cradle, and curled onto the bed. It was only then that her tears came. "Oh, God," she prayed. "Please, God . . . please, God . . . please, God."

Chapter 44

Anya and Braxton entered the townhouse, bodies stiff, like walking zombies. The inconceivable had hit them like a bomb. They had driven home in complete silence, each consumed by their own disbelief.

"You're pregnant." Dr. Moore's words kept reverberating through their minds, bringing different but still haunting thoughts. They were simple words that would change the course of their entire lives.

Pregnant. By a rapist. By a man who had not been captured. What would this mean? What would they do? They hadn't spoken a single word, yet their questions were exactly the same.

Braxton followed Anya from the living room into the kitchen. The air was dead space between them.

Anya began opening, then slamming cabinet doors. Finally, she asked, "Do you want anything?" Her voice tried to conceal the emotions that waged war inside. She searched the cabinets for something that would keep her from facing this remarkable truth—if only for a moment. But every part of her brain was firmly fixed on the doctor's report.

"Anya, whatever you need, I'll get for you." Braxton gently took her hand and led her from the kitchen into the living room. "Do you want something to eat or drink? I can make whatever you want. Or I can go out, but I don't want to leave you alone . . ." Braxton's voice trailed off.

Anya shook her head and rested her hand gently on her stomach. There was a baby there and the thought made her shudder.

Braxton sat down, removed her hand from her stomach, and held her hands in his. "You should eat something, honey."

"I don't want anything." She leaned back and closed her eyes.

Braxton leaned back as well and moved Anya's head to his shoulder. He buried his nose in her hair, pulling her as close as he could.

"It's going to be all right." He rocked slightly as Anya wrapped her arms around him. "I promise, Anya. I won't let anything else happen to you."

The sound that came from her was barely audible. Braxton pulled away and lifted her chin with his finger so that he could see her face clearly. "What's wrong?" She was chuckling or groaning, Braxton couldn't tell which.

"You won't let anything else happen to me. What else is there?" Her lips turned upward into a pained smile.

Braxton tried to return her smile. "I just mean that I will take care of you."

She leaned back into him. "I know you will."

They sat for what seemed like an hour, holding each other, and as each minute passed, Anya felt the weight slowly lifting from her heart. They had been through so much; they would find a way to deal with this.

"Braxton, we'll get through this, you know."

She could feel him nodding his head as he rubbed his hand along her arm. Finally, he stood and went into the kitchen. He combed the cabinets before he settled on a can of soup, emptied it into a bowl, and set it inside the microwave. When he returned to the living room, he paused, staring at Anya.

She was sitting back, eyes closed, head against the wall. She looked so peaceful, so beautiful. Braxton tilted his head back and mouthed a thank you to the Lord for keeping them, even with what they had to do.

Feeling him, she opened her eyes and smiled. She had been thinking about the baby . . . and what their lives would be like from now on. This was such a shock, and it was scary. Who was the father? But every time that question screeched into her mind, she suppressed it. She couldn't dwell on what was in her head. It was what was in her heart that would keep her going. The only thing she could do was think about the baby and know that the Lord would sustain them.

"Do you want to talk about it?" he asked after a few seconds passed.

She reached for him, and he moved toward her. "I still can't believe this. Braxton, I'm *pregnant*. It doesn't even sound real."

"I never thought this would happen," he said. "You know it *could* happen, but what are the chances? I was more concerned that you would catch a disease or something." He closed his eyes for a minute, then glanced at Anya out of the corner of his eye. "I didn't mean that. Anyway . . . Anya, I will be there for you the entire time. I'll handle everything if you want."

Anya frowned. Of course he would be there. This would be a great test, but they would pass it. They just had a tough decision in front of them . . . although she couldn't imagine giving her baby away. As she thought about giving the baby up for adoption, something deep inside of her stirred.

"Isn't it interesting?" she finally stated. "All this talk we've been having about children and Junior and now this—"

"But you don't have to worry, sweetheart," he said, putting his arms back around her. "We'll still have our family. An abortion won't change that."

Ping!

Anya wasn't sure if it was the sound of the microwave or Braxton's words that startled her. Her head moved in slow motion from side to side. "An abortion?" Surely she had misunderstood him.

"Yeah . . ." Braxton looked at Anya as if he were confused by her confusion. Then his eyes widened. "I *know* you're not thinking about having this baby."

"Well . . . I . . ." she stammered. "There are other options besides an abortion."

Braxton dropped his head. "You have got to be kidding. There are *no* other options. Why would you want to bring this monster into the world?" he asked angrily.

Anya flinched. "The *monster* that you're talking about is a part of me."

Braxton looked at her incredulously. "It is not! You were raped, Anya. You're not supposed to birth that thing."

"You don't have to remind me how I got pregnant, Braxton." Her words came out slowly. "And the *thing* that's inside of me is a living, breathing baby—my baby." Anya crossed her arms in front of her, resting them on her stomach.

"Anya, you're not thinking straight. One hour ago, a doctor tells us you're pregnant because you were raped. And now, you're calling this 'your baby.' It's crazy!"

"It's not crazy for me to look at all of my choices."

"Like what?" Braxton's expression dared her to say what she was thinking.

Anya's eyes had thinned to slits. "I could have this baby, Braxton. I could give it up for adoption or . . ." The rest of her sentence hung ominously in the air.

"Or what?" he yelled.

"I could have this baby . . . and we could keep it." She whispered the words uncertainly.

He slammed his fist on the couch and stood, pacing the floor in front of her. "You have got to be out of your mind!"

Anya glared at him but said nothing, only folding her arms tighter in front of her.

After a few seconds, he crouched in front of her and pushed out a stream of air from his puffed cheeks. "I'm sorry. It's just that . . ." He shook his head trying to search for the words. "Anya, you can't have this baby. We can't do it."

She took his hands. "We can do this if we stay on our knees."

"Oh, I get it." He pulled away from her. "This is a God thing for you!"

"This should be a God thing for you too. I thought you didn't believe in abortion."

"Abortion is fine in this case. God doesn't want you to have this baby."

"How can you say that when this is a life He created?"

He held his head. "You are so off-base. God didn't create this and He won't bless it."

"I think that God creates all life. We may not like the circumstances, Braxton, but the result—this baby— it's all Him. I'm as scared as you are, but we have to trust God."

"Honey," he stooped in front of her once more, "no woman in her right mind would have this baby."

"Besides the fact that I won't go against God, how can you ask me to have an abortion with everything I went through before?"

Braxton's head reared back. "I *knew* that was what you were thinking. But keeping this baby won't change what happened in the past."

She twisted her lips. "Maybe we shouldn't talk about this right now."

Braxton shook his head. He wasn't going to let her shut down. If they didn't talk now, this idea would spread like slow poison until it destroyed her. "You're not thinking straight and I have to get you to see that."

"Oh, I'm crazy and you're normal."

"Just listen to yourself, and you'll know I'm right."

Anya opened her mouth to protest, then just folded her arms. Braxton moved to the couch and sat as close to her as he could. He unfolded her arms and pulled her hands to his lips.

"I love you and there is nothing I wouldn't do for you. I'm just trying to get you to understand that you can have an abortion and no one would judge you."

"No one but God."

"Not even God in this case, Anya. He wants us to use common sense."

Anya felt every muscle inside of her tighten, but she remained silent.

"Anya, answer this. What are you going to do when you look at this baby? Think about it—every time you look at this child, you'll think about the rape. You won't love this child, you'll hate it!"

"I would never hate this baby!" she said angrily, although she was angrier with herself than him. With that one statement, he addressed the question that was tormenting her. What if that was how she felt? What if, no matter how much she relied on God, she did hate this baby?

She began to tremble, breaking under the emotion. She stood, and walked to the patio doors. "I would never hate this child," she repeated in a whisper. Her eyes burned from tears that had not yet fallen.

She couldn't listen to his words anymore. "I think you should leave." Her back was still turned to him.

He barely heard her, but knew what she said. With slumped shoulders, he nodded. He took a deep breath, stood, and started toward her, but then stopped. He turned to the front door but then went back to her and kissed her cheek. "I love you, Anya." His tone begged for understanding. "I love you more than I have ever loved anyone." He walked slowly out the door without looking back.

Anya waited a moment, then dragged herself to the couch and lay down. She had known the pregnancy was going to be hard to take, but never did she imagine this.

She closed her eyes. So much of what Braxton said made sense—the words he uttered were the same ones voicing themselves in her head. But they were not the ones in her heart. She couldn't kill this baby.

She believed, inside, Braxton felt the same way. She'd convince him, she had to.

With her eyes still closed, she rolled to the edge of the couch and dropped to her knees. She clasped her hands in front of her and said, "Lord, I have to turn this over to you. Please, Lord, open Braxton's heart and show him this is all you."

She wasn't sure how long she prayed, but when Anya rose, the house screamed its silence. She had to get away. It took less than a minute for her to grab her purse and jacket and run to the garage.

In her car, she called her office.

"Dianna, I won't be in today."

"Oh, but David needs to speak to you. Let me put you through to him."

A few seconds skipped by, then she heard his voice. "Are you all right, Anya?"

"I'm fine." She tried to put a smile into her voice. "I need to take care of some personal things; I'll be in tomorrow."

"Okay," he responded, unable to hide his doubt.

"Dianna said you needed me."

"No, you take care of what you have to do and I'll see you tomorrow." He paused. "Anya, you can count on me for anything. So if you need to talk . . ."

His voice was so soft, and filled with such care, that Anya wanted to spill everything that was inside of her. But instead she said, "You worry too much." She clicked off her phone before he could ask anything or before she could tell him everything.

But once she hung up, loneliness engulfed her and she turned her car in the direction of the only place where she knew she could find solace right now.

It took her just fifteen minutes to get to Madear's house. Before she got out of her car, Sasha was opening the front door. "What are you doing here?" she asked as Anya walked up the porch steps.

"I could ask you the same thing." Anya stepped inside.

"Madear had doctor's and cable appointments scheduled at the same time. So I did the house-sitting thing."

Anya smiled for the first time in hours. "You're kidding. Madear's getting cable?"

Sasha laughed. "It's only basic and I had to talk her into that."

Anya joined Sasha's laughter, glad to have something to take her away from the pain that pulled at her heart.

"Sounds like you and Madear are getting along."

"Of course we are," Madear said, as she entered the room. "And we'll keep getting along as soon as she takes off that short skirt."

Anya's eyes moved to Sasha, standing posed against the door in a black St. John's skirt that was high up her thigh. When Anya returned to Madear, her eyes were narrowed.

"Don't look at me like that," Madear said. "This has nothing to do with my baby's skin color. That skirt is just too darn short!"

Sasha rolled her eyes, and laughed with Madear. Anya only sighed with relief.

"Baby, I'm glad to see you," Madear said to Anya. When Anya leaned over to kiss Madear, she held her grandmother for a long moment, just enough for Madear to draw back and frown. "What's wrong?" Madear searched Anya's face for an answer.

The tug Anya felt in her chest was getting stronger, and she didn't have the strength to utter words without tears. So she only nodded.

"I've got to go to work," Sasha said, unaware of the exchange. "Anya, I might be a little late tonight. Joan, my manager, asked me out for drinks after we close. She wants to get to know me. You know the drill," Sasha chatted brightly. "I'll see you guys later."

"I have something to tell you." Anya squeezed the words from her throat. She spoke directly to Madear, but she added, "Sasha, stay for a minute."

Madear took Anya's hand, and led her to the couch. Her soft green eyes were squinted with concern and never left Anya's face.

"What's up?" Sasha asked, dropping her jacket and purse back in the chair.

Anya closed her eyes. "I'm pregnant." The brief statement was barely a whisper.

The audible gasps revealed their shock. Finally Sasha spoke. "Well, that's a good thing, right?" Her eyes darted between her grandmother and cousin. "You and Braxton are getting married in a couple of months anyway, so . . ."

When Anya turned to Madear, her grandmother's eyes told her she knew the truth.

Madear's hand was still over her mouth. "Baby" was all she could murmur.

Anya whipped away from her grandmother, and stared at her ring. "This is not Braxton's baby." Anya could see the confused thoughts turning over inside Sasha's head. "When I was raped—"

"Oh, my God!" Sasha jumped up and knelt next to Anya. She took her cousin's hand. "I'm so sorry," she cried.

For the first time, in the midst of women who loved her, Anya released tears that had been battling to be released. Madear and Sasha held Anya in their arms. Minutes passed before they broke apart.

When Madear rose to get tissues, Anya said to Sasha, "I shouldn't have told you before you had to go to work."

"I should call in and tell them I have a family emergency."

"Don't do that. This is your first week. I'll be fine with Madear."

Sasha glanced at Madear as she held a tissue to her nose. "Go on, baby," Madear said.

It took several more minutes before Sasha broke away, but when they were finally alone, Madear held Anya in her arms. "Does Braxton know?"

Anya nodded and pulled another tissue from the box. "But we have a big problem." When Madear remained silent, Anya continued. "I can't kill this baby, Madear."

"Sweetheart, you don't have to do that."

"That's what Braxton wants."

Madear faced Anya, holding her hands, but she didn't say anything.

"I don't know if I'm crying because I'm sad, or scared. I don't know if we should keep the baby or not, but I know that I can't abort it."

Anya wrapped her hands around her waist and let her eyes wander. Family history filled this room through the pictures that were scattered about. Now, inside of her, was a part of the family's future. But was this baby family? She squeezed her arms tighter around her waist.

"Braxton is so angry."

"But you know he loves you."

"I can't do what he wants."

"Come here, baby." Madear leaned back and Anya stretched out on the couch, laying her head in Madear's lap. "You're doing what you know is right. Braxton will come around."

"Braxton thinks that I've blocked out how . . ." Then she continued. "But I just can't block out the part of this baby that's me. Does that sound stupid?"

"Honey, you're doing what's in your blood. For generations, Black women have birthed, raised, and loved the babies from their womb. It never mattered how the baby got there; we love our children. It's who we are."

"Suppose I keep the baby and then I don't love it. That's what Braxton thinks will happen." Her voice squeaked.

Madear tisked. "You don't have to worry about that. But, Anya, you have choices—there's adoption."

Anya sat up and searched her grandmother's face. "Is that what you think I should do?"

"You should let the Lord lead you. Pray and He'll give you and Braxton the answers."

Anya nodded. "I'm leaning on God so much right now."

"That's how it's supposed to be. The Lord is your stronghold. He won't let you down. And neither will I."

She rested her head back on Madear's lap and allowed the peace that she always felt in this house to engulf her.

As she lay, Anya tried to imagine the future—the baby, what it would look like, would they keep it? But all she could see was the coldness of a room in New York, where a part of her died, all those years before.

"The one thing I know, Madear, is that I'm going to

give birth to this baby. I'm never going into an abortion clinic again."

It wasn't until she heard her grandmother's low gasp that she realized what she'd said. Anya's eyes opened widely, she held her breath and waited for Madear to speak. But Madear remained silent and continued stroking Anya's head.

Anya knew her grandmother heard her words, but after a few minutes, she knew there would be no questions. Not now. The present was more important than the past.

In the silence, it was Madear's touch that let Anya close her eyes and sleep. When she awakened, the living room shadows were longer—morning had turned to late afternoon. But she was still in her grandmother's lap, and Madear was still stroking her, just as she'd been doing for hours.

Braxton clicked the mouse on the print icon and listened to the hum of the computer as it prepared to spew forth the four pages he'd written in the last three hours. He skimmed through a few lines on each page, sucked his teeth, then tossed them into the wire trashcan. He didn't know why he was sitting at his computer. It had been weeks since he'd written anything and just when he thought he'd regain his writing groove, he'd been hit with this—the sequel to the nightmare.

He highlighted the text he'd written, and hit the DELETE button. Instantly, the screen went blank. He shook his head at the simplicity. That's what he needed, a DELETE button in his life.

"I know how Anya is," he said aloud. "I didn't approach her right." He stood and went to the window. The sun was still hanging in the late afternoon, filling the room with its brightness. He closed the miniblinds, bringing darkness to his office. Then he returned to his desk.

He thought they'd endured it all. But how much more was God going to put on his shoulders? How much more could he take as a man?

There was no way he was going to allow Anya to have this baby—even if she said she'd give it up for adoption. He couldn't trust that. Knowing Anya, at the last moment, she'd choose to keep the baby and then where would they be? The baby couldn't be a consideration at all. He'd have to convince her of that.

He was angry with himself—not with her. She had an excuse; hormones were storming through her. He should have been the calm, reasonable one. Demanding that she give up the baby would never work, she'd keep it just because he said to get rid of it.

He needed to talk to someone who could help him convince Anya to do the right thing. He eyed the Bible on the bookcase. Pastor Ford? No, she'd definitely agree with Anya. Madear? No, Anya had probably run to her already.

He smacked his palm against his forehead. Braxton reached for the phone, then put it down. This was something he had to do in person. With one click of the mouse, he shut off the computer and headed out the door.

"My man!" Carlos smiled as he came into the reception area. "Como está? What are you doing here?"

"I need to talk to you, buddy." Braxton kept his voice low as he glanced over at the receptionist. "Do you have a few minutes?"

Carlos glanced at his watch. "Sure, come on back."

They moved silently, past Carlos's secretary, finally into his office.

"You sound serious, my man," Carlos said, as he walked behind his desk.

Braxton sank into the chair opposite Carlos and shook his head slowly from side to side. "You're never going to believe this . . . this morning . . . we found out . . . from the doctor . . ." He paused as if he didn't want to say the final words. "Anya's pregnant . . ." He sat up straight and looked Carlos directly in the eye. "It's not mine—it's from the rape."

It was a moment before Carlos released a long whistle. Without saying a word, he stood, and sat in the chair next to Braxton. "Oh, man! I can't believe this. So . . ." Carlos left his unasked question in the air.

"Anya wants to keep the baby," Braxton answered him.

"You mean, have it and give it up for adoption?"

"I don't know what she's talking about, but it doesn't matter because she shouldn't have this baby at all. Even if she said she would give it up, I don't trust her—"

"Whoa, whoa." Carlos held up his hands. "You're not saying you want her to have an abortion?"

Braxton looked at his friend incredulously. "Carlos, I came here for support. Please don't tell me you agree with her."

"I'm not taking sides. I'm only saying that I'm not surprised at Anya. I'm surprised at you."

Braxton slammed his hand on the edge of the chair. "What is with everybody? Abortion is legal, you know."

"Man, you're asking Anya to go against everything she believes."

"Look at this from my side. If this happened to Michele . . . tell me you'd want her to have the baby."

"I wouldn't *want* her to have the baby, but if we were there—"

"Don't give me that crap!" Braxton said angrily. He stood and walked to the window, then turned back to face Carlos. "What am I supposed to do? Let her have this baby, then look at that monster every day!"

"Braxton, you have other options."

Braxton slammed his fist into the palm of his hand, hearing Carlos utter the same words Anya had. "We don't have any options!" he yelled.

"Okay, calm down. Let's talk this out."

"Talking won't do anything."

"That's why you came here."

"Well, I don't like what you're saying," Braxton growled.

"Then you don't want to hear the truth."

Braxton glared at Carlos for a few long moments, then slouched back down in the chair with a sigh.

"Man, I know this is tough." Carlos scooted his chair so that he was in front of Braxton. "Have you talked to anyone else? Have you talked to Pastor?"

"No," he replied quickly. "I know what she's going to say."

"Why are you so against adoption?"

"Because once Anya sees this baby, she's going to keep it. She's already talking about it's half hers."

"Try to see her side—"

"All I see is that man with his hands all over Anya, violating her in ways . . ."

Carlos put his hand on Braxton's shoulder. "Man . . ." Carlos took a deep breath. "Why don't you bring this up at Men's Prayer—"

"No!" Braxton jerked his head up before Carlos could finish. "I don't want *anyone* to know."

"We can help you talk through this and—"

"I said, no!"

Carlos held up his hands. "All right. Well, you and I can do that together—talk and pray . . ."

Braxton nodded, but he had already dismissed Carlos from his mind. His best friend had let him down.

"There is one thing I recommend, man," Carlos said. He paused, waiting for Braxton to look at him, but when he didn't, Carlos continued. "Don't push Anya. She needs your support right now."

Braxton turned to face Carlos. "That's why she can't have this baby. If she thinks it's tough now, how will it be later?" Braxton spoke as if he were presenting his argument in front of a jury.

"But back off, man," Carlos said strongly. "No matter what you think she should do, you can't push her. Or else . . ."

Braxton slouched in the chair, his eyes drooping from emotional exhaustion. The intercom on the desk buzzed.

"That's my four-thirty, but I can have one of the other attorneys handle this. We can go somewhere, maybe have a glass of wine."

Braxton shook his head and stood up quickly. "We can get together later."

It took a few moments for Carlos to agree. "I'll call you tonight. Are you going to be home?"

"Yeah," Braxton said, although he didn't know where he'd be.

They hugged in silence, and Carlos sighed deeply as he watched Braxton walk out the door.

Braxton moved quickly through the long dark hall, to the elevator bank. A man and a woman, holding matching briefcases and wearing navy pinstripe suits, chatted as they waited. Braxton looked toward the staircase and thought about walking down to the lobby. But the number 12 on the door reminded him how high up he was in the downtown building. He turned back toward the elevators.

As he waited, Carlos's words played in his head. *Don't push Anya.* Braxton shook his head. Carlos was wrong and Braxton was sorry he told him. He didn't believe for one moment that Carlos would live the words he spoke if this was happening to his wife. No man would keep this baby.

Braxton knew how to handle his woman; Anya had to be pushed to be convinced. But not in the way he'd done this morning.

The elevator pinged its arrival, and Braxton stepped inside with the two dark-suits who didn't seem to notice him. As they descended, a plan began to form. By the time Braxton stepped off the elevator, there was a new confidence in his step. He knew what he had to do.

Anya climbed the stairs, her legs weak from emotion. Without turning on the light, she sat on her bed and clicked the machine for her messages. "You have four messages," the mechanical voice said. "*Beep* . . . Anya, this is Braxton—"

She fast-forwarded to the next one. She did it again, then a third time, until her machine was clear. Then she did what she hadn't done in weeks—she turned off the ringer.

Just as she stood, she heard the patting of footsteps running up the steps. A few seconds later, Sasha appeared in her doorway.

"I thought you were working until closing tonight."

"I did. It's almost ten."

Anya looked at the clock. Had she been roaming around for that long? After she left Madear's, she'd driven around until the day's light gave way to the night. But even after darkness descended, she continued driving, finding her way onto the freeway. It wasn't until she saw the sign DIAMOND BAR NEXT 5 EXITS that she turned around and drove another seventy minutes back into Los Angeles.

"I could hardly work all day, thinking about this." Sasha sat on the bed. "Are you going to have an abortion?"

Anya held her cousin's gaze for a long moment. "No," she said softly, and turned away, waiting for Sasha's wrath.

"I didn't think so," Sasha said simply.

Anya raised her eyebrows. "I thought you'd be ranting about how I can't have this baby."

"If it were anyone else, I might be. But as I thought about it, I knew you guys wouldn't do that. It's a God thing, right?"

Anya released a bitter chuckle, remembering Braxton uttering those same words. "It's a God thing for me, but Braxton doesn't agree. If he had his way, we would have driven directly to an abortion clinic from the doctor's office this morning."

Sasha had been lying on the bed, but now she sat up and crossed her legs under her. "Wow! This could be trouble." She paused. "Anya, Braxton may be right. It might be better to have an abortion. Think about it; how are you going to actually have this baby?"

Anya didn't let a second pass. "I'm going to wait for my water to break, go to the hospital, get into one of those beds with stirrups and push."

Sasha rolled her eyes. "You just found out this morning and you've already made a decision. You haven't given yourself enough time."

A deep grunt came from Anya's throat. Sasha had no idea how much time she'd had. She looked at her cousin and, for the second time that day, thought about revealing her secret.

"Sasha, the main reason I can't abort this baby is because of God. I just know that all life comes from Him. But, there's something else." She bit her lip. "This is not the first time I've been pregnant. And that time, I did what everyone wants me to do now."

Sasha scooted closer to the window where Anya was standing. "I never knew that." Her shock made her voice go up a pitch.

"I don't want to go into the whole horrid affair, but imagine this." Anya paused and folded her arms across her chest. "A virgin freshman meets senior star football player. It takes a week to get her into bed and a month to get her pregnant. But it only took twenty minutes for him to forget that she exists."

"He just left you . . . pregnant?"

"Right after he told me that he knew the baby wasn't his. Sasha, I was so scared. I'd been away from home for two months and I was pregnant. I just couldn't bear the thought of telling Madear. So I scrounged around for the money, and went to a clinic where a faceless, emotionless doctor scraped that baby out of me." She said the words as if she were angry. "Then I went back to my dorm and cried for a week."

"So no one knows about this?"

"Braxton knows. He knows how that abortion affected me. He knows about the dreams I had every night where I could hear my baby crying. He knows that I thought I was going crazy. But interestingly, that turned out to be one of the best things that happened to me."

Sasha tilted her head like she was confused, but before she could open her mouth, Anya continued. "It landed me right in the arms of the Lord."

"Was the doctor a Christian?"

Anya chuckled. "I don't think so, but my roommate, Maria, was." Anya paused, remembering. "I was *so* ashamed. Here I was, a young woman raised in church and I had just had an abortion. I can't explain how empty I felt. But when I told Maria, she reminded me of what I just couldn't believe—that God still loved me and had already forgiven me. All I needed to do was forgive myself. It took a little while, but a few weeks later, I recommitted my life to the Lord, and my entire relationship with God changed." Anya paused.

"I've made a lot of mistakes in my life, but I'm not going to repeat that one."

"But, Anya, this is totally different. I understand your connection with the first baby but this—"

"The result is the same," Anya interrupted. "There's a life inside of me and this time, God knows I know better."

"It's hard for me to understand how you can put this in the context of God—it was a rape."

"I don't understand it either, Sasha. But I don't have to. The only thing I have to understand is that this"—she placed her hand on her stomach—"has to be from the Lord. I don't have to keep this baby, but I have to birth it."

Sasha shook her head slightly. "But what about Braxton?"

Anya looked out the window. Most of the lights in the homes across from her were darkened as families settled in. "I have to convince him because if I don't . . ."

"Anya, you and Braxton have come so far. Don't let this destroy your relationship."

"But I can't let Braxton destroy my relationship with God. That's the most important relationship to me."

Sasha stared at her cousin for a long moment, then stood and hugged her. They held each other silently, holding their thoughts inside. While Sasha closed her eyes and hoped that things would work out, Anya twirled the ring on her finger, and prayed that this wouldn't be the end that she had felt coming for a long time.

Chapter 45

It was already after nine when Anya awakened and tapped on Sasha's door. When there was no answer, she opened the bedroom door slightly and peeked into the room. She sighed with relief at the sight of the empty bed.

She dragged herself to the kitchen, where she automatically reached for the Mr. Coffee pot, but then stopped her arm in mid-air.

Instead, she poured a glass of orange juice, and made a mental note not to bring coffee into the house. No need to tempt herself now that she was pregnant.

Pregnant. All night she had tossed while that word turned in her mind. She'd gone from thinking this was a nightmare to believing it was a blessing, back to a nightmare, then blessing again.

Taking only a sip of the juice, she put the glass down, then rubbed her arms trying to massage the tiredness that had settled deep in her bones. Questions flickered through her mind like flash cards. Should she keep the baby or give it up for adoption? Would she love this child or hate it? Would she think of the attack every time she looked at the baby or would she be able to put that behind her? Would she wonder about the father? No! That would never happen. Braxton would be the father. He *would* be the father if she kept the baby. She sighed. The questions overwhelmed her.

Outside the morning light was brilliant. She was already late for work, but she couldn't handle work today.

She called her office.

"Dianna, I'm not coming in today."

"Didn't you say the same thing yesterday?"

Anya shook her head. She had the only assistant in America who would say that.

Aloud she said, "Well, I have something important to do, is that okay with you?"

"I didn't mean anything." Dianna whined. "It's just that you never take time off unless something's wrong. You're not sick, are you?"

Not in the way you think. "No," she replied, softening her voice. "Is David in?"

"Not yet. I just tried to page him, but he hasn't called in yet."

"Is he on his way?" Anya asked, wondering now if she should go into work.

"I think so."

Anya was thoughtful. "Tell him to call me the moment he gets in."

She hung up the phone, and headed straight for her bathroom. In front of the mirror, she slipped her oversized T-shirt from her body and stared at her bare stomach. It wasn't as flat as it used to be, but it was flatter than it was going to be.

She moved her hand gently across her abdomen trying

to imagine what she would look like. Inside, there was a baby with hands and feet and . . . she turned around abruptly, and started running the water in the tub, then sprinkled lavender bath salts into the water.

Just as she began to immerse herself in the steamy, bubbling water, the phone rang. She paused. Only one person would be calling her now. Second ring. It's probably Braxton, she thought and decided not to answer the phone. Third ring. Or maybe it was David. Fourth ring. She needed to know if he was going to be in the office today.

Grabbing a towel, she ran into the bedroom, shivering as the cool air hit her wet body. The answering machine beeped and instead of picking up the receiver, she turned up the volume.

"Anya, this is Detective Bush—"

She picked up the phone. "Good morning."

"Anya, I'm glad I caught you."

She sat down on the bed and pulled the comforter around her, covering the towel. "I was just coming out of the . . . kitchen. Do you have any news?" She hadn't spoken to Detective Bush in a few weeks and it wasn't until this moment that she realized she'd given up. It was a random rape and unlikely that her attacker would ever be caught.

"Actually, I do have some news. I need you to come to the station. We have a suspect in custody."

Anya jumped from the bed and both the comforter and towel fell, but she didn't notice. Her hand was covering her wildly beating heart.

"We got a break last night and we're pretty sure we have the man who assaulted you."

She needed both hands to hold the phone. "Oh, God," she breathed heavily into the phone. "Who is it?"

"It would be better if you came down to the station."

"Is it someone I know?" The question trembled from her lips. She didn't know why she asked that and it frightened her.

"Anya, I really prefer not to talk about this on the phone."

"Please."

The detective sighed. "All right." He paused, then told Anya who they had in custody.

Anya gasped, and dropped the phone.

The BMW's tires screeched as Anya turned west on Wilshire. She couldn't believe it. When she had picked the phone up from the floor, Detective Bush had given her little information, but she knew enough. She knew there had been something familiar that night. But why?

In less than twenty minutes, she pulled into the precinct parking lot, jumped from her car, and ran into the building.

"David!" she exclaimed. He was waiting in the lobby.

He grinned. "Anya, it's over." He hugged her.

"I can't believe it," she said, finally pulling back so that she could look into his face. "It was Alaister? And Detective Bush said that you found him. How?"

"Hold on. Detective Bush wants you to come to his office." He clutched her hand, and they almost ran down the long corridor.

Detective Bush was on the phone, but motioned for them to enter. Anya paced the small office until David pulled her to him, hugging her, calming her for the moment.

The detective finally put the phone down. "Well, Anya," he grinned as he came from behind the desk and enthusiastically shook her hand, "it looks like the first part of this might be over; this should be a slam-dunk for the DA. We have a confession. And, we have my man here"—Detective Bush slapped David on the back—"to thank."

"You said it was Alaister." Anya looked from the detective to David. "I still don't believe it. How——"

Detective Bush motioned for David to speak. "It was by accident really," he began. "Yesterday Alaister called in sick, and I needed some of the new business files. So, I went into his office and found the files, but inside one of them was a piece of paper with your name scribbled all over it. It seemed strange, but I put it aside. Then I thought about it and called Detective Bush. I didn't know if it meant anything . . ."

"*I* wasn't sure if it was anything," Detective Bush said, "but I wanted to talk to Alaister, because all along we suspected it was someone close to you. David told us that the night he found you, the office door was locked when he returned. Seems like a small thing, but it narrowed our suspect list. So I couldn't wait to talk to Alaister. We went over there last night, asked a couple of questions, and with a little probing, got what we needed."

"It sounds too simple," Anya said, still shaking her head. She laid her hand on her stomach and a chill filled her.

"It's usually like that," Detective Bush stated. "We work for weeks, months, and it's usually one simple thing that breaks the case. We've caught serial killers through traffic tickets. We don't usually catch these guys in the act, it's usually by accident."

"So he's going to jail?"

"Well, Alaister has to be arraigned and depending on how he pleads, things will move from there. But he won't have much of a case. He didn't try to hide anything, just started talking. We had to get him in front of a lawyer fast."

She looked down at her shaking hands. "Did he say why?" she whispered.

Detective Bush leaned forward. "Anya, there is no real why to this type of crime. At least not a reason that you or I would understand."

She shook her head not accepting his comment. Her mind searched for a motive through every conversation, every meeting she'd had with Alaister—the ones before and the ones after. But the only thing filling her thoughts was that she now had a face to go with those cold eyes that almost destroyed her that night.

"What do I do now?" She wasn't sure if she was asking the detective or herself.

Detective Bush shrugged. "Nothing yet. Alaister's in the holding cell downstairs." Detective Bush returned to the other side of his desk and missed the way Anya stiffened in the chair. He put on his glasses and opened a manila folder. "He's been arrested on suspicion of rape and battery and he'll be formally charged this afternoon. Bail will be set—"

"You mean, he'll be walking around?" She couldn't hide the shaking in her voice.

David reached for her hand and she gripped his tightly.

"You don't have anything to worry about," Detective Bush said reassuringly.

"How can you be sure?"

Detective Bush removed his glasses and stared directly at Anya. "Because rapists don't go back." He let his harsh words settle. "I don't want to sound rough, but he's done what he had to do."

Anya wondered if Detective Bush could see her fear. She nodded as if understanding, although she didn't understand at all.

Now that she knew Alaister was in the same building, she wanted to get away. She stood and forced herself to smile. Detective Bush had promised results, but now she wished she had never found this out.

Sensing her change, the detective came around the desk and took her hand. "This guy's going down, Anya." She nodded.

"The DA's office will contact you. This case hasn't been assigned yet, but the prosecutors will be helpful."

"Thank you for everything."

He shook her hand gently. Then the detective turned to David. "If you ever need another career . . ."

David and the detective chuckled; Anya didn't.

"This guy wouldn't let this go," Detective Bush said through his laughter. "I guess if I were engaged to you, I would have been relentless too. So when's the wedding?"

"Uh, no," David stammered. "I'm not marrying Anya. I mean, I would, but—"

"We're not engaged," Anya jumped in. "I'm marrying Braxton Vance. You met him. He spoke with you about my ring?"

It was the detective's turn to stammer. "I'm sorry, I forgot. It's just that David has been here all the time and the way you're together today . . ." The detective frowned. "Maybe I should just shut up."

"It was an honest mistake." She wanted to get out of there. "Thank you again, Detective Bush."

David held Anya's hand as they walked through the hallway, out of the building and into the parking lot.

"I have never been so fooled in my life." Anya leaned against her car and stared at the gray building. Alaister was in there. One part of her wanted to go in and see him. Face him and tear him apart. But a larger part wanted to run away. "I thought the man was familiar. But I didn't want to believe I knew someone who could do something like this to me . . ." Her voice trailed off. Should she cry? Should she feel relieved?

"He fooled us all, Anya."

She nodded.

"But it's over. There's nothing for you to fear. I'll make sure of that."

She smiled. "You're living up to your name? No matter how many Goliaths are out there, you're going to slay them all for me."

"I'll do my best." His smile didn't hide his seriousness.

Suddenly her smile faded. "What did I do to Alaister?"

She dropped her face into her hands and David put his arms around her. "You know this is not about anything that you did."

"It was easier for me to believe that when I didn't know who it was."

David held her close, trying to console her with his touch. They stayed that way until a car pulled into the empty space beside them.

Anya wiped her face, though no tears had fallen. "I'd better be going." She needed to tell Braxton, and she wanted to see Pastor Ford.

"What are you going to do for the rest of the day?" he asked.

She shrugged.

"I have an idea. Are you game?" He lifted her chin with his finger.

"I don't know . . . if you're not going to be in the office, then I need to be there."

"The troops can handle things for one day and I have something that I think will cheer you up. This is what we'll do," David said, taking charge. "We'll take your car to your house and then you'll ride with me. Come on," he urged.

She needed to call Braxton. But when she imagined his reaction, she knew she couldn't handle it right then. "Okay."

Determined not to give it any thought, she got into her car and drove, as David followed her home.

Chapter 46

He was surrounded by gray—from the walls to the floors, even the toilet in the corner—the drabness was sucking the breath from him. Americans said that London was colorless. But nothing could surpass this, even the air was gray.

Alaister held his head low, hanging between his knees. He'd hoped to stop the churning in his stomach. There couldn't be anything left; he'd vomited all night.

At least he was alone.

"Hey, buddy."

The ache in his neck made him raise his head slowly. It took a moment for his eyes to focus on the gray shadow on the other side of the bars.

"You want some of this?" The guard rattled the keys inside the holding cell's lock, then slid the tray along the floor. It stopped right under Alaister's nose.

He sat still until the aroma lifted to his nostrils, forcing him to run seven steps to the toilet. The guard's laughter echoed through the halls, but Alaister kept his head lowered until the guard's footsteps faded.

He shuffled to the low-lying cot and lay on his back,

with his feet hanging over the edge. He'd lain this way many times before, in the sanctuary he'd created. He should have stayed there. His secrets had been safe in that apartment.

The police were never even close. He had marveled at their ineptness, but now he was wondering how they'd found him.

It was her pictures in that room that had been his downfall. He'd kept evidence that should have been destroyed with the ring.

Carelessness was costly. Still there had to be a way to escape, just like he'd done in London, and in New York. But with what had happened yesterday, he didn't think he'd ever get out of this place. It was the sudden knock on the door that startled him. No one ever came to visit, and even a surprise guest had to be announced by the doorman.

So when he placed his hand on the doorknob, he figured a neighbor was on the other side. It had taken strength from deep within to remain composed when he opened the door. Even without uniforms, before they flashed badges, he knew who they were.

One was a tall Black man, with a shaved head, who looked to Alaister like he would have been comfortable on a basketball court. The other one—the white one—was shorter . . . and stockier—the one who did all the talking.

"Mr. Phillips, I'm Detective Bush. May we come in?"

"I don't know anything." Alaister's eyes had darted between the two.

The stocky one's thick eyebrows raised. "You don't know anything about what?"

The detectives were inside, but Alaister still stood at his opened door. "I . . . don't know . . . anything about Anya Mitchell," he stammered.

The detective's eyebrows raised higher. "Who said this was about Anya Mitchell?"

Alaister tried to steady his breathing, remembering that he was innocent. "Why else would you be here, Detective?" He'd been proud of his quick response, but pride turned to cold fear, when he noticed the other detective slowly walking around the living room, edging closer to the bedroom door.

"Excuse me." He had tried to get the detective's attention.

The Black cop finally turned around. "Do you mind if we look in there?"

Alaister closed his eyes. What were the rules in this country? Surely officers couldn't just walk into his home.

At the same time, the other detective held up a folder. "Is there something you want to tell us?"

Alaister had tried to count slowly in his head to calm the trembling that had taken over his body.

There was little that he remembered after that, until he'd been brought here. They kept him in a small room for much of the night, questioning him. Why did you do it? Have there been any others? What were your plans? Why Anya? There was no way to explain that he'd done nothing wrong. He tried to explain Shakespeare's thoughts on the matter— "I am a man, more sinn'd against than sinning." But, they could not see his innocence.

When they'd finally brought him to the cell in the early hours of the morning, fear kept his eyes opened and dread emptied his stomach. Now, he lay weak with fright.

"Mr. Phillips?"

He didn't open his eyes but frowned. When he heard his name again, his eyes shot open.

It had been thirteen years, but there was instant recognition between the two.

Alaister's eyes were wide as Sean Thomas held his finger to his lips. He didn't have to do that—the shock that filled Alaister was enough to choke all words inside him.

The guard opened the cell. Sean took only one step inside and waited for the guard to disappear down the hall.

"What are you doing here?" The question squeaked from Alaister's throat.

"I was about to ask you the same thing." Sean sat on the cot, then opened the folder in front of him. He shook his head as he read over the papers. "Your name was familiar, but I thought you were one of my old clients."

"Clients?"

Sean looked at Alaister. "I'm the lead attorney in the Public Defender's office."

"Here in the States?"

He nodded. "I've lived in Los Angeles for almost ten years."

Alaister stared at Sean in his tailored suit and silk tie. In that moment, a lifetime of memories flashed through his mind. How could this be? *He* was the brighter one.

Sean cleared his throat. "This is a bit unusual. I should excuse myself. You really need another lawyer."

Alaister didn't know whether to laugh or cry. Then one of his favorite lines from Shakespeare came to his mind—"They laugh that win." And he knew he would never laugh again.

Chapter 47

Anya felt like David was an old friend as they drove south on the 405 Freeway into Huntington Beach. When they exited on Beach Boulevard and turned into the Seaside Condominiums, Anya stiffened.

"This is where you live." She hoped she didn't sound as dreadful as she felt.

He nodded. "I want to change my clothes," he said, peering down at his suit. "That's okay?"

She barely nodded.

David maneuvered the Jeep to one of the two-story buildings. Without words, he opened her door and guided her to his apartment. She followed him inside, but then stood in the foyer, unsure of her next steps.

David continued through the enclosed entrance, under the arch that led to the living room. He turned back, looked at Anya, then held his hand to her. "Come in. It won't take me long to get out of this."

Anya glanced down at the long T-shirt dress she was wearing.

His eyes roamed her body. "You look fine. I just want to get comfortable."

She folded her arms in front of her and forced her eyes to turn away from him.

David chuckled, picked up a pillow from the floor, and tossed it casually on the couch. As he went into the bedroom, Anya settled on the edge of the couch, feeling the coolness of the leather against her bare legs. She clutched her purse, and with her legs so firmly sealed together, she felt like a young girl who had changed her mind about this first date.

But this is not a date, she said to herself.

"Would you like something to drink?" David yelled from a room behind her. She turned around and peered through the slightly opened door, then turned back quickly when she realized a mirror showed his reflection.

"No. I'll get something when we *leave*." She cringed as the words came from her mouth. She was a grown woman, why was she acting this way? Because she *was* a grown woman.

Taking a deep breath, she began to casually stroll the room. While everything in her townhouse seemed to be white, David appeared to have an affinity for black.

In that instant, music charged through the room, startling her for a moment, until she realized David had turned on the stereo from a remote.

She smiled, and then her smile widened when he stepped from his bedroom. She tried not to stare, but he was dressed in that black again—a muscle shirt that didn't leave her wondering and black jeans.

She took a deep breath. "Are you ready?"

He chuckled as if she'd told a joke. Then pointed to a stack of mail scattered on his dining room table. "I need a moment, do you mind?"

"No, I'm all yours today. I mean—"

He grinned at her, his dimple even deeper now. "I *know* what you mean."

She turned, needing something to focus on. She continued moving through the room, all the time ignoring the feel of David's eyes. In front of the fireplace she stopped, and picked up the single item that sat on the mantel. It was a yellowed photo in the center of a gold frame. From the way the two people were dressed, she knew it had been taken in the sixties. There was an attractive woman, dressed in a large-flowered minidress, holding the hand of a young boy. The boy's body had changed, but there was no mistaking that dimpled smile.

"You look so cute." She laughed. "You haven't changed a bit." She glanced at him. "Well, maybe a little."

"You don't think I'm cute anymore?" He walked to her.

"I wouldn't say that," she said, and wondered why she was flirting. She cleared her throat. "Is this your mother?"

He nodded, and took the photo from her. "She was so beautiful," he said sadly. "I don't remember this picture. I just kept it because it reminds me of a time when my mother was happy."

"Do you have any other pictures?" Anya kept her voice soft.

"No," he said abruptly, then handed the picture back to her. He returned to the dining room and shifted through the envelopes he'd been looking at. A few seconds later, he tossed them onto the table.

Anya took a deep breath, and went to him. "Every time we talk about your family, you go into a cave."

He said nothing.

She moved closer to him. "If you want to talk, I'm

here for you, David. Believe me, after all you've done for me . . ."

He finally smiled.

"You're not the only one who can be a good friend," she continued.

He chuckled, and the cloud lifted. "Well, if I'm a good friend, then I need to do what I promised and cheer you up. Let's get something to eat. There's a place on the beach called Adam and Eve's. I think you'll like the menu."

Anya wrapped the sweatshirt she'd been carrying around her waist, and they walked outside. It wasn't until they were on the street that Anya realized how close they were to the beach.

"I would love to live near the ocean. Let's walk for a while."

"That's one of my favorite things to do."

On the beach, they took off their shoes, letting their feet sink into the sand. The breeze made the air cool, and she covered up with her sweatshirt.

They strolled along the ocean's shore, shoulder to shoulder in comfortable silence. When the light mist tickled her, she sighed. Glancing up, she saw David smiling at her.

She smiled back and returned her eyes to the ocean. "David, I am so grateful for everything you've done. It's amazing how hard you worked on my case, but why did it interest you so?"

He glanced at her sideways. "You really don't know?"

She looked at him blankly.

He stopped walking and put his hand on her arm. He opened his mouth, then closed it and sighed. Finally he said, "I did it because you're a good friend and I care about you."

They continued walking for a few minutes, then Anya said, "Is that the only reason?" She kept her eyes straight ahead, not looking at him.

David pointed to some rocks. "Let's sit over there."

He laid his jacket down and they both leaned back against the hard surface. He picked up a small stone and tossed it into the ocean. "I helped the police because I wanted to get whoever had done this to you, and . . ." He picked up another rock and tossed it, this time throwing it farther than the last. "I didn't want them to suspect me."

Anya tucked her hands deep inside her sweatshirt. "You found me. Why would they suspect you?"

"There are things that you don't know. Things I haven't told anyone."

She didn't understand why her heart was beginning to pound. Suddenly she changed her mind. "David, if you don't want to talk about this—"

"My mother was raped." He breathed the words through clenched teeth.

Anya held her breath.

"She was raped over and over and many times all I could do was watch."

Anya's eyes widened in horror, while David's eyes were held to the ocean's waves.

"It was my father." He paused. "I remember wonderful times with my father. But when I was about ten, he lost his job and everything changed. He could never find steady work after that. And the more time that passed between jobs, the more he drank. That was when the beatings began . . ."

"Your father beat you?"

"Not me, my mother."

"Oh, God, David."

He shook his head. "My father wasn't a bad man. It was what life did to him. That's why when I saw you . . ." His eyes were pasted on the ocean as if the past was hidden in the waves.

She took his hand.

"There's more, Anya, but I can't . . . not right now." He closed his eyes, trying to block the memories, and at the same time trying to hold back his words. No one could ever know the complete truth.

She nodded, and rubbed her fingers along his hand, wanting to reassure him. His fingers gripped her tighter and, finally, he looked at her. She saw his pain deep in his eyes and tears filled her own.

"I'm here if you want to talk," she said softly. "You can trust me."

"I know."

Suddenly he leaned over, and brushed his lips lightly across hers. Anya closed her eyes, not daring to breathe, feeling the gentleness of him and waiting for more. But as suddenly as he moved to her, he pulled away. Her eyes snapped open, and she saw that he was smiling. "Thank you for being my friend." His voice was a raspy whisper.

"Thank you for being mine."

He kissed her cheek, then took her hands, and pulled her from the rocks.

"David, we have to talk."

He turned off the ignition and smiled. "Anya, it's almost seven. We sat in that restaurant until they kicked us out. We talked for the last hour as we sat in traffic. We've talked enough for today," he joked.

She took a deep breath. "We have to talk about . . ." Her eyes dropped, and she looked at her engagement ring.

"Are you trying to tell me that we have to talk about that little—"

"Kiss."

David drew his body back as if he were offended. "Anya, believe me. When I kiss you, you'll know it. That was not a kiss."

She slapped his arm playfully. "Whatever it was," she began, straightening her face into seriousness, "you know there are a lot of reasons why we can't go there."

"I know, you're engaged."

"Yes and—"

"You're my boss."

"David, imagine the complications this would cause."

"And, of course, you're not that kind of girl."

She looked into his eyes. "I'm not. I love Braxton."

"If you love him so much, what were you doing kissing me?"

She closed her eyes and sighed.

"I'm sorry," David said. "I put you in a bad position, and I didn't mean to. But you know what the little meeting of our lips was all about, don't you?"

Her expression questioned him.

"We had to get it out of the way. There was all of this . . . tension between us. It's been building, but now that our lips have met . . ." He took her hands. "Now we can really be friends."

She smiled. "You're a nice man, Mr. Montgomery."

"Make sure I get an invitation to the wedding."

"You'll be the first."

"So in the office tomorrow, I'll pretend that our lips never met."

She laughed. "Thank you for such a wonderful day."

They walked slowly to her front door. When she turned around to tell him good night, he put his finger to her lips. "I just want you to know one thing, Ms. Mitchell. If I *had* kissed you, you would have never made it home tonight." Then he walked away, leaving her standing with her mouth wide open.

Anya could hear the TV as she passed, but she didn't knock like she usually did. Instead she tiptoed into her bedroom and focused on the blinking light on her answering machine. She was tempted to ignore her messages and just slip into bed. But she knew she had to face Braxton. She owed this news to him.

She dialed his number and he answered before the phone fully rang once.

"I've been waiting for you to call," he said without saying hello and Anya remembered that he'd just purchased a caller ID box. "Where've you been?"

"I needed some time alone, I'm sorry."

"That's okay," he said quickly. "I just wanted to know that you were okay. I called your office and they didn't know where you were."

"I hope you weren't worried."

"I will always worry, I love you."

Her afternoon flickered through her mind, and she closed her eyes. Forgive me, Lord, she thought.

"Braxton, I have some news. Do you want to come over?"

"I can . . . I was on my way to Men's Prayer."

"Oh," she breathed relieved. "Go on . . . we can talk later."

"No, this sounds important. What is it?"

She took a deep breath. "Braxton, the police called this morning. They found out who did it—at least a suspect."

"Oh, my God, that's great. Now we can put this all behind us."

"Braxton, it was . . . someone I know." She stopped. This was as hard as when she found out she was pregnant. What would Braxton do?

"Who?"

She pushed the name through her lips. "Alaister Phillips, he works for me."

There was a pause, then Braxton exploded. "A man in your office attacked you? How could that happen?" he screamed.

"Braxton, I'm sorry," she cried.

"Oh, no, baby. No, I'm sorry. This has to be hard on you. I'm coming over—"

"No, I'm really tired and I want to go to sleep. We can talk about this tomorrow."

"I need to be there with you."

"I'm fine here. Alaister's in jail."

"Anya, it doesn't matter what you say—"

She sighed when she heard the dial tone. Braxton was on his way, and there was nothing she could do about it.

Before Anya hung up the telephone, Braxton was in his car. He floored the engine, then screeched into the street.

This nightmare was growing like weeds. What he wanted to do was run to the police station and beat that man until he begged for his life. But what he had to do was more important. He had to take care of Anya.

Just as he turned onto Santa Monica Boulevard, the light turned red. He closed his eyes as he waited. Alaister. Although he had a name, Braxton didn't have a face. He tried to force the memory of Alaister to his mind, but the picture was blank. One thing was for sure—this guy wasn't a brother. Not with that name. This was a white guy.

The blaring car horn startled him, and Braxton moved through the intersection, heading toward the freeway.

There was no way she could have the baby now. Anya would have to be convinced. But he had to be careful. He couldn't be demanding . . . he needed a kinder, gentler approach.

On the freeway, he breathed deeply, pushing his emotions beneath the surface. All he could let Anya see was his love. Anything else, would blow all that he had to do.

Anya tied her bathrobe tighter as she heard Braxton drive up. She massaged her eyes. There was no way she wanted to deal with this, but she opened the door before he could ring the bell.

"Hey." She smiled, hoping that helped to ward off any explosion.

He pulled her close and held her, softly rubbing her

arms and kissing her head. She felt her shoulders soften as relief filled her.

Minutes passed before Braxton took her hand and led her to the couch. She curled into him, comfortable in the silence. Wrapped in his arms, her breathing became even and not too long after, her eyes, heavy with emotion, closed.

Braxton knew she'd fallen asleep, but he held her for hours, until the clock ticked to midnight. He laid her down softly, got a blanket from the linen closet and covered her.

He brushed his hands through her hair. "I love you, Anya."

Then he closed the door gently behind him.

He sighed when he got into his car. He had made it past the first hurdle. Now he had to put his plan into action.

Chapter 48

"Anya, I want you to know that no matter what is going on over there, I still have confidence that you will be able to take care of my business," Jon Greene said.

Anya clutched the receiver tighter. Alaister's arrest was all over the news. Not that it was a front-page item, but there was enough coverage to keep the phones ringing. The only redeeming factor was that while the article had stated Alaister's name, her name was never mentioned.

Anya never suspected the challenges that would come with knowing her attacker. Yesterday she'd made the announcement to her office and then had to handle the gamut of emotions. Most were in shock. Geena had been downright hysterical, demanding to know where Alaister was being held.

Then clients began calling, although she'd been blessed: Not one account had left. She was holding things together, if only by a string.

The biggest challenge was Braxton. She hadn't heard from him since he'd left her sleeping on the couch.

Anya stood and went to the window. It seemed odd.

The way Braxton had held her the other night, she was sure they'd work this out. But now, she wondered.

"He's just giving me some space," she whispered.

She returned to her desk, when she heard the knock on her door. Braxton walked in and closed the door behind him.

"You look surprised," he said, as he kissed her. "I just wanted to see the woman I love."

She released a silent breath of air. "I was worried. You left the other night and then I didn't hear from you. But I'm glad to see you now."

"Then you're going to love why I'm here." He perched himself on her desk. "I'm here to take you away . . . and we're leaving right now." He snapped his fingers and called, "Dianna!"

Dianna came into the office holding a small bag over her head. "Sasha brought this by and filled me in. You have clothes to change into and I cleared your calendar."

"Dianna . . . I didn't tell you . . ."

"I told her to do it," David interrupted, as he stepped into the room. "I'm going to cover you, so there's no excuse for you not to leave with your fiancé." He grinned, making Anya wonder what was really behind his smile.

David picked up the bag and handed it to Braxton, who passed it to Anya.

"You might as well surrender; you're outnumbered." Braxton smiled. When she still hesitated, Braxton leaned forward and said, "I really want to do this." He dropped his eyes. "I have to apologize to you and we need to talk."

Anya smiled. She'd known it all along. From the way Braxton had held her the other night, she was sure he'd found a way to handle this. There would be no abortion.

David coughed. "Well, Dianna, I don't think they need us anymore."

When they were alone, Anya put her arms around Braxton's neck. "So, *if* I agree to do this, where are we going?"

"It's a surprise." He took her hand. "Come on."

Braxton held her as they rode in the elevator, and just as they stepped into the garage, Anya felt a flutter. She put her hand on her stomach. No way, she thought. She looked over at Braxton and he smiled.

As they pulled out of the parking lot, Anya rolled down the window, welcoming the warmth. Braxton took her hand and she knew it was going to be a great day.

The sky was the color of serenity, and as brush-stroked clouds glided aimlessly across the blue canvas, Anya sighed. They had driven almost an hour, along the Pacific Coast Highway, high into Topanga Canyon. The park was a green oasis, miles away from the bustling of the city.

Braxton tossed the last of their lunch into the basket, though he kept out the two crystal flutes and bottle of cider. He brought the glasses and bottle to the blanket where Anya was stretched out staring at the sky.

He joined her, lying on his back and staring into the heavens.

"I wish our life was like one of those clouds, where we could wander through without a care," Anya sighed.

"God has bigger plans for us." Braxton rolled onto his stomach and faced her. "I wish that you had married me a year ago, sold your business, and had not been in the office that night. I wish I had been able to protect you." He paused. "I love you so much."

She smiled. "I've never doubted that."

He dropped his eyes. "I am so sorry for the things I said the other day. I shouldn't have asked you to have an abortion." He closed his eyes, and Anya wondered if he was praying. He took a deep breath and continued, "So I will support you with this baby. Whatever you want to do—keep it or give it up for adoption, I'm behind you." His face twisted as if the words were painful to say.

It took every effort to hold back her tears. She hugged him. "Thank you." Her words came from deep inside. "I knew you would feel this way."

"You're thinking about keeping the baby, aren't you?"

She bit her lip. "I don't know." Then, she nodded.

Braxton opened his mouth to say something, then hesitated.

"What?" Anya asked, noticing that his face was creased in concern.

"Since we're going to do that, I'm going to withdraw my suit for Junior," he said mournfully.

Anya frowned. Inside, she knew to end the conversation here. She didn't need to know any more. It was his son, his choice. But she asked him why anyway.

"I'm worried about how this baby will affect Junior, and since I don't know what kind of person this child will grow up to be, I think it will be safer . . ." He didn't finish the sentence.

Anya shook her head in confusion. Only moments had passed, yet Anya felt as if an entire conversation had happened without her. Braxton was talking as if she would birth a monster. "This child will have my genes, and if we keep the baby, it will be raised by both of us—we won't have any problems."

"It won't matter. Roxanne will use this to keep Junior away from me."

"She won't do that." Anya paused. "We don't have to tell her," she whispered.

Braxton shook his head. "I would never keep a secret like that from her. Junior is her son too, and if I'm putting him in danger—"

"What are you talking about?" Anya backed away from him. Her heart was beating faster.

He moved toward her and laid his hands in her lap. "We don't know how this child will turn out."

"Braxton, you're making it sound as if this child will be a bad seed. No one knows how any child will turn out. You just do the best with what God gives you."

"But most children aren't born with all these strikes against them." He sighed and looked away from her. "It's sad because I really wanted to have Junior with me and now I don't know if Roxanne will even let him visit."

"If it comes to that, I'll talk to her. She's a mother, she'll understand. Junior will still be a part of your life."

"I'm not sure I want that anymore," Braxton began. "I don't know if I want him around this baby. We'll have to see how the child develops . . ."

"This is crazy."

"No, it's not, Anya. I've read things about the genetic factors. I've read about children of criminals. We have to be careful. I want to keep Junior away until we know. I don't think I even want him to come to our wedding."

"The baby won't even be born when we get married, Braxton. We're talking about a *baby*."

Sadness washed over his face. Anya took his hand, desperate to make this right. His son wouldn't be in danger, but if that was what he thought, he'd have no choice but to keep Junior away. "You're so wrong about this, believe me."

He looked down at her hands and rubbed his finger across her ring. "There is another thing . . ." He shook his head. "Never mind."

"You have to tell me what you're thinking."

He pulled her hands to his lips. "Anya, I don't want you to think that I don't want the baby. I want whatever you want, but . . ." He dropped her hands, and his shoulders slumped. "I read so many things that worry me. I keep thinking about those children killing other children in the schools—"

"Braxton!" Her hands covered her stomach. "My baby won't be like that."

"I hope you're right." He took her hands. "But Anya, I'm scared for all of us. Maybe I've read too much, paid too much attention to the news." He looked away. "But I will stand by whatever decision you make."

She pulled her knees to her chest, hugging her arms around them.

"And there's this too . . ."

Anya closed her eyes and pulled her legs closer to her body.

Braxton said, "Alaister could file for custody."

She twisted her face. "No judge would even consider such a case!"

"Don't be fooled, Anya. I saw this on *60 Minutes* or *20/20* or one of those programs. Even from prison, he could file papers forcing you to bring the baby to visit him."

She covered her face. "Oh, God."

"And, even if he doesn't try it from prison—even with the maximum sentence, he'll be out in eight years, tops. He could come looking for you and the baby."

"He won't even know about my baby."

"You never know what will happen . . . or who will be checking into records."

The tears began to stream down her face. Braxton fell to his knees and used his thumb to gently wipe her cheeks. "I want this baby as much as you do," he said gently. "But I'm looking at the whole picture, taking our entire future into account. We can still have our children, and the family we've dreamed about, but we need a clean beginning, without a child that we just don't know about."

"So you're saying that I should have an abortion." She couldn't bring herself to look into his eyes. Without looking up, she could feel him nodding.

Braxton said, "I tried to figure out ways to keep this baby because I knew that's what you wanted. I wanted to make it a part of our lives, but now that we've had a chance to talk, I think abortion is the only answer. And I'll go one step further. I think that God wants you to do that too."

The sound of laughter made them turn their heads, and they watched as children ran toward them. They were dressed in purple-plaid uniforms and from their size, Anya knew they were second or third graders. Three adults followed behind, huffing as if they were having difficulty keeping up.

"Yeah! I win!" one of the little girls shouted.

Anya's watery eyes followed them, as they played tag and circled around the teachers.

"God gives life," she whispered. "He doesn't take it away."

Braxton silently sighed in disgust. What were children doing here? He watched them for a moment. "Look at these children, Anya. They're happy, well-adjusted, that's the way we want our children to be. It's not fair to the child you're carrying to bring him into a world where he would never be happy. This baby will always be the child of a rapist."

She looked at him with soft eyes, pleading with him to stop. "I would never tell this baby that."

"Someone would. That happens with adoptions all the time. We would have to tell the child because it would be worse if it came from someone else."

He took her hands again and spoke. "You have to look at this from all sides. When you do, you'll know what to do . . . I'll be by your side no matter what."

He watched as her eyes roamed back to the children, sitting in a semi-circle now, around the adults who were reading aloud.

"This would be a great park to bring Junior to," he said.

Her eyes followed as Braxton stood and began to pack the remnants of their picnic.

They held hands as they walked to the car, but once inside, Anya stared silently out the window, her eyes never leaving the children.

"Is there any place else you want to go?" he asked as gently as he could.

She shook her head.

"We can stop somewhere for dessert."

"I want to go home."

He patted her hands and started the ignition.

Braxton stopped the car, then put his hand on the door.

"There's no need for you to come in," Anya said quickly. Her eyes still wouldn't meet his.

"Anya, if you still want to talk . . ."

"We've said enough."

"We have to decide."

She grabbed her bag, and jumped from the car. "I'll call you later." She ran to her door.

Braxton sat for a few moments, wanting to go after her, wanting to hold and comfort her. But after a while, he slowly pulled from the curb.

As he turned onto Stocker, he caught a glimpse of himself in the rearview mirror. He held his own stare for a few short seconds, then turned away.

"I'm protecting her," he said to himself, as their conversation played through his mind. He knew his words had been rough, striking all that was close to her heart. The key was Junior. It would kill her if she believed she was the cause of him not having a relationship with his son. That had been a stretch, but from the look in her eyes, it had been effective.

He shook his head and sighed, thinking about how much he'd hurt her. But it was all to prevent a life-long mistake.

He only had to wait for her call. He'd won, he knew that. But it wasn't winner's relief that filled him. Instead, his body was stiff with the pain in her eyes and the sound of those children in the park.

As he turned onto the freeway, he prayed for the relief he expected, but it never came.

Dry sobs heaved from her chest as Anya leaned against the door. Finally, she moved onto the patio where she rolled the steel grill aside, and pulled one of the green floral chaises into the sun. She stretched out and closed her eyes, wanting to clear her mind of the chaos that choked her.

When this day began, there was no way she would have even considered an abortion. And now . . . how did it happen? She rubbed her arms as the early evening breeze waltzed across the terrace.

Maybe Braxton was right. Obviously, he'd thought this through. He could see things that were hidden from her. Like the impact of her baby on others. She hadn't considered Braxton. And she had never considered his child. Was she being selfish?

Anya laid her hand across her stomach. "You're just a baby," she whispered.

She could feel tears stinging her eyes, but she forced them back. There was no room for emotion. This had to be a logical decision.

As the sun began to fade, she moved inside. The house was dim in the early evening light, but she didn't touch a lamp.

In her mind, she could see Braxton sitting, waiting for this call. Her legs weakened, and she slumped onto the couch. She'd give herself five minutes and then she'd call him. Her eyelids were closed, shut against tears that were fighting to release themselves, but in the end she lost the battle, and she cried until she drifted to sleep.

Darkness completely enveloped the house and she squinted to see the clock. It was after nine. Anya scurried up the stairs, glad that Sasha hadn't found her in her distressed state.

In her bedroom, she stared at the phone, before she picked it up, pushed the speed-dial, then hung up before it rang. A few minutes passed before she picked up the phone again and willed herself to allow the call to go through. It rang once . . . barely.

"Anya." His voice sounded as tight as a stretched rubber band. When she said nothing, he said, "Anya, sweetheart."

She wanted to hang up. "Make the appointment," she said softly. "Good night."

"Anya, honey, wait. Are you all right?"

She looked at her cold reflection in the mirror. "I'm fine."

"Sweetheart, this is the right thing. Let me come over."

"No."

"We're in this together. I want to hold you, and let you know that I love you."

She was still staring at her reflection—an empty face, devoid of emotion. "I don't want you to come over." Her voice was flat.

"Is there anything you need?"

I need to keep my baby, was what she wanted to say. "Good night, Braxton."

"Anya, wait—I have to tell you . . . I made the appointment." His voice dropped to almost a whisper.

His words tore at her insides, and she had to hold onto the headboard.

"When I didn't hear from you earlier," he continued with her silence, "I didn't want to chance missing the weekend appointments. So . . . I made a tentative appointment for tomorrow at ten. Is that okay with you?"

A pocket of air caught in her throat. She needed more time. "I'll be there."

She heard him exhale.

"They want us to be there a half-hour early—to sign some papers and . . ." He coughed. "They want to go over some things."

"Where?" her voice squeaked.

She didn't write the address down; she would forever remember the place where her baby would die.

"Anya, this is for the best. I'm only doing this because I love you."

She hung up the phone.

Chapter 49

nya pressed her legs together to try to calm the shaking. But then her hands began to quiver. Maybe if she didn't move, maybe if she closed her eyes, then opened them slowly, she would wake up from this hellish dream. She waited a second, closed her eyes, but when she opened them, it was still the same. It was still Saturday, she was still pregnant, and she was still going to go to an abortion clinic.

She heard the garage door open, then a minute later it closed—the sign that Sasha was gone. That's what she had been waiting for. How could she look into Sasha's eyes now, when she had tried to be an example?

Finally, she stood and walked from the bedroom. As she got to the first floor, she heard Sasha moving in the kitchen. She turned to go back, but Sasha called out her name.

"I thought you had left," Anya said when Sasha met her at the stairs.

"I'm on my way out," Sasha replied, crunching on half a bagel. "I needed a napkin." Sasha looked at Anya for a long moment. "What's wrong with you?"

She brushed past Sasha. If she had to answer that question, she couldn't look into Sasha's eyes.

Sasha followed her. "Are you and Braxton still fighting?"

Anya opened the refrigerator. "No, it's over." She faced Sasha. "I'm going to get an abortion this morning."

Sasha's mouth opened wide. "Are you okay with this?"

Anya pressed her lips together, holding back the emotion. "I can't talk about it right now," she quivered. "This is how it has to be."

"Anya, you can't do this if you're not sure. Don't do it today."

Anya shook her head. "There are things that you don't understand." She turned her back to Sasha and stared out the window.

"Have you talked to Madear?"

"No," Anya said, and turned to Sasha for just a moment. "And don't tell her. I have to handle this my way."

"Then I'm going with you." Sasha said, once again talking to Anya's back.

"I don't want you there," she said harshly. Then, she softened her voice. "Braxton's meeting me. The only reason he's not here now is because I asked him to give me some time. I need to be by myself."

"But, Anya—"

"Please, go, Sasha. I won't be able to stand it if you're here."

Without another word, Sasha hugged her cousin from behind, grateful that Anya couldn't see the tears that were building in her eyes. "Make sure this is what you want to do," Sasha whispered. "This is your baby." Sasha paused. "This is God's baby." Sasha blinked in surprise at her own words and she felt Anya flinch under her arms. But she turned, and walked away.

Anya stood at the window, with tears dripping from her eyes. Why did Sasha say that? Thoughts of the Lord had come to her all night, but she had pushed them away. She couldn't think of God, or even talk to Him right now. She was too broken to pray.

She laid her hands on her stomach and tried to calm the tremors that quaked within her. There was so much she wanted her baby to know. She had to explain that it was loved, but the time wasn't right. She couldn't keep it because it would mess up her relationship with Braxton, and it would never have a father, and it shouldn't be raised without one. She couldn't keep her child because it would never be loved the way it should be.

She recited all of Braxton's thoughts in her mind, not believing any of them. This baby would be loved—it was already loved more than she could have ever imagined.

But she knew that sometimes in love you had to do what you didn't want to do. Braxton was right—there were too many questions. How would her child feel knowing it was born from a rape? And, what if Alaister found out about the baby? But the question that cut her most—what would she see in her baby's eyes?

"I love you so much," she spoke to her hand that was still resting on her stomach. "But you'll be better off . . . with God."

She walked to the living room patio and opened the doors. "This is where you would've lived." She spoke as if the baby could see. Then, she moved through the living room, touching every piece of furniture, as if the baby could feel.

When the clock chimed nine times she stiffened, but then with quick movements, she picked up her purse and jacket. Tears flooded her, as she turned around the room one last time. She was trying to grasp the moment, hold onto it forever.

Then she walked out the door knowing that, no matter what, she would never be able to look back.

After checking in, Braxton took a seat that gave him a view through the tinted windowed doors of the clinic. He'd be able to see Anya even before she walked through the door. He glanced around at the others, mostly young girls waiting their turn.

He rubbed his hands together. Maybe he should wait outside. Then he shook his head slightly. Anya would come. He had planted deep seeds, ones she could never ignore.

He picked up one of the magazines on the table—*Family Life*. Chuckling, he tossed the magazine aside. He glanced at his watch. In just a few hours, this would be over. They would be able to move on. And he would be able to return to his goal—to make Anya the happiest woman alive.

Even with the rain pelting from the sky like machine gun ammunition, it hadn't taken her long to get to the clinic. No matter how slow she drove, every traffic light was green.

Pulling into the parking lot, she eyed the empty space

next to Braxton's car, then drove to one in the back, far from the front door.

She turned off the ignition and her eyes moved to the clock. She was five minutes early. Her eyes stayed on the clock, watching the second hand that barely seemed to move. But time was slipping quickly.

She took a breath and stepped from the car. The gravel crunched under her feet as she walked slowly across the puddled lot. But before she got to the front door, she stopped, turning suddenly, and ran back to the car.

"What is wrong with me?" She banged her hands on the steering wheel. She pulled down the visor and stared at her reflection, searching for the person she knew.

"Okay, God!" she cried aloud. "I need you like I've never needed you before. I know I haven't talked to you about this, but I'm coming to you now. You know what I'm feeling, but now please hear me. And talk to me, Lord. Please, in the name of Jesus, help me. I have this life inside of me that I know you put there. Why did you give me this baby?"

She paused, the words sticking in her throat. "I want to know what you want. I need to know and I'm trusting that you will tell me. Speak to my heart, Lord. Please." She paused, remembering how Jesus had prayed: *I thank thee that thou hast heard me.* So she did the same. "Heavenly Father, I thank you, for hearing me."

Then she leaned back, and waited. Closed her eyes, and listened. Calmed her breathing, and trusted. And as the rain began to slacken, she heard Him. She heard Him as clear as the silence surrounding her.

She remained still, allowing His message to sink into her heart. By the time she got out of the car, the rain had stopped. She maneuvered once again through the small circles of water covering the gravel, but halfway to the front door, she turned back.

Inside the car, she put her hand over her stomach and rubbed it in small circles. "I don't need to go in. They'll figure out that we're not coming." She turned on the ignition. "Come on, little one. We're going home."

She drove off, splashing water along the curb as she sped away from the clinic.

Braxton had only used the key that Anya had given him for emergencies a few times. Today, he used his key.

As soon as Braxton stepped in, he saw her. He held the door open for a few seconds before he let it slowly close behind him. Then he stepped to the couch and sat beside her.

Anya kept her eyes pasted on the mantel in front of her. But she could feel the glare of his stare.

Finally she whispered, "I couldn't do it, Braxton."

"Anya, you don't have a choice."

She simply shook her head.

"What about all the things we talked about?" he asked, keeping his voice steady. "You're going to hate this baby."

"That's not true."

He began to pace. "You're going to see the rape in the child's eyes." He crouched down in front of her. Finally, their eyes met. "I can't let you do this."

"Braxton, I can't explain it, but I love my baby already."

He cringed. For the first time, he noticed the Bible next to her, but he forced his eyes away. "You don't love this child."

She shook her head. "You don't understand, this child is a part of me."

"But think about the *other* part, Anya. How can you even think about bringing that man's child into the world?"

Her eyes pleaded for him to understand. "I wish I could find a way to explain, but there's nothing else for me to say." She paused and took his hands. "I'm going to have this baby."

"You're talking like this is just about you," he said, snatching his hand away. "What about the rest of us?"

"That's what makes this so hard, because I am thinking about you and Junior. But I don't see why I have to give up one person I want to love, for another person I love."

With his hands, he waved her words away. "You keep talking about love, but this is not about that. You can't love this . . . thing. You're in shock." He sat next to her again. "Anya, just remember that you were raped."

"Even without your constant reminders, I will always remember that."

He held his face in his hands. "I'm just trying to get you to understand."

"And I want *you* to understand. This baby is a part of me. Fifty percent of this child is me!"

"Okay . . ." He stood, his eyes flashing with anger. "Finish the equation, Anya. This baby is fifty percent you and—"

"This baby is fifty percent me and one hundred percent God."

Braxton sucked in air, then exhaled, letting silence visit them again. Minutes passed before he spoke. "Honey, this is not what God wants you to do."

"Braxton, I think this baby was in God's mind before it was ever conceived. He brought this to us."

"I don't believe that."

"I know you don't, but I've got to stand by my faith."

"We have the same faith."

She looked at him for a long moment, then turned away.

"So you're saying what I believe is wrong?" Braxton asked.

"I'm not saying anything about you. I'm talking about me and what *I* have to do for *my* walk of faith. I either believe in God or I don't. I can't do this halfway."

"That's what you think I'm doing?"

"I can't answer that. Braxton, I'm not judging you. I'm just walking the path that I believe God has set for me."

"While you're walking this walk, what about my son?"

"Junior will be fine, I promise you." She allowed a few seconds to pass. "I asked God for direction. And he gave me a scripture." She picked up the Bible and handed it to him, then recited the verse that she had already committed to memory. *"Before I formed thee in the belly I knew thee; and before thou camest forth out of the womb I sanctified thee . . ."*

Braxton sighed deeply. "Anya, God is not talking about your baby."

She took the Bible from him, then took his hand. "We don't need to keep going over and over this. We have to find a way to make this work for us."

He gently slipped his hand from hers.

"So you're willing to choose this baby over me."

"I'm not choosing the baby, I'm choosing God."

"Over me?"

"Braxton, would you want to marry me if I didn't put God first?"

"Anya, there's no way . . ." He stopped.

She clasped her hands together to stop their shaking. "Finish what you were saying."

He looked away. "This changes everything, Anya."

Immediately tears came to her eyes. "I know."

"I don't know how you expect me to live with this. You want me to bring that child into my home. That child is not mine."

"Junior is not my son either and I want him to be part of our home."

"That's different."

"I know you *think* it's different."

The present and the future were dichotomized only by the silence that fell between them. Finally, with a sideways glance, he spoke. "You need some time." He slowly nodded his head. "I know you'll change your mind."

Anya was unable to speak.

Their eyes didn't dare meet.

"I need to give you space," Braxton continued, his voice now beginning to shake.

When he finally forced himself to face her, the tears that stung his eyes matched the ones that were already streaming down her face.

"Just a little time . . ." his voice quavered.

She finally spoke. "I understand."

More minutes ticked by. Anya stared at her ring and began to twist it from her finger. A tear fell from her eye and covered the diamond. She wiped it away, then reached out, offering the ring to Braxton.

"No!" He shook his head vehemently. "It's not like that. I just want you to——"

She brought her forefinger to his lips. "When we work things out, you can put it back on my finger." Anya opened his closed hand and put the ring into his palm. She held his hand for a moment longer, then pulled away.

"I love you, Anya," he said, as a tear wavered in the corner of his eye.

"I love you."

When he kissed her on the cheek, his tears began to fall. Anya used her fingertips to wipe them away, then stood silently as he walked through the front door.

She clutched her arms as a lump expanded inside her throat, choking her until she had to gasp for each breath. And in that instant, she knew she would never experience a greater pain.

She heard the soft knock on her bedroom door and sat up immediately in the darkened room. "Braxton!" she yelled out.

The door opened and Sasha peeked inside. "Can I come in?"

Anya scooted up in the bed, pulled Madear's quilt over her, and turned on the nightstand light.

Sasha came to the edge of the bed. "I tried to call, but you didn't answer."

"I was trying to get some sleep."

Sasha took her hand. "Are you all right?"

"I didn't do it."

A slow smile crossed Sasha's face. "Oh, God, I knew you wouldn't do it." She hugged Anya.

"I thought you wanted me to."

"That's what I said the other day because I thought it was socially correct. But a lot of what you said made sense to me. I can't explain it, but somehow in my heart it seems . . . right for you to have this baby. I knew you guys wouldn't do it," she said, throwing her fist in the air like she had just won a prize. "So Braxton finally gave in, huh?"

Anya paused for a moment, then lifted her left hand and wiggled her fingers.

Sasha gasped. "No!"

"Yes." Even though she had cried most of the afternoon, the acknowledgment made her heart ache.

Sasha stood and paced the room. "He doesn't mean this, you'll work through it."

Anya sighed. "All I know is that I've shed a million tears today, but now I have to find a way to survive through this."

Sasha sat back down on the bed. "Are you scared?"

Anya nodded. "But I'm counting on God big time! He brought me here, so He's just going to have to pull me through."

Sasha shook her head. "Your faith amazes me. You act like you have God sitting in your back pocket."

Anya chuckled. "That's an interesting way of putting it, but that's how I feel. I know how God works."

Sasha hugged her again. "I know you're tired. Do you want anything to eat?"

Anya lay back on the bed. "No, I just want to sleep. I have church in the morning, and then I'll go by Madear's and tell her. So I need my rest." Anya grinned.

"Okay." Sasha moved toward the door, then turned around. "Where's your ring?"

Anya frowned. "I gave it back to him."

"You what? No, don't repeat that." Sasha closed her eyes and brought her hand to her forehead. "I think I'm going to faint." Then she put her hands on her hips and said, "Haven't you learned *anything* from me? You were supposed to keep the rock and let it give you solace in your moments of sorrow."

Anya laughed. "Get out of here, girl." Anya was still chuckling when Sasha left the room, still shaking her head in disbelief. And in spite of it all, Anya was still smiling when she turned off the light and went to sleep.

Chapter 50

Anya took an aisle seat and laid her Bible in the chair next to her. She was surprised at how good she felt, sleeping through most of the night. But now, she sat anxiously waiting. Service would begin in less than five minutes and Braxton had not arrived. It was becoming reality—he meant every word he said.

She used the bulletin to divert her attention, glancing at the announcements, when suddenly, she felt a hand on her shoulder. She smiled, relieved, and turned toward the hand. "Braxton."

It was his dimple that she noticed first. "David, what are you doing here?"

"Can I sit there?" he asked, pointing to the empty seat beside her.

She scooted over so that he would have the aisle seat. "I'm surprised to see you."

"You invited me, remember?"

"Weeks ago."

"So I'm a little slow. And now that we're friends," he whispered, "I thought it would be a good idea to visit the place that makes my friend so strong. Dianna gave me the address."

Before she could respond, the Praise Team began to sing and they both stood. Anya clapped, swayed, raised her hands to the Lord, and sang. But her eyes kept a vigilant watch on the door.

"Who are you looking for?" David asked, though she could tell by his smirk that he knew.

She turned her attention back to the choir.

Anya shared her Bible with David as the services continued, and at the end, she introduced him to friends as they made their way outside the church where the bright noon sun greeted them with open arms.

"I'm glad I came. Your pastor relates God to everyday living and I never heard Him talked about in that way before. I'm impressed."

"I hope that means you'll be coming back." She smiled.

"Yeah, it's a bit of a drive so early in the morning. Are there any other services besides this one?"

"There's an eleven o'clock, but this is the one I come to."

"Then this is the one I'll be attending."

She lowered her head. "That's not what I meant . . . I have friends who go to the second service. I can introduce you."

"No need." He grinned. "I'll be coming with you." They stopped in front of her car. "So . . . what are you going to do now?"

She shrugged her shoulders. "Go home . . . maybe go to the office . . . I'm going to my grandmother's later this afternoon . . ." Her eyes surveyed the street, looking for Braxton's car.

"Let's get something to eat." When she hesitated, he said, "Come on, I came all the way up here to visit you."

Before she could protest, he took her arm leading her to his car. "We'll pick up your car on the way back."

They had to wait for almost an hour at the Soul Train before they were finally seated at a corner booth.

"Now I remember why I haven't been here in a while," Anya chuckled. "Just inhaling adds two inches to my hips."

"Your hips look fine to me." He grinned. "Anyway, it's our birthright to have some catfish and collard greens, macaroni and cheese, with a little rice with gravy, some cornbread . . . this is the way Black folks are supposed to eat on Sundays."

She laughed, as they walked through the long buffet line, piling their plates high.

When they sat down, David waited while Anya bowed her head, and for a few seconds, he even closed his eyes.

Before she had a chance to savor her first forkful, David said, "I'm surprised that Braxton doesn't go to church with you."

She lowered her fork, still filled with yams, back onto her plate. "He does . . . normally."

"Today wasn't normal?"

She shook her head and looked out the window.

"I knew it wasn't a normal day when I noticed that you had forgotten your ring."

Anya glanced at her bare finger. "I gave it back to Braxton."

"Oh!"

"We're postponing the wedding."

"Oh!"

"Is that all you have to say?" She finally looked at him.

"Well, I don't want to be nosy."

She chuckled. "Yeah, right." She paused, then said softly, "Good friends can be nosy."

He placed his fork on his plate and leaned toward her. "Are you okay?"

She picked up her water glass and took a small sip. "I'm fine."

They ate for a while in silence, as others chattered and laughed around them.

It was Anya who spoke first. "Come on, Mr. Montgomery, you're dying to ask what happened."

"I don't want to know unless you want to tell me."

She breathed deeply, knowing that once she said these words, her reality would be in the atmosphere forever. "I'm pregnant, and it's not Braxton's."

"Ooohhh!"

"I got pregnant when I was raped." Her matter-of-fact tone hid the pounding in her chest.

There were seconds of silence. By the stiff look on David's face, and the way his jaw muscle jumped, she knew he wanted to ask her about Braxton. *How could he leave you?* was what she expected him to ask. But the only thing David finally said was, "Anya, I'm sorry."

"There's nothing to be sorry about. I'm fine with the baby."

His face showed his surprise. "You're going to keep it?"

She nodded.

He let out a low whistle. "I shouldn't be surprised." David pushed his plate aside and tapped his fingers on top of the table. "So what does this mean . . . for us?"

She leaned across the table and laid her hand on top of his. "It means that I have a very good friend whom I'm going to lean on now. And I thank God because I'm going to need my friends."

His dimple disappeared, but then he gave her a slight smile. "If that's what you want, that's what I'll be."

They allowed their conversation to drift back to business—the safer ground for now.

Anya took a deep breath, and stepped into the house. "Madear."

A few seconds later, Madear appeared in the hallway arch, smiling widely. Still wearing the cream dress she'd worn to church, Madear had small smudges of flour covering her face. She wiped her hands on her apron.

"Baby, what are you doing here so early?" Madear hugged Anya. "Are you all right?"

Anya smiled. "Yeah, but I wanted to talk to you before everyone got here."

"Well, come on back." Madear started down the hall to the kitchen. "You know I like to do this by myself, but I'll let you in this time," Madear chuckled.

Anya could smell the aroma from Madear's preparations at the front door. But as she neared the kitchen, her nostrils were assailed with the familiar fusion of scents. By the time she walked into Madear's cooking chamber, she was twelve again, returning home from church, and sneaking in to get a peek at the goodies that awaited.

Her stomach growled. Oh, no, she remembered all she'd eaten at brunch. She hoped she wasn't going to be the walking cliché of eating for two.

Madear pulled a muffin tin from the oven, and Anya

lifted the pot covers, drowning in the black-eyed peas and, then, collard greens.

"Get away," Madear playfully slapped Anya's hand. She dropped the pan on top of the stove. "Come over here." Madear led Anya to the small round table. "So tell me, baby. How are you really feeling?" Madear's eyes searched Anya.

Anya shrugged her jacket from her shoulders. "Fine."

Before Anya could add another word, Madear's eyes moved to her fingers. She lifted Anya's left hand and held it. "You're going to keep the baby, and he couldn't deal with it." Madear wasn't asking a question.

Anya nodded.

"Oh, Braxton," Madear whispered, as she continued to rub Anya's fingers. "Baby, I'm sorry. I'm not surprised though, I just hoped . . ."

"He never gave this baby a chance."

Madear nodded. "It's a hard thing for a man, but Braxton Vance should know better." She paused for a moment. "I need to talk to him about love and family and the Lord—"

"No, Grandmother. Braxton and I have talked about all of that and there's nothing more to say. He gave me a choice and I made it."

Anya pulled away from her grandmother and stood, leaning against the wall. "I'm a little relieved, Madear. I can't explain it, but it was getting hard with Braxton." She looked down at her bare finger. "I still love him," she said, feeling the soft surge of tears behind her eyes. "But . . . I know I'll make it."

Madear had been slumped at the table, and now suddenly, she pulled her shoulders back and went to Anya. "You're from strong stock, baby. You and I wouldn't be here today if my great-grandmother had aborted her baby. No matter how this happened, this is something wonderful because it's God's idea. You're going to come through this standing tall."

Anya tried to smile through lips that had begun to tremble.

Madear held her for several long moments, before she stepped back, and placed her hand on Anya's stomach. "That's my great grandbaby." Madear quivered with emotion.

Anya had planned to tell Madear about Alaister's arrest, but now she felt that news could wait. Instead, she leaned on her grandmother, and treasured the comfort she felt as Madear's strong arms held her.

"Madear, I'm scared."

"I know, baby, but as long as there is breath in me, I will be here for you." She leaned back and smiled. "You might not even get a chance to take care of this baby with me around." Madear's face turned somber. "But the most important thing for you to know is that the Lord is with you. God is not a spectator, Anya. He'll be all up in your business with this baby. God chose you for this because you are special, you are wonderful, and you are loved."

They held each other until they heard Donovan's voice boom through the living room. With the tip of her apron, Madear gently wiped the tears from Anya's face. "Use the back bathroom, sweetheart. We have to make sure the mother-to-be looks fabulous when we make this wonderful announcement to the world."

Chapter 51

The ringing would not stop, and Braxton peeked through the blinds. He couldn't see who was at his door, but Carlos's car was parked in the driveway. He waited a few more minutes, but the ringing continued, as if Carlos had no intentions of leaving.

Finally he went down the stairs. With one click of his lock, Braxton opened the door, and headed toward the living room, leaving Carlos still standing outside.

"Hey, it's good to see you, too, mi amigo. Qué pasa?" He followed Braxton. "Man, it's dark in here. What have you been doing?"

"I'm not in the mood for company, Carlos. I answered the door because you wouldn't go away." Braxton slumped onto the couch, and stretched his feet onto the table in front of him.

Carlos loosened his tie, then sat next to Braxton, matching his posture. "So how're you doing, my friend?" Carlos asked, ignoring Braxton's words. "I've been calling you for a week and you haven't returned any of my calls."

"I guess that means that you can't take a hint."

Carlos chuckled. "No, because I know what you really need is your best friend. Man, you've messed up big time."

Braxton looked at Carlos for a moment, then rolled his eyes. "Anya couldn't wait to tell you how I did her wrong, huh?"

"That's not your woman's style. What happened was, I called Madear to see how she was doing. *She* told me that you walked out on your pregnant fiancée."

"Remember the pregnant part has nothing to do with me."

"No one is going to forget that. You won't let us. But, man . . ." Carlos shook his head. "To leave her now, that was wrong."

Braxton brought his legs down and leaned forward. "You don't understand. I love Anya. I want to marry her. I just wanted her to make the right choice."

"The world according to Braxton."

He ignored Carlos's remark. "Anya was the one who told me that I wasn't part of her future and she gave me back the ring."

"So you left because she said she was choosing the baby over you . . ."

"She didn't say that." Braxton sighed, remembering the moment when she stated her choice. "She said she was choosing God over me."

Carlos whistled. "I knew she was a smart woman."

With a quickness, Braxton stood and stomped to the other side of the room. "I don't want to talk about this with you," he shouted, pointing his finger at his friend. "It's none of your business."

He turned his back and went into the foyer, heading toward the stairs.

Carlos jumped up but by the time he reached the landing, Braxton was already upstairs. "Let yourself out," Braxton shouted down coldly.

"Okay, I will. You can soak in this stuff by yourself, but let me ask you one question. Would you really want a woman who would choose *you* over God?"

Braxton looked back but only for a moment, then slammed his bedroom door.

Carlos shook his head, then walked out the door.

Chapter 52

Anya measured the passing of time in pregnancy weeks. She had her first official prenatal appointment in the seventh week of her pregnancy—the same week that she and Braxton broke up. In her ninth week, her agency acquired the Zytec account, which brought in a half million dollars in revenue. In the thirteenth week, at the coaching of Sasha and Madear, she bought her first maternity outfits. The fifteenth week was when she found out that Alaister had been sentenced to ten years on a plea bargain. And the seventeenth week found Anya working long hours, trying to forget that this would have been the week of her wedding. Now twenty-eight weeks had passed, and Anya was settled into preparing her life and her business for the baby.

"David's gone?" Sasha sang her question as she sauntered down the stairs. She was still twisting her hair into the tiny braids that she had perfectly squared off on her scalp.

Anya was sitting on a pile of pillows in front of the couch. Her new laptop and piles of paper were spread out in front of her.

"He just left." Anya didn't look up as she posted numbers onto a spreadsheet.

Sasha sat across from Anya and watched her cousin. "Don't you think it's time for a break?"

Anya removed her reading glasses and stretched, placing her hands in the small of her back. "I can tell by your tone you're not going to leave me alone, so . . . what do you want to do? Get something to eat?"

"Yeah, let's order in."

Anya replaced her glasses. "Good idea. Order anything. It doesn't matter to me."

But Sasha remained in place and said, "You and David have been working like crazy."

"We're trying to get everything ready so that I can take as much time as I need."

Sasha was silent for a moment. "Is it just about business with you two?"

Anya looked up, but said nothing.

"I really thought something would've happened between you guys by now."

Anya let her eyes drop to her bulging middle. "I'm not in the position for much to happen."

Sasha dismissed Anya's words with her hands. "That means nothing to David. He doesn't care that you look like the Goodyear blimp."

"Nothing is going to happen with me and David." Anya smiled.

"Don't be negative. You could drown your tears right into the lap of that fine man. You want each other anyway." Sasha stated her words as fact.

"Get over it, Sasha. We've already tested the waters

and decided we'd do better as friends." Anya laughed when Sasha's mouth opened wide.

"I can't believe that you actually slept with David."

Anya made a face. "You should know me better than that. It wasn't sex, but one day . . . our lips kinda met."

Sasha chuckled.

"But as a friend, he's been a blessing . . ." Then she added softly, "Just like you."

"Girl, I live to bless other people's lives." Sasha smiled. "I'm going to order Chinese." In her stocking feet, Sasha scurried into the kitchen to make the call.

Anya leaned back and closed her eyes. Indeed, her life was full of blessings. Her business was prospering, her doctor marveled at the ease of her pregnancy, and her family and friends were standing by. And then there was Madear, who called every day with a different scripture reminding her that she was surrounded by the favor of God—*Thou hast covered me in my mother's womb.* Psalm 139:13 had become one of her favorite verses.

She opened her eyes and reached for the Bible on the table. "I think it's in Ephesians," she said to herself.

"Did you say something?" Sasha came back into the room.

"I'm looking for . . ." She flipped through the pages. "Listen to this: *Now unto him that is able to do exceedingly abundantly above all that we ask or think, according to the power that worketh in us.* Isn't that awesome?"

Sasha shrugged her shoulders. "What does it mean?"

"I was just thinking about how God gets us through life. A few months ago, I was putting on a big-time front. I acted strong because that was the only way I could become strong. But I was scared. Now I see nothing but God's hands. Everything in my life is growing, especially this . . ." She put her hand on her stomach. "God is faithful."

Sasha squinted. "So you think it was worth it? Braxton was a good man. And he did love you."

Anya paused in thought. "Braxton *is* a good man . . . he was just the *wrong* good man. Or maybe he was the right man at the wrong time. I don't know."

"Aren't you afraid that you won't find that special love again?"

"It will take time because I'm still in love with him. So I'm not anxious to move onto anything else right now. But I'm not thinking about the future in those terms. There're so many other things on my plate . . . maybe one day I will be in a special relationship again."

"You're not angry at Braxton?"

"No, and never have been. He did what he had to do."

"But he was wrong."

"I don't know that. I'm not judging him or what he believes. We are all going to have to answer for ourselves. All I can worry about is what *I'm* going to say to the Lord about *me*."

Sasha looked thoughtful. "Umm, that's what being a Christian is really about, isn't it?"

Anya nodded slightly.

Sasha sat on the edge of her chair. "What about the baby though—aren't you a little scared to be doing this by yourself?"

"To tell the truth—I'm terrified!" she screamed playfully, and kicked her legs on the floor.

Sasha laughed too.

"But I don't feel alone because I'm truly standing on my faith and believing everything that God says."

"Believing in God gives you the perfect life, huh?"

Anya searched her cousin's face for signs of sarcasm, but there were none. "You can look at me and know that's not true."

Sasha leaned forward and put her elbows on her knees. "I guess I don't mean perfect, but look at how you handle everything. Even when we were kids, I knew you were different. You pulled through anything, always stronger than before. Just look at this. Anyone else would have dug a deep hole to crawl into. But you—" Sasha shook her head with amazement. "You just move on."

"What you see is my dependency on God. I don't have any other choice."

They both sat up when the doorbell rang.

"That's our food." Sasha stood.

Anya pushed herself from the floor. "I'm going to wash up a bit. I'll be back in a moment."

"Hey, Anya," Sasha said, her face deep inside her purse, as she searched for her wallet. "Wake me up for church in the morning." She finally lifted her eyes.

Anya nodded. "Okay."

"Oh, don't get any big ideas. I just think I should be with you, that's all."

"Sure." Anya started up the stairs. At the top, she paused to get her breath. No matter what happened now, something good was going to come out of all of this.

"You go, God!" Anya laughed as she waddled into her bathroom. "You are too awesome for me."

Chapter 58

"ongratulations, Braxton. You've never finished a manuscript so quickly." Carolyn flipped through the loose pages. "I can't wait to read it."

Braxton took a sip of water and smiled, saying nothing.

Carolyn pushed the pages to the side. "Do you want to order?"

The sun was shining directly into Braxton's eyes and he had to squint a bit. He looked into the hazel eyes of his editor. She was smiling, a bit flirtatiously, Braxton thought. He held her gaze. "No, I don't want anything."

Slowly she moved her hand and covered his. "You haven't seemed yourself lately, Braxton. Is there anything I can help with?"

First he looked at her hand, then back at her. He pulled his hand away. "I have to leave. I'll speak to you sometime next week."

"I'm more than just a good editor," Carolyn persisted. "I make a great friend."

Braxton said nothing.

"I don't get to Los Angeles often," Carolyn continued. "And I've done nothing but work these past two days. I was hoping you could take some time and show me around." With a gentle jerk of her head, she flipped her blond hair over her shoulder.

Braxton chuckled inside. Even if he wasn't still thinking about Anya, Carolyn would never be his choice. He didn't go that way.

He stood and put on his sunglasses. "Thanks for fitting me into your schedule."

"You're our best; I would do *anything* for you." Her voice was suddenly husky. "Why don't you stay? We could have a light lunch . . . and you never know how good dessert could be."

This time, he chuckled aloud. "See you later, Carolyn." As he walked away, he said over his shoulder, "Speak to you soon."

While he waited for the valet, he thought of all the women who had tried to slip into his life over the past months. He felt like he was wearing a sign: I'M A FREE MAN! But he wasn't free.

Many days, he spent his time trying to figure out a way to call Anya. But he could never do that. Friends told him that she was having the baby and making plans to keep it. He sighed. He'd taken the gamble and lost the bet.

When the valet handed Braxton his keys, he tipped him with a five-dollar bill, then jumped into his car and turned onto Wilshire Boulevard. A few blocks down, he slowed as he passed Anya's office. He didn't really expect to see her on a Saturday, though almost every day, he'd hoped for a chance meeting. It had never happened.

He punched the CD player button.

I thought that I was through, trying to find someone exciting and new

He reached to change the CD, then pulled his hand back. He hadn't listened to this song in a while.

You taught me how to love, showed me how simple things could mean so much
How to feel good without a touch, slow down and not rush

Anya had taught him how to love. She had taught him how to love, even though he couldn't control her. It was her independence that he loved, though in the end, it was her independence that allowed her to walk away.

He wondered if she ever thought of him.

I'd cry, I'd cry if you left my side . . .

He clicked off the CD, pushed the eject button, and tossed it over his shoulder into the back seat. He had cried enough tears, and if he kept playing this song and thinking these thoughts, there would be more tears to come. He didn't need that. It was time to find a way to get over Anya.

At the light, he made a U-turn. Maybe if he hurried back, he would be able to catch Carolyn. And, that would be a start.

He slowed as he approached the restaurant. She was still sitting at the table, sipping her glass of wine. Braxton turned into the valet area, but when the man came to take his keys, Braxton waved him away. He sucked his teeth as he headed home. When was he going to get over this? He had to find a way.

Chapter 54

The church service was almost over and Anya took a quick, but complete glance around the sanctuary as she'd been doing every Sunday for months. She was still looking over her shoulder when she felt Sasha stand. David was standing beside her.

Was it time to leave already? She hadn't heard the benediction. She closed her Bible, and reached for her purse.

"We're not leaving," Sasha whispered. "Pastor Ford just asked if anyone wanted to know Jesus as their Savior. That's what we're going to do."

Anya's eyebrows rose, but she moved aside, as Sasha and David stepped over her. All thoughts of Braxton disappeared, as Pastor Ford prayed over them and others who stood at the altar. When it was time for Sasha and David to be led to the counselors, Anya followed.

By the time she got to the back, Anya's surprise had turned to joy. She walked to Shirley Johnson, the head counselor. "Shirley, that young woman is my cousin. Would you mind if I counseled her?"

Shirley smiled. "Girl, go ahead. Isn't that wonderful?"

Anya took Sasha into the far corner of the counseling

room and hugged her. "I am so happy for you, but I'm surprised. You didn't say anything—"

"It's because of you, Anya. I know God's been trying to talk to me for a long time, but I didn't want to listen. But as I've watched you, this is the life I want. I want to have your peace."

They hugged again and Anya glanced to where David was sitting with Elder Watkins.

Sasha said, "Do you want David to join us?"

Anya was thoughtful as her gaze rested on David. The greatest gift she could give her good friend was to lead him to the Lord. But he was speaking with Elder Watkins, one of the older, true men of God.

As if he felt her eyes, David looked up, smiled, and nodded.

"David's fine," Anya said, feeling tears come to her eyes. She cried a lot these days, sometimes for no reason at all. But today, it was joy that brought this water.

She turned her attention back to Sasha. "Our pastor believes that everything must be done by the Word of God. I'm going to review scriptures that will help you understand what we're doing. Sasha, being born-again means that you're entering into a personal relationship with God. You're asking Jesus to come into your life and into your heart. You're saying that if Jesus died for you, you're going to live for Him. But most important, you're saying that you want everlasting life. That you know that this life is not the end; eternity is the most important thing."

"Wow!" Sasha exclaimed.

"Is it too much?" Anya asked worriedly.

"No, that's not it. I just never realized it was all of that. I can't wait for everything in my life to change. I need this."

Anya rubbed Sasha's hand. "Sweetie, that's what many people think. That accepting Jesus is going to be like being struck by a sudden bolt of lightning. It's not going to be like that. You're going to *be* different, not necessarily feel different—coming to the Lord is not about emotions; it's about a change that will come inside gradually. You'll grow in God. Do you understand?"

Sasha nodded, although Anya could see the questions on her face.

"Answers will be part of your growth. You're not going to know and understand everything today. Prayer and studying your Bible will bring revelation. Listen, instead of me talking, let's go through this."

Anya opened her Bible and began to read and explain scriptures. She had Sasha turn first to John 3:16, then to Romans 3:23, and Colossians 1:14. Finally, they turned to Romans 10:9.

"In this scripture, God tells us how to become saved. *That if thou shalt confess with thy mouth the Lord Jesus, and shalt believe in thine heart that God hath raised him from the dead, thou shalt be saved.*"

"You just say it and believe it?" Sasha asked, as if she missed something. "It can't be that simple."

"It is. We're going to pray something called the Sinner's Prayer, which simply asks Jesus to come into your heart and be your Lord and Savior. Once you do that, you're saved. You'll never have to ask God for salvation again. It's eternal."

Sasha inhaled a deep breath. "It sounds so heavy."

"It is." Anya took Sasha's hand. "This is the most important thing you will ever do."

Sasha bit her lip, then nodded. "Okay, I'm ready."

"Repeat after me. Dear Heavenly Father, I come to you as a sinner in need of a Savior. I confess with my mouth that Jesus is the son of God and I believe in my heart that God raised Him from the dead. I believe, Lord, that you died and shed your blood for the remission of my sins and I thank you for it. And now, Jesus, I ask that you come into my heart so that I may become your child. So that I can know your mercy, your glory and your power. I want to walk this walk of faith that leads to everlasting life. I accept you, Lord, and ask all of this in the name of Jesus. Amen."

And with the final words, Anya took Sasha into her arms and they cried.

Braxton picked up his ringing cell phone.

"Hey, are you on your way to Crossroads?" Carlos's voice boomed through the phone.

"Yeah, don't tell me you're going to be late?"

"On my way to church, I got a page. I'm at the office."

"Ah, man, so you're canceling?"

"Well, actually, I was hoping that you would still go to Crossroads and order take-out. We could eat a quick lunch here. Would you mind?"

"Naw, I'll do it. I'll be there in less than an hour."

Braxton clicked off the phone. At least he would still get to talk to his best friend. After what happened with Carolyn the other day, he needed someone to talk to.

He pulled up to the restaurant's valet, and jumped from the car.

"I am so proud of the two of you." Anya beamed across the table. They'd come to Crossroads straight from church for a celebration.

Sasha and David smiled at each other.

"What made you do it today?" Anya asked.

David said, "I planned to. God spoke to my heart a couple of weeks ago. It was time for me to take the next step. But what about you?" he asked Sasha.

She shrugged. "I don't know. I think it was all the things Anya and I talked about yesterday and then when you got up, there was nothing holding me back."

"I've been praying for both of you." Anya smiled.

"Well, then, that's what it was!" David laughed.

"And you can't be around Anya too long without picking up something. Thanks for the prayers, cuz. I can't wait to tell Madear. In fact . . ." She pulled her phone from her purse. "I'll call her now." She stood. "But, I'm not going to be like all these other L.A. folks. I'll go to the car."

After Sasha walked away, Anya took David's hand. "Congratulations."

"Thank you. It's because of you—"

"Oh!" Anya squealed.

David was startled. "Is it the baby?"

Anya waited a few beats before she spoke, "Yeah, the baby is happy for you too." She grimaced as the baby kicked again, then grinned at David. "Do you want to feel?"

He smiled sheepishly, as she took his hand and laid it on her stomach. At the first kick, he pulled his hand away. "Wow!"

She took his hand again, urging him to stay in place. "Can you believe that?"

"It's incredible." He smiled. "So no doubts?"

"No, but that doesn't mean I'm not a little scared. I guess that's normal for any first-time mother who's eight months pregnant."

He took her hand. "I'm getting as excited as you are."

She smiled. "David, I can't thank you enough for all that you've done. But, there is one more thing I'd like to ask." She took a deep breath. "If it's too much, tell me, and I'll understand because . . ."

"Anya," he laughed, interrupting her. "You know I'll do anything."

She bit her lip, then placed his hand back on her stomach. "I cannot think of a better man to be my baby's godfather."

David smiled widely. "Anya, I can think of only one thing that would make me happier. Thank you for asking me."

"I wouldn't want anyone else. You've been an incredible friend."

Very gently, he lifted their hands from her lap and brought her hand to his lips. "And if my godchild's mother ever wants to move beyond friendship, I'd love that more." Still holding her hands, he leaned over, and kissed her softly on the lips.

From the window outside, Braxton watched. Then, he turned around and ran, bumping into the Crossroads sign as he fled.

Braxton tried to open the heavy glass doors, but they were locked. He pressed the button and stayed on it until Carlos appeared in the lobby.

"Hey, man, what's the urgency?"

"I didn't feel like standing out there. I forgot the doors would be locked."

"Well, there's something else you forgot. Where's our lunch?"

Braxton stuffed his hands deep into his pockets. "Can we go into your office?"

"Sure."

Carlos led the way back, but as soon as they stepped into his office, he asked, "Qué pasa?"

Braxton dumped his jacket into the chair. He looked at Carlos, and shook his head. "I just saw Anya."

"Oh, that's why we don't have any food," Carlos said, trying to lighten the mood. "What did she say?"

He paced the entire floor from the window to the door. "She didn't see me. She was with David Montgomery." He stated the name as if it were a spoiled piece of beef. "They were holding hands . . . and kissing." He punched his fist into his palm.

"Ohhhh," Carlos moaned. "Well, what did you expect? Anya's an attractive woman. She's smart, she owns her business, is financially well-off, funny—"

"I don't need you to go down a list of her attributes," Braxton stated angrily.

"I thought maybe you'd forgotten. You're acting like you're surprised that she's moved on, and that there's another man who wants her in his life. Did you really expect her to sit back and pine over you?"

"*I* haven't rushed into anything! The other day, my editor threw every part of her body at me, and do you know what I did? I walked away, because Anya was on my mind."

"So Anya shouldn't move on because you're thinking of her? Man, you're a fool." He paused. "Look at what you've done to your life. You got rid of Anya, you've tossed most of your friends away—man, you don't even go to church. Not even the second service, not Men's Prayer, nothing. You have messed up everything!"

Braxton stopped, and looked at Carlos like he was crazy. "You have got to be out of your mind to talk to me that way."

"You're the one who's not making sense. You left Anya because she was doing something that she had to do, and now you don't want her to have a life?"

"I *love* Anya."

"Braxton, your definition of love is control and manipulation. Admit it, man. The reason you're upset is because this didn't turn out the way you planned. Because if you truly loved her, you'd be with her right now."

They glared at each other, then Braxton grabbed his jacket, and stomped out the door.

Braxton slammed his front door. He was still breathing heavily when he threw his jacket across the room like a football. His steps were hard, as he climbed the stairs to his bedroom.

"I can't believe Carlos." He slapped his fist into a pillow. "I should go back there and tell him what I really think of him."

He heard Carlos's words in his head. "You got rid of Anya."

"She gave me back the ring," he justified aloud.

Carlos's words continued to play in his mind. "You don't even go to church."

"I couldn't keep going to the same church. What was I supposed to do?" The image of Anya and David had planted itself in his mind and he closed his eyes, needing to expunge it. But it played repeatedly, like a bad song, over and over. He could see them—David's lips touching Anya's.

He sat on the edge of the bed and held his head in his hands. Oh, God, how he still loved her. Why couldn't she just get rid of that baby?

When he lifted his head, memories flooded him. Memories of how they dreamt together. Memories of their plans.

"I've got to get her out of my mind." His eyes wandered to the Bible on his dresser. He hadn't opened it in months.

That's what I need to do, he thought. I need to pray her away.

He got on his knees, clasped his hands together, but he couldn't think of what to say. What was he supposed to ask? He thought for a moment, then searched his heart for the right words. But as God spoke to him, all Braxton wanted to do was cry.

David turned into the gas station and stopped in front of the full-service pump. A man dressed in jeans and a blue jacket with a Mobil insignia trotted toward him. David handed the man his credit card. "Fill 'er up." Then, he leaned back, and closed his eyes.

The sun had already retreated and the blue-black of the first hours of darkness was drifting over the city. But as people were settling into their homes, David was driving aimlessly, as he had been doing for hours.

How had this day, with so much promise, turned out this way? A time that had been set aside for new beginnings, had dragged him deep into his past.

When he'd left Anya and Sasha this afternoon, he was still on the high from committing his life to the Lord. Even though Elder Watkins had cautioned him against expecting to feel anything, David had felt different immediately. Before they prayed, Elder Watkins told him coming to the Lord meant that he would be forgiven for any sins he had committed—that Jesus Christ had already paid the price. David felt like his shoulders were being freed from the burden he'd carried, and he was eager and grateful to accept God's mercy.

But by the time he returned home, his mind was riddled with images from his past. It was as if the burden had moved from his shoulders into his heart. And his heart was breaking with the secrets that yearned to burst forth.

"No!" he yelled, and slammed his fist against the steering wheel. "I can't go back."

"Did you say something?"

David opened his eyes, and stared into the curious gaze of the attendant. Without responding, he signed the credit slip, and drove away.

He headed toward the hills, still without a destination in mind. This weight had dropped on him like an oversized boulder blocking his passage to the future. But, he had to get to the other side. There was too much waiting there.

Anya was opening herself to him. And it was easy for him to respond—he long ago opened his heart to her. He was in love, but that love was driving him to the truth.

Even if it did come at a high price, he owed it to her no matter what the cost.

At Pico Boulevard, he made an illegal U-turn, causing two cars to hit their brakes hard. David ignored the blaring car horns and insults that were blasted toward him. Instead, he accelerated and headed toward Baldwin Hills.

"Come in," Anya whispered, and moved aside so that David could tiptoe into the townhouse. With only the wall sconces lighting the downstairs, the living room was engulfed in a soft, golden glow.

"I'm sorry to be stopping by so late." His low voice matched hers.

"It's not that bad," Anya stated, glancing at the clock on the mantel. She sat on the couch, and motioned for David to join her. "I told Madear that I asked you to be the baby's godfather, and she's thrilled. Sasha's going to be the godmother."

A pained smile crossed David's face. "That's nice," he said, sounding strained.

Anya took a long look at David. He was sitting stiffly, staring straight ahead, with his hands clasped tightly in front of him. His normally suave manner was gone.

"David, you sounded upset when you called."

It took a few moments before he turned toward her. "It meant a lot when you asked me to be your baby's godfather."

Anya sighed, relieved. "Is that what this is about? David, I am the one who's honored. We haven't known each other long, but you've stepped perfectly into my life. You're a great friend, I couldn't have asked for a better business associate, and now you'll be part of the family."

He shook his head slowly. "That's not going to happen." With his eyes closed, he breathed deeply. "I don't know if this is about what I did in church today or if it's because you asked me to be the baby's godfather, or if it's God dealing with me." He held his hands in front of his face as if he were praying. "I can't be the godfather."

"David, what's going on?"

"There are things about me that you don't know. Things, that if they ever came to light, would change my entire life . . ."

Anya crossed her arms in front of her, covering her stomach. She thought for a moment before she spoke. "Then maybe you shouldn't say anything."

David stood, moving away from her. "You brought me into your business, into your life. I owe you this." He breathed deeply again. "I've already told you part of it— about my mother and my father." When the frown on her face deepened, David's words came faster. "I told you that my father raped my mother, but the part that I didn't tell you—" He choked, and slowly returned to the couch. Anya reached over and touched his arm. "I killed my father."

Her hand jerked away and she covered her face. The soft ticking of the clock was the only sound in the room. She wanted to tell David that her ears had misled her, making her hear something that wasn't true, but she felt frozen in place.

David lowered his head into his hands. It was the first time he had spoken those words to anyone, though many knew the truth. Now in the silence, he wondered what he'd been thinking. There was much to lose with this admission.

But even the doubts that swirled through his head couldn't stop him from continuing. "It was one of those times when the rage inside my father found its way to my mother. He was beating her, and I begged him to stop. That was when my father looked into my fourteen-year-old eyes, and laughed in my face." David's eyes glazed as he took himself and Anya back to that time.

"Leave her alone!" David had screamed, as he beat his father on his back. But his father reached around and tossed him off the bed like a piece of paper.

David's head hit the ground, and it took a few seconds for his mother's screams to penetrate through the pain that enveloped his skull. With the pain still thumping, David lifted himself, and ran toward the closet. He knew where it was hidden—he and his friends had found it many years ago. David pulled down the shoebox, and took out the gun.

"Stop it, Daddy! Please, please, stop!" David cried.

His father turned toward him, and laughed. "Oh, you're a big man now."

He threw David's mother aside, and turned toward David.

As his father moved toward him, David's emotions flared. "I love you, Daddy!" he screamed. "Please, Daddy, please, please!"

Anya closed her eyes, trying to imagine what it was like for the boy.

"My father kept coming, and I was so scared—my mother was screaming, my father was laughing, and when he lurched toward me, I pulled the trigger." He gasped, trying to catch his breath. "It was only one shot. Just like I'd seen on TV. I only meant to stop him. What were the odds that I would hit him perfectly in his chest?"

"Oh, my God," Anya whispered, as she recoiled further into the couch's cushions.

"There are two things that I remember clearly about that night. The first is that my mother never stopped screaming. Even as she pried the gun from my hand, her cries shrilled through the apartment." He paused. "And then . . . the police. They kept asking me, where did I learn to shoot like that? My father was lying dead, and they were impressed with my skills."

Long, silent minutes passed before Anya said, "David—"

He held up his hands. "You don't have to say anything. I know everything changes now."

"It doesn't change anything for me. You were trying to protect your mother. Isn't that what the police decided?"

He shook his head. "They never got a chance. An investigation began, but then my grandmother came from North Carolina and took my mother and me away. My mother lived with my grandmother, and they hid me with a family who were members of my grandmother's church. They had so many children I lost count. I guess that was part of the plan."

"So what does that mean?" Anya asked confused. "Are they still looking for you?"

"I don't know. I guess they would have to be, although they didn't spend a lot of time or effort searching. Although . . . they weren't looking for David Montgomery." He glanced sideways. "My real name is David Collins. My grandmother thought it would be a good idea for me to have another name. She picked my last name from a store we passed in town one day."

Anya shook her head. She'd always known there was something dark hidden beneath David's confident veneer.

But she'd pushed her curiosity and doubts aside. What should she do now? Did this have to make a difference?

Before she could answer the questions that whirled in her mind, David continued. "That was why I was so persistent with . . . what happened to you. When I found you that night, I felt like it was happening to me again."

"And that was why you thought they might think of you as a suspect," she said, remembering his concern. "If they looked into your background . . ."

He nodded. "I had an alibi, but I was afraid that would raise more questions. That night, I'd gone to a therapist to try to settle my mind. But I was so shaken by that session that I couldn't go home. So I drove around for a few hours, and then went back to the office. That's when I found you."

For the first time in months, Anya allowed herself to remember that night. But all she could think about was how David had saved her. Even now, that was more important than what happened twenty years before.

"Anya, you've become so important to me, I felt you had to know. But I also know that I have to take care of this—there are things I have to face."

"Are you talking about going back to the police?"

He shook his head. "I don't know." He squeezed his hands together. "All I know is that it would be crazy for any Black man in America to turn himself in to the police. I don't know what I'm going to do. I think I'll go to North Carolina, and talk to my grandmother before I do anything." David made a sound halfway between a chuckle and a moan. "All these years that I've lived with this—I don't know why it had to come out today."

"David, this doesn't change anything for me. I still think you would make a wonderful godfather."

He took her hands, and for the first time that night, Anya saw the dimple that she loved so much. But there was sadness in his smile that scared her.

"I want you to hold that position for me. And while you're at it, do you think you could hold my job open too?"

"You're leaving now?" She couldn't hide the panic in her voice. He was her lifeline in so many ways.

"I haven't decided anything yet, but, I'll let you know."

She nodded and tried to fight back tears and emotions that surprised her. He helped her stand from the couch, and they held each other for several moments, before she followed him to the door. She opened her mouth, but before she could speak, he kissed his forefinger and placed it on her lips. "There is no need for us to say good-bye."

She nodded and bit her trembling lip. Then she watched him walk out her door.

Chapter 55

It had been a while since Braxton had stood on the balcony outside his bedroom. The city lights didn't seem to glow as brightly as he remembered. Even the decorative lights that had been put up early for the holidays did little to improve his spirits.

Braxton rubbed his hands along his arms, trying to warm himself against the chill of the November night. A few minutes later, he stepped inside, closing the French doors behind him.

He wasn't looking forward to the holidays. A year ago, he was making plans for a long life with Anya. Now he was sitting in this darkened house alone, just as he'd been doing for months.

"A year ago?" he said aloud.

He walked quickly to his office and turned on the lights. At his desk, he looked at the calendar—November 13. He was sure this was the date.

He opened the file drawer, pushing aside folders until he found the papers he was looking for. He scanned the mortgage agreement. There it was—November 13. A year ago, he had bought this house.

As he tipped the folder to return it to its place, a picture slipped out. Slowly, he picked it up. The Realtor had taken this picture of him and Anya. He held a bottle of champagne, while Anya held the deed high above her head. They were standing with their cheeks pressed together and Braxton remembered that, in that moment, he had never been happier.

He returned the file to its place but kept the photo out. Where had it all gone wrong? There was really no reason that he and Anya should have broken up. He should have been able to convince her not to have that baby.

But he hadn't, and according Carlos's updates, the baby would be arriving any day. Anya had moved on, while he was acting like a sad character in a blues song, still trying to figure out how his love had gone wrong.

Carlos had told him that he would never be able to move forward until he made his past right.

The Rolodex on his desk caught his eye. Carlos was wrong. All he needed to do was get out more, make friends, meet new women. But as he scrolled through the cards, there was no one who he wanted to call.

It had taken him months to get here, to realize that he was truly alone. His decision had left him with no one to call, or visit or no one who even cared. Just like when he was a child.

He wasn't going to live this way anymore. He scrolled through the cards again and picked one: Desiree. He read the notes—met at a booksigning, no kids, legal secretary . . . he liked that part. A business that wouldn't put him second. He took in the other notes he'd made, then glanced at the clock. It was really too late for that first call tonight. But tomorrow, he'd call her first thing. Yes, tomorrow would be his new start.

Chapter 56

nya stood, and tried to stretch, but the pain came sharper than before. "Argh!" she yelled.

No more than five seconds passed before Sasha was standing at her door. "Is it time?"

Anya tried to smile through the sharp jabs in her back. "I was stretching and I think I made things worse."

"What are you doing up anyway? I thought you were going to rest."

"I tried, but I thought it would be a good idea for me to pack. Dr. Moore told me to do that a couple of days ago."

"I can do that for you." Sasha plopped on the bed.

"No, I need something to do." She stopped in front of the mirrored closet and turned sideways, stretching her shirt over her rounded stomach.

"I feel so fat and ugly," Anya whined, turning away from her reflection.

"Honey, you are not hardly ugly." Sasha laughed. "Hey, Madear called a little while ago. Wanted to know if it was time."

"I feel like an amoeba being studied under a microscope."

"Anya, amoebas are tiny things."

"Okay, enough of the fat jokes." She reached into the back of her closet and felt something on top of the suitcase. "What's this?" It took her a moment to recognize the blue garment, and a low moan escaped from her throat.

"What's that?" Sasha asked.

Anya sat next to Sasha. "This is Braxton's robe. He must've left it here . . . when he was staying." She lifted the bathrobe to her nose, closed her eyes and inhaled the faintness of the slight scent that remained.

"Oh, sweetie." Sasha rubbed Anya's back. "You really do miss him."

Anya nodded. "I've been trying to be so strong, but I guess somewhere inside, I thought Braxton would come back, because I thought God wanted us together."

"Well, there are many things that God wants, but He still gives us free will and most of us mess up."

Anya sniffed back tears that hadn't fallen. "When did you get so smart about God?"

Sasha shrugged, but smiled widely.

Anya placed the robe in the chair. "I'll mail this back to Braxton."

"Why don't you lay down?" Anya shook her head, and Sasha said, "It'll be better for me if you do."

Anya laughed, as Sasha pulled back the comforter, then helped Anya into the bed. Sasha lay next to her and rubbed her stomach.

"You know what," Sasha said. "You haven't said a word about the baby's name."

Anya sighed. "A part of me thought that I should wait, just in case Braxton—"

"Oh, sweetie . . ." Then Sasha jumped up. "Well,

we've got to do something. I'm not going to call my cousin Baby for the rest of its life."

Anya tried to laugh, but nothing would come through the thoughts that had suddenly invaded her mind.

"I have an idea." Sasha reached for Anya's Bible. "I was reading something that was so beautiful. But now . . ." She turned the pages. "How am I going to find it?"

"Maybe I can help."

"Ssshhh."

It took her a few minutes, but Sasha suddenly let out a shriek. "Here it is!" She turned to Anya. "Listen to this. *Weeping may endure for a night, but joy cometh in the morning.* Isn't that beautiful?" Sasha gushed. "Wouldn't that make a great name?"

"You want to name my child 'Morning'?"

Sasha laughed, but then frowned when Anya squeezed her eyes together. "What's wrong?"

"I think we're going to have to discuss this on the way to the hospital."

"Oh, my God! Is this it? Finally! The baby is going to come! Oh, my."

"Sasha!" Anya giggled. "Could you help me up? We better get out of here."

Anya grasped the bed handle and moaned.

"Breathe, baby," Madear said softly as she wiped Anya's forehead. "Remember all of those breathing exercises?"

Anya slowly turned toward her grandmother's voice. If she says that to me one more time, Anya thought before squeezing her eyes shut.

"Hey, sis, wanna hear a joke?"

She turned to the other side of the bed. With her eyes barely opened, she could see Donovan bending over the railing. His wide grin couldn't hide the concern on his face and that almost made Anya smile. From their childhood, Donovan had never allowed the fact that she was older to get in the way of protecting her, shielding her from every pain. Anya was sure he was trying to figure out a way to even transfer the pain of childbirth from her to him.

"I'm sure I've heard all of your sorry jokes," she squeaked, running her tongue against her dry lips.

"You're going to love this one. His mother is so stupid, it took her two hours to watch *60 Minutes*."

"Ohhhhh!" Anya groaned, and tried to lift herself from the bed.

"It wasn't that bad." Donovan chuckled.

"Madear, please tell the doctor that I need something."

"But, sweetie, you wanted to do this naturally—"

"I want drugs!" Anya hollered in a bass that would have made Barry White proud.

A smiling nurse came into the room. "I heard you," she said cheerfully to Anya. "Let me just check the monitor and do a quick examination and I'll get the doctor."

"I can't stand this." Sasha had been standing in the corner, as far away from Anya's bed as she could get. "Shouldn't the doctors be taking her now? Anyone can look at her and see that she's going to have a baby."

Madear gave Sasha a long glance. "Now, you be quiet. Anya is going to be just fine."

"But she's in pain!" Sasha exclaimed, whining as if she felt each stab that went through Anya's body.

Madear smiled. "It's natural," she said. She turned back to Anya. "Hold on, baby. The doctor will be here. Hold my hand if you need to."

At that moment, Dr. Moore entered. "Well, Anya, how are you doing?"

She shook her head. "I'm ready to get this over with, Doctor."

Dr. Moore looked at the chart at the foot of the bed. A slight frown crossed her face, and she quickly glanced at the monitor. But when Dr. Moore looked at Anya, the smile that she had walked in with returned. "Okay, let me take a look at things."

As the doctor put on the thin plastic gloves, Madear moved away, and motioned for Donovan to do the same.

Sasha had backed herself into the corner. Madear chuckled and hugged her. "Baby, what's going to happen when you have to go through this?"

Sasha shook her head. "Uh-uh . . . I don't think this is for me," she whispered. "Anya's the strongest person I know and look at her."

Donovan joined in. "Madear, do you think Anya's all right?"

"You two are something else. There's a baby inside of Anya who's trying to come out. It's going to hurt a little."

"I guess it depends on what's your definition of 'little,'" Sasha moaned.

"Excuse me." They hadn't noticed the doctor. "Can I speak to you?"

It was Madear's turn to show concern. "What is it, Doctor?"

The doctor motioned for them to leave the room. As they got to the door, Madear looked back. Anya's eyes were closed and the nurse was hovering nearby, checking the monitor.

"Is everything all right?" Madear asked the moment they were in the hall.

"Yes, but there is a small problem," Dr. Moore said, but then she quickly added when she saw their horrified glances, "The baby hasn't turned fully and I don't know why. I'm concerned because I didn't see this coming. It may be because the baby is a bit premature, but only by a few days."

"This sounds serious," Sasha said.

As another pregnant woman was wheeled past them, the doctor motioned for them to sit on the bench across from the nurse's station. "What we're dealing with is what's termed a breeched birth."

Madear gasped, and Donovan put his arm around his grandmother.

"Breeched—the baby is not in the right position for birth," Donovan said.

"That's right," Dr. Moore smiled, trying to reassure them. "I'm going to take a number of steps. First, we have to find out why this has happened. If it looks clear, then I'll try to turn the baby. But I don't want to get too far into labor. I might decide to deliver the baby by cesarean." The three gave a collective sigh. "There's nothing to worry about, but now I have to get back in there with Anya."

Madear stood. "I'm going with you," she stated, in her schoolteacher's tone.

When Sasha and Donovan stood behind her, the doctor's brow creased.

"It's just going to be me," Madear assured the doctor.

She turned to Sasha and Donovan. "You two stay out here. Everything is going to be all right." Then Madear started down the hall and the doctor followed her.

Sasha fell back onto the bench and covered her mouth with her hand. "Oh, God, Donovan. Anya gave up so much for this."

Donovan nodded, and pulled Sasha into his arms. "I know, but she is going to make it."

Sash nodded in agreement, taking comfort in his confidence.

"But there is one thing we can do," Donovan said suddenly.

"I know. It's time for us to pray."

They closed their eyes, held hands, and spoke to the Lord.

Sasha's heels played a slow rhythm on the tiled floor. She glanced at the clock again. More than forty-five minutes had passed. She sighed loudly, and the nurse behind the desk smiled sympathetically. Sasha smiled back, determined not to ask the question she'd asked at least a dozen times—how much longer.

"Here you go, cuz," Donovan said, handing Sasha a cup of coffee. "Any news?"

Sasha took a sip from the plastic cup, crinkled her face, and placed the cup on the floor. "Nothing and I can't stand this."

Donovan took a sip of his coffee and made a face that matched Sasha's before he placed his cup on the bench.

The large steel door to the room opened and Madear

came out with her hands covering her face. Sasha and Donovan jumped up.

"Madear!" Sasha called, her voice shaking.

Madear looked up, gave them a long glance, and a slow smile spread across her lips.

"The Lord has blessed this family with a healthy, beautiful baby girl."

"Oh, thank you, Jesus!" Donovan yelled.

"Can we see her?" Sasha asked.

Madear nodded. "The doctor asked that we give her a few minutes. She wants to clean up the baby and make sure Anya is okay. Cesarean births are tough on the mother."

"How is Anya?" Sasha asked.

"She's fine. She was awake through the birth and is in a bit of pain, but we have a lot to be grateful for."

"Oh, yes," Sasha gushed. She paused for a moment. "Donovan and I have been praying. I feel like we owe God a big thank you."

Madear's face was shining with pride. She ran the palm of her hand across Sasha's cheek. Then, she took Donovan's hand. "That's a great idea." When Madear lowered her head, her grandchildren followed. And in the middle of the hallway as nurses and paramedics wheeled patients by, Madear led the Mitchell family as they poured praise to the Lord.

The nurse helped Anya sit up a bit in the bed, then settled the baby into her arms. Dr. Moore smiled. "I'll tell your grandmother that they can come in now."

Anya said, "Doctor, can you give me just a few

moments?" She squirmed against the pillows trying to find a comfortable place. But she didn't take her eyes off the baby.

The doctor smiled knowingly. "I'll keep them at bay for a while. You did great, Anya."

When she was alone, Anya allowed herself to breathe deeply. She peeked under the blanket and looked at the baby's feet, then took the small hand into hers. The baby's face was framed by straight brown hair, and through the half-opened slits, Anya thought her eyes were light brown. She pulled the baby closer letting it feel the pounding in her chest, then gently pulled back to stare at the tiny infant.

This was the moment she had secretly feared—what would she feel like the first time she saw her baby?

As she stared at this life in her arms, tears came to her eyes. All she saw was the baby, and she was consumed with an overwhelming feeling of love.

She brought her lips to the baby's forehead. The baby made a light sound and squirmed. Anya held her breath, hoping the baby wouldn't start to cry. But a few seconds later, the baby settled comfortably in the crook of her arm.

"I may not know how to feed you," Anya said softly, "or change your diaper or even hold you, but I know how to love you."

She kissed the baby again and then raised tearful eyes to the ceiling. "Thank you, Lord."

"She is so precious," Sasha cooed.
They nodded their heads in agreement.

Madear stroked the hair on the baby's head. "She is beautiful. She's so light—"

Their eyes turned to Madear.

Madear looked at her grandchildren. "What? I was just saying that she's so pale, I hope she darkens up soon," Madear said sternly, then let a smile cross her face.

They laughed. "I think she's beautiful just the way she is," Anya said, bringing her baby closer and kissing her forehead.

"So how does it feel?" Sasha sat on the edge of the bed. "You're a mother."

"It's pretty amazing, huh? Madear, I'm going to need a lot of help."

Madear beamed. "Baby, by the time I finish, you'll be begging me to hold your own child."

Anya laughed, but it was only a short one. She knew her grandmother was serious, and she would have to set the rules from the beginning.

"We have to let the mother and baby get some rest," the nurse said as she came into the room. "The sooner she rests, the sooner we can get her home."

Anya nodded, grateful for the nurse's reprieve. She was exhausted. She allowed the nurse to lift the baby from her arms, but she watched until the nurse placed her into the bassinet.

"Okay, sweetie," Madear said, kissing Anya. "I'll call you later. I'll be back tomorrow."

"Me too," Sasha kissed her next.

"Thanks for making me an uncle." Donovan lingered behind for a moment. "You know, Mom and Dad are proud." He hugged her tightly.

After they left, the nurse rolled the bassinet closer to

Anya's bed. "I'm going to be right outside. If you need anything, push this button." The nurse pointed to the device on the side of the bed.

Moments later, when the nurse stepped outside the room, Anya raised her head to take another look at her baby. She smiled and closed her eyes. It was over, but she knew it was all just beginning.

Anya heard the steps in her room and opened her eyes.

"I'm sorry to wake you," the nurse smiled. "Just wanted to check on you and the baby."

"That's okay, I was awake. How's the baby?" Anya whispered.

"She's just fine. I wasn't going to wake you, but there's a gentleman here to see you. He's been waiting for a while, and even though it's past visiting hours, I thought I'd let him in for a few minutes. He said it was important that he see you."

Anya grimaced at the pain as she pushed herself up. Her chest began to pound.

"I'll get him now," the nurse said.

She ran her hands over her head, trying to smooth down her hair. Then she tightened the robe around her chest. The door opened and he entered.

Anya stared at him for a long moment, and then she smiled.

"David."

His dimpled smile was wide as he walked toward her. Without a word, he hugged her gently, before he glanced at the baby, then sat on the edge of the bed. He took her hands. "They said I only have a few minutes." He spoke softly. "It's so good to see you."

"When did you get back?"

"Today. Dianna called a few days ago, and told me that you were having the baby any day. It looks like you did a great job." He glanced at the baby again. "She's beautiful."

"Thank you." The two of them gazed at the baby for a moment. "So . . . are you back for good?" She searched his face for answers before he spoke.

He nodded. "And I didn't come a moment too soon. I've gotta jump back into things so that you can spend time with this little one."

Anya squeezed his hands. "I'm so glad. So everything . . ."

"Is fine," he said, finishing her sentence. "I'll tell you about it later, but I've been cleared of all charges. I'm officially not a criminal."

She was surprised when a wave of relief washed through her.

"And for the first time in many years, I feel truly free."

"So what are your plans?" Her steady voice didn't reveal her anxiety.

His eyes bored into her in a way that she had become accustomed to, but that still left her unsettled. "Do you have to ask? I came back here because of you."

She wondered why her heart was beating so fast.

"I promised the nurse that I wouldn't stay long."

He hugged her again.

"I'll come by tomorrow during regular hours." He kissed her forehead, but as he backed away, she held him close. It only took a moment for him to move his lips to hers. It was a soft kiss that lingered.

When they pulled apart, he was smiling. "Don't do this to me, Anya . . ."

This time, she kissed him, and allowed their tongues to meet. He drew back only when the nurse came into the room.

"I'm sorry, but—" the nurse began.

"I have to go." David's voice was husky, but his eyes hadn't left Anya. "What does this mean?" he whispered.

Anya smiled. "I don't know."

He chuckled. "I know."

He kissed her cheek, then glanced at the baby before he left the room.

"So that's your man, huh?" The nurse smiled. "Girl, that is one fine man you got."

Anya's eyes were still glued to the door. "I know. I think I finally know."

A bit later . . .

Anya pulled her leather jacket tighter as she leaned on the rail, looking at the numerous yachts and sailboats that lined the marina. The breeze kicked up the water and Anya stepped back, away from the water's target. She continued her stroll along the dock, but kept her eyes on the shops behind her. The restaurants and shops were overly crowded for a winter afternoon, and she preferred the cool winter air to the stuffy stores.

"Anya." Her back was to the familiar voice, and she froze for a moment before she involuntarily turned to face the sound.

And there he was.

She put on a smile. "Braxton." She stated his name as if she'd seen him yesterday.

He walked over and stood close, staring at her, then took her into his arms.

She jammed her hands deeper into her coat pockets. "How are you?"

"Fine." His eyes roamed her body. "You look terrific. You cut your hair."

Anya ran her fingers through her shorter curls. "It was time for a change."

For a few moments, silence hung awkwardly between them. "I can't believe it's you," he said softly.

She shifted from one foot to the other. "So everything is going well with you?" She tried to hold her voice steadier than the pounding in her chest.

"Yeah, what about you? How's your business?"

"Things are great. I've been blessed."

His eyes seemed to pierce hers. "You certainly have been."

Again, silence.

Finally, he said, "Do you still attend Chapel of Hope?"

"Of course, that's my church home. I thought it was yours too. I'm sorry that you felt you had to leave. I hope it wasn't because of me . . . us."

"No, that wasn't it." He paused. "So what have you been up to?"

"Mommy, Mommy!"

Braxton's eyes widened as a young girl with golden curls ran toward them and wrapped her arms around Anya's legs.

"Hey, sweetie." Anya lifted her daughter and from the corner of her eye watched Braxton.

"Mommy, I thought you got lost."

"You did?" Anya playfully rubbed her hand through her daughter's Shirley Temple curls. "Where's Daddy?"

"Here I am." David joined them, and held out his hand to Braxton. "How are you, Braxton?"

Braxton remained still, overwhelmed with the sight in front of him. Finally, he took David's hand. But his eyes were fixed on Anya.

"So who is this pretty little girl?" Braxton asked.

"This is our daughter," David said.

Braxton reached for her hand. "And what's your name?"

She snatched her hand away and nestled her face inside the crook of Anya's neck.

"She's just tired," Anya explained to Braxton. "We've been out here all morning."

Braxton nodded, then looked from David to Anya. "I understand . . ."

"Mommy, I wanna get down. I wanna get some ice cream."

"Okay. David, would you mind?" He hesitated, then smiled and kissed Anya lightly on her lips. She smiled. "I'll be just a few moments, darling."

David lifted his daughter into his arms, then turned to Braxton. "Nice to see you again." He walked away, leaving Anya and Braxton to share more seconds of silence.

"She is really a gorgeous little girl," Braxton finally said. "How old is she? Almost three?"

She nodded.

Braxton gazed down the boardwalk, following David. "Anya, how could such a beautiful child have come between us?"

Her eyes thinned into slits. "Is that the way you remember it?"

He cleared his throat.

"How is Junior?" she asked, softening her voice.

"Getting grown." He beamed.

"Is he living with you?"

"Yeah, most of the time. My wife—"

"You got married?" she asked without surprise in her voice.

"Uh, yeah. Her name is Desiree."

"I didn't know. I don't see anyone in the gang anymore. That's nice. Are you happy?"

He stared into her eyes and seconds fluttered by before he spoke. "Not as happy as I thought I would be, but happier than I probably deserve." He waited a few beats before he asked, "What about you?"

"I'm very happy. Our family has been blessed."

His smile didn't conceal the sadness in his eyes. "I always thought you were my soulmate."

She returned his smile. "I'd better go find David . . ."

He nodded somberly. "I hope it won't be another three years before we see each other."

She hugged him. "It was good to see you, Braxton."

His arms tightened, holding her longer than he knew he should. When they pulled apart, he said, "Maybe one day we could get together."

She shook her head. "There's no need for that."

"I'd like to give you a call . . ."

"I don't think so," she said, then smiled her good-bye. She could feel Braxton's eyes on her as she walked away and she wondered how many regrets were stabbing at his heart. She smiled, pleased that the only thing in her heart was love.

They were waiting at the corner.

"Are you all right?" David frowned.

"I'm better than that!" She kissed him. "Do you know how much I love you?"

He smiled. "I know."

"Mommy, who was that man?"

"An old friend, honey."

"I didn't like him."

David and Anya exchanged glances, then David lifted her into his arms.

"Did I ever tell you how you got your name?"

"Daddy, you tell me all the time. It came from God's book."

"And do you remember where it is in God's book?"

She frowned and pursed her lips together deep in thought. "Mommy, do you know?"

Anya smiled. "It's in Psalms."

"Right! Can we say the words together like we always do?"

"Okay, on a count of three," Anya said.

"One, two, three: *Weeping may endure for a night, but joy cometh in the morning.*"

"That's me, Joy!"

About the Author

Victoria Christopher Murray is a graduate of Hampton Institute and has an MBA from New York University. Originally from New York City, she now lives in Los Angeles, California.

Reading Group Guide

themselves that it was justified because they loved each other. What are some ways that Christians are tempted

ANYA

1. David, and others, initially found Anya to be a paradox as she was a successful Christian businesswoman. Why do some people believe that Christianity means a life of mediocrity or even paucity with regard to material successes? Read **Deuteronomy 29:9; Jeremiah 29:11; 1 Chronicles 4:9–10.** Think of (you may use your Bibles!) at least three biblical examples of righteous persons who were also rich in earthly things. How can Christians who are successful in temporal endeavors use their achievements as a testimony of what it means to be a Christian?

2. Should Anya's hesitance to set a wedding date have been a clue to her that Braxton—even though he was a Christian—may not have been God's best for her? Read **Psalm 86:11; Proverbs 2:7–8.** Was she ever in danger of compromising her faith in order to stay in a relationship with Braxton? Read **2 Corinthians 11:3; Ephesians 5:6.**

3. What should have tipped Anya off that she and Braxton might not be equally yoked regarding their spiritual growth in the Lord? What does God's Word say about spiritual compatibility? Read **2 Corinthians 6:14.** How might their relationship have been used for a greater purpose? Read **Genesis 50:20; Judges 14:3–4.**

4. Braxton and Anya had been sexually active earlier in their relationship and in the heat of passion convinced

themselves that it was justified because they loved each other. What are some ways that Christians can work to avoid the trap of premarital sex and avoid such deceptive thinking? Read **1 Corinthians 6:9–10; 2 Cor. 7:1.** Discuss what it means to be in a "compromising position" and discuss the wisdom of **Proverbs 6:27.**

5. Anya lied to Braxton in order to avoid him. Why do people, even Christians, sometimes lie to avoid unpleasant situations? What does God's Word reveal about truth and honesty? Read **Psalm 15:2; Psalm 43:3; Proverbs 24:26.**

6. Anya's faith remained constant, even after her attack, yet she wondered why God allowed the assault to happen to her. How can believers find consolation through difficult situations and turn it around to help build their faith and trust in God? Read **Exodus 5:22; 1 Kings 17:18–22; Psalm 10; Mark 15:34.**

7. Immediately after her attack, could Anya have been using her faith as a means of avoiding the painful reality of what happened to her? Or was her faith simply so strong that it did not affect her as many would have expected? Read **Genesis 25:22.** Why do some Christians fail to understand that God can use trained professionals to help His people and that counseling is not the antithesis of faith? **Exodus 28:3; 1 Chronicles 25:7; 2 Chronicles 2:7 (NIV); Proverbs 22:29; Isaiah 6:8.**

8. Do you think that most Christian women would have made a similar choice as Anya—even if they risked losing the love of their life? How can God's Word encourage us to make such difficult choices? Read **Psalm 9:10; Psalm 125:1.**

9. By the end of the book, Anya's life had changed drastically, yet her faith in God remained constant. How can we use circumstances, both good and bad, to affect positive change in our lives and help our faith to grow? Read **Genesis 45:4–5; Psalm 34:17; Isaiah 12:2.**

BRAXTON

1. Despite the fact that Braxton was successful in his own career, he was intimidated by Anya's success. How can godly men be confident with their mate's successes and support their efforts instead of discouraging them? Read **1 Samuel 1:22–23; Ruth 2:10–16; Psalm 40:4.**

2. Think about some of Braxton's actions, (some of which on the surface looked good! That boat ride was the bomb!) that demonstrated his desire to manipulate people and circumstances—like when he hired the private yacht to seduce Anya or wanting her to be a stay-at-home mom so he could attempt to win custody of his son. How does such manipulative behavior reveal immature faith and a believer's lack of trust in

God? Read **Proverbs 14:8; 1 Corinthians 3:3; 2 Corinthians 4:2; 1 John 1:6.**

3. How did Braxton's actions hint that his love for Anya was conditional, based on her willingness to do what pleased him? Why must Christians be willing to extend unconditional love in their relationships? Read **John 13:34–35; Romans 12:10; Romans 13:10.**

4. Why did Braxton interpret Anya's choice as wrong? Read **Proverbs 16:3; Proverbs 21:2.**

5. Braxton thought he could find happiness by marrying a woman who would do what he wanted. How do people cut their blessings short by refusing to leave comfort zones and follow God's way rather than their own? Read **Psalm 37:5–6; Proverbs 3:5.**

SASHA

1. What might have been some things that contributed to Sasha's worldly attitude toward men and her disinterest in God? Read **John 4:7–19.**

2. How did God use Anya to show Sasha the kind of life that is available to Christians? How can believers remember that our lives are living testimonies to those who do not know Christ? Read **1 Corinthians 10:32; 1 Peter 2:5.**

3. Sasha found Anya refreshingly different from other Christians she had encountered. How can believers strive to be an inspiration rather than a "turn-off" to unbelievers? Read **Matthew 23:23–28.** What can believers do to make sure they live God's Word so that it is understood as more than just a collection of rules that people must follow? Read **John 3:16; John 9:25.**

4. Why did Sasha choose to ignore the warning signs about Hunter Blaine? What are some reasons why people ignore their inner signals and choose to follow their earthly desires? Read **Ecclesiastes 4:13; Isaiah 8:11.**

5. Sasha's attempt at a relationship with God began with her wanting God to get Hunter Blaine to fall in love with her. Were her efforts an attempt to bargain with God? How could her attraction to Hunter have drawn her closer to God? Read **Psalm 51:10; Matthew 6:8–13; Hebrews 5:12.**

6. Sasha was a beautiful woman who had the potential to be anything she wanted, yet her self-esteem was extremely low. Among other things, she believed she had to settle for a "sex only" relationship with Hunter. How does Satan attack our self-esteem to make us feel we are unworthy of the abundant life that comes from obedience to God and His Word which in turn puts us in a position to receive His blessings? Read **Luke 7:38–44; 1 Peter 3:3–4; James 4:8.**

DAVID

1. Initially, David was held in bondage by secrets in his past. How does Satan use secrets and deception to keep people from reaching their fullest potential? Read **Genesis 3:1–6; Isaiah 43:18–19; Luke 4:1–13.**

2. Through his association with Anya, David came to accept Jesus Christ as his Lord and Savior and resolve past secrets that were dominating his life. How can believers resolve to allow God to use them to reach others and help them find the way to Him? Read **2 Corinthians 5:20; 2 Corinthians 11:3.**

PASTOR FORD

1. In a sermon, Pastor Ford admonished her parishioners to "practice the presence of God." How can living in constant awareness of God's presence help believers to abstain from sin? Read **Psalm 143:8; 1 Timothy 5:22; 2 Timothy 2:22.**

2. Pastor Ford explained to Anya that as she grew in the Lord, she no longer experienced being angry with Him. Is anger at God a sign of spiritual immaturity? How can believers learn to allow God's will to manifest without anger? Read **Psalm 40:8; Psalm 143:10; Matthew 6:10; 26:42; Hebrews 10:9.**

*S*urprise!" Kyla beamed as her startled husband jumped back. Friends shouted their greetings from the restaurant tables adorned with silver and black "Over-the-Hill" balloons.

"I don't believe this!" Jefferson grinned. He grabbed Kyla around her waist and hugged her close.

Kyla's skin tingled at his touch. After many years, he still turned her on. "We got you, didn't we?"

"That's for sure. I can't believe this."

"Happy birthday, darling!"

Cheers echoed through the restaurant again as Jefferson kissed Kyla. They lingered in the embrace and the crowd applauded.

"Hey, hey Dr. Jefferson!" A voice from the crowd interrupted their moment. "There's no room for that here, Ky. Dr. Jefferson has to be shared with everyone," Jasmine, Kyla's best friend, scolded playfully.

Laughter filled the room as Jasmine wiggled and nudged herself between Kyla and Jefferson. Standing on her toes, she said, "Here's something for your birthday I know you'll never forget." She kissed him, full on the lips.

As friends pushed Jasmine aside to offer their congratulatory wishes, Kyla frowned and remembered her husband's recent complaints about Jasmine. Now, she wondered if she should have so lightly dismissed his concerns. Taking his hand a bit too firmly, Kyla moved alongside her husband, past a smiling Jasmine as Stevie Wonder blasted birthday wishes from speakers around the elegantly decorated room. After a few body-crushing minutes, Kyla loosened her grip and allowed Jefferson to be pulled further into the crowd. He caught her eye and reluctantly let her fingers slide from his.

Kyla leaned against the restaurant's blue-suede wall and her eyes roamed through the crowd of the ninety invited guests, personal friends as well as colleagues, present to celebrate the fortieth birthday of her husband, a well-respected pulmonary specialist.

Kyla took a glass of sparkling cider from a passing tuxedoed waiter, then moved to a table, away from a swell of guests. Watching her husband over the rim of her fluted glass, she saw him stride confidently through the maze of tables on his mission to greet every guest. She was content to watch it all from the sidelines. "Thank you, Lord," she whispered as her eyes continued to follow Jefferson. "Thank you for giving me sixteen wonderful years with this man."

"Girl, things are heating up in here," Jasmine said, interrupting Kyla's prayer as she bounced down into a chair. Kyla's eyes swept over Jasmine in her red knit, hip-squeezing mini-dress and, although it was a little too short for her taste, she had to admit that Jasmine did look good.

Jasmine fanned her face, then took Kyla's glass and sipped her cider before Kyla could protest. Kyla got another glass from a passing waiter and crinkled her nose as the cider's bubbles rose and tickled her. She fixed her eyes on the couples on the dance floor, doing her best to ignore Jasmine and the feelings of anger she felt brewing inside.

Jasmine was tapping her fingers atop the silver tablecloth. "Well, it looks like it's going to be the party of the century, Ky." Jasmine's tone belied her words.

"At least the party of the week."

"Well, I'm not as important as you and Jefferson. I don't get invited to all those posh affairs. It's the first time I've been to a p-a-r-t-y since my separation."

Kyla's light brown eyes softened. "Are you okay? You know you can talk to me."

"Nothing to talk about. I'm fine, look at me." Jasmine made a sweeping gesture with her hand across her body. "Do I look like I'm suffering?"

Kyla smiled. "Jas, you look great."

"Yeah. The Commodores called it a brick house. And to think in a little while *I'll* be forty."

Kyla laughed.

"What's so funny?" Jasmine smirked. "Remember, two weeks after *I* hit that big number, *you'll* be joining the club."

"But, we still look good, girl."

They laughed together. "We do, don't we?" But a second later, Jasmine's smile slid away. "I just hope someone else will notice."

"Don't force it, sweetie. It might be a little too soon for you to get involved with anyone."

"Easy for you to say. You have a man."

Kyla reached over and squeezed her friend's hand. "I'm just trying to pass on some good advice."

"How can you give me advice on something you don't know anything about? All you know is perfection and I don't feel like being perfect right now."

"I'm not perfect, Jas."

"Umh. You're as close as any human being on earth will ever be. Just ask my father, my sister, anyone we know, they'll tell you!" Her words sounded bitter.

"How can you say that? You know me better than anyone, except for Jefferson, so you know my laundry stinks just like everybody else's."

Jasmine couldn't suppress a laugh.

Kyla half smiled. "I just want you to be okay."

"I'm fine." Jasmine sighed. "I'm not going to sit here and talk all night when all of these fine men are waiting for me."

Kyla's eyes followed Jasmine as she sashayed across the room. She shook her head. But right now, she didn't have time to worry about Jasmine. Standing, Kyla edged toward the crowd, knowing it was just as important for her to meet and greet the guests as it was for Jefferson. She moved shyly along the perimeter of the room, watching as the waiters bustled around, clicking glasses, making sure none were ever empty and plates were never bare. The guests gathered in clusters and the conversation and laughter mixed with the music to form a melodic hum that floated through the air. Stepping forward, Kyla finally entered the arena and paused to chat warmly with each person, spending a little extra time with the guests she knew might later become benefactors of the Medical Center.

As she continued her stroll, Kyla was embraced and kissed at every turn as if it were her birthday. She picked hot hors d'oeuvres from the trays and, with a fixed smile, searched for Jefferson, finally spotting him at a table with a few of the other doctors. As if on cue, Jefferson turned and looked directly at her with a twinkle in his eye. Heat rushed to her face and Kyla instantly thanked God their nine-year-old daughter, Nicole, was spending the weekend in San Diego with Jefferson's mother. She turned away, afraid that others at the party would be able to discern their telepathic messages. Jefferson's gaze fortified her and she continued her stroll, pausing at the stage that had been set for the DJ.

"The music is great." She smiled at the deejay as Marvin Gaye crooned "What's Goin' On." A small circle had formed in the center of the dance floor. Jasmine was in the middle, with her arms high above her head as she cha-cha'ed with Ian Hollis, the accountant for the Medical Center, who was swaying more like an exotic dancer than a numbers cruncher. As the crowd cheered and Marvin continued to ask about picket lines and brutality, Jasmine's hips swiveled deeply.

"I had a feeling you'd like the old school theme." The deejay's words snapped Kyla back.

Turning away from the dance floor spectacle, Kyla chuckled. "I can't imagine music that I love is considered old."

He laughed. "I know how you feel!"

With an audible sigh, she shook her head. It seemed like a short time ago, but almost twenty years had passed since she had met Jefferson at Hampton Institute. Only five minutes after they had met, Jefferson had proposed to her. The memory of that night was still so clear.

She had wandered out from the Kappa Alpha Psi party, seeking refuge from the suffocating heat inside where the rooms were packed with students celebrating the completion of finals. She was squinting through the dim streetlights when a tall, mocha-skinned brother dressed in red and white fraternity paraphernalia swaggered toward her.

"Some party, huh?" the man with the huge Afro said, as he sloped against the wall.

Kyla nodded and smiled. "A little hot though."

"I like hot things," he said with a half-smile.

Ignoring his innuendo, Kyla walked across the wooden porch and perched against the rail. He followed and leaned on the fence, facing her.

"My name is Jefferson, by the way."

"Nice to meet you." She extended her hand and waited as he switched the Budweiser can from his right hand to his left.

"The pleasure is definitely all mine . . ." he answered as he took her hand. When Kyla remained silent, he continued. "So, are you a student here? I haven't noticed you before."

"I haven't noticed you either."

He laughed.

Kyla ran her hands along her corduroy jeans. The smooth voices of the Ohio Players blasted through the opened windows and Kyla snapped her fingers.

"Fire! Fire!" Jefferson sang, as his eyes danced with the music. "Fire! The way you walk and talk really sets me off to a full alarm . . ."

"It was nice meeting you, Jefferson," she said and started back toward the house.

"Wait, we haven't finished yet."

"Haven't finished what?"

"Making all of our plans. You're gonna be my wife," he said as he brought the beer can to his lips.

"You don't even know my name," she chuckled.

"Okay, wife, tell me your name."

She stepped closer so that she could see his face clearly through the streetlights and spoke with a smile. "Kyla. Kyla Carrington."

"That's all I need to know. Everything else I'll learn over the lifetime of our long and happy marriage," he said as his hand traveled gently down the sleeve of her polyester blouse, until his fingers laced through hers.

Her eyes blinked with surprise, but she kept her hand in his. "So, Jefferson. If we're going to be married, don't you think I should know *your* last name?"

"Does that mean you *will* marry me?"

They shared their first laugh together in a scene not too different from this one.

"Hey, girl," a voice came over her shoulder. "I saw you over there talking to that Jasmine person. I was going to rescue you, but decided it would serve you right to be stuck with her all night."

"Now, Alexis. You promised you would behave," she said hugging her friend.

"I am behaving." Alexis raised her thick eyebrows, feigning innocence. She paused, lowering her voice conspiratorially. "If I wasn't I would tell Jasmine that her dress is so short, you can see what she had for breakfast!"

"Stop it," Kyla said trying to hold her laugh.

"Pastor says, 'Tell the truth and shame the devil,'" Alexis drawled as she held up one hand as if she was about to shout Hallelujah. "Anyway, sorry I'm late. Things were crazy at work. Was Jefferson surprised?"

"I think he was stunned."

"No problem getting him here?"

"That was the easy part. You know how much he loves this place."

"You worked it, Ky," Alexis said as she reached for one of the black balloons that floated above her. "Memphis restaurant has never looked better. Louise did this, right?"

"Of course."

"She's the best in L.A. She used to cater everything for my office, but recently, she's been hard to get. Hollywood has been calling her."

"I wasn't about to try to do this without Louise. But enough about this stuff," Kyla said grabbing her friend's hand and pulling her into the corner. "There are a lot of good-looking, single, successful men here."

"Kyla . . ." Alexis whined.

"Now, I'm not trying to set you up or anything."

Alexis raised her eyebrows in doubt.

"I just want you to know . . . you have *options* here."

"That's a new way of putting it."

"I just want you to be happy."

"I *am* happy. I don't need a man for that."

"But . . ."

"Kyla!" Alexis interrupted before her friend could continue. "Not everyone is going to find her Prince Charming, have the perfect child and wake up sixteen years later just as much in love as the day she married. That only happens in fairy tales and at *your* house."

"Well, you never know who you'll meet."

Alexis closed her eyes, slightly irritated, and tilted her head toward the ceiling. "Lord, please have mercy! And, please keep this chilè out of my love life!"

"What are you two over here conspiring about?" Jasmine wiped her sweaty face, then tugged at her dress, trying to smooth it down over her hips. "Hello, Alexis," Jasmine said in a slow drawl, imitating Alexis's southern accent.

"Hello, Jasmine," Alexis said curtly. "Anyway, Kyla," Alexis continued, turning her back to Jasmine. "How are things going with the expansion at the clinic?"

"Great. The final proposal goes in next week."

"Does that mean they're going ahead with it?" Jasmine asked, leaning forward so that she could be heard.

"Uh-huh. Can you believe it?"

"Of course!" Alexis said. "As hard as you guys work, you deserve it."

"Yeah, just what you need—more success," Jasmine whispered and rolled her eyes.

"Hey, you," Jefferson appeared, and grabbed Kyla's arm. "We haven't danced all night."

As they stood in the center of the dance floor, Jefferson wrapped his arms around Kyla and they swayed to Lionel Richie's sexy voice. "Zoom! I'd like to fly away!" Jefferson sang softly into her ear.

"Umm," Kyla sighed and leaned in closer.

Jefferson brushed her thick bangs from her face and kissed her forehead. "Kyla, I can't believe you did this for me. Thank you." He leaned over and brushed his lips against hers, then pulled her tighter. As Jefferson sang Lionel's words into her hear, Kyla knew this would be one of the best nights of her life.

"Louise, you outdid yourself this time, lady," Kyla exclaimed as she signed her name with a flourish and handed the check to the caterer.

"I'm glad you're happy. I haven't done many private parties since I opened the Pie Shoppe. But how could I refuse this for Jefferson? By the way, I have a gift for him. I couldn't remember which was his favorite, so I baked two things—a pecan sweet potato pie and a pineapple cheesecake. They're in the kitchen."

"No, you didn't!"

Louise laughed. "I know his sweet tooth."

"He'll think he's walking around in heaven! Thank you!" As she hugged Louise, she glanced around the empty room.

"Jefferson's out front with some of the guys," Alexis said reading her friend's expression as she sat down at the table. "I just saw him. Kyla, this was a *great* party."

"I was just thanking Louise for everything. So, did you . . . meet anyone?"

Alexis rolled her eyes and ignored the question. "Anyway . . . how have things been with you, Louise?"

Louise laughed. "Great. I've been busy. In fact, I have a wedding to do tomorrow, so I've got to get going." Standing, she hugged Alexis, then Kyla. "Tell Jefferson I said enjoy the rest of his birthday."

Kyla remained silent until Louise left the room, then scooted her chair closer to Alexis, but before she could say anything, she heard Jasmine's voice.

"Still here, Alexis?"

Kyla glanced up and saw Jefferson and Jasmine walking toward them.

"Hey, you," Jefferson took Kyla's hand and pulled her to him. "Honey, everyone is raving about this party."

"It was all Louise. She left you a special surprise and said to tell you to enjoy the rest of your birthday." Kyla brushed her lips against his neck, drinking in his scent. "I want you to enjoy the rest of your birthday, too."

"Well . . . I guess that's my cue. I'm out of here." Alexis stood, readying herself to go, and glared at Jasmine when she didn't do the same.

"Hey, Alexis," said Jefferson. "Brian told me you guys had a great time together. He's a good brother."

"Brian!" Kyla said, opening her eyes wide.

"What about Brian?" Jasmine asked. She hoped they weren't talking about Brian Lewis, the doctor who had just joined the Medical Center. Jasmine had spent quite a bit of time tonight trying to get his attention, but he hadn't shown any interest in her. Now, she hoped that they weren't talking about Alexis getting together with him. That would be a dire end to this dismal evening.

"Jefferson, don't say another word!" Alexis commanded, softening her words with a smile. "You know how your wife is."

"Sorry. I was only passing along some information."

"But Alex, we can help. Jefferson has known him since they were kids, right, honey?"

"Leave me out of this. I don't want Alex killing me."

"You're a smart man, Dr. Blake."

"What are you guys talking about?" Jasmine piped in again.

"Like I said, I'm outta here." Alexis hugged Kyla and Jefferson. "Happy birthday, again. I'll call you tomorrow, Ky." Alexis looked over her shoulder. "Aren't *you* coming, Jasmine?"

"I was hoping that Jefferson and Kyla could drop me home."

"I think they want to be alone," Alexis said stating what she thought was obvious. "Where's your car?"

Jasmine grimaced at Alexis's cutting tone. "I came with some friends. Not that it's any of your business," she snapped. "Ky, would you mind giving me a ride?"

"No!" Alexis interjected before Kyla could answer. "I'll take you home."

"Alexis, that would be great!" Jefferson exclaimed. "I do want some time with this beautiful lady," he said pulling Kyla closer. "I want to thank her and I have a very special way to do that." Jefferson kissed Kyla as if the two of them were already alone.

Jasmine grabbed her jacket from the table and stomped out. Alexis followed, leaving Jefferson and Kyla totally unaware of anything that was happening around them.

The Publisher's Diary

Dear Faithful Reader,

At Walk Worthy Press we realize that true joy in the Lord" is not simply happiness but it is instead the consciousness of our victory in Jesus Christ — no mater what the circumstances. The novel, *Joy*, by Victoria Christopher Murray, unflinchingly demonstrates this principle.

"Many readers will savor this novel of romance, intrigue, and faith," said *Publishers Weekly*.

Joy, tells the story of Anya Mitchell, a woman who is prosperous in every area of her tile. Her fiancee, Braxton Vance, is a man of God, who, although they occasionally have differences over the direction of their future, she is sure she loves him. Trying to live a good example before her wild, unsaved cousin, Sasha, Anya is confident that her faith is unshakable ... until the night she is brutally attacked in her office. Reeling with anger and fear, Anya finds herself questioning everything she has ever believed—including her

relationship with Braxton.

How can she now stand when her circumstances now make her only want to hide?

But it is when Anya draws on a strength only found in her relationship with God hat she is indeed able to take the most di fficult stand of her life and finally tap into the true meaning of joy.

Be blessed in your reading,

Denise Stinson